Dr. Dempsey

A Novel

by:
Grace Maxwell

Cover Design: Jennilynn Wyer Designs
https://www.jennilynnwyerdesigns.com
Cover Model: Andrew Biernat
Photographer: WANDER AGUIAR

Dempsey Follies: Dr. Dempsey/Grace Maxwell—1st edition

One

Liz

I've been to Paradise a thousand times, but it looks different when you're arriving to stay.

The highway curves along the lake, where sheets of ice cling to the edges and fog drifts low over the water on an early-January morning. Sunlight slants through the evergreen trees, turning their shadows silver across the snowbanks. The air smells like pine, diesel, and wood smoke. I crack the window just enough to breathe it in, cold air biting my lungs, the kind of clean that feels like permission to start over.

"New job, new town, new life," I whisper. "No drama. No men."

That last part matters.

My best friend, Trinity Paradise, called about an opening in her department at the hospital where she works part time, and the timing was perfect in that tragic, poetic way that life sometimes offers mercy disguised as chaos. The guy I'd been dating—three dinners, one forgettable night of lousy sex, and an expensive bottle of wine I regret sharing—had ghosted me. My parents had retired to Mexico. My brother, Mark, and his family had already moved here. I was the leftover piece on a chessboard when nobody wanted to finish the game.

But Trinity dangled an escape, Assistant Director of Hospital Administration for one of the top health systems in the province. Two interviews, a final meeting with the board, and a handshake later, I broke my lease in Vancouver, packed my car, and assured myself this move was about ambition, not loneliness.

Snow dusts the rooftops as I crest the hill. The sign flashes past—*Welcome to Paradise, B.C., the Wine Capital of Canada*—half buried under a crust of ice. My stomach flips. The irony of "wine capital" in the dead of winter isn't lost on me. The vines are asleep. I just hope my judgment is not. *You're just nervous*, I assure myself. *Change is never fun.* And coming to Paradise doesn't have to mean anything more than that. This is just where the job happened to be.

I cross the bridge over Black Bear Lake into downtown Paradise. Everything appears in soft gray tones, storefronts glowing behind fogged glass, icicles glinting from awnings. A plow rumbles past, spraying salt. I pull into the market lot for supplies, tires crunching over packed snow. The rental cottage Trinity found for me is small, but it's within walking distance of the hospital and has a stone fireplace, a view of the lake, and an empty fridge.

Coffee, milk, and something edible. That's the plan.

Inside the market, the air smells like bread, cinnamon, and wool wet from melting snow. Locals push carts and chat near the produce section. A corkboard by the door advertises the winter carnival and the hospital's blood drive. I shake the cold from my scarf, grab a cart, and tell myself again that today is the first step toward the life I want. *Don't overthink, keep your head down, and avoid complications, especially the male kind.*

I move toward the coffee aisle. The heater vents hum

overhead. It's almost cozy. I'm reaching for coffee beans, proud of how functional and normal I'm being, when a voice cuts through the music overhead. Low. Warm. Threaded with laughter that once curled through my chest and stayed there.

I freeze. *No, no, no. That can't be him.*

I tell myself it's someone else. There must be other men in Paradise with voices that sound like warm whiskey. But my heart already knows. It's racing, traitorous, remembering too much.

I turn my head, slow and unwilling. And there he is.

Alaric Dempsey.

Tall. Broad-shouldered. The kind of man who makes winter seem deliberate, like he was built for it. His hair is damp, sleeves pushed up on a navy sweater that shouldn't look that good under fluorescent lights. He's standing in front of a display of apples, smiling at a brunette in yoga pants. She laughs too loudly, touching his arm.

He looks older than the last time I saw him three years ago, but better. His smile used to be mine, and I hate that I still feel the echo of it.

Every bit of healing I've done since then fractures.

But I am thirty-one, a professional woman with an MBA and a career that demands composure. I can handle seeing an ex. I can nod politely, walk away, and buy my milk. I even take a step forward.

Then panic grips me. I haven't washed my hair in three days. I have a coffee drip on the front of my sweater. There's a pimple on my chin, and my period has me bloated. I wanted to see him when I looked my best, so he'd know he didn't break me.

I duck behind a display of cereal boxes and peek through a gap.

Brilliant move, Liz. Real dignified.

Somewhere inside, the rational part of me asks, *What are you doing?* The rest of me whispers, *Survival strategy.*

The brunette leans closer. Alaric says something that makes her laugh again.

My stomach twists. "I'm invisible," I whisper. "Just

another shopper." I take a breath. I can do this. I'll wait until they leave.

Except what if I can't?

I shift, trying to get feeling back in my legs, and bump the cereal tower, which wobbles. *Oh shit!*

Too late.

The display tips in a glorious slow-motion disaster. Boxes tumble and crash into the apple pyramid. Honeycrisps scatter like marbles, rolling across the tile. One bounces off my boot and spins under a cart. A man in a puffy jacket swerves to avoid it.

The brunette yelps. Someone gasps.

Alaric turns.

Our eyes meet through the chaos.

Recognition hits like a power line sparking in the snow. Surprise. Then that slow, dangerous smile that used to be my undoing.

He mouths something—maybe my name—but I've already abandoned my cart and headed for the exit. I don't need groceries that bad.

The blast of cold air slaps my cheeks as I hit the parking lot, breath steaming.

I dive into my car, slam the door, and grip the steering wheel. "Well done, Liz. Ten minutes in Paradise and you've committed a grocery-store hit-and-run. And you didn't even buy coffee."

The windows fog as I rest my head against the seat. *His face. His voice. That smile*. Three years, and he still looks like trouble disguised as comfort.

I thought time would dull it. It hasn't.

My phone buzzes. Trinity's name flashes, and I answer with frozen fingers. "Please tell me you're available for emotional triage."

"Define emotional," she says. "You made it? Are you alive?"

"Alive is debatable. I think I've sustained psychological injuries."

"Oh no. What happened? Did the cottage flood? Did you lock yourself out already?"

"Worse." I take a breath. "I saw him."

A pause. *"Him?"*

"Alaric. In the flesh. Buying apples. Flirting with a yoga-pants-wearing woman who was laughing like she got paid to giggle."

Trinity snorts. "You're kidding."

"I wish. I tried to hide behind a cereal display. There was...fallout."

"Liz."

"It fell and took out the apple pyramid. I panicked and ran."

She's laughing so hard now she can barely breathe. "You've been here how long?"

"Thirty-seven minutes."

"Oh, Liz." Her voice softens. "You realize you're going to see him again, right? He's Paradise royalty."

"Not if I schedule my life carefully. I'll shop on Thursdays, work late, wear sunglasses indoors."

"That might be tricky, considering you start at the hospital tomorrow."

I blink. "I beg your pardon?"

"He's head of Behavioral Health. You'll cross paths."

My forehead thuds against the steering wheel. "Kill me now. Why didn't you tell me this?"

"Hey. You've got this. You didn't move here for him. You moved here for you."

I groan. "Right. The empowering, career-driven, independent-woman step."

"Exactly. And maybe skip the cereal avalanche next time."

"Not helpful."

She laughs. "Well, I love you. Greyson, Theo, and I will bring dinner around five. You can tell us all about your escape from the grocery store."

"Perfect. Nothing says new beginning like recounting my

humiliation."

"See you soon." She hangs up, still laughing.

I stay parked, watching the market doors slide open and shut. Every time they do, I expect Alaric to walk out—calm, collected, the man who broke my heart and never explained. Not that I reached out to ask…

The ache is smaller now, more bruise than wound, but it's still there.

Snow flurries drift across the windshield. Across the lot, an older couple loads groceries into their hatchback, moving in quiet rhythm. That easy partnership twists something in my chest. I need to be over wanting that too.

I start the engine and adjust the heater as I exit the parking lot. The road ahead is slick with slush, but the lake shimmers beside it.

I tighten my hands on the wheel. "You've got this, Liz."

Trinity will give me a pep talk this evening, and tomorrow, I'll walk into that hospital with my head high and my heart locked down. I'll act like seeing Alaric Dempsey didn't rattle me at all.

If I can survive the produce aisle, I can survive anything.

Maybe.

Two

Alaric

The scenery flashes by as I drive, but I barely see it. I can't get her out of my head. The woman in the grocery store this morning, the one who tipped the cereal display before bolting, looked exactly like Liz. Same blonde hair, same confident posture that dared people to underestimate her. The kind of woman who could silence a room just by walking through it.

It's ridiculous, of course. Liz lives in Vancouver, and she's made that perfectly clear. She wants nothing to do with anything outside the city. It's been almost four years since I packed up my apartment in North Van and came home to Paradise, British Columbia. Three years since I ran into her at a christening, her arms crossed and her eyes full of disappointment I'd earned. She was the one person in my life who made me feel, and I never was very good at that.

I shake my head, but the image won't let go. It could've been the light, or the way she tilted her chin. I might've imagined it entirely. Maybe it was a stranger wearing her perfume—a trace of jasmine threading through citrus and floor polish.

The store was crowded, and my brain filled in what it wanted to see. I was distracted, catching up with my cousin Kaitlyn about family gossip and our grandmother's increasing volatility. But Liz? No. It was recognition bias. Projection. I teach this stuff to my interns, but knowing the psychology doesn't stop the sting of memory.

I should be thinking about my patients, not ghosts from another life. I've got three reports due tomorrow, two intake summaries to finish, and a patient at the clinic. No time for distractions.

Still, as I pull into the narrow parking lot behind my office and the hospital, the thought follows me. If it was her, what would she be doing here? Liz's best friend, Trinity Paradise, lives in town... Maybe she's visiting, but those two are usually attached at the hip, and that woman was alone. I cut the engine, pocket my keys, and stare up at the snow-heavy sky pressing low over the valley. The air is crisp with the bite of winter, but for a moment, I swear I can still smell jasmine on the wind.

Inside, the office is quiet in that Sunday kind of way—still air, muted light, and the faint smell of peppermint tea from the mug I forgot to wash yesterday. The waiting-room lamps glow against the frost-laced windows, and my only patient of the day sits hunched in a corner chair, scrolling her phone until I open the door.

"Come on in, Kara," I tell her.

She's a nurse from the emergency department at Paradise General—exhausted, overworked, and barely holding it together. I've seen that look a hundred times this winter.

She tucks her phone away and forces a smile. "Sorry. I was just checking messages."

"No apology needed." I nod toward the couch as she enters. "Rough weekend?"

Her laugh is brittle. "They're all rough these days. People don't stop needing care just because we're short-staffed or it's the holidays."

She talks for a long time—about double shifts, the lack of sleep, the guilt of leaving her kids with her ex so she can work nights. I listen, scribbling notes I'll probably never read again, because it's not the paper that matters. It's the way her voice cracks on the words she doesn't mean to say.

When she stops talking, I give her a moment before speaking. "You're carrying too much alone," I tell her. "You know that, right?"

She looks at her hands. "If I let go, people get hurt."

I wish I had better answers. The truth is, I'm right there with her—different field, same exhaustion. I guide her through breathing work, offer a few grounding techniques, and schedule another session for next week. As she leaves, she hesitates in the doorway.

"Thanks, Dr. Dempsey." Her voice softens. "You always make it feel like I'm not losing my mind."

I smile, but her words linger after the door clicks shut. The quiet that follows isn't peace. It's emptiness.

I sink back into my chair, rubbing my face. My eyes ache. My brain buzzes with the constant noise of other people's pain. On the desk, my computer screen glows with unanswered emails. I click through them—messages from colleagues asking if I can take new referrals, continuing medical education reminders flagged red because the hours are required for my license renewal, research articles I'd love to read if I ever had the time.

My jaw tightens. I don't have the time. I don't even have the energy. But I'll say yes to much of this. I always do.

I scroll back up to a renewal notice from the College of Health and Care Professionals of British Columbia—sixteen hours of continuing education due by next month's end or my license lapses. They've even copied hospital administration for good measure. Who has time for professional development when you're one of three psychologists covering half the valley?

I close my laptop without reading the rest. It just feels impossible. And anyway, it'll still be there tomorrow, along with the growing pile of things I'm pretending I'll get to.

Out the window, daylight is fading fast. Snow drifts down in thin white ribbons, catching on the ledge. The heater clicks on with a soft groan. Maybe I should go home, but home doesn't feel like rest anymore. Not with all the added drama circling my family's winery and the mess we might be in, thanks to my grandmother and her particular way of being the matriarch.

For a long moment, I just sit. My mind loops back to the woman in the grocery store—the curve of her jaw, the familiar spark in her eyes. The memory shouldn't feel this raw. But Liz was never easy to forget. Leaving her was the right decision, but that doesn't mean it's stopped hurting. She wanted to stay close to her family, and I knew mine needed me here.

The office feels too big, too quiet. I built this space to help people heal, but some days it feels like I'm patching holes in everyone else's lives while mine quietly frays at the edges. Everyone in this valley depends on someone too tired to say no.

I pull out the reports I've fallen behind on. Patient charts stay current—I don't let those slide—but the rest stacks up faster than I can manage until the weight of it all feels crushing.

I'm about to give up and power down for the evening when my phone lights up—a name that guarantees my day isn't over.

"Hi, Evie," I say, bracing for the tempest that is my grandmother.

"Alaric, thank God you answered," she says, voice sharp. "Do you have any idea what's going on in this valley?"

I close my eyes and lean back. The storm has arrived.

Breathe in. Count to four. Breathe out. Count to four.

"I'm not sure," I say, rubbing the bridge of my nose. "What's happened now?"

Evelyn Dempsey sighs so loudly I have to pull the phone from my ear. "What's happened is incompetence, that's what. The investigators are useless. They still haven't questioned anyone at Paradise Hill. Not one. You'd think after everything that happened with the vineyard, they'd have enough sense to look closer."

I spin the chair toward the window, watching the parking lot lights blink through the falling snow. "They're still reviewing the reports. These things take time."

"Time is what they want us to waste," she snaps. "Mark my words, Alaric, someone over there is covering it up. Those Paradise people have friends in every office from here to Victoria. They're aiming at me to take our land."

I've heard all this before. Still, there's something new in her voice tonight, an edge of desperation that cuts through her usual fire. "You don't need to get involved," I tell her gently. "If you think it's serious, talk to your lawyer. Let him handle it."

She scoffs. "Lawyers only care when there's a bill to send. No, I'll handle it. I always do."

I want to press harder, ask what kind of sabotage she's talking about this time, but experience tells me that will only feed her anger. I've spent years, probably decades, fielding calls from her filled with gossip, complaints, and theories about the Paradises. I love her, but her approach drains me in a way no patient ever could.

"Evie," I say softly, "please just be careful."

Her tone softens. "I'm fine. Serafina's running the day-to-day and Dylan and Scott are helping out."

Sera is my sister, and Dylan and Scott are our cousins. Them helping out is news to me. I'll have to check in with my sisters, though probably only three of them because Evie wouldn't tell Ginny anything since she's married to a Paradise. We saw each other for breakfast at Evie's on Christmas morning, but that's not the place to talk.

I fight a sigh. "That's great."

She harrumphs. "If Trace and Max Paradise think they can intimidate me, they're sadly mistaken."

"They know better," I lie, hoping to steer us clear of another argument. She's in her mid-eighties and has been angry with the Paradise family as long as I can remember. She likely knows I'm lying, but this time she lets it go.

When I hang up, silence floods back in—heavy, bone-deep. I lean forward, elbows on my knees, staring at the faint reflection of my face in the window.

I used to love this work—the problem-solving, the connection, helping people find their way back to themselves. Now, it feels like I'm pouring from an empty cup. I've taken on too many clients, filled too many gaps at the hospital, and there's never enough time or energy left for me.

Outside, the snow has thickened, now lit by the glow of the streetlight. I tell myself I'll take a day off next weekend. Maybe even two. But I already know I won't.

Before I can set the phone down, it buzzes again. Same name on the screen. I sigh and answer, leaning back. "Hello?"

"You hung up on me," she accuses.

"I thought we were done."

"Done? Hardly. You didn't let me finish." Her voice sharpens. "You never let me finish."

I swivel the chair toward the window again. "All right, Evie. Finish."

"Do you know who I saw at the market this morning?" she asks.

I freeze for half a beat. She didn't see Liz. Couldn't have. But the coincidence tightens something in my chest. "Who?" I ask carefully.

"Vicky Paradise," she says, disgust dripping. "Parading around like she owns the valley. I swear, those people never quit showing off. And after all the damage they've done…" She trails off with a sigh that's half grief, half venom.

I press my thumb into the bridge of my nose. "Evie, Paradise Hill's been hit hard over the last year. Good for her for not hiding at home. And maybe she just needed groceries."

"You think it's a coincidence our irrigation lines were cut the same week their cottage burned? That we're losing bottling contracts we've held for twenty years? Someone's playing games, and it isn't us."

This again. The feud, the sabotage, the endless comparisons between our Black Bear Winery and Paradise Hill. I grew up on it—two families locked in competition so old no one remembers how it started. Most people in town stopped caring years ago. Everyone except Evelyn Dempsey.

"I really think you should call your lawyer," I tell her. "If there's something wrong with the irrigation, he can handle it before it gets worse."

She makes a dismissive noise. "I'm not wasting money on some man who barely remembers which side he's on. You think lawyers in this town don't drink Paradise wine?"

I almost laugh. "You make it sound like a conspiracy."

"Because it is," she says flatly. "And I *will not* sit by while they take what's ours. This winery has been in business for eight generations. I won't see it destroyed by people who think they can buy their way out of every mess they make."

Her voice trembles at the end, and that's what undoes me. The fire's still there, but so is fatigue. She's not the same woman who used to walk the rows at sunrise, coat unbuttoned, boots muddy, commanding foremen like a general. She sounds smaller now.

"Evie," I say gently, "you're not alone in this, okay? You've got Sera and Josie helping, and Addie's art exhibit at the diner is bringing good press."

"They're girls," she says, dismissing her granddaughters. "They don't understand what this land means. Ginny married a Paradise. You're the only one who's been true to this family. If you won't do it, I'm beginning to wonder if Dylan and Scott aren't better suited to take over when I'm gone."

"I think Sera and Josie are doing a great job—"

"They're too close to the Paradise family."

My sisters would be crushed if she handed the vineyard to my cousins, but arguing usually digs her heels in deeper. So I say nothing, but the guilt lands like a weight I can't shrug off. I moved home to help people, to build something that didn't depend on barrels, harvests, and grudges. But every time I hear the spite in her voice, I wonder… If I had agreed to take over the family vineyard, would it be different?

"I'll come by this week," I say softly. "Check on things. Maybe walk the rows with you."

That seems to placate her. "Good boy. Bring coffee. That fancy kind I like."

"I'll pick some up."

We talk a little longer about the weather and the neighbor's dog digging in her flower beds. By the time we say goodbye, her mood seems to have evened out, but the call leaves a heaviness behind.

I set my phone down and stare at it, my chest tightening with the familiar pull between duty and distance. I don't want any of this. I've tried not to be involved, but I haven't mastered that. Anyway, she's not wrong about one thing. Everyone in the valley is trying to protect what's theirs.

I look around the office, realize I'm not getting any more work done, and decide to head home.

Outside, the world feels muted, as if the valley itself is holding its breath. I lock the office door and pocket my keys, my boots crunching as I walk to the car. I picture my grandmother alone in that big house, stewing in her suspicions. She's stubborn, but she's also afraid, and that's the part that worries me.

Inside the car, I sit for a moment before starting the engine. The heater wheezes to life, fogging the windshield. My phone buzzes with another reminder about my CME credits being overdue. I swipe it away.

The phantom from this morning flickers again in my mind—the turn of her head, the way she brushed her hair behind her ear. But it had to be someone else.

Still, as I pull onto the road, the doubt lingers. Paradise isn't a town you end up in by mistake. And if Liz is here, crashing two store displays might be better than having to see me.

Three

Liz

The doors of Paradise General Hospital slide open with a hush of warm air and the faint scent of coffee and antiseptic as I step inside on my first Monday. I pause just inside the lobby, taking it in—the cacophony of voices, the echo of footsteps on tile, the way the morning light bounces off the polished floors. Everything here feels new, organized, and predictable. I like that.

After a short conversation with the woman at the front desk, I'm ready to go. I smooth my coat and glance down at my new hospital badge, which was waiting for me this morning. Elizabeth Ward, Assistant Director of Hospital Administration. That looks…right, like I finally found a place that sees me the way I've been trying to see myself.

Nurses move in clusters, staring at electronic medical records. A maintenance worker pushes a mop bucket past me, whistling softly. The whole place has a rhythm—steady, pulsing, certain. The opposite of the chaos I left behind in Vancouver, where everything was politics first, medicine second.

I draw a deep breath and let it fill all the way to the base of my lungs. My heartbeat slows. I follow the green line on the floor to the elevators and wait until I can step inside. Pushing the fifth-floor button, I catch my reflection—hair pulled tight, expression calm, but the pulse at my throat gives me away. When the doors slide open again, sunlight spills across a long corridor lined with frosted-glass doors and framed photos of smiling staff at charity events and holiday galas.

The reception desk stands before me, and I step forward to introduce myself. The woman behind the counter checks a clipboard and points me toward my new office. My heels click against the floor as I walk, nerves buzzing louder with each step. I was here for the interviews, but I was so nervous that nothing looks familiar.

First day. Don't screw it up.

The view from the window at the end of the hall catches me. Black Bear Lake is gray and choppy in the wind, mountains rising behind it like sentinels. The beauty of it steals my breath for a second.

"Hey, stranger."

I turn and find Trinity walking toward me, cheeks pink from the cold, a paper bag in her hand. Her scarf's half untucked, and her hair's loose around her face, the picture of effortless charm. She grins, though she looks a little pale. Trinity works here part-time on projects now so she can stay home with her son, Theo.

She hands me the bag. "It's pan au chocolat to celebrate your first day. Sorry about last night," she says. "After I spent the afternoon hugging the porcelain god, I thought it best just to send the boys with your dinner."

I laugh, taking the bag she offers. "Thanks. We missed you last night. I loved the hugs from my godson, and the pasta dish was fantastic. But I'm sorry for you. That doesn't sound like a great way to spend a Sunday."

"Right? Theo's daycare plague. He's fine now, of course, but I was down for the count." She presses a hand to her stomach and groans. "I think I saw my soul leave my body."

I raise an eyebrow. "Are you sure it's just a bug? You know Greyson has a certain…effect on women."

Her mouth drops open. "Don't you dare."

"Maybe you caught something else." I bounce my eyebrows at her.

"Absolutely not." She points at me with mock outrage. "Theo just turned three. One toddler is plenty. I'm not ready to chase another one while he's still climbing the furniture."

"Fair," I say, grinning. "Though I'm betting the nurses already have a pool."

She snorts. "They'd better not. If anyone asks, I'm just sleep-deprived."

It feels good to laugh like this, and to feel something other than the weight of what I left behind. Trinity's been a steady friend through all my worst decisions, and seeing her here, happy, makes me believe I can be that kind of grounded again.

"Come on," she says, motioning down the hall. "Let me give you the tour before Hudson gets you. He's punctual to a fault, so we've got about ten minutes."

We walk the maze of corridors together, and she points things out as we go. "Your office is here. The coffee station that actually works is there. The break room is down that hall. If you ever need quiet, the north stairwell is your best friend. No one uses it except a few residents hiding from rounds."

I try to memorize the layout of the place. There's life here—purpose—and I can already feel it catching under my skin.

"Hudson's great," she says as we approach a glass door marked Roger Hudson, Director of Hospital Administration. "Intense but fair. You'll be managing vendor contracts, budgets, accreditation reports, and one or two projects at a time. All the glamorous stuff no one else wants."

"Perfect," I say. "Give me spreadsheets over drama any

day."

She laughs, opening the door for me. "You might eat those words, but I admire the optimism."

Inside, Roger Hudson rises from behind his desk as we step in. He's tall, solid, silver-haired, the kind of man who looks like he's been running hospitals since before I finished elementary school. His office is spotless, the files color-coded, not a paper out of place.

"Elizabeth," he says, shaking my hand. "Welcome to Paradise General. We're glad to have you."

"Thank you," I reply, aware of the flutter in my chest. "Please call me Liz."

"And you can call me Hudson. It's a holdover from school where there were three Rogers in my class." He gestures for me to sit. "Trinity gave you the grand tour?"

I nod. "She's an excellent guide."

Trinity gives me a quick thumbs-up before slipping out.

Hudson opens a thin folder with my name on it. "Your experience at North Vancouver Hospital will come in handy here—budget restructuring, vendor negotiations, process improvements. That's exactly what we need. We're expanding with a new trauma wing, tech upgrades, and accreditation renewals. You'll find this place rewarding and demanding."

He slides a printed list toward me. It's long—vendor audits, contract reviews, staffing projections. My fingers itch for a pen. "I'll prioritize these by department," I tell him. "Starting with facilities and procurement. If we're heading into expansion, they'll set the pace."

A smile flickers across his face. "I like initiative. Just keep communication open. I don't micromanage, but I don't like surprises. We'll meet every Monday before the leadership meeting, which you may occasionally attend. But let's try to touch base daily before you leave for these first few weeks so I can answer any questions you may have."

"Understood."

"Trinity will be your point of contact for clinical

coordination," he adds. "Misty Bryant is our admin, and she will be a great help to you. Otherwise, my door's open."

The meeting ends efficiently, and when I leave his office, I feel the pressure and possibility settling over me. There's work to do, and that's exactly what I want. I see Misty's on the phone, so I wave, and she gives me a tight smile. She's busy.

Trinity's waiting by the elevator. "How'd it go?"

"He's all business," I say. "Which is perfect."

"Good. You'll fit right in." She presses the button. "You'll meet the department heads next week. For now, breathe. First days are supposed to be overwhelming."

"I'm fine," I say, mostly meaning it. "Honestly, this is the good kind of overwhelming."

We step into the elevator, and the doors close as monitors beep somewhere distant, a voice calls for Dr. Singh, and someone laughs near the nurses' station. It's a rhythm I could learn to love.

"Come on," Trinity says. "I'll buy you a coffee. You'll need the caffeine to survive orientation."

She walks me over to human resources by way of the cafeteria for fuel, and they give me a stack of paperwork to fill out, my new email address, a meeting time with IT in my office, and a list of videos to watch. Workplace Safety and Emergency Procedures. Privacy and Confidentiality. Respectful Workplace and Anti-Harassment. I'm in administration, so I should be excited, but these are the same everywhere, and we go through them once a year.

I spend the afternoon watching the videos, doing my best to stay awake and paying enough attention to pass the quiz at the end. If I fail, I'll have to sit through in-person training. *No thank you.*

Ready for a break, I text Trinity and find my way down to the hospital cafeteria to meet her. We grab a corner table near the window, and Trinity stirs cream into her herbal tea, watching the swirl before she looks up.

"You're doing great today," she says. "Hudson already told me he's impressed."

"That's a relief," I say, smiling. "I've had enough of bosses who make you guess."

She laughs, and then sobers a little. "There's one thing I should probably mention."

The way she says it gives me pause. "That sounds ominous."

"It's not," she hedges. "Just…something you should know." She leans closer. "You'll probably see Alaric soon. Like I told you, he's head of Behavioral Health. Brilliant, respected, patients adore him. He works seven days a week. But his family's complicated."

I nod. "They were difficult when we dated. His sisters are great. But his grandmother is an acquired taste. She didn't like me."

"To make matters worse, there have been investigations into Paradise Hill over the last couple of years. Sabotage, fires, property damage—at Black Bear Valley and at Paradise Hill. Supposedly, they're building a case, and people whisper. Around here, that kind of gossip sticks."

A shiver runs through me. Such an ugly mess. Trinity and I talked about this when she was dating Greyson and I was dating Alaric. Those families have a hatred that goes back generations.

Trinity sighs. "He's not a bad guy, Liz. Just…the feud. I didn't want you caught off guard."

"Thanks for the heads-up," I say, wrapping my hands around my cup. The heat seeps into my palms. "I can handle myself."

"I know you can." She studies me. "Just…stay focused. You've worked too hard to let anything derail that."

"I plan to."

Her phone buzzes, and her eyes travel over the screen. "I've got twenty minutes to get home so the nanny can make it to her evening class on time." She grabs her coat. "We'll catch up soon."

"Can't wait. And don't worry about me. I'll be fine."

She pulls her coat on. "What are you doing tonight?"

"Dinner with my brother and his family."

"Okay. Have fun and we'll get together soon."

When she's gone, I linger at the table, watching the snow pile in soft ridges along the glass. A truck with a sand and salt spreader rolls through the lot, making sure there are no slippery places.

I vow to take Trinity's words to heart. No distractions. No complications. Men with secrets and shadows have cost me enough already.

It's getting late, and I need to get my new-start packet over to human resources if I expect to be paid. I clear away my trash and head out of the cafeteria down an administrative hallway.

I'm on my way back from dropping off my paperwork when I nearly collide with someone rounding the corner outside the main elevators.

"Liz?"

My head snaps up. Josie Dempsey, one of Alaric's sisters. My smile falters, for barely a breath, but I feel it.

Her dark hair's shorter than I remember, a sleek bob that frames her grin before she sets her clipboard aside and pulls me into a hug. The scent of vanilla lotion and hospital soap hits me at once, familiar and strange all over again.

"Josie! Oh my God." I pull back to see her face. "I can't believe I ran into you. What are you doing here?"

"I needed to visit my cousin Scott. He was in a car accident over the weekend and broke a rib. I didn't expect to run into you here in Paradise."

"Oh! I hope your cousin is okay, and that makes sense. I never expected to be here, but Trinity found an opening at the hospital that hit me on the right day."

She smiles. "You're going to love it here. I know the pace isn't like Vancouver, but it really is a great place to live. Does…Ric know you're here?"

I tilt my head, lips pressing into something that isn't quite a smile. "I don't know. Today's my first day."

"He's going to go crazy when he finds out. I swear he's

still hung up on you."

I snort. "Somehow, I doubt that. He left and never looked back."

"I'll tell him I saw you. He's going to want to show you where all the locals go."

I force a smile, pretending her answer doesn't make my pulse trip. "That sounds great. I was planning to reach out once I got settled."

She nods, studying me for a beat longer than feels comfortable. Her face softens. "You look good, Liz. Happier."

"Trying to be."

"Good." She squeezes my arm. "Let's catch up properly. Coffee? Soon?"

"Absolutely."

She flashes that easy, knowing smile that used to make secrets impossible between us. "Perfect. I'll text you."

Then she's gone, disappearing through a side corridor.

So much for staying invisible. Alaric will know in five minutes that I'm here. Maybe he already does after the scene I caused at the market yesterday.

I straighten my badge, swallow the knot in my throat, and keep walking.

Time to prepare for the inevitable.

By the time I return to my office, the afternoon light has gone pale and gold. I set my bag down and stand by the window, tracing a line through the condensation on the glass.

This office isn't much—just a desk, a bookshelf, and a window—but it's mine, and it isn't a cubicle. It's my space and a chance to restart. Before I go, I take a minute to unpack a few personal items, including a framed photo of my nephew, Nicky, a small succulent I nearly killed during the move, and a notebook. On the first blank page, I write the words that feel truest.

Day One – Don't look back.

The ink soaks into the paper like a promise. Outside, snow flurries twist through the fading light. No more men who vanish when things get hard. Just me, this job, and a hospital that might finally give me a place to stay.

Four

Alaric

I don't even need to check my phone when the first text buzzes through this morning. I already know it's one of my sisters, probably the three I haven't heard from.

Josie's call last night to tell me Liz is here in Paradise knocked me off balance. Turns out what I saw at the market is exactly what my mind said it was.

Liz is the one who got away. I loved her. I wanted forever with her. But my family was coming apart at the seams, and my grandmother was in full crisis mode. I couldn't hold anything together, least of all my own relationship.

And anyway, the Dempseys are always in crisis mode. No one wants that in their life if they can avoid it. I did Liz a favor, keeping her away from all this. Only now she's here…

I pick up my phone, and sure enough, Addie, Sera, and

Ginny are lined up like a firing squad.

Addie: Don't be an idiot. She's here. Be nice.

Sera: It wouldn't kill you to show her around. She doesn't know anyone but Trinity.

Ginny: If you don't, I will. And you know how much I love stirring up hospital gossip.

I toss my phone onto the kitchen counter and lean against the sink, watching snowmelt trace thin rivers down the window. They're all thrilled that Liz Ward—*the Liz Ward*—is back in my life. She's moved to Paradise and is working at the hospital, the same one I walk into every morning pretending to have my life together.

The Dempsey women seem to think this is some kind of second-chance miracle. They don't remember the details—the way I left, the things I didn't say. My life was falling apart even back then, and dragging Liz into it would've been cruel. Now, four years later, they want me to pick up where I left off, as if love is a song you can just unpause.

The kettle clicks off, and I pour hot water over an English breakfast tea bag. The scent tugs at an old memory—Liz sitting cross-legged on the counter of her Vancouver apartment, teasing me for buying "*grown-up tea.*"

I stir the mug and tell myself to focus on the day ahead. But every thought finds its way back to Liz and our time together.

By the time I hit the road, the caffeine's barely kicked in, and my tea's already gone cold. I crank the car heater higher and try to focus on the snow-lined highway curling along the lake, on anything that isn't her.

Halfway into town, the car speakers light up with a call from my grandmother. Of course. "Good morning, Evie," I say, though I know better than to think this will be a good-morning kind of conversation.

"Don't you morning me," she fires back. "I heard your ex is working at the hospital."

I sigh. "News travels fast."

"News like this always does. I warned you about women tied to the Paradise family. Trinity Paradise is her best friend, isn't she?"

"She was when we were dating."

"Then she's trouble," she says simply. "And you've got enough of that to last you a lifetime."

I almost laugh. "You don't even know her."

"I met her, and I know you," she says. "And I know how evil that family is. They brought her here to spy on us for them. Stay away from her. You hear me?"

This is why I can't be with Liz. Nothing has changed.

By the time I'd finished my practicum in Vancouver, the Dempsey name was hanging by a thread. We look put together, but underneath we're carrying generations of resentment and attempts at control. Silence feels safer than honesty, and even our desire to protect each other usually backfires.

Not drawing Liz into this was my choice. She had her life in Vancouver—friends, a close family, stability. I told myself I was sparing her when I ended things. Yet even now, the memory of her eyes—quiet, steady, breaking without a sound—makes my stomach knot. I couldn't face that kind of honesty then. Maybe I still can't.

"I'm not planning anything," I say.

"You'd better not," Evie warns. "You've got too much to lose."

"I understand," I murmur, though we both know she means the family's reputation more than my heart.

Breathe in. Count to four. Breathe out. Count to four.

"Good." She pauses. "Keep your head on straight, Alaric."

The line clicks dead, but her warning lingers, and I feel that familiar squeeze of duty in my gut. It's not her words that stick. It's her tone, the same one she used on my father right before he cracked. Maybe that's the problem with being a

Dempsey. We mistake control for safety until it smothers everything else.

I get myself to work and start the day, but by midmorning, I'm already behind schedule. My inbox is a nightmare, and the one thing I'd been counting on—a quiet hour between appointments—has been hijacked by a calendar invite.

Hospital Compliance Meeting at three in the Administrative Conference Room.

Of course, that's where it is. The admin floor is where I hide when I need to breathe. But not today.

I hover over Decline, sigh, and hit Accept. Responsibility wins again.

My next patient, Shelly Martin, is already waiting. Mid-forties, overworked, invisible in her own home. We've been working on communication, getting her to use I statements instead of keeping everything bottled inside.

When I walk into the treatment room, she's sitting on the edge of the couch, shoulders tight. "Sorry I'm late," she says. "Traffic was bad."

"You're fine," I tell her, sitting down in my chair across from her. "How's your week been?"

"I tried what you said. Told my husband I feel ignored when he spends all evening on his phone."

"How'd he take it?"

"He said I'm too sensitive," she mutters, twisting her hands. "Then I felt guilty for saying anything."

I nod. "You don't need to feel guilty for wanting to be seen, Shelly."

Her eyes flick up, searching mine. "You look like someone who hasn't been seen either."

That catches me off guard. I almost laugh. "Rough night, that's all."

"Well," she says softly, "maybe try your own advice."

That earns her a smile. "Touché."

We talk for a while longer, and when we finish her session, she leaves looking lighter. I jot a note in her chart, though my pen drags across the page. My brain's miles away, caught between dread and curiosity about that meeting invitation I wish I hadn't accepted. Something in my gut tells me Liz Ward will be there, and I am absolutely not ready for that.

The afternoon slides by in a blur of charts and consultations until I look up and realize my appointment has run long and I'm now ten minutes late. *Fantastic*. I shove papers into a folder, grab my jacket, and jog down the hall, muttering apologies to passing nurses.

By the time I reach the admin wing, the corridor is quiet, the meeting already underway. The glass door to the conference room stands open, and I catch a glimpse of her before she notices me. Liz is at the head of the table, hair swept back, posture straight, tablet in hand. Calm. Controlled. Everything I'm not.

I freeze for a heartbeat before my mouth catches up to my brain. "You're the new assistant director?"

She glances up and recognition flashes, but her expression smooths before I can read it. "You're the noncompliant psychologist."

The words crackle like a spark between us.

I clear my throat. "Guess that memo forgot to mention I'm also punctual?"

One brow lifts. "And defensive. Not a good start."

She's still Liz. Still impossible.

I take the empty chair across from her, willing my pulse to settle. I didn't realize this meeting was just me. "When did you move into compliance? What happened to physiotherapy?"

"I moved into hospital administration several years ago." Her tone is clipped. "My team handles continuing-education credits, certifications, and licensing renewals. Including yours."

She pushes a piece of paper across the table. "You're missing nineteen hours of compliance."

"Wait." I look down at the paper. "That includes three for this year. I'll be compliant with sixteen hours."

She shakes her head. "You're already out of compliance, so they've tacked on the three that should be done by now. You need them completed by the end of next month."

I stare at the sheet. She's all business, but I know that tone, a thin edge of frustration hiding under professionalism.

"We don't have enough psychologists here in Black Bear Valley," she continues. "If patients don't get their mental-health needs met, we're in trouble."

"I couldn't agree more. I'll work with HR on recruiting."

Her gaze flicks up, cool and unwavering. "We'll be in a bigger hole if you stay noncompliant. Are you aware that any session you bill right now could be rejected by BC Health? And your malpractice insurance won't cover you if there's an issue?"

I hang my head. I've been ignoring notices from the insurance company too. "Okay. I'll do some research and find somewhere to get my credits."

She slides a small stack of papers across the table. "Already done. You're going to Kauai for six days to earn twenty CME hours. I convinced accounting to merge last year's and this year's CME allowances to cover it. You just need to book your flight."

For a moment, I can only blink at her. "You—what?"

She finally meets my eyes, the faintest glint of challenge there. "You're welcome."

A reluctant laugh escapes me. "I don't know how I'm going to fit in a week off, but...maybe a break's what I need."

"Maybe it is," she says, collecting her folder.

"Thank you," I manage.

She stands to leave, but I stay seated, watching her gather her papers, the pen sliding behind her ear like she used to do when she was studying late.

My chest tightens. "Liz..." I say before I can stop myself.

She pauses but doesn't turn back. "Dr. Dempsey."

"Can we talk?"

"About your CMEs?"

"No." I stand. "About before."

Now, she turns, slow and measured. "Before what?"

"You know what," I say quietly. "Back in Vancouver."

A breath leaves her like a laugh. "You mean when we talked about getting married, and then you showed up at my apartment and broke it off as you were driving out of town?"

"That's not— " I start, then stop. "Okay, it is. But it wasn't because of you."

She folds her arms. "That's the classic line, but I already knew that."

"I mean it. Things were falling apart. I'd gone to Vancouver because I was running away from my family, but realized I needed to come back. I couldn't drag someone into that."

"I wasn't just someone."

"I know." The words scrape my throat. "That's why I couldn't ask you to come with me. You had a life there. I wasn't going to ruin it because mine was burning down."

Her eyes soften for half a second before she straightens again, the professional mask sliding back into place. "You don't get to decide what I can handle," she says quietly. "You just left."

She's right. And I've known it every day since.

"I wanted to call," I admit. "Every day for months. But I knew if I did, I wouldn't be able to hang up."

Her gaze flicks to the folder on the table, then back to me. "Well, now you don't have to. We work in the same building. Congratulations."

She turns, heels clicking across the floor. I should let her go, let professionalism win, but the apology forces its way out anyway. "Liz, for what it's worth," I say softly, "I'm sorry."

Her voice is low, almost gentle. "Apologies are easy, Alaric. Change is harder."

The door closes behind her, and the silence that follows feels like the punishment I've earned. I sink back into the chair and press my palms over my face. I've spent four years telling myself I did the right thing, and one meeting with her blows it all apart.

Someone laughs down the hall, a cart rattles over the linoleum, and life goes on as if my world didn't just tilt off its axis. Maybe Evie was right. Maybe I should've kept my head straighter. My heart's a lousy listener, and it just remembered exactly what it lost, and what it still wants back.

Five

Liz

After I've finished the afternoon's meetings, I step into Hudson's office, clutching my notebook, and he glances up from his monitor with a smile that makes me think he's waiting to be impressed.

"Is it that time already?"

"Well, I'm done with the meetings, but if you need some time, we can talk tomorrow."

"No, no. Sit. I'll be here for hours figuring out how accounting messed up the budgets we put together last fall."

"Sounds like fun."

"Hardly. But tell me, how's it going? Feedback has been super positive."

"Already? Well, thank you. I've got a lot to learn." I look down at my notes. "I sat down this afternoon with everyone who was out of compliance. Grace Nishida wants to retire. Her vision isn't as sharp as it used to be, and she doesn't want to risk malpractice."

Hudson sits back. "Is she even fifty?"

"Forty-five."

He makes a quick note. "Good catch. I'll meet with her and see if she'd move into a mentoring role for the surgical interns. She's too good to lose."

I nod. "I think anything's worth a try. All she can tell you is no."

He types something into his computer and looks at me again, so I continue. "Dr. Wells and Ryker Paradise already scheduled their CMEs. They were short two hours, so they're doing a BC Health course up north."

"Great." He leans forward. "How about our biggest offender?"

I smile. "You must mean Alaric Dempsey."

"Exactly."

"I've confirmed that he's all set to fulfill his continuing medical education requirement. Twenty hours next month in Hawaii."

Hudson blinks. "Hawaii? You got him to commit to something in Hawaii?"

"It's all done."

He laughs, shaking his head. "Unbelievable. We've been sending him emails for months."

"I might have nudged things along." I slide the file across his desk. "The hospital's portion of the registration is complete, and the conference approved him. He still needs to book his flight, but everything else is finished."

Hudson flips through the paperwork. "How did you manage this?"

"I figured he's too busy to deal with logistics. He's working seven days a week right now, filling in shifts, running Behavioral Health, probably putting out fires no one tells you about. So I took care of the setup myself."

He looks up at me, clearly impressed. "Liz, this is incredible. We can't afford to lose him. You've solved one of my biggest headaches."

"I just made it easier for him to do something good for himself," I say, tucking my pen under my notebook strap. "He won't take time off unless someone pushes him. Now, he has no excuse."

Hudson laughs again, leaning back until his chair creaks. "You might be the first person who's ever managed to out-organize Alaric Dempsey."

Hearing his name out loud does something strange to my chest. I force a smile. "I'll take that as a compliment."

"It is. Keep this up and I'll have to change your title from Assistant Director to Miracle Worker." He nods, still studying the papers as he hands them back. "Seriously, nice work."

"Thank you." I stand, tucking the file back into my binder. "I'll follow up next week to make sure he booked the flight."

"Please do. And if you can get him to actually relax once he's there, I'll personally nominate you for sainthood."

"Let's not get carried away. One miracle at a time."

He chuckles, waving me off, and I can't help smiling to myself. If only he knew how complicated that miracle really was.

"Hey, Liz, wait a second." Hudson's voice stops me halfway to the door.

I turn back. "Yes?"

"When exactly is that conference in Hawaii?"

"Next month. The third week of February. It's the Western Alliance for Medical Innovation."

His eyes light with recognition. "That's the one I signed up for. The administrative track."

"You're going?"

"I was," he says with a sigh. "Now, I can't. The board rescheduled the quarterly budget review for that week." He leans back, thoughtful. "But someone should go. Someone organized. Someone who can make sure Dr. Dempsey actually attends the sessions and gets his required hours."

The way he says this makes my stomach tighten. "You mean…me?"

He gives me a calm, managerial smile. "You've already done all the groundwork. You know the itinerary, the program director, and the credit requirements. You're the logical choice."

"I set it up so Alaric—Dr. Dempsey—could relax and take a real break. The last thing he needs is someone from admin shadowing him with a clipboard."

He shakes his head. "You make it sound like I'm asking you to babysit. I just want someone there who can make sure the hospital's investment pays off. And I've already booked a spot in the admin sessions. Consider it professional development. Besides, Hawaii in February isn't exactly punishment."

"It's work," I say automatically, though my voice wavers. I haven't taken a real vacation in years.

Hudson catches the hesitation and pounces. "Perfect. You can attend a few administrative sessions, represent the hospital, enjoy the sun, maybe a luau, and make sure Dempsey checks in at his classes. I'll authorize the travel today and have Misty get it moved into your name."

Misty Brandt hasn't said two words to me thus far and hasn't been very helpful. I'm not sure how that will go. "I really don't think—"

He raises a hand, ending the conversation. "I do. Pack something tropical and bring your badge. You're going."

I exhale, knowing I've lost. "Fine. But if Dr. Dempsey skips out for surfing lessons, I'm not chasing him down the beach."

Hudson grins. "Deal."

A few moments later, the elevator doors slide open at the end of the hall, and as I step inside, my reflection stares back—wide eyes, a faint flush. *Hawaii. With Alaric Dempsey. What could possibly go wrong?*

Back in my office, I'm not sure if I should scream in frustration or celebrate a free week in the islands. Instead, I text Trinity.

Me: Hey, are you around? Can I come by after work?

Her reply comes quickly.

Trinity: Come on over. Greyson's working the late shift tonight. We can order pizza.

I finish my last few tasks and pack my bag, frustration growing with every step. By the time I pull into Trinity's building's guest parking, the sun's gone and the cold has that sharp edge that sneaks in once the snow starts to refreeze. I buzz her unit, and the click of the lock feels like an exhale I've been holding in all day.

I've spent the entire drive over working myself up about Alaric Dempsey—why Hudson thinks I should keep an eye on him in Hawaii, why I agreed, and how on Earth I'm supposed to survive a week in Hawaii with the man my heart once belonged to.

Upstairs, Trinity opens the door before I even knock, holding out a glass. "You sounded like you need this."

"Desperately." I step inside and take the drink, something pale and citrusy with a sugared rim. Warmth hits instantly, both from the cocktail and the fire flickering in her living room.

Before I can launch into my rant, something on the dining table catches my eye. Blueprints, sketches, and color samples are spread across the surface, anchored by a mug and a tape measure. "What's all this?"

Trinity grins, brushing a stray curl off her cheek. "Greyson and I are thinking about building. We inherited a plot up on the cliffs overlooking the lake, just west of where Ryker and Beckett live."

"On Paradise Hill land?" I ask, circling the table.

"Technically, yeah. But it's the rocky stretch that can't support vines. Useless for wine, perfect for a house. Greyson keeps saying it's the best view in the valley. Their grandparents gave each of them a plot of land, so he's probably right."

Seems like they're more than just thinking about it. These plans are detailed—big windows, a wraparound deck, and an open kitchen that spills into a living area with floor-to-ceiling glass. I can already imagine the sunsets pouring through. "It's beautiful."

Her face softens. "We've outgrown the condo. Between his hospital shifts, my admin work done mostly from home, all of Theo's toys, and the constant parade of family dropping by, it's starting to feel small. This seems like the next step."

I smile, caught up in her excitement. "It looks like home already. And I see extra rooms for when your family grows."

She nudges my shoulder. "Enough about me. What's going on? You sounded stressed."

I take a long sip, letting the sugar melt on my tongue. "Let's just say our boss has a sense of humor, and it involves sending me to Hawaii with Alaric Dempsey."

Her eyes widen. "Oh, this I've got to hear." Trinity moves into the living room and pats the sofa. "Sit. Start from the top."

I sink into the cushion, kicking off my heels and curling one leg beneath me. She tucks her feet under her, glass in hand as well, and waits, the picture of patience and quiet curiosity.

"How was your day?" she prompts.

I laugh softly. "Busy. Productive. Infuriating."

"Infuriating sounds interesting."

"I arranged for Dr. Dempsey to catch up on continuing education hours next month at a conference on Kauai, and when I told Hudson about it, he assigned me to go along in his place."

Her lips twitch. "You and Ric? I told you you'd run into him."

"You were a little late since you waited to tell me until after I moved here."

"Hawaii sounds lovely." She doesn't push. She just waits until I fill the silence.

"Yes, Hudson realized Dr. Dempsey will be attending the same conference he was supposed to go to but can't."

Her brow furrows.

"The board scheduled a budget review, so now I'm going instead. He wants me to attend a few admin sessions and make sure Alaric gets to his classes." I add air quotes around the last part.

"You know that's how Greyson and I met."

I shake my head. "No, it isn't. He sat down next to you on the ferry. You two just hooked up after that. Not the same thing."

She laughs. "Still, conferences are magical."

"Yes, for one-night stands. And before you suggest it, Ric and I have been there, done that."

Trinity leans back, biting her grin. "So your boss wants you to babysit your ex-boyfriend in Hawaii?"

"I didn't tell Hudson he was my ex-boyfriend. I didn't think there was a reason to." I rub my temples. "It's not professional. But this is not healthy. And it's definitely not my idea of a vacation."

"Why didn't you tell Hudson you didn't feel comfortable with this?"

"I'm not going to tell my boss about my personal life. This is part of my job. I can do it."

She hums, seeming unconvinced. "Are you sure?"

"It's fine," I say too quickly. "I'm just getting used to him being around. The last time I saw him was three years ago at Leah and Trey's twins' christening in North Van, and he disappeared before the party. But we've both moved on."

Trinity studies me over the rim of her glass. "And yet here you are, worked up enough to come over the minute your day ended."

I open my mouth to argue, but I can't. My thoughts tumble back to Alaric's sharp eyes during our meeting, the way his voice still finds that nerve I swore I buried. "I just don't want to dredge up the past," I say finally. "It ended for a reason."

She nods slowly. "Sometimes healing means facing what broke you."

The words land like a pebble in still water, rippling outward until something deep inside me shifts. *No. That can't be true. I've built a life, a career, a new version of myself.* But even as I think it, I know she's right. I'm not over him. I never really have been.

I look down at my glass, watching the ice swirl. "Then I guess it's time to face it."

Trinity smiles. "Or at least survive a week in the tropics without losing your mind."

"Strictly by the book," I say, nodding, as if I can convince myself. "Professional. Civil. That's it."

"Sure," she says with a teasing glint. "What could possibly go wrong?"

Six

Alaric

Mikey's is alive with Friday-night noise. Laughter mixes with clinking glasses and the low strum of a guitar sliding through the speakers. Snow melts off boots by the door and puddles on the worn wood floor. I hadn't planned on stopping. The idea was to go home, microwave something sad, and fall asleep in front of the game. But I ran into my sister Ginny and Ryker, her husband, as I was walking out, and somehow, that turned into a beer in my hand and a booth in the corner.

Ryker leans back, one arm stretched across the seat. Ginny sits across from him, cheeks pink from the cold, smiling into her drink. They make it look effortless, being part of something.

"You look like someone told you year-end reports are making a comeback," Ryker says. "Is that scowl permanent now or just your resting face?"

I take a slow sip, mostly to buy time. "Some of us work real jobs. You just play with toddlers and call it medicine."

He laughs. "That's Dr. Toddler to you."

Ginny snorts into her wine. "Oh, don't start that again. You two are like kids on a playground."

"Pretty sure kids have more fun," I say. "I spent half the week buried under compliance reports. Red tape everywhere. Bureaucracy's a lot like an ex. Keeps coming back to remind you of your mistakes."

Ginny almost chokes on her drink. Ryker slaps the table, laughing. "That's one way to put it. Sounds like you and the hospital's new assistant director are on great terms."

"Admin and I have an understanding," I say. "They keep sending emails, and I keep ignoring them."

"You need to lighten up," Ginny tells me. "Come over tomorrow. Everyone will be at our place to watch the hockey game. Join us. We'll order wings, yell at the TV, and pretend we don't have jobs."

I let the invitation hang. There's an easy warmth between them I'm not sure I remember how to fit into, and also, that's Paradise territory. I tell myself I don't care what Evie thinks of my life, but I also avoid picking fights when I can. "I'll think about it," I say, which means I won't.

Ryker grins. "Translation is he'll sit at home working on patient charts."

"Someone's got to keep the world turning."

Ginny taps her finger against my hand. "You know, for a guy who tells other people how to live, you're terrible at doing it yourself."

"Occupational hazard."

She laughs again, and for a moment, I almost forget the week, the weight, the way this town still looks at my family like we're the villains in someone else's story. The noise of the bar throbs around me, warm and alive. I let it. But when Ryker signals the server for another round, I check my watch.

He excuses himself to grab the drinks, leaving me and Ginny alone. She swirls what's left of her wine and studies me. "Have you heard from our dear grandmother lately?"

I let out a short laugh. "Entirely too often. She's on edge about something, more than usual."

Ginny arches a brow. "That narrows it down."

"She mentioned that Dylan and Scott are working at the vineyard. Do you know what they're doing? I didn't want to unpack that box with her. Not that she'd give me a straight answer, anyway."

Ginny groans. "God help us. If those two are learning the ropes, they'll hang themselves with them."

"Evie's been hinting that she might not see Sera or Josie as the ones to take over when she steps down."

Ginny snorts. "She'll step down when they put her in a pine box and not a second before. If Dylan or Scott ever ran Black Bear, it'd be over in a month. The feud with the Paradises would become a five-alarm fire. And they'd probably end up in jail."

"Agreed," I say. "Disastrous doesn't begin to cover it."

Ryker returns with fresh drinks, sliding a pint toward me and setting another glass of wine in front of Ginny. "You two look serious. Who died?"

"Just talking about our family," Ginny says. "Specifically the part that's still trying to outlive us all."

Ryker chuckles. "Ah, Evelyn Dempsey. Still terrifying?"

I pick up the glass, the condensation cold against my palm. "More than ever."

He sits down, lowering his voice. "Is she talking about the investigation?"

I look over at him. "What investigation?"

"The one into her supposed involvement with the Paradise vineyard sabotage."

"You mean the Zach stuff?"

Ginny rolls her eyes. "That, plus a dozen other things, including the fire before Christmas. I heard the police are poking around again."

My head snaps back. "You're kidding."

"Wish I was," Ryker says. "We're leaving that to Tarryn and my dad, but still. Has she said anything?"

I shake my head. "Not to me. She's nervous about something, but she's not talking about it."

Ryker studies me. "You think that's because she's behind it?"

That sends a rock to my gut. I set my drink down, watching the foam settle. "I don't speculate about my patients or my family," I say carefully. "But I do know when someone's losing sleep."

Ginny frowns. "Meaning?"

"Meaning she's worried. Whether it's guilt or pride or just fear of losing control, I can't say. But something's eating at her."

Ryker nods. "Then maybe someone needs to watch her a little more closely."

"Someone always is," I say, forcing a small smile. "We just try not to let her notice."

Ginny laughs under her breath. "Good luck with that."

Ryker clinks his glass against mine. "To surviving family politics."

I lift mine. "Barely." And then I stand, leaving my half-full glass behind. "I need to get home. If I don't work out first thing in the morning, I start falling asleep mid afternoon."

"Come over tomorrow night," Ginny insists. "The Vancouver Bears are heading toward playoffs, and Jacob Wheeler's playing."

Jacob is from Paradise, and all of Black Bear Valley follows his success.

"I'll do my best," I say.

Ryker rolls his eyes. "You're hopeless."

"Consistent," I say, tossing a few bills on the table.

Outside, snow spills through the streetlights. Behind me, their laughter trails out the door. It's easier to keep walking than admit I wish I'd stayed. Maybe that's why I keep my distance. Any kind of relationship seems complicated to me. With Evie, even silence feels like a negotiation I'm losing.

I remember how our dad used to tense up whenever his mother called. Now, I get it. She fired him and both of his siblings from the vineyard and cut them off completely. She now focuses on her grandchildren. Dad moved up north years ago, runs a smaller vineyard operation, and is in a much better place with his second wife and their business. I'm glad he got out.

I take the long way home, down the hill past the darkened storefronts and the bakery that I imagine still smells faintly of sugar and yeast. It's quiet in a way that leaves too much room for thinking.

I reach the overlook near Black Bear Lake, and the town lights shimmer below. I park and look out over town, trying not to think about how small it all seems from up here. But my mind goes exactly where I don't want it to.

Liz Ward. Every time I hear her name, something in me tightens. She's not supposed to matter anymore. Four years should be enough to dull anything. But all it takes is someone saying *Ms. Ward* in a clipped, professional tone, and I'm right back there, watching her close the door, calm as ever, while everything in me cracked.

Maybe that's what really gets me. No matter how long I've been home, I can't escape the shadows. The Dempsey name hangs over me like storm clouds. Everyone smiles, but I see it in their eyes. The feud. The whispers. My grandmother's voice behind every headline.

She's too frail to run the vineyard, not that she'd ever admit it. Yet she still runs the narrative. She calls me relentlessly, and probably most of my siblings too. And it isn't affection. She calls to maintain control. Her contact isn't nurturing. It's surveillance, manipulation, and grooming.

She's the reason I became a psychologist. But I'd never tell her that.

Maybe it's easier to play the grumpy recluse than admit I can't walk away. Because walking away means leaving my sisters to deal with her alone. And being present means getting pulled back into the dinners, the gossip, the expectations—the name I'm supposed to defend even when I don't believe in it anymore.

I stay until my fingers are frozen and then I get back in the car and head home.

Snow is falling heavier by the time I turn onto my street. Headlights sweep across my driveway, and for a second, I think they're mine until I see the silver Mercedes sedan idling at the curb, engine purring. A woman stands in the porch light, coat buttoned to her throat, posture straight as a ruler.

Of course, she's here.

Breathe in. Count to four. Breathe out. Count to four.

I park and climb out of the truck, my breath misting in the cold. "Evening, Evie."

My grandmother turns, hair dusted with snow. "You don't answer your phone."

"That's usually a clue," I say, pushing past her toward the door.

She follows, uninvited, the same way she always has. By the time I hang up my coat, she's in the kitchen, flicking the light on, scanning the place like she's evaluating an acquisition.

Evelyn arches a brow. "You missed our family dinner tonight. You didn't even send your sister a message."

"I've been busy."

"With what? Avoiding responsibility?" Her tone sharpens. "Do you have any idea how it looks when you don't show up? The Paradises are whispering again about that fire, the water rights, the shipments, and a dozen other things."

"Same gossip, different year," I say. "They'll move on."

"You're a Dempsey," she snaps. "You don't vanish when people start talking about your family."

"Our integrity's not something you fix with a photo op," I say.

Her smile turns thin. "You think this independence makes you principled. It makes you naïve. Everything you are exists because I built it."

"I'm not denying that."

"Then act like it," she says. "Show up. Remind them who we are."

I shake my head. "You can defend the name without me."

She steps closer. "Without you?" Her voice dips low, dangerous. "You think you can stand apart from this family, but you're still wearing the name. You walk into that hospital, and they see me. Don't forget that."

"I'm not getting involved," I say, quiet but firm. "You can keep fighting your battles without dragging me into them."

Her eyes narrow. "You'll regret this," she says. "When it all collapses, you'll wish you'd chosen the winning side."

She doesn't wait for an answer. Her heels click, coat flaring as she walks out.

The door shuts behind her, but her perfume lingers, sharp and suffocating.

I stare for a long time at the patch of melted snow on the floor where she stood. My body feels heavy, not from guilt, just fatigue. She's exhausting, manipulative, impossible, and somehow, still the center of gravity we all keep orbiting, even when we swear we're done.

The heater clicks on, and I pour what's left of the whiskey in my cabinet into a glass and flop into a chair at the table. Outside, the snow keeps falling, and the world looks clean, like maybe I could keep it that way if I just stay out of her reach.

I tell myself I don't need anyone, that solitude's easier. Predictable. But the truth of the matter won't fade. I'm here to keep the others safe from her.

I take a slow drink, watching the amber light fade from the surface of the liquid, and let the quiet settle.

Maybe freedom's just another kind of servitude.

Seven

Liz

The administrative wing of the hospital feels different on Saturdays. Quieter. A different energy. I push through the main doors, and my sneakers suddenly seem squeaky as they echo down the hall. The lights are dimmed and a maintenance cart rattles somewhere in the distance, the only sign of life.

I tell myself I'm here because I'm still learning the systems and it takes me longer to get things done. That's the practical reason. But the truth is, I don't really know what to do with free time yet.

I'm still proving—to Hudson and to myself—that I belong in this position, that I'm not just the woman Trinity recommended. I want to earn it, every bit of it. And anyway, I can't expect Trinity to entertain me all the time.

I hang my coat in my office, boot up my computer, and let

the rhythm of work settle around me. This is the kind of Saturday I can manage—productive and safe.

I open the spreadsheet Misty keeps on the shared drive with the figures Hudson needs for his leadership meeting next week. The numbers stare back in neat rows, color-coded and perfectly aligned, at least at first glance.

It doesn't take long to spot the trouble—a column total that's off by a few thousand. A date transposed in a header that shifts a quarterly figure into the wrong fiscal year. Nothing catastrophic, but enough to raise questions if Hudson uses it as-is.

I correct each line carefully, noting every change in my log. No need to rock the boat. No reason to make a big deal out of it. I enter the right numbers into the slides Hudson asked me to use and send them off to him, copying Misty. I'll let her know what I found quietly next week.

By the time I finish, the coffee in my mug has gone cold. I'm rereading a slide deck when I hear a voice behind me.

"You haven't been here long enough to give up your weekends."

I glance over my shoulder, smiling at Hudson. "I'm still getting my bearings. The learning curve's steep, and I didn't want to fall behind. Plus, I wanted to get the slides ready for your leadership presentation."

He steps closer, leaning over the back of my chair to scan the open file. His brow lifts. "This is great. Exactly what I was hoping for." He scrolls through a few slides, nodding. "The numbers line up perfectly. Nice work."

The praise catches me off guard. I thank him, and he continues down the hall, already on to the next thing. I let out a breath. I've been here a week, and I'm already cleaning up someone else's mistakes. If I miss even one of my own, I won't get the same benefit of the doubt. Hudson seems to trust me, but I'm still new so that trust feels fragile, something I have to hold carefully or risk watching it crack.

By the time my stomach reminds me it's past lunch, the

administration wing feels almost asleep. The cafeteria tables sit mostly empty. A few nurses cluster near the window, laughing over something on a phone.

I pick a seat by the far wall with my salad and an energy bar. The quiet stretches between every sound, amplifying how alone I feel. Everyone else has somewhere to be, something waiting for them outside these walls. Weekend plans. Families. Friends. I have an inbox full of half-finished reports.

I scroll through a few emails before giving up and texting Trinity.

Me: How's it going? I'm at work. Trying to get ahead before Monday eats me alive.

Her reply comes quickly.

Trinity: You're at work? It's Saturday! People in Paradise have balance. We don't work weekends unless absolutely necessary.

I chuckle and start to send a reminder about my short tenure and steep learning curve, but another message pops up before I can answer.

Trinity: Ginny told me this morning that she invited you over for the hockey game tonight. You know all the guys and their partners are great.

I smile despite myself. My first instinct was to say no. I'm tired, and my idea of recovery usually involves laundry and a quiet evening with my laptop. But the thought lingers.

I don't know many people here. Maybe through Trinity's sisters-in-law I can meet some. Maybe I can stop being the woman who spends her Saturdays with spreadsheets and lukewarm coffee.

Me: Send me their address. I'll be there about five.

When the message sends, I stare at it for a moment, surprised by my own decisiveness. Maybe saying yes is how things start to change.

I tuck my phone away and finish my lunch slowly, feeling a little better about my place in the world.

In the late afternoon, as the last of the daylight fades through the frosted windows, painting long shadows across my desk, I finish one more task, save the file, and power down my laptop.

The screen goes black, and for a second, my reflection stares back—hair pulled into a messy twist, faint circles under my eyes. I look tired. Not the kind of tired a nap fixes, but one that comes from running too hard after something I haven't caught yet.

I think again about this evening's invitation and almost type out a polite excuse. *Next time. Maybe.* But the thought of another night alone in the cottage makes my chest ache a little. I'll go to meet new people, to start building a life here. I don't want to be alone.

I put on my coat and step out into the cold. The drive to Ryker and Ginny's place takes me across the bridge and through the Paradise Hill vineyard. Snow blankets the winter-bare rows of vines on both sides, drawn like faint pencil lines against the white. A few leftover holiday lights blink in windows, cutting through the dusk.

The longer I drive, the more the tightness in my shoulders starts to ease. The town looks smaller at night, gentler somehow. By the time I turn onto their street, I'm feeling excited.

I step through the door, following the sign's direction to *just come in,* and find Ryker and Ginny's house brimming with noise and warmth. Laughter erupts from the kitchen, and someone cheers as the TV blares. The smell of garlic and melted cheese fills the air, mixing with woodsmoke and the faint bite of winter that clings to my coat.

Trinity spots me before I can even take off my boots. "You made it!" she says, pulling me into a hug. "Come on. Everyone's here."

She leads me into the living room where the Paradise family has gathered. Greyson's brothers—Kingston, Beckett, and Ryker—have claimed the couches, teasing each other over plays like the outcome of the game depends on their commentary. Their sister, Tarryn, joins in from the kitchen island, laughing as Trinity introduces me around.

I already know Elise, Kingston's fiancée, from the time I've spent with Trinity. She smiles warmly and hands me a glass of wine. Beckett's wife, Sadie, sits beside her, her baby boy, Will, asleep against her shoulder. "Six and a half months," she says proudly when I ask.

Ginny waves from across the room, grinning. "We met when she was dating my brother back when they lived in Vancouver," she says, and there's mischief in her tone that makes Trinity roll her eyes.

Tarryn's husband, Declan, is at the stove, flipping sliders like a man in his element. He offers me one over the counter with a grin. "Welcome to the madness."

The noise, the teasing, the comfortable rhythm—it all pulls me in. I find myself smiling, relaxing into it. Still, part of me feels like I'm watching through glass, half in and half out of something I haven't earned yet.

Then the door opens.

The cold rushes in, followed by a familiar voice. "Sorry I'm late. Traffic was—"

Alaric stops when he sees me. For a moment, we just stare. His eyes widen, then narrow slightly.

Sadie doesn't miss a beat. "Well, this is a surprise. You two know each other?"

Ginny smirks from her spot by the counter. "Oh, they more than know each other."

My face heats instantly. "We work together," I say, hoping that'll end it.

"Used to date," Ginny corrects, grinning wider.

Alaric rubs the back of his neck, clearly wishing the floor would open up. "It's fine, Ginny. You don't have to narrate."

The teasing fades into laughter, and then the Bears score a goal, so we're left in our own little awkward bubble in the corner of the room.

"I didn't expect to see you here," I say quietly.

"I could say the same," he replies. "But that seems to be a theme for me lately. It's nice to see you beyond the walls of the hospital. Can I get you a drink? It would be nice to catch up a bit in a non-professional setting."

Nothing wrong with being polite, I remind myself. "I'd love a drink. Thank you."

He nods and goes over to examine the series of wine bottles set up on the counter. After a moment, he returns with two glasses of red. Of course, he remembers what I like.

"Let's see if this stuff is any good, shall we?" he asks loud enough to get a rise out of the sports fans on the couch.

Ryker snorts. "Careful. If Evie hears you compliment Paradise Hill wine, she'll have a stroke."

Laughter rolls through the room. Someone mutters something about loyalty clauses and family bylaws.

Alaric takes a measured sip, his expression giving nothing away. He glances around the room—at the familiar faces, the unspoken rules, the lines that never stop being drawn—and I catch the flicker of something restrained in his eyes. Not annoyance. Resignation.

"Anyway," Alaric says, turning his attention to me once the ribbing dies down. "What made you trade Vancouver for Paradise?"

I steel myself to look him in the eye and be pleasant. It's much harder without the armor of professionalism around me. "My parents moved to Mexico a while back, and my brother, Mark, and his family moved here. Trinity's been after me for years to come to Paradise, so when admin at the hospital started expanding, she let me know, and I jumped on it."

His expression softens. "You always did land on your feet."

I shrug. "I rented a little cottage a few blocks from the hospital. It's small, but bigger than my apartment in Vancouver, and I can walk to work. No commute, no traffic, just me and the smell of cedar in the mornings."

"That sounds…very you."

There's a pause that's heavy with all the things we're not saying. Better to return to more work-related ground.

"So," I continue, "Hudson was supposed to go to Kauai for that hospital leadership conference you're attending to get your CMEs, but the board scheduled a big budget meeting at the same time. Now, I'm going in his place."

Alaric raises an eyebrow. "Funny. I just booked my flight yesterday."

I blink, caught between surprise and relief. "Well done. I guess I'll see you there."

He laughs. "Paradise is a small town, Liz. You'll see me plenty before then."

Before I can respond, Ryker yells something from the couch about a penalty, and the room erupts again. The moment breaks, but the air between us doesn't quite settle. After a moment, though, Alaric moves closer to yell at the television, and I step back to chat with Trinity and Ginny near the snacks.

As the night goes on, the room grows more comfortable, the tension thinner. I find myself joining in, passing plates, cheering at goals. Everyone's kind, and they make sure I feel included.

In the end, I'm glad I came tonight. Perhaps belonging isn't as hard as I've made it out to be. And I suppose this proves Alaric and I can coexist. Maybe everything starts with just showing up.

Eight

Alaric

I'm already late when my pager goes off again. *Behavioral health consult needed.* There's a mother in triage with a teenager who won't speak. I check the clock—eight minutes until the leadership meeting on the other side of the hospital. If I try to hand this off, it'll most likely sit until I can return. If I go now, I'll be late.

I go.

The kid's half-vanished inside an oversized hoodie, strings pulled tight so only the tip of her nose shows. Her sneaker taps a nervous beat against the floor. The mother sits beside her, twisting a tissue into white threads.

I drop onto a crouch so I'm eye level. My knees pop. "Hey," I say. "I'm Dr. Dempsey—Ric's fine, if you'd rather. You don't have to talk if you don't want to. We can just breathe."

No answer. The sneaker keeps tapping.

I glance up at the lights. Too bright. The air too dry. "Want me to dim the lights?" Nothing. "Is it too loud in here?" Still nothing. I try one more. "We can step outside if it feels crowded."

The foot stops. A tiny nod.

"Okay. Let's take a break." I pull the curtain aside. The mother stands, clutching her purse strap, and follows.

We stop in a quiet alcove near the vending machines. The atmosphere here is softer, the air less busy. "Here's the deal," I say. "You get to pick. Sit or stand. Stay or walk."

"Walk," she whispers.

"Good call." I match her pace down the hall. One lap. Two. Gradually, her shoulders unclench.

"It's the teacher," she says suddenly, voice muffled. "She keeps calling on me."

"Even when you ask her not to?"

A small nod.

"My dad says it's just a phase," she adds.

"And your friends?"

"They stopped texting back." Her words hitch.

We stop near a bulletin board full of outdated posters. "When the panic starts," I ask, "what does it feel like?"

"Like my chest's on fire."

"Hard to breathe?"

"Yeah. Like I'm running and not going anywhere."

I pull a sticky note from my pocket and click a pen. "Let me show you something." I draw a small square, holding it out so she can see. "In for four," I count along the first line. "Hold for four." Second line. "Out for four. Hold again." I tap the last corner. "You can trace this whenever your chest gets too tight. Nobody has to know you're doing it."

She studies the note, finger hovering over the ink. "Okay," she whispers. She slides it into the sleeve of the hoodie.

The mother exhales, her shoulders shaking. "Thank you," she says, voice frayed. "Thank you so much."

"She did the hard part," I tell her. I nod toward the kid.

"Keep the sticky. Tomorrow morning, a social worker will check in. Same time. And reach out to the teacher who insists on calling on her during class. Bring in the principal if you need to."

They both nod. As they leave, I catch a glimpse of the yellow note peeking from the cuff of the hoodie. I rub the back of my neck. The wall clock says 9:12. The leadership meeting started twelve minutes ago. I pull my phone from my coat pocket and type one-handed to the leadership message group while I walk toward the stairs.

Running two consults behind. Save me a chair. – Ric.

The message sends. I take the stairs two at a time, pulse running on overload. When I hit the second floor, I can see the glass wall of the boardroom and the reflection of my own rushed outline. Through it, the long table is full—CEO, CMO, heads of departments, and Liz at the far end, near the screen. She's in a charcoal dress, hair pulled back in a knot.

I open the door as quietly as it will allow. It still gives a soft thud that makes three heads turn.

Hudson glances up, one eyebrow lifting like a punctuation mark. "Nice of you to join us, Dr. Dempsey."

"Sorry," I mutter, sliding into the last open chair beside Radiology. My heart hasn't caught up with my body yet. I flip the agenda over and pretend to read, hoping no one notices the sweat cooling between my shoulder blades.

Liz's gaze flicks to me long enough to register I'm here. No smile. No judgment either. Just a quick read and back to the presentation.

After a moment, Roger Hudson stands before the group. The projector clicks through slides while he moves through the first few topics—new equipment, volunteer recruitment, department budgets. My breathing steadies, and for a second, it almost feels normal, like the morning chaos hasn't followed me in here.

Then the CMO clears his throat. "Before we move on, I'd

like an update on accreditation, specifically, CME compliance."

Hudson nods toward Liz. "Liz has reviewed the files and can give you a full report."

Every head turns. Liz doesn't flinch. "All departments have been audited for CME completion and renewal schedules. Most are on track. A few shortfalls remain, but plans are in place to address them."

The CMO leans back. "Plans are nice. Actions are better. What's being done?"

"Surgery is booked for an advanced trauma refresher next month. Imaging registered for an online diagnostic series. Pediatrics is attending the regional update in March." She glances down at her notes. "Behavioral Health was the farthest behind and is attending a conference in Kauai next month."

A stylus freezes mid-tap. Laptops pause. In the glass wall, I count three reflected faces aimed at me and one at the clock.

I feel it before I look up, the shift in the air. The CMO's gaze lands on me. "Farthest behind and now you're off to Kauai, Ric?"

Heat crawls up my neck. I rest my palms on the table, careful not to curl them into fists. "We're short psychiatrists and therapists. I've been covering crisis consults. That's why I was late today. And that's how I got so far behind on my CMEs. Liz came to me with a solution, and I realized I needed to get it done."

The CMO's mouth twitches, not quite a smile. "I somehow doubt staffing shortages prevent you from opening your email. And now, you have your own travel agent? Kauai should be…restorative."

Restorative? I'll be earning credits, not vacationing. I have nearly sixty days of paid time off accrued but no time to use them. All I do is work.

A few people shift in their chairs, pretending to read their notes. Hudson murmurs something to change the subject. The meeting moves on, but the burn doesn't fade.

When it finally ends, chairs scrape and conversation

bubbles up again. I gather my papers more slowly than I need to, giving myself a minute to breathe. Liz unplugs the HDMI cable, winding it in perfect loops. Her posture's still straight, and I can see tightness in her shoulders.

I step closer. "You put me on display."

She looks up fast, eyes bright. We're nose to nose, and her perfume is clean citrus. I hate that I notice it.

"I answered a question," she says.

"In front of everyone."

"I didn't name you. And I know Misty sent you nearly a dozen emails. Nothing I said was a lie."

I laugh once, sharp. "Next time you want to throw me under the bus in front of the leadership team, at least warn me before you announce it."

Her chin lifts a fraction. "I wasn't doing your job, Alaric. I was doing mine."

The way she says my name registers in a way I wish it didn't. She used to call me Ric, but she doesn't anymore. I start to walk away, then stop. It would be better to be angry with the CMO. He's my boss. He's the one who clearly doesn't get it. Yet attacking Liz is my answer. Is it cowardly? Absolutely. Is it effective? Not at all.

But now, I don't have anything to say that won't sound like an excuse. "Enjoy running the place," I manage.

"Enjoy running yourself into the ground," she fires back.

I leave before I say something worse, the words trailing me like static.

When I reach the hallway, my phone buzzes again—two new consults, both marked urgent. I shove it into my pocket and start moving, the echo of Liz's voice still ringing in my ears.

By the time I reach Behavioral Health, the caffeine in my system has worn off, and the fluorescent lights hum behind my eyes like bees. The waiting room's packed—one patient arguing with the receptionist, another pacing near the vending machine. A nurse intercepts me halfway down the corridor. "Dr. Dempsey, the teenager from this morning's back. Said she can't breathe again."

I take a breath of my own, long enough to dissipate the leftover heat from the meeting. "Okay," I say. "Let's get her a room."

Behind the curtain, the girl is curled in the chair again, hood up, hands shaking. The sticky note's balled in one fist. The nurse clips on a pulse ox, and we watch her numbers climb, right along with her panic.

"What caused this?" I ask her mother.

"She said she'd go back to school, and it started again as we drove up," she replies.

I crouch. "Hey," I say gently. "Remember the square?"

A weak nod.

"Good. Let's slow it down. In—two, three, four. Hold—two, three, four. Out—two, three, four. Hold—two, three, four."

When her breaths even out, I drop my voice. "Pick a color," I tell her. "Find three things that match it." Her eyes begin moving around the room. "Let's check her chart," I murmur to the nurse. "See if she's already on something for anxiety."

Her eyes dart—ceiling tile, blanket, the edge of my badge. Shoulders ease another fraction.

Her mother's hand shakes around a tissue. I slide the box toward her. "She's okay," I say quietly. "Let's take the rest of the day off from school. Tomorrow, our social worker will meet you both, and they can help you figure out how to manage the school and other issues. If she feels this tight before then, call."

I turn toward the girl and meet her eyes before I go. "We're going to sort this out," I assure her. She gives me another nod.

Outside, the corridor noise rushes back in—a phone ringing, a gurney rattling by. I glance at the clock. It's one thirty. I haven't eaten since dawn.

In the break room, the coffee's burned but hot. I'm halfway through a cup when my pager goes off again. Room six—agitated patient. I dump the rest in the sink and head out, bitterness on my tongue.

When I arrive, room six is chaos. A man's pacing,

muttering about cameras in the ceiling. A resident's frozen by the door.

"Step out," I tell her.

She disappears like she's been waiting for permission.

I keep my distance, hands visible. "Hey, I'm Ric. Rough day?"

"They put something in the meds," he says, voice shaking. "I can feel it crawling."

"Feels like bugs?"

He nods.

"Yeah. That sounds awful." I point to the chair. "Sit. Let's figure out how to make it stop."

He hesitates, then sits. We talk until his pulse slows enough for the nurse to step in with a shot of fast-acting sedative. His breathing evens, eyes growing heavy.

I order a complete workup on him, checking for drugs and alcohol in his system as well as blood work for electrolytes, kidney function, and infection markers. When the nurses have him covered, I step into the hall and scrub a hand over my face. My phone buzzes again—with an email from Liz.

Coverage for your week off.
Let me know if you need adjustments.

That's all it says. I don't open the attached file. I'm sure it's fine.

The rest of the afternoon blurs—patients, paperwork, interruptions that bleed together. By six, the clinic's finally quiet. I stretch, bones popping, and check my email. I now look over the coverage Liz arranged, detailed down to the minute. These are the locums I would have requested. I'd get them here on staff if I could. Maybe I should take a day or two off after the conference and just relax.

A knock hits my doorframe, and when I look up, Liz stands there, folder under one arm, her hand braced on the wood. Her hair's come loose, a strand curling near her cheek. "Can I come in?"

I nod. "Door's open."

She steps inside and sets the folder on my desk. "Backup copies, in case the email bounced. And some shorter CME modules if you'd rather stay local."

I lean back. "You didn't have to."

"Hudson asked for actions, not promises. I wasn't trying to embarrass you."

"I realize that. It's the CMO who doesn't get it." I sigh. "I'll go to the conference. I'll just try to fly under the radar next time."

Her mouth curves, not quite a smile. "Good luck with that."

I swallow pride that tastes like rust. "Thanks."

She nods, leaves the folder, and walks out, heels clicking down the hall.

I sit for a long minute, and my pulse finally slows. Then I pack up, slide the folder into my bag, and flip off the light. The walk to the parking lot feels longer than usual. Outside, snow melts around puddles that mirror the sodium lights above. I climb into my car, rest my forehead against the steering wheel, and breathe…

In for four. Hold for four. Out for four. Hold for four.

The same square I drew this morning.

For the first time all day, the air goes all the way down.

Nine

Alaric

On Saturday mornings, Paradise looks a lot like it did ten years ago before the population bloomed. When I step into Dot's Diner, a bell jingles overhead and the scent of bacon, brewed coffee, and maple syrup is so familiar I can almost forget how long I stayed away. Families crowd the booths, with kids in hockey jerseys kicking their heels under the tables. Two men in ball caps argue about the weather and whether the vines will freeze if this cold keeps up. A server with a pencil stuck behind her ear calls out an order over the hiss of the griddle.

I scan the room for Sera. She's not here yet. Not a surprise. My sister runs on vineyard time, which means nothing starts until the sun hits the vines. I step into the line that snakes along the counter, hands shoved in my pockets, watching the dance of the place.

Dot's Diner has survived every new coffee shop and brunch spot that's tried to compete with it. There's comfort in that. Cracked vinyl booths, walls the color of butter, a chalkboard listing pie flavors that never change. It's the kind of place where everyone knows you or, at least, knows enough to fill in the blanks.

The server behind the counter flashes me a grin. "You back again, Doc?"

I nod. "Couldn't stay away from your pancakes."

She laughs and slides a menu toward me. "You want the open spot at the counter?"

"Waiting for my sister."

"Then you'll need a booth," she says, scribbling my name on her pad. "Give me five minutes."

I nod as I move aside and lean against the wall, arms crossed. Even with the familiarity, I don't belong here, not completely, but it's the closest thing to belonging I've felt in a long time. My reflection appears in the window, and for a second, I catch a look at the tired version of myself I keep pretending doesn't exist.

The bell rings again, and cold air sweeps across the floor. I glance toward the door, and everything inside me goes still.

Liz Ward.

She's framed by the morning light, hair loose over her shoulders, cheeks pink from the cold. A scarf hangs around her neck, soft and neutral, the kind she used to wear when we'd stop for coffee after long shifts. She looks exactly the same and nothing like I remember.

My pulse does a strange hiccup.

She spots me and hesitates just long enough for me to notice. Her expression shifts, polite but cool, the kind of look that says she's already decided this conversation will be short.

I straighten and force a casual smile, even though it feels like my body forgot how to move.

She gives me a nod and steps toward the counter.

"Morning," she says, voice even, a touch warmer than her eyes.

"Didn't expect to see you here," I say, trying for light. "Thought hospital administrators didn't believe in weekends."

Her mouth curves, but it's not quite a smile. "And I thought psychologists preferred quiet places to drink their tea, not crowded diners where everyone listens."

Her bag brushes my arm as she shifts, and the faint scent of her perfume pulls up memories I'd buried deep—mornings in Vancouver, the two of us fighting over who'd get the last blueberry muffin.

I lean back against the wall. "Paradise doesn't have quiet places unless you count the cemetery."

"That your professional recommendation?" she asks. "Spend my Saturday with the dead?"

"Could be peaceful."

She huffs a laugh. "You always had strange ideas of peaceful."

The line moves forward, and she brushes past me. For half a second, her sleeve catches mine. Static snaps between us. I tell myself it's just the winter air, not everything I never said.

She glances over her shoulder. "Enjoy your pancakes, Dr. Dempsey."

"Enjoy your breakfast, Ms. Ward."

I need to let her go, but my eyes follow her across the diner anyway. She stops near the window where a man stands, waving. Mid-thirties, neat haircut, pressed shirt, the kind of guy who looks like he irons his socks. He steps around the table as she approaches and folds her into a hug.

My jaw tightens. She laughs at something he says and tilts her head the way she used to when she was comfortable. I don't know the man, but I already don't like him.

The bell over the door sounds again, and a rush of cold air pulls my attention back.

"Ric!"

Sera waves, cheeks flushed from the cold, dark curls under her knit hat. She reaches me in two strides and gives me a quick hug that smells like wine and winter. "Sorry I'm late. The guys forgot to cover the pruning gear last night, so I had to deal with a minor frost tantrum."

"Sounds fun."

She follows my gaze toward Liz's table. "Who's she having breakfast with?"

The hostess appears with two menus and gestures for us to follow her to the corner booth. We slide in. I already know what I'll order. Across the room, Liz leans forward, talking with her hands, and the man nods like he's hanging on every word.

"No idea." I keep my voice even. "Work thing, maybe."

Sera gives me a knowing look, the kind only sisters have mastered. "Right. A work thing that requires laughter, and he just touched her arm."

I shoot her a warning glance, but she just smirks. "Come on," she says. "Let's figure out what we're going to eat before you sprain your neck."

The server pours coffee for Sera, promises to bring water for tea, and asks if we're ready to order. I nod, barely hearing her.

Sera studies me. "You're subtle as a tractor in a vineyard, you know that?"

"Just hungry," I mumble, though we both know it's a lie.

The server leaves with our order, and Sera keeps watching like she's waiting for me to slip. She's always been the one who sees too much.

"So," she says, stirring cream into her coffee, "how's life in hospital land? Still saving souls one therapy session at a time?"

"Trying," I say. "Some days it feels like more paperwork than people."

She grins. "At least you get to sit inside where it's warm. I've been in the vineyard since before dawn. Frost on the wires, mud up to my knees, and Josie barking orders like we're in boot camp."

"You love it," I say. "Admit it."

"I could never work inside like you do."

"How's the winter pruning?"

She shrugs. "We're behind schedule after the holidays, and the snow doesn't help. Once pruning's done, we'll start blending and bottling last year's reserve. Then comes the real chaos when we start the process all over again."

She talks with her hands, animated and alive in a way that always pulls me in. The vineyard is her oxygen. Even when she complains, she glows.

"Do you ever take a day off?" I ask.

"Not when there's work to do." She sips her coffee. "You should tell Evie that. She thinks I don't spend enough time at the vineyard, and I rarely get away."

"The only one who's perfect in Evie's eyes is Evie. Don't let her get to you."

Her laugh draws a few glances from nearby tables. She doesn't care. Paradise has always watched everything we do and then gossiped about it.

I lean back in the booth. "Are you seeing anyone these days?"

She raises an eyebrow. "What's this? Concerned big brother energy?"

"Curiosity."

"No time," she says. "Men don't mix well with long days and cold nights. Besides, I'm not sure I'd trust anyone who wanted to date a woman who smells like fermentation."

"Someone will appreciate that someday."

She nudges my foot under the table. "What about you? You and Liz have actual conversations now or just those awkward hallway nods?"

"We talk. Work stuff."

"Uh-huh. And that's why you're glaring at the guy sitting with her?"

"I wasn't glaring."

She smirks. "Sure. If you say so."

I drop my gaze to the table, giving me an excuse not to look across the diner.

Sera sets her cup down. "She's the one that got away, isn't

she?"

"No." The word comes too fast, too sharp. I take a breath and try again. "We had our chance. It didn't work."

She tilts her head. "Didn't work, or you didn't fight for it?"

I look out the window. "Does it matter?"

"Only if you still care." The silence stretches, and eventually, she softens. "You deserve to be happy. You always carry everything like it's your job to fix it."

"That's exactly my job."

"You were miserable when you returned to Paradise without Liz. Maybe it's time for you to take care of yourself, rather than worrying exclusively about the rest of us."

The server returns with our food and my tea. The smell of butter and maple syrup cuts through the tension. Sera digs in, unbothered by my quiet. She's never needed me to talk to understand what's going on.

By the time we've made a dent in our pancakes, Sera's energy has shifted. The sparkle fades from her eyes, replaced by something tighter, heavier. I know that look. It always means one thing. She's gotten to the main business of this breakfast.

"How's Evie?" I ask.

Sera sighs and pushes her plate away. "Up to her same tricks. You know how she gets when she's bored."

"Duplicitous and dramatic?"

"Add conniving, and you've got the full set." She folds her napkin and sets it beside her plate. "She's angry at the world. Angry that she's getting older. Angry that she can't control every decision we make. She blames Josie and me for everything."

I take a long sip of tea. "What's Dylan doing for her these days?"

"As far as I know, nothing. But if she promised him a share of the vineyard, he'd come running."

I take a breath. I don't want to make the situation worse, but I wonder if Sera knows Evie has said as much to me. "You think she'd do that?"

"She's done worse." Sera's voice drops low. "She turned

on Dad and the rest of her children? She's unpredictable."

I remember—the shouting, the slammed doors, the way the house never felt safe. "You and Josie need to protect yourselves."

Sera's jaw flexes. "We've tried. But if Evie wants to make things ugly, she will. She likes the power. The constant guessing. Some days, I think she pits us against each other just for entertainment."

"That sounds like her."

"She told me last week she was revising her will."

I meet her eyes. "And?"

"She didn't say anything else. Which is worse than knowing. I'm tired of jumping through her hoops, but if she gives the vineyard to Dylan and Scott, the business will be gone in two seasons."

So she has put the pieces together. Of course, she has. "If Evie leaves that vineyard to anyone other than you and Josie, she'll tear the family apart."

"She already has." Sera exhales. "I love that land. Every inch of it. If she hands it to Dylan or Scott, I'll survive, but it'll break something inside me. We've worked so hard to make Black Bear what it is."

I reach across the table and rest my hand over hers. "You and Josie have made a small local vineyard into something incredible. She can't take that from you."

"She'll try."

I sit back. "You don't have to handle her alone," I say, even though part of me wishes my sisters could do just that.

Sera gives me a small smile. "You know she won't change."

"True. But I can make sure she doesn't destroy you."

Her smile falters. "You already came back for us. That's enough."

For a moment, I see the little sister who used to follow me through the vineyard rows, skipping between the vines, trusting that I could make everything right. I wish I still believed I could do that.

Sera's phone buzzes, and she flips it to look at the screen. After a moment, she frowns and slides it into her pocket. "Josie. She's asking if I'm on my way."

I look around the diner, and most of the breakfast crowd is gone. Only a few stragglers linger with half-empty mugs.

Across the room, Liz rises from her booth. Her companion stands too, resting a hand at her back as they walk toward the door. The sight knots my stomach before my head can reason with it. He says something that makes her laugh, and she touches his arm—light, familiar. They pause at the door, the bell chiming as they step outside. Then he leans in, and she hugs him. For too long.

Sera follows my line of sight. "You want to tell me who's with Liz?"

"No idea," I say, reaching for my tea. "Probably someone from work."

She snorts. "You're terrible at lying."

"Just trying to drink my tea in peace."

"Uh-huh." She gathers her coat, still smiling. "You seem jealous."

"Not jealous."

"Sure." She shrugs into her jacket. "Whatever helps you sleep at night."

I watch her adjust her scarf. "Are you heading back to the vineyard?"

"Yeah. We've got tanks to check and a few blends that need attention. And I have to finalize our entries for the International Wine and Spirits competition before Josie panics."

I nod as I rise as well. "Paradise Hill entering again?"

"Of course. And Evie won't miss the chance to gloat about our incompetence if we lose." Her tone softens. "But we won't. She thinks it's all a waste of time, even though we've taken more gold medals than Paradise Hill four years running and I can prove it's valuable to our bottom line." She shrugs. "Doesn't matter, though. I plan to make it five because that's what I want."

"That'll drive her wild."

"That's the plan." She grins fiercely, a glint in her eyes. "We leave for London in two weeks. I can't wait to get out of here for a bit."

"Try to have fun while you're winning medals."

"Always do." She leans over and hugs me. "Thanks for breakfast, big brother."

"Anytime."

She disappears outside, and I stay a moment longer, nursing what's left of my tea. But I have nothing to hold my attention now. Liz and her mystery date are gone, leaving only empty plates and a tip folded under the sugar caddy.

I tell myself it doesn't matter. It's none of my business who Liz spends her Saturday with. But the thought follows me as I slide out of the booth and drop a few bills on the table.

Outside, the morning has brightened. Snow melts on the sidewalks, turning to puddles that reflect the pale blue of the sky. I pull my jacket tighter and start toward the hospital. That's why I'm here. That's my life's work.

Lately, I can feel the slow pull of things I've tried to leave behind. Family drama. Old wounds. And Liz—always Liz.

I walk faster, as if somehow I can outrun it.

Ten

Liz

The office has quieted, but as has become my habit, I'm still here. It's a Friday night, and I've worked here for over a month. The rhythm is familiar now, so I'm not staying because I'm worried about getting up to speed. I've just found I like doing it. It's after five, and the building has emptied. Perfect. No interruptions. Just the sound of paper sliding into neat piles and the soft tap of my pen against the desk.

Four folders wait in front of me—manila for my travel information, blue for the sessions I'll attend, green for open projects in case someone calls, and red for tracking CME compliance. I pause and then flip each one closed. Everything is aligned. Everything controlled.

I double-check the last flight confirmation before shutting down my laptop. My six-a.m. flight to Vancouver is booked, the connection to Kauai confirmed, and my seat assigned—window because aisle seats feel too exposed.

It's been three weeks since I ran into Alaric at Dot's Diner. Since then we've only exchanged short, polite emails about hospital business. "Approved." "Noted." "Attached for review." Nothing more. Safe. Professional.

The word *professional* has become my armor, and I wear it at all times.

My phone buzzes against the desk.

Trinity: Are we still on for dinner tonight? Don't bail.

I lean back in my chair. I'd completely forgotten we made plans.

Me: I can't. I haven't even started to pack. The flight leaves at six am. Rain check?

Trinity: I'll bring Paradise Grill to you. You can pack while we eat.

I debate that for a moment. My shoulders ache from the day, and my head's full of last-minute details. A night to myself would be nice, but relaxing feels elusive when I'm not prepared.

Me: You're impossible.

Trinity: And you're boring. See you in an hour.

A smile tugs at my mouth. Trinity never takes no for an answer.

I glance around the office one last time, making sure everything's in order. Papers stacked, pens capped, floor spotless. I shut off the light and tell myself the same thing I always do before I leave. *I'm fine. Everything's fine.* The echo that follows me down the hallway doesn't sound convinced.

Hudson's office door is half open, light shooting into the

quiet corridor. He's still at his desk, sleeves rolled, glasses low on his nose as he studies a spreadsheet. I knock lightly before leaning against the doorframe.

"Still here," he says without looking up. "You're as bad as I am."

"I just finished. Thought I'd wish you luck with the board meeting next week."

He glances up and smiles. "Thanks. I'll need it."

"You'll be great," I say. "If it helps, I'm bringing you back chocolate-covered macadamia nuts. They're supposed to bring good luck."

"That's a new one," he says, laughing. "I'll take whatever luck I can get."

I wave and head down the hall. Misty is at the copier, a stack of papers in her arms. The air between us always feels slightly charged, like static that won't dissipate no matter how many times I try to ground it.

"I'm heading out," I tell her. "If you think of anything you need for the board meeting, email me tonight. I'll check before I go in the morning."

She nods without meeting my eyes. "Everything's covered."

"Okay. I'll bring you something from Hawaii," I say, too brightly. "Chocolate-covered macadamia nuts sound good?"

Her smile is polite but thin. "Sure. Thanks."

The conversation stalls. I wait a beat before giving up. "All right, then. See you in a week."

"Safe travels."

Her voice is even, but I can't shake the sense that I've done something wrong.

The elevator drops, and my ears pop. The car smells faintly of lemon cleaner. In the mirrored doors, I look composed. But that's not how I feel.

I tell myself not everyone has to like me, that it doesn't matter as long as the work gets done. I pretend that helps. It doesn't. The doors slide open in the empty lobby, and I step out, adjusting the strap of my bag. I close up my coat and pull on my gloves, ready for the walk home.

Trinity's car is already in the driveway when I arrive. The porch light glows against the fading sky, and through the kitchen window, I can see her moving around like she owns the place, setting out plates on the counter. I breathe deep as I open the door—roasted chicken, honey-glazed salmon, warm bread. Comfort in edible form.

"You're ridiculous," I say, kicking off my heels. "You realize I was going to have cereal for dinner, right?"

"That's exactly why I'm here," she says, unpacking a paper bag. "I told Greyson you were trying to cancel on me, and he said to bring reinforcements."

I laugh, hanging my coat on the hook. "Remind me to thank him later."

"You can start by eating." She slides a plate toward me. "I brought the good stuff because I knew you'd pick this one."

She's right. I take a bite of the salmon, and the taste pulls a small sound from my throat. "You're a saint."

"Don't forget it," she says, grabbing a piece of chicken for herself. "You weren't really going to skip dinner, were you?"

"I have a six-a.m. flight, and half my clothes are still in the laundry," I admit. "I was trying to be responsible."

"Responsible is overrated."

She moves through my kitchen, familiar and at ease, while I pull my suitcase from the hall closet. My packing style is efficient—rolled clothes, labeled toiletry bag, everything in its place. I just have to get everything ready first.

Trinity leans against the counter, watching me. "You know, for someone who spends her life telling other people how to manage stress, you don't seem very good at it."

"I'm fine," I say automatically.

"You're always fine."

I pause with a shirt in my hands, caught between a retort and the truth. "It's a lot right now. This trip, the new systems, the staff. I just need to get through next week."

She nods. "I get it. But you've been here a month, and I barely see you anymore. The hospital has swallowed you whole."

"I know." I close the suitcase and survey my pile of laundry. "After this trip, I'll be home more. I promise. We'll go for dinner somewhere without paperwork or fluorescent lights."

"I'll believe it when I see it."

Her tone is teasing, but her eyes are kind. She's reminded me what it's like to exhale. For the first time all day, I do.

Trinity helps me fold a few more shirts while I refill our glasses with sparkling water. The fizz catches the light, tiny bursts of silver. She's quiet for a long stretch, which has me studying her. "What is it?" I ask.

She hesitates, then smiles nervously, which gives her away. "I wasn't sure if I should tell you yet, but you'll find out soon anyway."

"Now you have to tell me," I say, laughing.

She bites her lip, eyes bright. "I'm twelve weeks pregnant."

For a second, the words don't register. Then they do, and I let out a startled laugh, covering my mouth. "What? Trinity!"

"I know." She shakes her head. "We didn't plan it. We were just getting our lives back, but Greyson's over the moon. He's already talking about finishing the new house before the baby comes."

I pull her into a hug, laughing against her shoulder. "I can't believe it. You're going to have two kids. That's insane."

"Tell me about it," she says, sinking into the couch. "I was so sure we were done for a while. Guess the universe had other plans." Her hand drifts to her stomach, and her expression softens.

The sight tugs at my chest. Joy, fear, acceptance, all tangled up in one small motion. "I'm really happy for you," I say quietly. "You're going to be great."

She looks at me, the corners of her mouth lifting. "You forget I can be a mess too."

"That's why I like you. It makes me feel less alone."

She laughs, and it fills the small room with warmth. For a moment, the lists and deadlines and travel plans fade into the background. All that's left is this. Two friends, food on the table, and new beginnings.

Trinity squeezes my hand. "Don't work too hard while you're gone, okay? You've earned some time to breathe."

"I'll try," I say.

Trinity follows me to my room and leans back on the bed while I flop the suitcase at the foot and pull the rest of my wardrobe options from the closet. I open my suitcase at the end of the bed, half-packed with neutral tones and pressed dresses that scream business trip. I hold up a navy sheath dress. "What about this for the opening reception? It's professional but still relaxed."

She tilts her head. "Relaxed for a tax audit, maybe."

I laugh. "It's classic."

"It's boring." She stands and goes to a shopping bag she left near the doorway. "You're going to Hawaii, not to a staff meeting."

"I'm there to work."

"Work can still have color." She pulls out a floral sundress, bright and unapologetically loud. "Here. Borrow this. You need it."

I stare at the explosion of coral and yellow. "I can't wear that. I'll look like a walking hibiscus."

"That's the point," she says, holding it up against me. "I picked it up on our last trip to Hawaii, and it will look fantastic on you. You spend your life blending in. Try standing out for once."

I can't help laughing. "You're relentless."

"Someone has to save you from yourself."

I take the dress and drape it over the chair. It's soft under my fingers, lighter than anything I'd normally wear. "Maybe I'll pack it," I say, which makes her beam.

"Progress," she teases.

We eat a few more bites of our dinners while I fill up the

suitcase. Trinity eyes the list I've taped to the dresser. Clothes, toiletries, backup charger, travel folder. "You're a machine."

"It's called being prepared."

"It's called not knowing how to relax," she says, smiling.

I roll my eyes, but there's no heat in it. "I can relax."

"Sure," she says. "And I'm the Queen of England."

She glances at the pile of clothes again and lowers her voice. "So…are you going to see much of Alaric while you're there?"

The question sends a ripple through me. "I doubt it. He left today, so we're not even on the same flight. And the schedule's packed. Chances are slim we'll do much more than cross paths, as we're in different cohorts."

"Still," she says, drawing out the word. "Six days in Hawaii. Anything can happen."

"Not that," I say quickly. "Definitely not that."

Trinity grins. "You never know."

I throw a balled-up sock at her, and she ducks, laughing.

When she finally stands to leave, she hugs me tight. "Promise me something. Have a good time in Hawaii. And if you get the chance, get laid."

"Trinity," I groan, laughing.

"What? You can't tell me you don't need it."

I shake my head, still smiling. "It's unlikely."

"Then at least wear the dress and pack Bob," she says, heading for the door. Bob is our nickname for my battery-operated boyfriend.

I send her home with the leftovers and look at what else I need to do before I leave in the morning. I rinse the dishes and stand for a moment with my hands on the counter.

I should finish up and go straight to bed. Six-a.m. flight. Long day tomorrow. Instead, I wander back to the bedroom and stare at the open suitcase. Everything is in its place. Folded shirts, a navy dress, the floral one sitting neatly on top like a dare.

I smooth the fabric with my fingers. Maybe she's right. Maybe I could use a little color.

The clock on my nightstand glows past nine. I move through my final checklist. Chargers, toiletries. Each item slips into its spot—precise, predictable. The rhythm of order usually calms me. Tonight, it doesn't.

My thoughts keep circling back to Alaric. He's already there, maybe walking the beach. Maybe he took someone with him. Maybe he's not thinking about me at all. That should help. It doesn't.

When the packing's done, I open my bedside drawer to find my travel adapter. My fingers brush something else instead. Bob, in the small velvet pouch I tucked there when I moved in last month. I unzip the suitcase and slip it between the layers of my clothes. Just in case I need some stress relief.

But as I zip the case, I know it's more than that. I'm not as sure of myself as I pretend to be. Tomorrow, I fly to Hawaii. And the man who still makes me come undone is already there.

Eleven

Liz

The airport parking lot is half ice, half slush, and my breath curls in the air when I step out of the rideshare. I planned for an easy morning—coffee, a quiet drive, no surprises—and a checklist kind of day that ends with a window seat, a view of clouds, and, at the other end, a mai tai on the beach.

I board on time, which feels like a small victory. I slide into my seat, pull out my planner, and tell myself everything's running exactly as scheduled.

Then the captain's voice crackles over the speaker, calm and cheerful. "We're just waiting for de-icing before we can take off."

Of course, we are.

Outside, a bright orange truck rolls up and starts spraying the wings with some mysterious green slush that looks like it belongs in a science experiment. I watch the liquid streak down the metal and remind myself to be grateful. Safety first. Delays mean I'll live to complain about them later.

Still, my jaw tightens as I check my watch. Every minute we sit here cuts into my layover in Vancouver. I've got an hour and a half between flights—if everything runs perfectly—and I still have to go through U.S. Customs and Immigration. It's going to be tight.

I take a deep breath and paste on my patient face. The man across the aisle opens a breakfast burrito that smells of onions and regret. The universe has a sense of humor.

I knew it was cold, but apparently, the weather has decided to compete with Antarctica this morning. I pull out my phone. The connection in Vancouver is looking borderline impossible. I'm going to have to sprint through customs and security like it's an Olympic event, not exactly how I like to start a twelve-hour travel day.

Across the aisle, a kid kicks his carry-on as if it owes him money. His mother scrolls on her phone, unbothered. A man behind me coughs. For some reason, the air smells faintly of cigarettes and fried food.

I open my laptop because that's what I do when I'm nervous. Numbers and spreadsheets feel controllable. But the Wi-Fi panel spins, refuses to connect, and then drops me completely. *Perfect.* I close the lid before I throw it.

Finally, we take off, and the flight is short and bumpy. I stare out the window and pretend not to care that the man beside me smells like garlic. I've read that traveling calmly reduces jet lag. Whoever wrote that never sat in row fourteen of a prop plane that feels held together with duct tape.

When the wheels finally touch down, I have thirty-five minutes before boarding for Hawaii begins. I'm half out of my seat the second the seatbelt light dings off. A man in front of me blocks the aisle to check his phone. I count to ten. It doesn't help.

By the time I hit the terminal, I'm running. My boots slap the tile, bag bouncing, heart thudding. I dodge a group of teenagers in matching sweatshirts and a woman with a dog in a carrier. Customs takes forever. The officer looks at my passport, looks at me, and then looks again, as if we're in a bad spy movie. I smile like a normal person who isn't panicking about missing a flight.

Finally, I'm done. I sprint past duty-free in a blur. Naturally, my gate is at the end of the longest concourse. I reach it just as the display flickers.

Air Canada Flight to Lihue—delayed four hours.

I stop so fast the man behind me nearly crashes into me. Sweat slides down my back, and my hair's sticking to my neck. I feel ridiculous, like a marathon runner who trained for months only to find the finish line has moved elsewhere.

I drop into the nearest seat and laugh under my breath because it's either that or cry. I smooth my blazer, pull in some air, and try to look composed as I open my phone again. Four hours to kill.

The Vancouver airport is a maze of polished floors and glass walls that makes everything echo. I drag my carry-on down the U.S. concourse, looking for somewhere that isn't crowded or loud. The whole building smells like coffee and jet fuel, which would be fine if it didn't remind me that I'm still stuck on the ground.

I pass sushi, burgers, overpriced smoothies, and a store selling neck pillows with Hello Kitty faces. None of it feels right. My stomach grumbles anyway. I settle for a sandwich that tastes like Styrofoam and a cup of coffee so cold it should come with ice. But I do find a seat near a window. Outside, rain smears across the glass in long streaks. Planes taxi in slow motion, lights blinking like they're taunting me.

I try to check my email, but the Wi-Fi cuts in and out. The universe clearly wants me to experience growth, build some character.

Fine. I'll grow.

I pull out my conference folder instead—perfectly organized, color-coded tabs and all. *Focus will make the time pass more quickly,* I tell myself. It doesn't.

The family across from me has a full-blown argument about whether the mom should've packed extra snacks. The kid cries. The dad looks ready to abandon his luggage and start over somewhere new. I give him a sympathetic nod.

By hour three, I'm wandering again. I buy a magazine I don't want and a bottle of water I don't need. I consider splurging on one of those massage chairs, but the idea of being that person in public is too much for me.

When the loudspeaker finally announces boarding, I could cry with relief. I gather my things, straighten my blazer, and join the line. My boarding group is somewhere near the back, which feels symbolic. And then I see him.

Alaric Dempsey, standing in the first-class line like a travel brochure come to life. He's in dark jeans and a gray sweater that looks expensive, hair a little messy in a way that seems intentional. He glances over, spots me, and that familiar half-smile curves his mouth.

Of course.

He steps out of the line and closes the distance between us. "Why aren't you flying first class?" he asks. "Hospital policy covers it for international flights."

I blink. "When Misty booked my ticket, they must've been out of first-class seats."

His brow lifts. "You didn't check?"

I bristle. "I trust the system." This is a lie. I just didn't want to be the person who complained about seating arrangements.

He nods toward the boarding door. "I was in the lounge. They would've fixed it for you."

I stare at him. "The lounge?" My voice jumps higher than I mean it to. "You've been in there for a day and a half?"

Confusion flickers across his face, then clears. "No. I came in early to see Trey, Leah, and the twins."

That brings a smile to my face. Trey is Alaric's best friend back in Vancouver. He was one of the few people who didn't treat me like collateral damage when Alaric left. "You saw them?"

"Yeah." A small smile touches his mouth. "The twins are so big now. I forgot how loud their house can get."

Something in my chest shifts, but I cover it with a tight nod. "Good for them."

"Yeah," he says again, and the warmth in his voice makes me look away.

A boarding announcement crackles over the speaker. Alaric's group is called first, naturally. He gives me a polite nod and steps back to his line. I watch him hand over his ticket and disappear through the door, already planning the six hours I'll spend breathing recycled air in the back of the plane while he sips Champagne up front.

Perfect.

The economy line moves slower than molasses. The flight attendants look exhausted already, which doesn't inspire confidence. I shuffle forward inch by inch, pretending I don't care that first class boarded fifteen minutes ago and probably has hot towels by now.

At the door, the flight attendant smiles apologetically. "We're out of overhead space," she says. "We'll need to check your carry-on."

Of course. I surrender the bag, as if I'm handing over a child and tell myself to stay calm. It's fine. Totally fine. The bag will be waiting for me in Hawaii, safe and intact. Probably.

I edge down the narrow aisle to the last row. The middle seat. My personal circle of hell. The man in front of me reclines before I even sit down. My knees hit the seatback, and I bite my tongue to keep from swearing.

To my left is a woman with a floral neck pillow and a stack of romance novels. To my right, her husband, who looks like he hasn't smiled since the early nineties. They lean forward to talk over me, passing mints back and forth like I'm invisible.

"Would you two like to sit together?" I offer.

She shakes her head. "He likes the aisle. I like the window."

Naturally.

I wedge myself between them, plug in my headphones, and close my eyes. The air-conditioning rattles. The couple starts arguing about their son's wedding seating chart. I try deep breathing, but all I can smell is tuna from somewhere nearby.

When we finally take off, I want to rip my hair out, but instead, I remind myself that I'm heading to Hawaii and the hospital is paying for it.

Turbulence hits just after we level off. The seatbelt sign dings back on. A baby starts crying three rows ahead.

I glance toward the front curtain, picturing Alaric in first class. He's probably sipping something sparkling and chatting with the flight attendants, not being slowly crushed by a reclining seatback.

It doesn't matter. I'm independent. Capable. Completely comfortable back here in exile.

Another jolt shakes the plane. The man beside me groans and grabs the armrest—my armrest. Our elbows clash and I lose.

Six hours stretch like taffy. I drift in and out of half-sleep, waking every time someone bumps me. My neck aches. My phone battery dies. The flight attendants run out of snack boxes before they reach our row. The woman beside me tuts like she's been personally betrayed.

By the time the pilot announces our descent, I feel like I've aged ten years. My hair is flat, my clothes are wrinkled, and my patience evaporated somewhere over the Pacific. When the wheels hit the runway, a ripple of applause breaks out. I almost join in.

The woman next to me beams. "Wasn't that smooth?"

"It was something," I say.

The curtain to first class opens just long enough for me to see Alaric stand and stretch, calm and unbothered, like someone who's had the kind of flight I only dream about. Of course, he looks refreshed.

When the plane stops, people leap up, as if the floor is lava. I stay seated. There's nowhere to go. It takes fifteen minutes before the line moves, and by then, my spine feels permanently curved.

But the airport in Kauai feels like another world. It's open to the air, just covered overhead. Warmth presses against my skin the moment I step off the plane. The scent of salt and flowers hits next, sweet and heavy, almost dizzying after the canned air of the cabin. My shoulders drop. Everyone around me is thrilled to be here. They smile, they stretch, and they take selfies under the Aloha Hawaii sign.

I feel like I've been run over by the beverage cart.

I follow the crowd to baggage claim, and the carousel jolts to life, its silver belt groaning under oversized suitcases and surfboard bags. I tug my jacket tighter and stand back, pretending I'm calm even though sweat sticks my shirt to my spine.

Then he appears again.

Alaric leans against a column near the carousel, phone in hand, looking like the travel gods made sure he didn't get a single wrinkle. His sweater is gone, his T-shirt looks freshly pressed, and somehow, he already appears tan. He glances up, catches my eye, and nods. I nod back, aiming for polite neutrality while my brain grumbles.

The first bag off is his. Then a parade of other suitcases ride past, none of them mine. The crowd thins. Finally, I spot my bag. Or what's left of it. The zipper is split wide open and half my clothes hang out like laundry on display. My toiletry bag has burst open, and Bob has rolled out of its velvet pouch. It sits right on top like a shiny red beacon of humiliation.

Someone snickers. Then another. The sound spreads like static.

Heat floods my face. I step forward, hoping I can grab it before anyone gets a better look, but Alaric is faster. He lifts the bag off the carousel without a word. His expression gives away nothing, which somehow makes it worse.

"I can—" I start, reaching for it.

He shakes his head once. "I've got it."

My throat tightens. "You really don't have to—"

"I know," he says. "But I'm doing it anyway."

He tucks the broken side against his leg, shielding it from view. No one would notice now unless they looked closely. He doesn't say a word about the toy, thank God.

The carousel groans to a stop. My dignity is somewhere underneath it.

"I'll grab a cab," I say, needing distance, but he's already shaking his head.

"Come on. We're going to the same hotel. We'll share one."

I'm too tired to argue properly. "Fine. But I'm paying for it."

He doesn't respond, just starts walking, my bag held effortlessly in one hand. I hurry to keep up, half mortified, half grateful.

The humid air intensifies around us as we step outside. A line of taxis waits at the curb, engines idling. Alaric opens a door for me, and for a second, I consider refusing on principle. Then my body reminds me I've been awake for nearly twenty hours, and pride can wait.

I sink into the seat, eyes closing as the driver loads our bags. Alaric slides in beside me. The door shuts with a solid thud, sealing us into quiet.

We glide past palm trees and dark stores glowing under streetlights. Soft Hawaiian music plays on the radio. I try to let the rhythm calm the buzzing in my brain, but my body won't stop replaying the day. The delay. The sprint. The flight. The humiliation.

Alaric scrolls his phone, thumb moving slow and steady. I steal a glance. His jaw is relaxed. He looks like someone who could fall asleep anywhere, no matter the chaos.

"How was your flight?" he asks after a while.

I snort. "Transformative."

He smiles faintly. "That bad?"

"Let's just say I learned new limits of human patience."

He doesn't push, and I'm grateful. Silence settles again. Outside, waves crash against the dark shoreline. I lean my head back and let my eyes drift closed, breathing in warm air and ocean.

When the cab finally turns in to the long, curving drive of the Grand Hyatt Kauai Resort and Spa, I sit up. The place looks like a postcard—torches flickering, fountains sparkling, palm trees swaying. I should feel lucky. Right now, I just want a shower, a mai tai, and a bed.

Alaric pays the driver before I can protest. I make a weak grab for my wallet. "You didn't have to—"

"You can buy the first round of drinks later."

"Assuming I'm awake then."

Inside, the lobby glows soft and gold, the scent of plumeria drifting through the air. I step up to the counter, determined to handle this myself.

"Hi. Elizabeth Ward. Checking in."

The clerk smiles and starts typing. "Of course. Just a moment." The pause is too long. The smile fades. "I'm not finding a reservation under that name."

My stomach dips. "Can you check again? Maybe under Liz Ward or Paradise General? Or maybe it's still under my boss's name—Roger Hudson?"

He tries again, frowning. "I'm sorry. Nothing's coming up. Do you have a confirmation number?"

I pull out my travel folder, flipping through the neatly organized pockets. Flight info. Conference schedule. Emergency contacts. Everything except a confirmation number. Misty's handwriting stares up at me from the page with the hotel address.

"There has to be something," I say, keeping my voice even. "Can you check for any available rooms?"

He winces. "We're sold out for the conference."

Of course, they are.

Behind me, Alaric steps forward. "She's with me." His voice is calm, steady, annoyingly confident.

The clerk's entire posture changes. "Dr. Dempsey, welcome. We have you in an ocean-view room."

I turn to him. "You don't have to—"

"You need a place to sleep," he says with a shrug. "I have a sofa."

Heat creeps up my neck. "I'll find something else."

He shakes his head. "You won't. It's late. You're exhausted. We'll figure it out tomorrow."

The clerk slides him a set of key cards, clearly entertained. I grab my broken suitcase, wishing I could sink through the polished floor.

We walk toward the elevators. His stride is long, unbothered. Mine is three steps for every one of his. The air feels thick, full of things I don't want to name.

At the elevator, I finally say, "You must love this."

He presses the button, glancing at me. "Love what?"

"I'm still a mess."

He shakes his head as the doors open. Inside, soft music hums through hidden speakers. Our reflections stare back from the mirrored wall—him, relaxed and put together; me with frizzy hair, a wrinkled blouse, and raccoon eyes.

I look like I've survived a natural disaster.

Twelve

Alaric

I unpack my bag while Liz is in the shower. The sound of running water fills my mind, but I force myself to focus on something I can fix—folding shirts, lining up toiletries, anything that keeps me from thinking about her behind that door. Naked.

She said I must love that she's still a mess. The truth is, I don't see her that way at all. Not really. She's strong and stubborn and more put together than she gives herself credit for. And I can't ignore the quiet pull between us. She's beautiful, though there's still no path forward for us if she's even interested. Nothing has changed with my family.

I glance toward the couch and let out a quiet laugh. It's not a couch at all. It's a loveseat, barely wide enough for one person to sit comfortably, never mind sleep. That means the floor. *Perfect*.

The shower shuts off, and every thought in my head goes

still. I can hear Liz moving around, the faint rustle of a towel, the soft click of bottles on the counter. I picture her, skin flushed, steam rising. I swallow hard and turn away, grabbing my wallet just to give my hands something to do.

I walk over to the bathroom door and knock lightly. "The opening reception and conference check-in goes on for a while longer. I'm going to head down," I call. "I'll be back in a bit."

A muffled "Okay" comes through the door.

That's all I need. I'm out.

The conference check-in is filled with noise from the moment I step off the elevator. Voices overlap, laughter echoes, lanyards and badges clink together. The smell of the ocean and plumeria filters through everything.

I join the line at the registration table, half listening to the chatter around me. Doctors of every flavor. Administrators. People catching up after a year apart. It feels strange to stand here in all this noise when my head's still back in the room upstairs.

"Alaric Dempsey?"

I turn and see Denise Miller walking toward me, smiling wide. It takes a second for my brain to catch up. Graduate school. Late-night study sessions. Too much caffeine and not enough sleep.

"Denise," I say, returning the smile. "Wow. It's been a while."

She looks exactly the same. Sharp suit, perfect hair, eyes that miss nothing. "I didn't expect to run into you here. Still saving lives and stealing hearts?"

"Mostly paperwork these days."

We laugh, and it feels like she's already scanning for her next conversation. Then her gaze stops and something shifts in her expression.

"Wow, Alaric," she says softly. "I didn't know you'd settled down with Liz Ward."

I turn, and the world narrows.

Liz steps into the lobby wearing a floral sundress that looks like summer somehow snuck into February. The light catches her hair, and even with the conference crowd buzzing around her, it feels like everyone stops to look.

My pulse jumps. "We work together," I say quickly. "Not *together* together."

Denise raises an eyebrow, a knowing smile tugging at her lips. "If you say so."

I do, but even I don't sound convinced.

Liz doesn't make it three steps into the lobby before a tall man stops her. He's got that easy, confident smile that comes from knowing he'll be welcomed.

"Liz Ward, Administrator at Paradise General Hospital," he says, reading her badge. "Where's that?"

"British Columbia, Canada," she answers, smiling.

"Mitchell Van der Ahe," he adds. "Neurology, Los Angeles."

She laughs, warm and genuine, and I catch the sound even over the noise of the crowd. I recognize him from past conferences—always front row, always talking like he's on stage.

They look comfortable together.

I remember her saying all she wanted after the flight was a mai tai on the beach, and before I can talk myself out of it, I'm at the bar ordering one. I add a glass of fresh pineapple juice for myself because it feels safer than anything stronger.

When I approach and hand her the drink, she blinks, surprised. Then she smiles. "You remembered."

"I pay attention," I tell her.

She laughs under her breath and turns toward the man beside her. "Alaric, this is Mitchell Van der Ahe."

He offers his hand, grip firm, eyes calculating. I know that look. He's trying to decide if I'm competition or just background noise.

"Good to meet you," I say.

"Same," he replies.

A beat passes, long enough for him to realize Liz isn't alone.

His smile shifts. "I should check in with a few people," he

says. "I'll see you around, Liz."

"Of course," she says as he walks away.

I take a sip of my juice, not looking at her, but I can feel her smile lingering between us.

We move through the room together, weaving between clusters of people with drinks and half-empty appetizer plates. It's a blur of faces I feel like I almost recognize—people from other conferences, quick conversations, names that sound familiar but don't quite stick.

But Liz makes it look easy. She smiles, listens, laughs in all the right places. It's the first time I've seen her looking truly relaxed since she arrived in Paradise, and the sound of her laughter does something to me. It's lighter, unguarded, and for a moment, I forget why this trip feels so complicated.

When the crowd starts thinning, I lean closer. "You hungry?"

"Starved," she admits, hand pressed lightly to her stomach.

The hotel restaurant is just off the lobby. The host greets us with a practiced smile and leads us to a small table by the window. Outside, rain sprinkles, softening the edges of everything it touches and blurring the lights from the boardwalk below.

The host hands us menus. Liz glances down, and her expression shifts.

"Wow," she murmurs, eyebrows lifting. "This is…pricey."

I shrug. "Don't worry about it. I've got it."

She shakes her head, lips pressing together. "Only if the hospital's paying."

I grin, knowing better than to tell her the truth. The hospital's allowance only covered my conference fees. The rest is on me. "Something like that," I assure her.

If I tell her I'm covering it, she'll argue. I don't want to fight about money. I just want a quiet dinner with her. No interruptions, no emails, no chaos. Just the two of us.

What I don't say is that she's worth it.

The server comes back. I order the mahi-mahi, and she orders the ono special.

We talk easily, conversation drifting without effort.

"Where are you living?" he asks. "I mean, in Paradise. Are you staying with Trinity?"

"No. I found one of those cute little cottages not far from the hospital. It's easier to walk than fight for parking."

I laugh because she's not wrong. Employee parking is a nightmare.

"What about you? Are you living at your family's vineyard?"

"God, no."

She settles back, brown eyes narrowing slightly.

"I didn't mean it in a bad way. I just... If I lived there, they'd expect me to work there. And I don't want that." I shrug. "I've got a place on the west side of the lake. It's probably bigger than I need, but..."

My words trail off. I realize I'm babbling, and I don't quite know why.

Our dinners arrive just in time to stop me from saying something stupid, and we dig in.

"With everyone here, Paradise seemed like the logical place to move," she adds. "Or maybe the only one that felt like home. What about you? How are your sisters?"

"I still have four of them," I say. "And they're all still talking to me, which feels like an accomplishment."

Liz smiles. "That bad?"

"Let's just say family politics are still alive and well." I lean back. "Sera and Josie have taken over the vineyard. They've got the place running better than Evie ever did, but don't tell her that, or she'll give the vineyard to someone else. Every time I visit, they hand me a to-do list and tell me not to touch anything."

She laughs softly. "Sounds like sisters."

"Addie's still painting in that tiny apartment downtown. Half her stuff's stacked against the walls, but she swears the mess is part of her process. She's happy, though. Makes enough to scrape by, and every now and then, I slip her a little help and she pretends not to notice."

"That's sweet." Liz nods. "And the youngest?" she prompts.

I shake my head, smiling. "As you know, Ginny went and married a Paradise. You can imagine how that went over. My mother's still recovering, and my grandmother pretends she doesn't exist." I chuckle. "Which is ironic, considering I've spent enough time with Paradises lately to know they're not nearly as terrible as we were raised to believe." My eyes meet hers. She already knows that part. She's seen it.

Liz laughs, shaking her head. "It's poetic, really. Your families can't seem to avoid each other."

"You fit in Paradise," I say before I can stop myself. "I'm starting to think it's fate."

Her eyes flick up to mine, seeming amused.

A shadow crosses the table and a voice calls, "Dr. Dempsey? Liz?"

I glance up to see a tall man in a dark suit and his partner approaching. "Dr. Patel," I say, standing to shake his hand. "Good to see you. It's been a few years."

"Too long," he says, giving Liz an easy smile. "It's great to see you again. I heard you got the job at Paradise General. I'm sure North Vancouver misses you."

Liz laughs. "They moved an excellent person into the job."

He motions to the woman beside him. "This is Monica Cutler. She's in the administration program track."

We make polite small talk for a minute before they move on to another table.

Liz leans back, still smiling, the light catching on her glass. "I forgot how charming you can be."

I raise an eyebrow. "That was all you."

She shakes her head. "You make it look effortless."

I shrug, ignoring the warmth that rises in my chest. "You must be confusing me with someone else."

She shakes her head again, gaze steady. "No. You're the one who remembered my drink and made this whole thing feel…manageable."

I don't know what to do with that, so I just nod.

"Thank you," she says quietly, "for taking me in."

"Anytime," I tell her.

The rain has intensified and is now a steady curtain against the windows. When we've finished, it turns the walk back into a sprint between windows. By the time we reach the elevator, Liz is laughing, hair damp, eyes bright. The sound follows us all the way up.

Back in the room, she kicks off her shoes with a sigh. "I don't think I've ever been this tired."

"You take the bed," I tell her. "I'll sleep on the floor."

She looks at me like I've started speaking another language. "We've shared a bed before. We can do it again."

"That was different," I say.

"Fine." She crosses her arms. "Then I'll sleep on the floor."

"No, you won't."

We go back and forth until she finally wins, mostly because I'm too tired to keep arguing. We agree to share the bed.

She disappears into the bathroom to brush her teeth, humming under her breath. I pull out clothes for tomorrow and tell myself none of this means anything. It's just logistics. Two colleagues in one room. Nothing more.

When she's done, she heads into the bedroom, and I enter the bathroom. By the time I'm out of the shower, the lights are dimmed, and she's already asleep, a neat wall of pillows dividing the bed. Her breathing is soft and even, and the faint scent of citrus lingers in the air.

I'm grateful. It saves us from the awkwardness of saying goodnight.

I switch off the last lamp and lie on my side, close enough to hear her breathing but far enough to pretend the space between us is adequate. I tell myself not to think about what it would feel like to reach across that barrier.

Fortunately, sleep comes quickly.

Thirteen

Liz

I wake to warmth—heavy and solid and alive. Soft air moves across my skin, carrying salt and something woodsy. For a second, I think I'm dreaming…maybe back in Vancouver, wrapped in a bed that isn't mine. Then the world sharpens.

There's an arm around my waist.

My breath catches.

The weight is steady, the hold sure. The body behind me is unmistakably male—solid chest, slow breathing, and the subtle grind of hips with each exhale.

I'm not dreaming.

The fortress of pillows I built last night—my safety line, my careful control—is gone. His body is flush against mine. The hard length of him fits snugly between my ass cheeks, barely disguised behind the thin barrier of my sleep shorts.

Oh God.

I freeze, caught between shock and something else. Something low and traitorous that makes my pulse flutter.

"Liz," he murmurs.

The sound melts through me before reason catches up. His arm tightens, his hand shifting until his palm cups my breast. His thumb brushes the fabric—light, unthinking—enough to pull a gasp from my throat. My nipple hardens, and I shiver with excitement I don't want to feel.

It's instinct to move, but I freeze. His breath whispers across my shoulder, warm and slow, and my mind is a war—whether to scream or lean back into it.

Then he kisses me.

Barely a kiss—a half-asleep press of lips to my shoulder—but it lands intimate and uninvited. Heat burns down my spine.

I hold still, afraid to wake him, afraid not to. Every inch of me is aware of him—the roughness of his jaw against my neck, the solid muscle at my back, the rise and fall of his chest syncing with mine.

Then he grinds against me, hard enough to steal my breath. It would be so easy to turn, open my legs, and let muscle memory take over. For a dizzy second, I imagine it—his mouth, his hands, that old rhythm of want and surrender—and the ache pulses through me, sharp and terrifying.

Move, Liz.

I inch forward, slow and careful, slipping out from under his arm. He shifts, mumbling something I can't make out, then rolls onto his back. Cool air rushes in where his body was.

I stand beside the bed, heart hammering. Sunlight filters through the curtains, catching on his skin where the sheet's fallen to his waist. He looks peaceful. Completely unaware.

It was nothing. A sleep reflex. Two people too close.

But the truth vibrates under my skin—the ghost of that touch, how right it felt before he disappeared from my life.

He stirs. His eyes open, blinking against the light. He looks at me, confusion knitting his brow. "Liz?" His voice is rough, still wrapped in sleep. "What…where are the pillows?"

I glance at the floor. "They didn't survive the night."

He sits up, rubbing the back of his neck, his expression sliding from confusion to horror. "Did I—"

"It's fine," I cut in. "You were asleep."

He shakes his head. "I didn't mean to—"

"I know." I crouch to pick up a pillow, using movement to hide the heat in my face. "Seriously. Don't worry about it."

"I feel like I should—"

"Apologize? Already done." I force a small laugh. "Let's just forget it."

I tuck a pillow back onto the bed and keep my hands busy, gathering my clothes. I showered before I went to sleep, but I need another to rinse off the night.

He watches me for a long moment. The silence stretches.

"I'll find another room," I say finally. "There's got to be a cancellation."

"You don't have to do that." His voice softens. "I'll take the couch."

I glance at the loveseat—small, pretty, useless. "You're not sleeping on that. It'll destroy your back. I'll handle it."

"Liz—"

"I mean it." I try for a smile. "It's fine. Really."

He opens his mouth like he wants to argue, then nods. "I'm sorry."

"Me too."

The words hang between us. I straighten the last pillow—our wall rebuilt—and head for the bathroom.

The door clicks shut behind me, and I lean against the counter, palms pressed into cool marble. My pulse still races. The mirror throws back a version of me I barely recognize—flushed cheeks, wild hair, lips parted like I'm caught in a secret.

"Get it together," I whisper.

I turn on the shower. Steam fills the room, fogging the mirror until I disappear.

When I step under the spray, the heat hits my skin, chasing

away the chill. I wash quickly, but the memory clings—his hand, his weight, the whisper of his breath at my neck. It shouldn't matter, but it does.

Just biology and bad timing. Still, I can't shake the echo of it, the way it felt safe before it felt dangerous, the part of me that wanted to stay.

I scrub harder, like I can rinse the thought away. The soap smells like plumeria and coconut—sweet and tropical and too soft for the sharp edges of my thoughts.

When I step out, the room is still thick with steam. My reflection is a blur as I towel off and dress. My hair goes up, makeup on, my face settling into something professional. Controlled. Safe.

I can do this.

When I open the door, cooler air rushes in. The bed's made, perfectly smooth. I stand there, towel in hand, looking for any sign of him.

Nothing.

He's gone.

And even though I said that's what I wanted, a small hollow opens under my ribs.

But it's better this way—cleaner. No awkward good mornings. No more apologies. But the ache doesn't care. It lingers as I pull my bag over my shoulder and grab my badge and notebook.

I ride the elevator down with two nurses from the mainland who are laughing about the time difference—their bodies still thinking it's ten a.m. Mine too. Maybe that's why everything feels off-kilter, stretched between exhaustion and adrenaline.

The doors open onto the lobby downstairs, and morning light filters through palm leaves and wide windows, painting the marble floor in gold and green. My ears fill with the rush of waterfalls spilling into the koi pond.

I stop at the front desk, clinging to hope. The woman behind the counter wears her hair in a glossy twist with a pink plumeria tucked behind her ear. Her smile is warm.

"Hi," I say, leaning in. "Any cancellations? Anyone not checked in? I'm looking for a room."

Her smile softens. "I'm sorry. We're at full capacity."

I exhale slowly. "Right. Of course. Do you have a list of nearby hotels?"

She pulls out a laminated sheet and winces. "Here you go, but… Well, there's a Comicon on the island this week. The news said there isn't a free room anywhere."

I blink. "You're kidding."

Before she can answer, a couple strolls past in full Starfleet uniforms. Behind them, a group of Stormtroopers clatters across the marble like they're late for battle.

I shut my eyes and rub the bridge of my nose. "This can't be happening."

She tries not to laugh. "I'm afraid it is."

"Thank you for your help," I say. "Can I leave my info in case something opens?"

"Of course." She writes as I dictate.

Five more nights like this – how?

I thank her again and head toward the conference center. When I arrive, people are lined up for coffee and breakfast, the air full of chatter about the beach.

I bypass the buffet, grab a cup, and follow the crowd into the ballroom. The banner across the stage reads *Healing the Healer: Understanding the Self in Service.* That feels uncomfortably close.

I find a seat near the back and after a few minutes, the lights dim as a woman in a bright floral dress steps up to the podium.

"Good morning, everyone," she begins. "We're thrilled to kick off the first day of sessions with a topic that matters to every one of us. Please welcome our guest speaker, Joy Love."

Applause rises. I open my notebook and prepare to disappear.

Joy adjusts her mic. "Good morning. Today, we're talking about how trauma can mirror itself in our relationship patterns."

The words stop me cold.

She smiles. "I once worked with a nurse who couldn't understand why she kept ending up in the same kind of relationship—different people, same pattern. She'd take care of them, anticipate every need, and eventually burn out—hurt, exhausted, wondering what went wrong."

Heads nod.

"She said, 'I'm a professional caregiver. I should be good at this.' And I told her, 'That's exactly why it keeps happening.'"

Soft laughter.

"When we spend our lives caring for others, we learn to read pain before people speak it. We learn to fix things fast, stay calm, be dependable. But those instincts can pull us into relationships that recreate the very wounds we've spent years helping others heal. We fall into what's familiar because familiar feels safe, even when it isn't."

She pauses. "Healing the healer starts with understanding the self in service. It's not about judging our patterns. It's about tracing where they come from and gently rewriting them."

Her words ripple through the room. A murmur spreads.

"When you grow up managing chaos," she continues, "control starts to look like safety. You micromanage emotions. You over prepare. You don't trust ease because ease feels like the calm before the storm."

Control. Safety. Familiar pain.

Each word hits like a pulse. My pen hovers but doesn't move.

I think of the pillow wall I lined up, believing boundaries would keep me safe. How fast they fell. Breath at my neck. A hand sliding close. My name spoken like a secret.

My body remembers before my mind does.

My mind wanders—I'm not even sure where—and when I focus again, Joy is finishing up. "Remember, you don't have to decide anything immediately," she says. "Just notice when you feel safe and when something in you tightens and wants out. Both responses make sense. Our work is learning which one deserves your trust."

Applause breaks out, and people rise, gathering bags and coffee cups, murmuring about the next session. I stay seated, staring at the mostly blank page.

Control. Safety. Repetition.

The words blur, and beneath them, I write something small, barely legible.

I don't know which kind this is.

The room empties until only the scent of coffee and ocean air lingers. I close my notebook and take one last sip, letting the rhythm of waves beyond the windows steady me.

Finally, I rise and exit. Outside, the day is bright. Palms sway in the breeze. Somewhere down the path, laughter carries, a reminder that life keeps moving, no matter what happens in the dark before dawn.

I square my shoulders, breathe in deep, and tell myself I can learn a different kind of safe.

Fourteen

Alaric

The air smells like salt and roasted pork as I step onto the sand. The last streaks of sunlight stretch across the water. It's been a long day of lectures. I look around, but no one looks familiar. That's okay. I'm here to learn—and to relax.

A woman in a red hibiscus dress greets me with a smile bright enough to match the firelight. She loops a lei around my neck. "Aloha," she says, pressing a drink into my hand. "Welcome to the conference luau."

The glass sweats against my palm and the scent of pineapple and rum hits before I take the first sip. Strong, sweet, dangerously easy. A mai tai. The official welcome to Hawaii.

I thank her and move farther in, shoes sinking into warm sand as I look over the spread. Long tables run under a white tent strung with lights, making everything look softer. People gather in groups, laughing, clinking glasses, voices rising over the surf.

The sun eventually drops behind the horizon, leaving a soft bruise of purple across the sky. My phone buzzes in my pocket, a reminder that I promised to check in with my office, but I silence it. *Not yet.*

I scan faces. Too many leis, too many bright shirts, too many people pretending they're not reading badges for titles they recognize. I should be mingling, talking, maybe even enjoying myself. Instead, my chest tightens with that familiar pulse of anticipation I don't like to name.

She's here. I know it before I see her.

It's been years since that hospital in North Vancouver, but I can still picture her leaning over her computer, brow furrowed, lips pressed together while she worked through a challenge. The thought catches me off guard, stirring something I came here hoping to leave buried. I take another sip of my drink, ice clinking against the glass, and tell myself it's just nostalgia, a trick of air and music.

But even as I think it—and especially after this morning—I know it's a lie.

"Alaric Dempsey?"

I turn, blinking against the torches until the face clicks into focus.

"Dr. Sato," I say. "I'll be damned."

He laughs, clapping a hand to my shoulder. "Please call me Peter. Haven't seen you since your practicum days at North Van. You're looking good, man. Hawaii suits you."

I huff a quiet laugh. "I've been here less than a day."

"I'll trade our rain for this heat any day," he says. "Are you in town for the whole week?"

"Yeah. Keynote tomorrow, panels Tuesday and Wednesday." I pause. "You still working in Vancouver?"

"Emergency department in Surrey," he says. "Teaching part-time at UBC. You?"

"Still in Paradise, balancing a private and hospital

practice."

"Good for you. That's a solid hospital." He nods, and then leans in a little. "We should catch up. I'll be at the bar after the hula show. You remember how we used to close down O'Malley's back in North Van?"

I smile despite myself. "I remember the hangovers."

"Then I'll see you later." He's already backing into the crowd.

I lift my glass in acknowledgment, but my thoughts drift—to the practicum, sleepless rotations, and the woman who made all the noise fade. The one I left because I thought it was the right thing to do.

I inhale slowly, trying to shake off the memories. The ocean wind catches the torches, and they flicker like they're waving.

When I turn back toward the tent, the laughter feels louder. I scan the rows of tables. She's easy to miss at first. The tent is crowded, but then my eyes find her.

She sits halfway down one of the long tables, hair loose around her shoulders, a flower tucked behind one ear, and a purple orchid lei at her neck. The light catches the gold in her hair, and for a moment, I forget to breathe.

She's talking to someone. A man. He's sitting too close, leaning in, his hand resting a little too near hers. She laughs politely at something he says, but I know that look. The polite smile. The slight tilt of her shoulders away from him. She's being pleasant, but she's not interested. When he touches her arm, I see the faint stiffening, the tiny pause before she pulls back. It's subtle, but I catch it.

The sound of the luau fades. I can't look away.

It shouldn't bother me. She doesn't owe me anything after the way I left. But the sight of his hand on her arm twists something hot in my gut.

I take a slow sip, ice melting against my tongue, and try to talk myself down. We slept in the same bed last night, but it means nothing. We're here for work. She deserves to be happy.

Still, the possessive thought slips through. She was mine once.

Her head turns, maybe catching movement in the crowd, and her gaze sweeps past me. My pulse jumps, as if she's caught me doing something I shouldn't. But she doesn't see me. She's already smiling again, tight, polite.

The man leans in closer, saying something I can't hear. Her fingers curl around the stem of her drink, knuckles pale.

That's enough.

Before I know it, I'm moving. Across the sand, through the tables, past clusters of colleagues talking shop. My pulse beats in time with the drums from the stage, fast and low, each step tightening the line between memory and impulse.

By the time I reach her table, I've already decided what I'm going to do.

I stop beside her before she even looks up. The man's hand is still on the table, too close to hers. Her shoulders tense again.

I lean down, close enough to catch the faint scent of her shampoo and press a light kiss to her temple.

"Sorry I'm late, sweetheart," I say, just loud enough for him to hear. "The kids wouldn't stop talking about their day. You know how they are."

Her head jerks up, eyes wide. For a heartbeat, she just blinks at me, stunned. Then I see it click—the slight lift of her brow, the way her lips twitch into a small, knowing smile. "They did okay, though?" she asks. "How was school today?"

The guy's mouth opens and closes once. "Oh," he manages, glancing between us. "Didn't realize you were, uh—"

"Married?" I offer with a grin. "Yeah. Still getting used to it myself."

Liz hides a laugh behind her glass. The man mutters something about grabbing another drink and disappears into the crowd, leaving a trail of awkward behind.

When I glance down, Liz is shaking her head, fighting a smile. "You just scared off a perfectly decent human being."

"He didn't look decent to me," I say, sliding into the

empty seat beside her.

She tips her head, conceding without giving me the win. "I can't believe you did that," she murmurs.

"I can't believe I had to."

Her eyes flick up, sharp but curious. "You don't have to protect me. But I'm glad you stepped in. He was a little friendlier than I like."

"Old habits." I swirl what's left of my drink. "You didn't look like you wanted him there."

She doesn't argue. Just exhales slowly, fingers tracing the edge of her napkin. The light catches her face, softening her jaw, and I realize I've missed this. Her calm in the noise. Her focus. The way she always seemed more grounded than anyone in the room.

I clear my throat, aiming for casual. "You look good."

Her gaze lingers a beat too long. "You too."

Then applause breaks out as the host steps onstage, thanking everyone for coming.

Liz sits back, lips curving. "Guess the show's starting."

I smile, but my pulse hasn't settled since I touched her.

The lights dim, and the crowd quiets, anticipation rolling through the air like the tide.

A dancer in traditional Hawaiian clothing and ankle shells steps into the firelight, skin gleaming, smile wide. With a shout, he scales a palm tree barefoot, muscles bunching. The crowd gasps as he swings one arm out, machete flashing, and slices clean through the top of a coconut.

He slides down in a rush and lands light. With a showman's grin, he pulls a straw from behind his ear. He scans the crowd, eyes catching on Liz.

Of course.

He struts toward our table, holding the coconut high like an offering. The crowd laughs and claps as he stops in front of her and bows.

"For the lovely lady," he says, presenting it with a flourish.

Liz laughs, cheeks pink, and accepts it. "Thank you."

I watch her take a sip, her lips wrapping around the straw, and something unreasonably primal stirs in my chest.

"You okay over there?" she asks, eyebrows raised.

"Fine," I lie. "Just wondering if I should get a machete."

She laughs, shaking her head. "You're impossible."

"So I've been told."

The drums kick up, echoing off the surf. A line of dancers step onto the stage, hips swaying, arms flowing like waves. The smell of roasted pork drifts closer as servers appear with trays, moving between tables.

Plates land in front of us—kālua pork wrapped in ti leaves, laulau, lomi lomi salmon, bowls of poi, squares of haupia gleaming white like moonlight.

Liz murmurs a quiet, "Wow," and I can't tell if she means the food or the dancers.

We eat, drink, and watch. The firelight paints her skin gold, the ocean rumbling just beyond the tent. Every so often, she glances my way, half smile, half question, but neither of us says what we're thinking.

By the time dessert arrives, the night feels softer. The noise around us fades.

Liz leans back, fingers tracing the rim of her glass. "This is beautiful," she says quietly.

"It is."

She looks at me. "You're not talking about the beach, are you?"

I shake my head. "No."

Her breath catches, small but real, and she looks away. The drums fade, the crowd claps, and torches flare as the dancers take a final bow.

The moment slips, but the air between us doesn't move. If anything, it thickens, like everything we've never said is right here, waiting.

When the music fades and the crowd scatters, the beach feels different. Eventually, the torches burn low, smoke curling into the night sky.

I pull off my loafers, Liz slips out of her sandals, and we carry our shoes as we wander down the shoreline. The sand's still warm, the tide inching higher with each wave. I shove my free hand into my pocket, unsure what to say, afraid of saying the wrong thing.

She breaks the silence. "I called every hotel on the island," she says. "There's another convention this week. Some kind of comic thing. Everything's booked solid."

I look at her, already knowing what I want. "Then stay with me."

She stops walking. The ocean fills the space between us. "Alaric…"

"It makes sense," I say. "The room's big enough. It's just for the week. I don't want you stranded."

Her gaze holds mine, wary and steady. "You think this is a good idea?"

I shrug, chest tight. "It's practical."

She gives a short laugh. "You always were good at making things sound reasonable."

"Is that a bad thing?"

Her voice is quiet, but it cuts clean. "It was when you left."

I let the words land. Don't argue. I already did that once, and it didn't save anything. "It wasn't that I didn't care," I say. "I was wrong." I don't know how to explain this to her.

She exhales, shoulders sinking. "You don't get to say things like that, Alaric."

I take a step closer, careful not to touch her. "I'm not asking for anything. Just…stay. Let me make sure you're okay while you're here."

She studies me, searching for the angle. "Nothing can happen between us."

"I know."

"Do you?"

The corner of my mouth lifts. "I'll behave. Mostly."

That earns the smallest smile. Not forgiveness. Just permission.

We stand there, the water sliding in and out over our feet. I want to reach for her. But I don't. I stay beside her instead, close enough to feel her warmth without claiming it.

When she finally nods, it's hesitant. "Okay. I guess that's my best option."

"I guess it is," I repeat.

I really hope that's true.

Fifteen

Liz

The ocean sounds seep through the quiet between each of our steps. My sandals dangle from my fingers, the sand cool now that the sun's gone, the night soft and blue around us. The luau music still drifts through the air, but out here, it's mostly waves and distant laughter fading into dark.

All day my attention has kept drifting to Alaric, whether I wanted it to or not. I noticed when he wasn't around, and I felt it when he was. Whatever chemistry there was between us didn't fade just because we were apart for so long. But I've changed, grown. Now, I can separate what my body wants from foolish ideas my heart has in mind. And it's a good thing too. Because telling him nothing was going to happen has only strengthened the pull of what I desperately want from him.

The words scrape up my throat before I can stop them. "When you left, it broke me."

His breath catches. It's small, but I hear it. The truth hangs between us, trembling in the air, and suddenly, I wish I could pull it back into my chest and lock it away again.

"We had that weekend in Victoria," I say, quieter now. "It meant something to me. And then you cut things off, disappeared, and left Vancouver like none of it mattered." I swallow, take a breath. "I'm not ruined, Alaric. But I had to rebuild myself without you."

He steps close enough that his arm brushes mine as we walk, and those light touches pull my thoughts in too many directions. He stays quiet, measured, careful. "I'm sorry," he finally says. "I didn't know how to explain what was happening with me."

"I'm not looking for you to fix it," I clarify. "And I'm not here to pretend we're picking up where we left off."

He watches me, waiting.

"I'm serious," I say, meeting his eyes. "I'm not stepping back into what hurt me."

His gaze softens, but his voice stays steady. "I won't assume anything. I understand."

"Good," I say.

Even as I nod, I have to keep telling myself this is fine. That I'm choosing it with my eyes open. Yet I'm also aware of how close he is. Of how easy it would be to lean in.

But this is a truce, born of an unfortunate situation, not a reunion.

Still, I don't move away.

I can sleep beside him without falling back into the mess we used to be. I can keep my footing. Except my chest still feels too tight every time he looks at me.

We turn closer to the resort, and the torches along the beach path flicker gold on his skin. It hits me how familiar all of this feels—his stride, the tilt of his head.

"Okay?" he asks finally, voice low.

I nod. "Yeah. I just needed to walk it off."

"Me too." The corners of his mouth lift, just enough to soften the shadows. We walk a few more steps. "For what it's worth, I don't want to hurt you again."

I want to believe him. God, I do. But belief feels like a luxury I can't afford twice.

"I know," I say because I can't give him more than that.

We pass a stack of beach chairs by the lifeguard hut, the smell of salt thick in the air. The sky's a deep navy now, a few stars pushing through. His hand twitches once, like he wants to reach for me and stops himself.

That restraint is new. It's also the only thing keeping me from unraveling. If he can stay strong, I can too. I can be near him without losing myself.

I'm here on behalf of my boss and because I'm supposed to be making sure Alaric completes his CMEs. People think I'm the one who can keep him in check.

That's a bit laughable if you know our history, but nonetheless, if I stay inside those limits, I'm still doing what I came here to do.

I'll just also be lying beside him.

The hotel lights bloom ahead, golden against the night. I focus on that—the walk back, the promise we made, the fragile balance we're pretending we can keep.

But when he looks over, a small, quiet smile tugging at his mouth, the part of me that swore she was done with him doesn't feel so sure.

By the time we get back to the hotel, the night air feels heavier, warm against my skin. The soft thump of drums fades as we climb the short steps to the lobby. I slip my sandals back on and shake sand from my hem, trying to seem composed, even as my conversation with myself continues. I was honest with him. We've cleared the air so we can move forward without tension. We can be professional. We can share a room without it meaning anything more.

A man's laugh cuts through the quiet, and before I can

place it, a familiar voice calls out.

"Dr. Dempsey!"

Alaric and I turn together. Dr. Sato waves from across the foyer, a lei hanging crookedly around his shoulder. A woman stands beside him, petite, dark hair in a sleek bun, her smile quick and kind.

"We were just coming in from the beach," Alaric murmurs, his hand brushing the small of my back as we cross the lobby. The gesture is protective and instinctive, and I tell myself not to read into it.

"Dr. Sato," I say when we reach them.

"Please, call me Peter. It's nice to see you. This conference is popular with the Canadian crowd," he says, grinning. "I ran into someone I went to medical school with in Montreal."

"Who can blame us? Winter in this paradise beats the one back home," Alaric says.

"Definitely beats the rain and snow." Sato laughs. "And look at you two. Still together after all these years. Megan, you remember Alaric Dempsey from my North Van days, and this is his partner, Liz Ward."

Partner lands like a pebble in my shoe, small and impossible to ignore.

I freeze, every nerve flaring. *Still together.* For a second, I consider correcting him. But Alaric laughs, easy and warm, and I can't bring myself to comment.

Megan's smile widens. "It's great to see you both. We were just going for a drink. Come join us."

I glance at Alaric, expecting him to decline, but he tilts his head, leaving the choice to me. I hear myself say, "We'd love to."

A few minutes later, we're gathered around a low table on the open-air lanai. The bar's strung with white lights, and everything feels a little magical, or maybe it's just the mai tai set in front of me.

"So," Peter says, lifting his glass. "Another conference, another year of pretending we're not all avoiding the American medical billing and accounting sessions."

Megan laughs. "You're not pretending at all. He actually switched out of one of his afternoon sessions for the Waimea Canyon tour."

"The canyon was incredible," Peter says. "Have you gone yet?"

"I did," I say. "This afternoon after the first session. The colors—it's like someone painted the earth with rust and emerald."

Megan lights up. "Yes. That's exactly how I'd describe it."

We compare photos—hers with bright smiles, mine more cautious—but the conversation flows easily. They talk about tomorrow's dinner cruise up the Na Pali coast, which includes sunset along the cliffs, open water, fresh fish, and live music. We don't have a reservation for that. I didn't want to go by myself, as it seemed romantic. I catch Alaric watching me over the rim of his glass, his expression soft.

When Peter jokes about how grateful he is for Canada's system, Megan nods. "I never appreciated universal healthcare until I left. The paperwork alone nearly crushed me."

"Paperwork is awful wherever we practice," Alaric says. "Half my job feels like arguing with Provincial Health. I miss medicine being about patients, not policy."

"At least here the biggest concern is deciding whether to sit in on the cardiac symposium or sneak out to the beach," Peter adds.

I smile into my glass. "I know which one I'd choose."

They laugh, and the talk shifts to travel again—Waimea Canyon, snorkeling at Poipu Beach. Megan's eyes shine when she describes what she's heard about the cliffs glowing red at sunset. "They say it's the most romantic view in Hawaii."

My heart skips. "It sounds beautiful."

Alaric glances at me, and for a moment the space between us feels smaller, the air charged.

The night drifts by around us, and when the check comes, my cheeks ache from smiling.

Peter stretches. "We should all get some sleep. Big day

tomorrow."

Megan squeezes my hand. "It was lovely meeting you, Liz. We hope to see you both on the boat?"

"Have a good night," I say, rather than responding.

Megan squeezes once more. "You two are such a lovely couple."

I manage a smile. "Thank you. You too."

As they walk toward the elevators, Alaric catches my eye. There's amusement there, but something else too. Something tender.

The warmth blooming in me is not from the drink.

We linger at the table. The bar's almost empty now, staff stacking chairs near the railing. I trace the rim of my glass, watching ice melt into amber swirls.

He leans closer, voice low. "You looked like you had fun tonight."

"What do you mean?"

"Meaning you smiled. You laughed." His mouth curves. "You looked happy."

"I am," I say quietly. Then, after a beat, "For now."

He nods.

We stand and walk side by side through the open doors. The lobby's quiet, just waves and distant music. The elevator hums as we ride up, the air thick. My heart hasn't settled since we left the bar. I can still feel the warmth of his knee brushing mine, the sound of his laugh, the way his eyes caught mine when I said I was happy for now.

He stands beside me in the elevator, hands in his pockets, a faint smile on his lips like he's lost in the same memory. The lights slide up the mirrored wall, flashing across his reflection—open collar, faint tan at his throat, the exhaustion softening his features. I can almost see the man I first fell for, the one who made me believe love could fix anything.

When the doors open, I step out first. The carpet muffles our footsteps, and the hall lined is with tall palms and soft light. I tell myself to breathe, to stay calm, to remember our agreement.

Just sharing space. No falling back into what nearly destroyed me.

But as we unlock the door and step into the dim hotel room, I can feel it—the pull.

The curtains are open, the ocean beyond the glass black and endless. I drop my purse on the chair and turn to say something casual, something safe, but Alaric's in the doorway, watching me like he's trying to memorize the moment.

I shouldn't. I know that. But suddenly I can't find any other option.

My fingers catch his shirt and tug him closer. He comes without hesitation, his hand sliding to the back of my neck, his mouth finding mine. The kiss is soft for half a heartbeat, and then deepens, years of space collapsing between us. It's desperate and careful all at once, leaving no room for thought.

His breath is warm against my cheek. My heart pounds, every nerve lit. I taste salt and something sweet, maybe from the drink, maybe from him. His hands skim down my sides, and I press closer before I remember the promise.

"Alaric," I whisper, pulling back enough to breathe. "We said—"

"I know." His forehead rests against mine. "I know."

He sits on the bed only when I press against his chest, and even then, he keeps his hands to himself, like he's waiting for permission. His restraint should make this easier. But it just makes me ache.

I step between his knees, and his palms finally rise to skim along my thighs, slow enough to test whether I'll pull away. I don't. If anything, I lean into the touch, my breath catching in a way I hope he doesn't notice.

"Liz…" he murmurs, voice low, almost rough.

"Don't," I whisper. "Not tonight."

That's all it takes. His hands tighten at my hips, guiding me closer, and when I slide onto his lap, the sound he lets out vibrates straight through me. His mouth finds mine again, deeper this time, no hesitation left, and the tension that's been building since this morning snaps cleanly between us.

His fingers trace up my spine, unhurried, deliberate, and my whole body shivers in response. I try to stay quiet, try not to give him the satisfaction of knowing how easily he unravels me, but it's useless. He can surely feel every breath, every tremor.

He pulls back to look at me, eyes dark, focused, unbearably gentle. "Tell me if you want me to stop."

Stopping is the last thing I want, the last thing I've wanted since the moment I saw him standing in that doorway, looking at me like the years hadn't managed to burn this out of us.

"I'll tell you," I say.

His thumb brushes my lower lip, slow and reverent, and then his mouth is on my neck, tracing a line of heat that pulls a sound out of me I can't swallow down. He breathes against my skin like he's memorizing it, and my pulse stutters helplessly.

When his hands move to the hem of my dress, he pauses again, waiting.

I nod once, barely, and that's enough.

He lifts the dress over my head and drops it to the floor beside us.

Leaning in, he puts his mouth over my hard nipple. I cry out in ecstasy.

My panties are wet, and he moves them aside, fingers sliding easily between my folds. He pushes inside me, pivoting in and out. My internal muscles tighten.

"Oh God," I cry as I grip his shoulders.

I want more. I want to feel the way he used to light me on fire. I lift my hips, and he slips my panties down my legs. He draws a deep breath. "You smell so good. God, I've missed this."

I paw at his shirt and lift it over his head. I'm already working on his belt buckle and jeans. He lifts me off and pushes his pants to the floor. Then his hands are all over me, skimming my stomach and heating a trail to my breasts as he captures my nipple and suckles. I whimper and moan, rubbing against his hand, and my bliss returns once more.

I spread my legs, and his thumb finds the hard nub. He

circles, coming closer and closer, but not actually touching it—until I cry out. "Please..."

"Are you sure?" he rasps.

"Yes." I groan, moving his fingers out of the way so I can stroke it myself as three of his fingers plunge into my wetness. I arch as he bites my nipple, my body lifting off the bed, balanced only by my head and heels as pleasure rushes through me.My wetness covers his fingers, and he doesn't stop until I'm boneless. Then he watches as I regain my breath.

I reach for him. "It's your turn," I whisper. "I want you inside me."

He scrambles to his pants and pulls a condom from his wallet. I lick my lips as he rolls it on. "You can change your mind," he says.

"No way." I pull in a deep breath as he lines himself up. When he pushes in, the stretch burns for a second before my body gives way, pulling him deeper. He rocks in and out of me as I adjust to his size, and my nails sink into his back. He's the perfect lover, an aberration. I hold on, drawing him deeper as I arch my hips up to meet his thrusts.

"So fucking tight," he groans.

He's inside of me, pushing deep, hard and fast, pounding mindlessly. It's what we want, what our bodies desire. I explode again, and this time, it's more intense because of the frantic way he's moving inside me. He follows, and our climax together is complete.

I gasp, my body once again limp and exhausted. He rolls to the side, taking the bulk of his weight off of me, but our legs and lower bodies remain intimately locked.

"We do that well," I breathe.

"I agree."

Laughter breaks through the tension, and the comforter rustles as I settle against him. He wraps an arm around my waist, his palm warm against my stomach. My head fits beneath his chin the way it used to.

Outside, waves crash relentlessly against the shore. Inside, the only sound is our breathing, slowly syncing. I should move. I should say something. But exhaustion slips in, warm and heavy.

"Goodnight," he murmurs, his lips brushing my hair.

I nod against his chest, eyes already closing.

Sixteen

Alaric

I wake to warmth that doesn't belong to me, a soft press of skin against my arm, the faint hitch of a woman's breath. For a second, I breathe in the mix of hotel linen, salt air, and coconut lotion—and then it all rushes back. *The conference. The flight. Liz. Last night.*

I keep my eyes closed and try to rewrite it in my head. Maybe it didn't happen. Or maybe it was just two overworked people too tired to think straight. Pretending is easier, safer.

She shifts beside me, the mattress dipping as she rolls onto her back. "You're awake," she says, her voice still rough with sleep.

I clear my throat. "Barely."

We don't talk about last night. Instead, we slip into the easy rhythm we've always had, built on sarcasm and carefully measured distance.

"Snore much?" she asks, reaching for the pillow she must have thrown at me during the night.

"You're one to talk. You stole all the covers."

"Liar." She smirks, brushing her hair back with her fingers.

"Evidence suggests otherwise."

Our banter is light and sharp. I can see it in her eyes too, the relief that we're pretending. Last night doesn't need a postmortem.

She sits up and stretches, the sheet sliding down her bare shoulder. I look away because I'm a coward—or because if I don't, we'll spend all day here in the room and I'll remain short on my CMEs.

She catches me looking anyway and raises an eyebrow. "You planning to stare all morning, or are you going to shower before I call room service?"

"Shower," I say. "You should order coffee for yourself and tea for me. I'll be quick."

"I'll make sure they make it strong," she says. "You look like you need it."

I force a laugh and grab my clothes, escaping to the bathroom like a man dodging an ambush. The door clicks shut behind me, and for one second, I lean against the counter—palms flat, heart pounding—and remind myself that this is temporary and shouldn't have happened in the first place. We're at a conference. It's a truce. Nothing more.

Still, there's a flicker of guilt because I liked it. Because I want more. Pretending this means nothing might be the biggest lie I've told myself in a long time.

Outside, Liz hums softly, some tune she probably doesn't realize she's making. *It's just background noise*, I tell myself. But as the mirror fogs, I can still see her behind my eyelids, soft hair, sleepy smile, the faint taste of last night burning on my tongue.

I step into the shower, twist the handle to cold, and wait for the sting. When the water hits, it's brutal. Cold shocks are supposed to wake up your nervous system, lower your blood pressure, clear your head. That's what the studies say. I need all three.

The first rush steals my breath but then steadies it. I focus on that instead of the image of Liz in white sheets, her hair fanned across the pillow, her mouth curved in a smile.

I stand under the spray until my skin feels raw and my thoughts are quiet. No more heat. No more want. Just water, white noise, and control.

When I finally turn it off, the air feels warmer, the world smaller. I towel dry quickly, pull on a pair of slacks, and take one last look in the mirror. My reflection looks calm, composed—a man who hasn't been undone by a single kiss. I almost believe it.

When I return to the bedroom, the smell of coffee engulfs me. Room service has already arrived. A silver carafe and a tea pot with tea bags sits on the table beside two mugs and a plate of fruit.

Liz looks up from her phone. "You survived."

"Barely," I say, running a hand through my damp hair. "That water's straight from the Arctic."

She smiles, and something soft flickers there, something that could undo all the distance I just rebuilt.

I dunk a bag of strong orange pekoe. "Sessions start in an hour?"

She nods, still smiling. "Plenty of time for you to remember how to act normal."

"Define normal."

"Not looking at me like that would be a good start."

I glance away, pretend to check the schedule on my phone, and tell myself the conference will reset everything. Seminars. Colleagues. The illusion of balance.

Liz disappears into the bathroom, still humming as she gets ready. The sound is faint through the door, and I take the chance to breathe.

I button my shirt, tuck it in, pull it out, then re-tuck it and stare at my reflection. My collar's fine. I still look like a man who hasn't slept properly in days. She's in there brushing her teeth, and the space feels too small for both of us.

The door opens, and she steps out wrapped in that quiet confidence she wears like armor. Hair up. Lip gloss faintly pink. She's wearing a sundress she bought in the gift shop that shows off the start of her tan. Conference badge clipped to her lanyard. Professional. Contained. Safer than last night.

"You're awfully happy for someone who hates mornings," I say.

She gives me that half-smile that could start a war. "Fear of bad lighting, not mornings."

I let out a short laugh. "I'll make a note."

She moves toward the table, slipping on her sandals. "We should head down soon. I want good seats for the keynote."

"You mean the ones with the best exit strategy."

"Obviously." She grabs her tablet and glances at the door. "You ready?"

"As I'll ever be."

We fall into step, the hallway echoing with soft footfalls.

The elevator doors open with a polite chime, and we step inside. We're two professionals heading to a conference, nothing more. I focus on the floor numbers ticking down. She folds her arms, looking straight ahead. The quiet isn't awkward. It's charged, like the air before a storm.

Then my phone rings, and I glance down at the screen. *Evie.*

Liz catches the look on my face. "You can answer," she says, her voice careful.

"I should."

She nods. "I'll look for you later."

The elevator slows, the lights flicker with the shift in power, and she steps back.

As the doors open on the lobby, I lift my phone. "*Sorry,*" I mouth.

Her eyes soften. "*Good luck,*" she mouths back.

Then she's gone, heels clicking across marble, disappearing into the crowd—while I hit accept and brace myself for the hurricane on the other end of the line.

"Do you have any idea what's happening at the vineyard?" Evie doesn't bother with a greeting. Her voice is full of outrage and disbelief. "They're tearing through my people like vultures, calling it an investigation. Half of them couldn't find a corkscrew without a manual, and they're questioning me as if I have time to pour vinegar into barrels."

"Max Paradise named you as a co-conspirator. It's standard procedure."

"Don't patronize me." Her voice sharpens. "I built that place from dirt and debt. There was no procedure when everyone else was too busy doubting I could pull it off. Now, suddenly, I'm the villain because he said so? I can't stand the man. I had nothing to do with their made-up drama. Please."

Breathe in. Count to four. Breathe out. Count to four.

"They have to follow leads."

"Leads?" She lets out a bitter laugh. "They're chasing ghosts. You know what this really is? Weak men covering their incompetence with suspicion. They think they can drag my name through the mud, and I'll sit quietly, polishing my medals. I don't sit quietly, Alaric. Not ever." Her breathing changes, short and uneven, the edge of fury giving way to something colder. "You've got that calm voice, that reasonable tone everyone loves so much," she continues. "Use it. Talk to them. Make this disappear before it grows teeth."

I sigh. "That's not how it works."

"Then learn how it works. Because if they think I'm going down for this, I'll take the whole goddamn hill with me."

The line goes dead.

I lower the phone and stare out at the ocean. The tide is high, and the waves are big, crashing in slow motion under the morning sun. For a moment, I can't tell if the sound in my ears is surf or blood.

I hope I still look composed, but I don't feel it. Instead, I feel cracked open.

The air in the lobby feels thick as I put my phone in my

pocket. I pull in a breath. Years of psychology training whisper the same list I always run through when it comes to Evie—narcissistic grandiosity. Paranoia under pressure. Deflection of blame. Classic traits. Textbook. Predictable. And still, she lands a punch every time she opens her mouth.

I take a deep breath in and hold it for four, doing the box breathing I preach to my patients with anxiety. It's the only way to get beyond talking to my grandmother.

I pause at the edge of the crowd and let the noise close in around me. Voices. Clinking mugs. The faint echo of the ocean. But inside, I'm still standing in the eye of the storm, wondering how many more people Evelyn Dempsey will pull into her mess before the wind finally breaks everything down.

Then I see Liz. She's by the coffee station, laughing with a few other attendees. The sound is soft, warm, the opposite of everything I just heard. When she spots me, her expression shifts to concern a moment before returning to composure.

"Everything okay?" she asks when I reach her.

"Fine," I say with a sigh. "Family drama."

"Evie?"

"Evie."

Her eyes narrow. "I can tell by your jaw you didn't win that round."

I almost smile. "No one wins with Evie. You just try not to drown."

Liz hands me a cup of dark tea. "Here. Fuel. You could use it."

"Thanks."

She tilts her head, studying me. "First keynote's on physician burnout. Think you'll make it through without diagnosing yourself?"

"Doubtful."

Her laugh is quiet, and it cuts through the static in my chest better than caffeine ever could. For a second, I forget about Evie, the vineyard, and everything waiting back home.

Liz glances toward the conference room doors. "We

should go in. They're starting soon."

We fall into step together, the crowd funneling around us.

The room is full of large tables, and we find one in the middle where, hopefully, we can see. As we sit, I set my phone face down on the table. Evie's words still echo at the edges of my thoughts, sharp as broken glass. If she's under investigation, things are worse than she's admitting. And if she means what she said about taking the whole hill with her, there won't be a clean way out.

But for now, I do what I've spent a lifetime perfecting. I take a breath, pull my shoulders back, and pretend I'm fine.

Seventeen

Liz

Alaric and I managed the conference day together, but after we return to the room at the end of the day, I don't sleep well. Every time I drift off, I wake again—too warm, too aware of the space beside me. It's ridiculous. Unlike the previous evening, we didn't even touch. But knowing he was there, close enough to hear him breathe, messed with me.

Last night, I told myself I was fine with it. That great sex was great, and it didn't mean anything. But lying there in the dark, I kept wondering if I wanted it to. The thought looped relentlessly. Wanting more from Alaric is dangerous, and I know better than to rewrite our past into something it wasn't. Still, the sound of his breathing and the weight of his presence blurs lines I promised myself I'd keep clear.

I have to remember that this isn't just about wanting him

or not. It's about wanting something steady, and I've already learned he can disappear without warning.

Light slips through the curtains before either of us says anything. I'm already awake, so I rise and get ready, as does he. Eventually, I sit on the edge of the bed, debating whether brushing my hair twice will make me look more awake. He's already dressed, shirt half-buttoned, dark circles under his eyes.

He glances at me. "You look like you slept about as well as I did."

I arch a brow. "So…not at all?"

"Maybe an hour," he admits, tugging at his cuff. "Turns out sharing a bed with a pillow wall to cuddle isn't exactly restful."

I shoot him a look. "You talk in your sleep, you know."

He pauses, his tea halfway to his mouth. "Do I?"

"Yeah. Something about statistical variance and emotional boundaries."

He gives a dry laugh. "That tracks."

I stand and reach for my sandals. "For the record, you also hog the blanket."

"I was defending myself," he says, deadpan. "You kept stealing it."

"Because you built a fort with it," I say, crossing my arms.

His mouth lifts, that hint of a smile I both love and hate. "Well, it worked. Mostly."

I grab my bag and nod toward the door. "Breakfast?"

He opens it for me, still smiling. "If the caffeine's as strong as the hotel Wi-Fi, maybe we'll survive the day."

Downstairs, the banquet room smells like burned toast and coffee. Rows of silver trays line the counter, full of lukewarm eggs and something pretending to be sausage. At least there's fresh pineapple juice.

"I'm going to miss this juice when we get back home."

Alaric nods. "It's not the same when it's not fresh." He leans against the buffet with a plate in one hand, scrolling through his phone with the other. His Hawaiian shirt shows off his biceps, and for some reason, I can't stop noticing.

We end up at a small table by the window, sunlight making the white tablecloth glow. Outside, palm trees sway while a few other early risers with conference badges wander toward the shuttle stop.

"You still up for the tour to Waimea Falls this afternoon?" he asks.

"Yes. I can't wait. The tour should take us places I didn't get to on my own." I spear a piece of pineapple. "You?"

He nods. "Looking forward to it."

"Okay then," I say, standing. "I'll meet you in the lobby after our session."

We head in different directions, and I try to focus on why I'm here.

After a session I nearly napped through, Alaric and I meet in the lobby again.

"How was yours?" he asks.

"It was okay." I glance around, making sure no one's listening. "Pretty boring. What about yours?"

He grins. "The same. Someone actually fell asleep. When the presenter asked if he was boring, the guy blamed jet lag."

I laugh, shaking my head as we make our way out to the bus. The air smells like ocean and plumeria, warm enough to cling to my skin.

The bus is small, its paint fading under the Hawaiian sun. I climb aboard and slide into a window seat halfway back. Alaric follows a minute later and sits beside me. He doesn't ask—just sits, his knee brushing mine as he tucks his bag under the seat. The bus feels even smaller.

"You could've sat anywhere," I say as the engine roars to

life. There are others on the bus, but it's far from full.

He tips his head toward the window. "And miss the commentary?"

I roll my eyes but smile anyway. Soon, the road winds through a thick green forest, flashes of the ocean between the trees. The driver talks about movie sets and waterfalls, but I barely hear him.

"So," Alaric says after a while, "what did your session teach you?"

"That doctors should communicate like normal humans," I say with a laugh. "Apparently, that's groundbreaking."

He smiles. "Mine was worse. Two hours on dealing with trauma. I think I lost brain cells."

"That's tragic," I tell him, and he laughs. The sound fills the bus, warm and easy, and for a few seconds, it feels like old times—before everything between us got complicated.

The bus slows for a sharp curve, and our shoulders bump. Neither of us moves away. I turn toward the window to hide the warmth spreading through me. The island blurs by—green and gold, hibiscus blooming wild, the air thick and sweet. I let myself enjoy the quiet.

When the driver announces Waimea Falls, everyone stirs, collecting hats and cameras. Alaric stands and offers his hand to steady me as I step into the aisle. His palm is warm and steady, and I let him grasp my fingers longer than I should.

"Ready?" he asks, tone gentle.

"Yeah," I say, though I'm not sure what I'm ready for.

The trail curves beneath a canopy so thick it swallows the sunlight. The air smells like wet leaves and earth, heavy with moisture. Birdsong echoes through the branches, and Alaric walks beside me, close enough that our arms brush when the path narrows. We fall into a rhythm, stopping when others pause for photos.

"This place doesn't feel real," I tell him, looking up through the tangle of green. "I've been to the Big Island, Oahu, and Maui, and this is different from all of them. They're all so different but beautiful."

"Paradise back home doesn't come with this view or this Wi-Fi," he says with a grin. "I can't decide if that's progress or blasphemy."

I laugh, and when I turn toward him, he's looking at me. Not the quick glance from breakfast but one that lingers.

The trail opens, and the sound of rushing water surrounds us. Waimea Falls spills white and wild over black stone into a pool that looks painted. Mist drifts through the air, cool against my face. People scatter along the bank, wading near the rope line, taking photos, laughing. For a minute, I forget everything else.

"This was a good idea," I say, watching sunlight shatter across the water.

He nods, voice quiet. "Yeah. It was."

Then his attention shifts. The looseness in his shoulders vanishes. I follow his gaze to a couple on the far side of the clearing—voices sharp, hands gesturing. Behind them, a little girl stands alone, her lips turning blue, chest rising in shallow, panicked gasps.

A cold prickle runs through me. "Oh no."

Alaric is already moving. He crosses the grass, dropping to his knees beside her. The parents keep arguing, lost in their worry.

"She's allergic," the woman stammers. "To nuts."

"Has she been exposed today?" Alaric's tone is calm but clipped.

"I don't know," the mother says, voice breaking.

"Where's her EpiPen?"

That stops them both. The father blinks. "You had it."

"No, I gave it to you."

Alaric's voice cuts through. "She's going into anaphylaxis. We need that pen right now."

They freeze, panic swallowing logic.

"Where's her bag?" I ask, scanning the ground.

The mother points to a pink backpack near a bench. I grab it, drop to my knees, and dump everything onto the grass.

Sunscreen. A stuffed rabbit. Juice box. A clear case with the epi pen rolls free.

"Got it," I call.

Alaric doesn't look up. "Good. Take off the blue cap."

I do it, hands steady even though my heart's racing. He stays focused on the girl, his voice low and soothing. "Hey, sweetheart. Look at me. You're okay. I know it feels scary, but I've got you. You're safe right here with me."

Her breaths come too fast, high and broken. Her tiny chest jerks with each one. Alaric holds up the injector so she can see it. "This is going to help you breathe, all right? Just a quick poke and you'll start to feel better soon."

I press the injector into his hand. He counts softly, "One, two, three," and presses it into her thigh. The click sounds sharp in the humid air. The girl flinches but doesn't cry.

"There we go," he murmurs. "That's it. You're brave. Keep breathing for me."

Her breathing deepens. Color creeps back into her cheeks. My throat loosens.

The mother's crying now, whispering her daughter's name, but Alaric doesn't waver. "You're doing so well," he says, voice soft and sure. "Can you squeeze my hand? That's it. The medicine's working. Just keep breathing with me, okay? In and out. Like this."

He breathes slowly, exaggerating each inhale and exhale until she starts to copy him. The panic in her eyes fades. "See that waterfall?" he says gently. "Let's count the drops. One, two, three. Good girl. You're safe now."

It's barely a minute, but it feels like time stalls around them. The air shifts. Her breathing steadies. Through it all, Alaric stays right there—steady hands, calm voice, eyes full of quiet focus.

I've seen him lecture, argue, flirt. But this gentleness and calm is something else entirely.

The father drops beside them. "Is she—"

"She's okay," Alaric says, checking her pulse. "She'll need

to be monitored, but she's out of danger."

The park medic arrives with a first-aid kit, and Alaric steps back to let him take over. He explains what happened, his tone level, posture still protective. When he hands me the empty EpiPen, our fingers brush. His touch is warm, solid.

"You were incredible," I tell him softly.

He shakes his head. "You found it. That's what mattered. Her parents were in panic mode."

For a second, we just stand there in the mist. The girl's parents thank him over and over, and when the medic leads them toward the ambulance path, the crowd slowly disperses.

The falls roar on, steady and endless. Alaric wipes his palms on his pants and exhales, the tension finally leaving his shoulders.

"That was…" I start, but the words won't come.

"Intense," he says, meeting my eyes.

"Yeah," I whisper. "And kind of amazing."

A small smile tugs at his mouth. "It's nice when things go right."

We start back along the trail.

As we walk, I replay the drama of the afternoon and realize he has an amazing way of making people believe they're safe. It's a kindness and a gift I'm not sure he understands he has. But the warmth I feel soon gives way to the same old confusion as I remember how safe I once felt with him—right up until I didn't.

He's said he thought he was doing what was right, and that maybe that was a mistake. But I still don't really understand what he means. And I don't know whether it's wise or just inviting more pain for me to ask.

Eighteen

Alaric

The ride back from Waimea Falls is quiet. Liz sits beside me, her sunglasses pushed up on her head. She leans her shoulder against the window, eyes half closed, and I can't tell if she's tired or just letting herself drift. Maybe both.

When the bus arrives at the hotel, I stand and step back to let her pass.

"Thank you."

"Do you have the energy to make the social this afternoon? It's happy hour."

She sighs. "Not really. But we should go."

The lobby is cool after the heat outside. The marble floors gleam beneath the slow turn of ceiling fans, and the faint scent of orchids drifts through the air. I stop at the concierge desk while

Liz waits beside me.

"Can I help you?" the woman asks, her name tag polished bright against her white shirt.

"Yes, please." I give her our room number. "I'd like dinner reservations for two. Somewhere nice."

She smiles. "I have just the thing. Seafood all right?"

I glance at Liz, and she hesitates a moment, but then nods. "Perfect."

The concierge jots something on a card. "I'll text you the details once I get them confirmed."

Liz arches a brow at me. "You're planning ahead."

"Just making sure we eat something that isn't hotel buffet food," I say.

"Somewhere nice, huh?"

"You deserve a decent dinner after all that hiking."

She shakes her head, smiling. "All right. I'll hold you to that."

We head toward the ballroom. Liz glances at me like she wants to say something but doesn't, and I let the silence stretch.

Before we even get to the conference, my cell phone pings with the concierge's dinner details. This is going to be good.

Inside, the room is packed. We start side by side, but I barely manage to give Liz our dinner reservation time before she's pulled away by a group of women from her track. I let her go as Peter Sato waves me over.

"Alaric," he says warmly, "have you met Dr. Raj Poon from Calgary and Dr. Jim Lee from Montreal?"

We shake hands. Someone jokes about the humidity ruining their slides. Another mentions jet lag. The conversation turns to healthcare systems.

"It's not perfect," Raj says, pushing up his glasses, "but at least I can focus on my patients instead of billing codes. That counts for something."

Jim nods. "You can't measure how much lighter that feels until you've worked both sides."

I nod and contribute where I should, but my focus drifts.

My gaze keeps scanning the room, searching for Liz.

When I don't see her, I check my phone.

Liz: I'm heading up to the room to get ready for dinner. See you soon.

My pulse kicks up. I tell Sato and the others it was good to see them and make my way toward the elevator. The music and laughter fade as the doors close behind me.

Upstairs, the hallway is cool and still. I swipe the keycard and step inside. The scent of jasmine hits me, and for a second, I just stand there, letting the scent pull me back in time.

Then the bathroom door opens. Liz steps out and the sight knocks the air from my lungs. Her black dress catches the light, the neckline low, the skirt brushing her thighs. A slit reveals more skin than I should be noticing. The diamond pendant I gave her years ago rests at her throat, glinting softly. "You look…stunning," I manage.

Color rises in her cheeks as she tucks a strand of hair behind her ear. "Thank you."

The way the fabric moves when she breathes. The way her blush deepens. It's torture.

I clear my throat. "Give me five minutes to change. Our ride will be here soon."

She nods. "Sure."

I move through my wardrobe shift. Slacks, clean shirt, loafers. I can feel her watching me in the mirror. When our eyes meet, my body remembers, even if my mind tries to forget.

"You ready?" I ask, offering my arm.

She slips hers into mine and nods. "Yeah. I'm ready."

The elevator is crowded, and the doors open on every floor. Eventually, Peter and Megan step in.

Megan beams at Liz. "You look lovely tonight."

Liz blushes again, her arm still linked with mine.

Peter grins. "Date night?"

"Just dinner," I say.

When the elevator stops, Megan squeezes Liz's arm. "Have fun, you two."

Outside, a rideshare idles at the curb, headlights washing over the hotel steps. I circle around to Liz's side and open the door. She hesitates for a beat, eyes lifting to mine, then climbs in.

Once I'm seated, the driver pulls away. Storefronts, palms, and neon are reflected in the window glass. Liz sits close enough that I can feel the warmth of her arm.

When the ocean comes into view, the lights thin out. The restaurant glows ahead, small and warm under strings of white bulbs swaying in the breeze.

We step out into the sound of the surf. The hostess leads us through the open deck to a table by the railing. Beyond it, the beach fades into darkness, the waves flashing silver under the moon. She lights a candle between us, painting Liz's skin in gold.

Liz studies the menu, tilting her head so the light catches her hair. "To not getting lost on the trail," she says when the wine arrives, lifting her glass.

We order, and I clink my wine against hers. "And to surviving the bus ride back."

After a few minutes, the server returns, setting down our meals, Liz's grilled ono with macadamia-nut butter and lime, and my opakapaka, crisped golden, both with jasmine rice and grilled pineapple.

She takes a bite and closes her eyes, a quiet sound escaping. "Oh, this is ridiculous."

I take a bite and agree. "Indeed. This is definitely somewhere nice."

She smiles, and the breeze stirs the candle flame, lifting the edges of the tablecloth. For a while, we talk easily. The waterfall, the hike, the little girl with the nut allergy. Safe topics that fill the air without touching the fault lines between us.

I think about telling her the truth, that I've spent years trying to outrun what happened, that no matter how far I go, it finds me. Instead I ask, "You ever think about what it would've been like if I hadn't left?"

She studies me for a long moment, then looks down at her plate. "I did when it first happened. But not anymore. We were different people then."

"I guess we still are."

"You think so?" she asks.

I don't know how to answer that. I know I have perspective I didn't before, but I'm not any closer to knowing how to make space for what I want in the stifling grip that is my family.

The quiet settles again. When the plates are cleared, the server leaves dessert menus we ignore. The candle burns lower, wax pooling at its base.

When the bill comes, I pay without thinking. She doesn't argue, just watches the dark line of the surf beyond the deck.

"Thank you for dinner," she murmurs.

"It's my pleasure," I say.

Outside, Liz slips off her shoes as we walk along the sand toward the road. We don't talk on the drive back. The windows are down, warm air rushing in. She stares out at the dark water, yet I can feel something between us—soft and electric.

When the car pulls up at the hotel, she turns to me. "Shall we go upstairs?"

We reach the lobby just as a group of women sweeps in. Bright laughter, half-empty cocktail glasses, perfume in the air. Liz exhales a quiet laugh.

"They're in the admin track," she murmurs. "I met them this morning."

One of them spots her. "Liz! There you are! You disappeared after the mixer!"

"Just dinner," Liz says, her voice friendly.

They close in, chattering, bracelets clinking, talking over one another. When the elevator opens, they surge forward, then realize it's full. The doors slide shut, leaving them giggling and pressing the button again.

We wait. The tension between us crackles like static.

When the next elevator arrives, we step in with the group,

louder now, joined by another couple. Someone presses too many buttons.

"Oops!" One of them laughs.

The elevator lurches upward. First floor, second, third. Each stop peeling them away in waves of perfume and laughter.

Finally, the doors close again, leaving only us and the other couple behind.

"That was chaos," Liz says, laughing softly.

"Welcome to conference life," I say.

The couple steps out on the next floor, and the doors shut behind them. The space feels smaller now. The low buzz of the light, the faint scent of her perfume, the quiet rhythm of our breathing as the elevator rises.

Inside the room, jasmine greets us again. Liz turns on the lamp beside the bed, golden light spilling across her shoulders. She sets her clutch on the dresser and exhales like she's been holding her breath all night.

I close the door and lean against it, watching her unclasp the necklace. The diamond catches one last glint of light before falling into her palm.

"You're staring," she says, voice low.

"Yeah," I admit. "Guess I am."

Her lips part, and she takes a slow step closer. "You shouldn't look at me like that."

"Then stop being impossible to look away from."

She doesn't move.

I reach for her, giving her time to change her mind.

It seems she doesn't.

The kiss starts soft, cautious, then deepens as her hands find my chest. She tastes like wine and salt and memory.

When her fingers slide to the back of my neck, everything else fades. The room. The ocean. The years we lost. All of it falls away as we stumble toward the bed, her laugh caught between our mouths before it dissolves into a sigh.

I unzip the back of her dress. "Leave the shoes on and get on the bed on your knees."

She disrobes and presents her ass to me.

My cock stands at attention. I reach into the bedside table and turn the vibrator on. “I can see you’re wet.” I shake my head and force myself to breathe. “Let me know if you’re nervous or uncomfortable.”

She nods as I run the vibe up her legs and move to her nipples.

She moves her ass around, and I want to lick her into a frenzy.

I push the vibe in, and her pussy pulls it deep. I rub my fingers over her throbbing clit. I know exactly what it takes to make her climax. After a moment, I pull the vibe out. Her sounds tell me she’s close.

“Roll on your back and open wide.”

I look down at her, arms high above her head and legs spread wide, her pussy open and flexing. “I wish I could take a photo of you like this.”

“Don’t you dare.” She starts to close her knees.

I push them wide and shake my head. “I can wish. Instead, I’m committing it to memory.”

She relaxes, and I tap her hip. She lifts so I can place a pillow under her. I pick up her vibrator.

“So you thought you might need orgasms while you were in Hawaii?”

She shrugs. “It’s better than planning a one-time hook up.”

I lean the vibe against the outside of her pussy lips. She can feel the sensation, but I don’t think it will be enough to get a release. She whimpers, her hips looking for the friction she needs.

My cock is weeping in my pants, but her toy will make the task ahead so much more fun. “Does this feel okay?” I adjust the vibrator, and her hips move, pleading for more. “You’re so responsive. This gives me ideas.”

I stand and undress for her. I give my cock two hard tugs to keep it from exploding. Tonight is about Liz.

I join her on the bed and circle the vibrator with a light

touch around her clit. She tries to grind into the toy.

"What do you want, Liz? Use your words and tell me."

"Ric. Ple—aaah—" I put the vibrator into her with one sharp push. "I need you inside me."

"Do you like this?"

She nods, and her hips rock.

I pull out the vibrator, and she whimpers.

My fingers roam her body, careful not to touch her breasts or her beautiful slit. If I wait too long, I'll come without ever pushing into that stunning pussy, but I can't stop yet. Her body is so responsive. I return the vibrator to her vagina and twist it to a faster setting. She moans.

"You like this plastic cock inside you."

Her breathing is labored, so I know she's close. I pull the vibrator out, and moisture escapes.

I tap her lips with the toy, and she opens her mouth. "That's it. Clean this off."

She licks it. "Holy fuuuuuck."

"Do you use other toys?" I ask.

"Sometimes."

"What else do you like?"

"I love my clit sucker and my nipple—"

I place the vibrator on her clit and her voice fades. "Don't stop."

I reach for her nipples to pinch and pull as her hips undulate.

"I sometimes like nipple clamps."

"Did you bring those too?"

"No, but don't stop what you're doing. My pussy's on fire, and I'm ready to hump anything for some friction."

I lean down and kiss her. I can taste her on her lips. I lie down beside her to continue the kiss. "Do you want to come?" I whisper.

She shivers. "Yes, please."

"I'll let you," I promise. Although probably not as quickly as she'd like.

I move down her body, kissing reverently as I go—her clavicle, nipples, belly button, and hip bones all get little pecks, unlike the bruising bites of back in the day.

"Please. Please. Make me come," she begs.

My tongue licks a path down to her center and moves gently across her pussy. It's time. "I want you to watch me."

My fingers move to her clit, matching the rhythm of my tongue. I suckle the bud. She's so close.

With two fingers, I push inside and find that special spot. I rub it hard while increasing the sucking on her nub.

"Come for me," I command, barely taking my mouth away from her pussy. I press my tongue into her, and she can't hold back. I'm bathed in her bliss, the nectar I was eager for.

I continue to strum her clit as I reach for a condom and roll it on as the last waves of her orgasm move through her. Then I turn her over and push into her pussy. "You're so fucking tight."

I spank her, and she moans her delight as we push and pull together. "I'm close," I say through gritted teeth.

"Harder," Liz demands.

I push into her and spank her again, and I can feel the twitches inside her. As she reaches her climax again, her pussy grabs my cock and pulses out my seed.

"Holy shit!" she yells. "These are the best orgasms I've ever had."

My dick rises to the occasion, proud of himself. I hold her tightly. "Me too."

When it's over, I stay close, bracing my weight beside her. Her chest rises and falls.

I roll to my side, and she rests her head against my chest like it's the most natural thing in the world. Her hair spills across my arm, warm and soft, her scent mixing with salt air and candlelight drifting through the open balcony door.

The room is still.

I stare at the ceiling, tracing the shadows the light makes across the plaster. I know how fragile this is. How easily it could break. How quickly one wrong move could ruin it all.

After all, we specifically agreed not to do this—right before we did. Yet she's here. Curled into me. Breathing with me. Choosing to stay.

And that feels like something.

Maybe an opening.

Maybe this only exists for tonight. Maybe it lasts the week. Maybe it burns out as fast as it flared.

I just know I don't want to waste a second pretending it doesn't matter.

Nineteen

Liz

The light is soft when I wake, filtered through gauzy curtains that move with the breeze.

I should get up. I should shower, get coffee, and find something to do that doesn't involve staring at Alaric. Instead, I linger. The morning is still in a way that feels rare—no phone notifications, no work, no pretending. Just the soft hush of the ocean through the open balcony doors and the steady sound of him breathing.

When I finally move, I slide out of bed and pull the sheet up over him. The floor is cool under my bare feet. In the bedroom mirror, I can see whisker burn.

After a minute, I hear him stir behind me. A rough sound escapes his throat, half a groan, half a sigh, and I turn to see him stretch, his hand dragging across his chest before falling back to the mattress. His hair is a mess, sticking up in a way that makes me smile.

"Morning," I say.

He blinks at me, still somewhere between sleep and waking. "You're up early."

"I couldn't sleep." I curl into the armchair near the balcony. "Too many thoughts. And I just called for coffee and tea."

He sits up slowly, the sheet slipping down to his waist and his glorious morning erection. I have to look away before my thoughts turn back to last night.

"Are you regretting what we did?" he asks quietly.

"No," I say. "Just wondering what it means."

He nods like he understands, and maybe he does. At least we're acknowledging what we've done this time. That feels like progress.

There's a knock at the door, and I open it to find room service and our morning beverages. Once we've gotten our caffeine, we go through the morning routine. The conference doesn't have sessions for us to attend this morning, so we can be tourists or just do more of what we did last night. It feels a little reckless, but a big part of me wants to stay in the room and have more mind-blowing sex all day.

We decide against that, but it does take some time to get out of bed. By the time we make it downstairs, the breakfast buffet is nearly empty. A few couples linger over coffee and fruit.

Alaric gestures toward a table near the open windows, sunlight spilling across the linen. "Does this work?"

"Perfect." I drop my bag on the chair and glance at him. "You cleaned up nice today."

He looks down at his crisp shirt and conference lanyard. "You're saying this like I had a choice. It's the uniform of professional suffering."

I laugh and grab a plate. "Right. Because nothing says cutting-edge psychology like scrambled eggs and a name tag."

He smirks but follows me to the buffet, waiting while I

debate between fruit and pancakes.

"You're overthinking breakfast again," he says.

"It's a talent." I scoop some fruit onto my plate. "You should see me at a salad bar."

He chuckles as we move through the line together, our shoulders brushing now and then. When we sit, the ocean stretches wide behind him, blue and endless. He steals one of my pineapple slices before I can stab it with my fork.

"Hey," I protest. "That was mine."

"I'm conducting a quality check." He chews thoughtfully. "Approved."

I shake my head, trying not to smile. "You're insufferable."

"I've been called worse."

We eat in companionable silence and every so often, our eyes meet and the air shifts a little.

He gazes out the window. "Do you think they ever tire of that view?"

"I don't think you can." I rest my chin on my hand. "If I lived here, I'd eat breakfast outside every day and pretend I didn't have to be anywhere."

He nods. "You're the one who always said she wanted to live by the water."

"Yeah." I look out at the waves. "Back when I thought dreams were things you could just manifest whenever you wanted."

His expression turns thoughtful. "Maybe you still can."

I don't answer right away, just watch the sunlight catch the edge of his smile. This feels different. Not that our past has gone away, but somehow, I've stopped running from it long enough to breathe.

I glance down at my coffee, realizing it's gone cold. The shift in light across the table tells me we've been here longer than I thought. But still, I trace my finger along the rim of my cup, not ready to move yet.

He leans back in his chair, eyes on the horizon. "Are you

glad you left?"

I look at him. "Left where?"

"Vancouver." His voice is quiet. "Some days, I think about leaving Paradise and moving back there to start over."

That catches me off guard. "You'd leave your family?"

He shrugs, his thumb brushing the handle of his mug. "I became a psychologist to figure out my own stuff, and I came back home to help my sisters and maybe understand my grandmother, but I've realized that will never happen." He lets out a soft laugh. "I think maybe I'm tired of being the one who always fixes things."

I watch him, surprised by the honesty in his tone. "You have always been the fixer," I say. "You were like that even when we were dating. Your family came first, especially when we were in Paradise."

"Yeah. But maybe I don't have to be." He looks down at the table, then back up at me. "Sometimes, I picture a place on the edge of the city. Maybe a practice near the water, fewer patients, more time to actually live."

He looks away for a moment. There's something wistful in the way he's speaking.

"That sounds…nice," I tell him.

He gives a faint smile. "You used to talk about moving to Salt Spring Island with a big house on the water."

I smile. "You remember that?"

"Of course, I do. You said you'd fill your whole place with color and noise so it never felt empty."

The memory makes me laugh. "That sounds like me."

He tilts his head, eyes warm. "You still could, you know. Do something for yourself. Doesn't have to be the same dream."

"Maybe," I admit. "I moved to Paradise General for myself. Paradise doesn't move as fast, and working weekends and long days here feels unnecessary. It's not the same as it was in North Van. I need to adapt."

He nods, eyes softening. "Maybe we both need to stop striving so hard."

He goes quiet for a while after that, just watching the water.

He catches me watching him. "What?"

I shake my head. "Nothing. You look…lighter, just talking about it."

He smiles, and something soft unfurls inside me. "You deserve to be happy, Ric."

He goes still, the words settling between us. For a second, I think he'll look away, but he doesn't. He just holds my gaze. Then he reaches across the table, his fingers brushing mine. It sends a ripple through me.

"I think we both do," he says.

Despite my better judgment, I turn my hand, letting my fingers fit between his. His thumb traces small, absent circles against my skin.

For as long as I've known him, I thought his calm was coldness, that his ability to step back meant he didn't feel. But now, looking at him, I see what it really is. He feels everything too deeply, and that calm. It's armor. This is the part of him I needed to know existed. The part that listens and softens enough to let someone in.

We linger long after the plates are cleared, the table now just scattered crumbs and cold coffee. No one rushes us.

This is our last full day. Tomorrow is only a half day before we fly home, back to Vancouver, and then on to Paradise and everything waiting for us.

Ric leans back in his chair, eyes closed, face turned toward the sunlight. He looks content, maybe even peaceful, and the sight knots something in my chest. I can't remember the last time either of us looked like that.

When he finally stands, he holds out his hand. "Come on. Let's hit our last session this morning and then make the most of today."

I let him help me to my feet, feeling the warmth of his palm against mine. As we walk toward the lobby, the sound of the ocean follows us, wrapping everything in quiet. It feels like the stillness before something shifts again. And I still don't know what that means for us.

Twenty

Liz

On the morning of our last day, Ric stands by the window in our room, one hand resting on the curtain. The light catches the edge of his jaw, dark with stubble. I lie back against the pillows and watch him pretend to study the view.

Neither of us says what we're thinking. The conference is ending. Our bubble of whatever this has been is going to pop. We're taking a red-eye home tonight. Back to the same city, the same people, the same complicated mess that waits for us there. And we'll be sleeping at our own places.

"Beautiful morning," he notes.

"It is." My voice sounds lighter than I feel.

He turns toward me. "You slept okay?"

"Better than I thought I would after all those orgasms

you've given me." I smile a little. "You?"

He shrugs. "Didn't want to waste it."

I sit up, pulling my knees to my chest, trying not to think about how good it feels to have him this close. We talk about small things—how the ocean looks different here, what time the shuttle leaves, how the air smells like plumeria even inside the room. Anything but what happens next.

Eventually, he sits down beside me on the bed. I can feel the heat of him through the thin sheet, that familiar warmth that shouldn't still make me nervous.

"Feels strange," I say. "Like we've been living in a bubble."

"Maybe that's what we needed." His hand finds the edge of the blanket, tracing it with his thumb. "A place where no one expects anything from us."

I look at him, and he looks back, and for a second, the whole world narrows to that line between his mouth and mine.

"Liz," he says, voice quiet.

"I don't know what we should expect from each other either."

We both know we're on borrowed time. This kind of peace never holds for long.

He leans back on his palms, eyes on the ceiling. "It's easier here."

"Yeah," I whisper. "It's not real."

The clock ticks softly on the nightstand, and the breeze lifts the curtains. For a heartbeat, it feels like we could stay. As if the real world won't find us if we just keep pretending.

I glance toward him, catching the way his shoulders rise and fall with a deep breath. "We still have a few hours before checkout."

His eyes meet mine, and something flickers there. A decision, maybe. Or a goodbye we're not ready to say.

He pushes off the bed and stands by the dresser, pretending to check his phone. The light hits his shoulders, turning the thin cotton of his shirt almost sheer. I can't look away.

"We should probably get ready for the flight," he says without turning around.

"Probably," I answer, though neither of us moves.

He sets his phone down and exhales, slow and uneven. Then he faces me, and the careful distance he's been keeping all morning is gone. "Liz."

Just my name. Nothing more. But it lands like a touch.

I rise from the bed before I can think about it and cross to him. He doesn't reach for me right away. He waits, giving me the chance to step back. I don't. "I don't know what this means," I whisper.

"Maybe we don't need to know right now." He brushes a strand of hair behind my ear, his fingers trembling slightly. The scent of him—soap, salt, something warm and clean—wraps around me.

When his thumb grazes my jaw, I close my eyes. The touch is careful, almost reverent. Then his hand slides to the back of my neck, and the careful part disappears.

The kiss starts slow. Soft. Questioning. Then it deepens, breaking past everything we've been trying to hold together. I taste the salt from his skin. His hand fists gently in my hair, and I forget why we ever stopped touching each other.

He presses me against the dresser, his breath rough against my mouth. Every inhale feels like it might undo me.

I break the kiss first, just enough to breathe. "This is crazy."

He smiles, eyes dark and unsteady. "It's us. It's always been crazy."

I laugh softly, and he kisses me again, harder this time. There's no logic left in it, no caution. Just the familiar rhythm of something that never really ended. *Though I know how easily it could end again*, I remind myself.

When we finally pull apart, I rest my forehead against his chest. His heart beats fast beneath my hand, matching mine. "I missed this," I say quietly.

He whispers against my hair, "Me too."

The world outside keeps moving—waves, wind, the faint sound of doors closing down the hall—but in here, it's just us, caught between the past we can't change and the future we haven't decided on yet.

Then a sound drifts in from the room next door. Soft. Indistinct. A low moan that makes the air between us go tight all over again.

I pull back just enough to blink at him. "Was that—"

He exhales a quiet laugh, shaking his head. "I think it was."

Heat creeps up my neck, equal parts mortified and amused. I press my forehead back to his chest, laughing under my breath because it's either that or do something reckless.

"Of course," I mutter. "Last day in Hawaii."

He laughs too—low, breathless—his hand sliding to my waist like it knows exactly what it's doing even when he's pretending he doesn't.

But then he brushes his thumb over my lower lip, eyes still tracing me like he can't quite believe I'm real. "We should probably eat," he says.

"Now you think about food," I tease.

His mouth curves. "I'm starving."

He picks up the phone and calls room service, eyes locked on me. "Coffee and a pot of tea—orange pekoe," he says, "and something sweet."

When he hangs up, he crosses the room and pulls me back into him. I melt into the touch, the warmth of his skin against mine. His hands skim my back, slow and steady, grounding me before he steps away.

We don't talk anymore, just move around the room gathering our things and packing our bags.

Room service arrives twenty minutes later—fresh fruit, croissants, a pot of dark coffee, and a kettle of hot water and several tea bags. The server's polite enough not to look at us too closely. When the door shuts again, Ric pours my coffee and passes it over. His hand brushes mine, causing a familiar spark.

He then pours hot water into his mug and adds a tea bag. "To not thinking too much," he says.

I lift my cup. "To bad decisions that feel good."

He laughs, the sound deep and soft, even as he winces.

We sit on the bed, sharing bites of flaky pastry and bits of fruit off the same plate. Every small thing—his smile, the warmth of his knee against mine—feels sharper, more dangerous.

He watches me for a long time. "I do think this is what we needed."

I set down my cup. "A vacation."

"A reminder," he says. "That we still fit. It doesn't have to be complicated."

I want to believe him. I want to hold on to this feeling and pretend it's enough to carry us home. But wanting isn't the same as keeping.

"Maybe we're only possible when the world's far away," I suggest.

He reaches for my hand. "Maybe we could work again if we try."

His thumb strokes over my knuckles, slow and thoughtful. I lean against him, letting the quiet settle around us. I consider what it would look like for us to actually make it.

By the time the coffee pot and tea kettle are empty, the sun is higher, and the spell of the morning starts to thin. Ric checks his watch and sighs. "We should probably finish packing."

I nod but don't move right away. He folds his clothes, methodical as always. Eventually, I do the same, but my hands keep pausing over each piece, as if touching fabric could slow time.

"Do you ever wish we could just stay?" I ask quietly.

He looks up. "Yeah. But we both know we wouldn't."

I put a shirt into my suitcase and smooth it flat. "We're terrible at pretending."

He closes his bag halfway, then crosses to me. His hand settles over mine. "Then let's not pretend anymore."

I meet his eyes. There's no hesitation there, just a steady

resolve. "What do you mean?"

"When we get home," he says, "let's start over. No rules. No walls. Whatever this is, we see where it goes."

My chest tightens with something that feels dangerously like hope. "A clean slate."

He nods. "If you want one."

I let out a slow breath. "I do." But then I add, "When we get home, though, I need this to stay ours. At work. In public. I'm not ready for anyone else weighing in."

His expression doesn't change. "Professional," he says.

"Yes," I agree. "Private."

He leans down and kisses me, like sealing an agreement neither of us fully understands yet. When he pulls back, he's smiling. "Maybe we'll finally get it right."

"Maybe," I say, but I'm still not sure how.

Twenty-one

Alaric

The plane's cabin lights come on too early, washing everything in a gray glow that makes the red-eye feel even longer. I managed to upgrade Liz into first class so we could sit next to each other. Now, nearly six hours later, my neck aches, my eyes burn, and Liz hasn't said more than five words to me since we left Lihue. She's kept her head turned toward the window, snoozing with her earbuds in, body angled just enough that I feel the distance as clearly as if she'd moved to another row.

We were fine when the flight started. Better than fine. Then somewhere between takeoff and cruising altitude she folded in on herself, quiet and unreachable. Every time I try to catch her eye, she shifts, pretending to adjust the blanket or look at something on her phone. It's as if the closer we get to Paradise, the more she withdraws into her professional demeanor.

The flight attendant walks down the aisle, asking everyone to prepare for landing. Liz nods without looking up. Her jaw is tight. Her hands stay wrapped around the straps of her bag like she's bracing for impact.

I clear my throat. "Are you doing okay?"

She nods. "Fine."

I tell myself she's tired. Jet lag. The emotional hangover of the last few days. But there's something else, something I can feel even though she won't say it out loud.

The wheels hit the runway with a soft thump, and Liz gathers her things before we even taxi to the gate, still turned away from me.

When the seatbelt light dings off, she stands quickly. I stand too, giving her space even though every part of me wants to close the gap that wasn't here yesterday. She doesn't look back as we file toward the front of the plane.

The moment feels like slipping back into the life we left behind. The same city waiting. The same people. The same troubles that kept us apart for years. And she's already drawing the line again.

The jet bridge opens into the terminal, and the bustle of Vancouver hits us all at once. People push ahead of us, dragging carry-ons and pulling on hoodies, everyone moving fast because it's early and no one wants to be here longer than they have to before racing to customs.

Liz walks beside me, but not with me. There's a difference, and I feel it with every step.

We end up in two different customs lines, and I get through faster. I look over to find her, and the border agent is flirting. I can't believe we didn't go through together.

She walks through the sliding glass doors a moment later, pulling her bag behind her, scanning for me. "What gate is our flight home?" she asks.

"C twenty-four. Can I get you a coffee from Steaming Mugs?"

I can see her thinking it over.

"We have more than an hour. Why don't we sit for a minute before the flight takes off? We have some things to figure out."

She gives me a strange look, and for a moment, I'm sure she's going to turn me down. But then she nods. "I think that's a good idea," she says.

We walk together, and she finds a table while I secure our drinks.

"I had a lot of fun while we were in Hawaii," she says as I sit across from her.

"Me too," I agree. "I want to make sure I understand what happens when we get home? What would you want this to look like? Or would you prefer to pretend it never happened?"

She doesn't answer right away, and I can feel my nerves fraying. I shouldn't have put that second option on the table. Clearly, she's already stressed. She studies me, as if she's weighing the cost of honesty. "My job matters to me," she says finally. "And I don't want to be the reason people start talking."

I nod, though I wish she didn't care about any of that.

She looks away, then back again. "At work, we'll be professional. No gray area. Outside of work…" Her mouth tilts. "We figure it out as we go."

I lean closer. "Does figuring it out include you coming over tonight?"

She lifts her coffee, takes a slow sip, and meets my eyes over the rim. "We'll see."

It's definitely not a no, so I guess I should feel good about that.

And for a few minutes, I do. But when we prepare to board the plane, a former patient of mine says hello, and Liz immediately puts distance between us. I don't like how that feels. I get it, but I'm not going to be happy about it. My heart lurches every time.

Our seats are once again next to each other in first class on the short ride to Paradise, and once we're on the plane, Liz seems to relax again. She's warmer, more present. It feels like we might actually pull this off—professional at work and together at night.

Back in Black Bear Valley's tiny airport, we turn the corner toward the baggage carousels, and Jeannine Jennings appears. I drop Liz's hand.

Jeannine is a surgical nurse who knows every secret in Paradise, not because she pries but because people love how kind she seems. She freezes for half a second when her eyes land on us, then beams like we just made her morning.

"Dr. Dempsey. Liz Ward. Look at you two," she says with genuine delight. "Back in one piece. Travel can be so exhausting."

Liz stiffens next to me.

"We're just returning from a conference," I say. "What about you?"

"I've been visiting family up on the Sunshine Coast." She gives Liz's arm a soft squeeze like they're old friends. Her eyes travel over our rumpled clothes and our matching rolling luggage. "You poor things. You look wiped. Those conferences run you ragged. And you know what they say, *what happens at conferences stays at conferences*."

She laughs like she's telling a fantastic joke. Harmless. Sweet. But Liz shuts down so fast it's visible. Her shoulders tighten. Her face becomes neutral. She offers a polite smile.

Jeannine tilts her head. "Where was your conference? I hope it was somewhere warm. I once had a view of a dumpster out my hotel window, but I didn't care because it was snowing at home and the temperatures there were toasty."

"We were very lucky. We stayed at the Grand Hyatt on the island of Kauai," I say, forcing my voice into something easy.

Her whole face lights up. "Oh, that sounds beautiful. And together. How fun."

"We just attended the same conference," I say, trying to clarify when I really shouldn't.

"Oh, of course," she says, nodding enthusiastically. "But still. A familiar face on a work trip is such a comfort. Did you get to explore a little? You must have. Those islands are impossible to resist."

Liz opens her mouth, and then closes it again.

I step in. "A few things. Mostly after sessions."

Liz's eyes flick toward me in surprise. Or warning. I can't tell.

Jeannine clasps her hands together. "Kauai's so romantic. Not that I'm suggesting anything. Just that the beaches are gorgeous. The falls. The sunsets. Anyone would want to see them." When we don't respond, she just keeps going. "Well, it sounds like a lovely trip. Productive but fun. Those are always the best, the kind that bond colleagues in unexpected ways."

Liz's silence becomes heavy. Solid.

Jeannine never notices. Or pretends not to. "I can't wait to hear more once we're back at the hospital. People always love the travel stories. They bring everyone together."

"We were there for work," Liz says softly.

"Oh, sweetheart, of course, you were," Jeannine says with a warm smile. "That's exactly how I'll tell it."

She gives Liz another pat on the arm and heads off with a wave.

When she disappears into the crowd, Liz releases a slow breath. She adjusts her bag and widens the gap between us. Just like that, Hawaii feels farther away than the ocean we flew over to get home.

Our carousel roars to life, and Liz's roller bag comes around quickly. She grabs it and moves toward the exit without looking back.

When my checked conference materials finally appear, I pull the bag off and head toward the exit as well. I spot Liz just as she's climbing into a rideshare. She pauses long enough to adjust her purse strap and meet my eyes.

"Thanks for the trip," she says. Her voice is polite and distant, as if we barely know each other. "See you at the hospital."

Before I can answer, she ducks into the car.

I stand there with nothing but my suitcase handle to

steady me, watching her go. After a minute, I call a car and drag my suitcase toward the rideshare pickup zone, shivering against the early morning air. When my phone buzzes with my driver's arrival notification, I slide into the backseat, exhaustion settling over me like a weight.

The city outside the window looks washed out. Empty sidewalks. Gray sky. A few taxis lined up at the curb.

I open my messages and type because I'm not sure what else to do.

Me: Do you want to come over later? We could talk about this.

I stare at the screen, waiting for the dots to appear. Nothing. The message sits there in the bubble, unread.

The driver attempts conversation, but my voice sounds rough, tired as he pulls into traffic. It's not long before he gives up.

I keep my phone in my hand the entire drive. Every time it vibrates, I look down expectantly. But it's flight delays. Promotions. Spam. Everything except Liz.

By the time we turn on to my street, I know she's not going to reply. Her silence settles into the space between my ribs and stays there. I'm already losing her again.

As the driver pulls up in front of my house, I spot Evie's Mercedes in my driveway. The cherry on top of the sundae.

Breathe in. Count to four. Breathe out. Count to four.

My front door sticks a little when I push it open, the wood swollen. I drag my suitcase inside. "Hello, Evie," I announce, finding her at my kitchen island, wrapped in one of her expensive shawls and drinking from my mug with zero shame.

She gives me a sharp once-over. "You look terrible."

"Red-eye flight," I explain. I close the door behind me and fight the urge to rub my face. "What are you doing here?"

"I needed to talk to you," she says. Her tone is clipped and dramatic, the one she uses when she's dropping a grenade into the middle of the family. "Your sisters are driving the vineyard straight into the ground."

There it is. I set my suitcase aside and lean against the counter, bracing.

The second I set my keys down, Evie launches forward. "Josie let the bottling crew change the rotation again," she says, stabbing the air with her finger. "Just let them do it without even thinking about the long-term impact on efficiency. She's too soft. Always has been. She lets everyone walk all over her."

I open my mouth, but she barrels on.

"And Sera. Don't get me started on her. That girl has no sense of pacing. None. She's talking about expanding the sparkling line as if money grows on trees. Impulsive. Reckless. She thinks ideas are the same as strategy."

She pushes off the counter and starts pacing, her shawl swinging behind her. "I told them both to slow down. I told them to listen. I've run that property longer than they've been alive. Do you think they care? No, they nod and smile and do whatever they want anyway." She throws her hands up. "They don't respect the legacy. They don't respect their grandfather's work. One wrong decision, and it all falls apart. That's how fast it happens."

Her voice rises. She's not looking at me anymore. She's staring at the window like her reflection has personally offended her. Then she turns, eyes narrowing like she's reaching the point she's been circling around. "Maybe it's time for Dylan and Scott to take over," she says. "At least, they understand discipline. Structure. Authority. They wouldn't let sentimental nonsense ruin the estate."

There it is. The grenade. Pulled. Thrown. And she watches my face like she's waiting for the explosion.

I almost laugh. Not because it's funny, but because it's so transparent. "You want me to tell my sisters that?" I say.

She lifts her chin. "They need to hear it."

"I disagree," I say. "But if you feel they do, you can tell them yourself."

Her eyes narrow as she realizes her usual tactics aren't going to work on me. She tries again, louder this time. I've been on this merry-go-round before. I know what she's up to.

If the town's talking, if people are whispering about what she may or may not have done with Paradise Hill, she needs to redirect the attention. Stirring up family drama is her favorite smokescreen.

"I'm not getting involved," I say. "I'm not playing messenger so you can start a fire and pretend you didn't light the match."

She slams the mug down. "You always take their side."

"They're my sisters, and you're wrong," I explain calmly. "And because this is about you wanting the town to talk about something other than everyone thinking you sabotaged Paradise Hill."

Her lips pinch. She hates hearing it said plainly, hates being caught before the game even starts.

I move past her and grab a bottle of water from the fridge. "I'm going to unpack. Stay if you want, but I'm not discussing this."

She huffs, offended, but she doesn't follow me. For once, she has no leverage.

In the bedroom, I finally scrub my hands over my face. The only thing louder than my grandmother's silence is the thought of Liz not answering my text.

Twenty-two

Liz

We've been back over a week, and I've avoided Alaric nearly completely. He's texted and called, but Jeannine didn't waste a moment, and the gossip around the hospital has been at full throttle. No way am I contributing to that. I feel a bit of panic now when I think about Hawaii. I can't believe I got caught up in things like that. All it takes is a little proximity for me to completely lose my head? Nothing about my reality with Alaric has changed, and now, I just hope a few days of walking down memory lane haven't derailed my career and wrecked my heart.

The bell over the door jingles as I walk into Steaming Mugs, and I spot my older brother Mark already at a booth by the window. He waves me over with a grin.

"Look at you," he says as I slide into the seat across from

him. "You're tanned. Like, actually tanned."

I snort and peel off my jacket. "The sun in Hawaii kind of forces itself on you. It's only a week since I got back, and it's already starting to fade."

"Still, you look good." He lifts his mug. "Refreshed."

"I don't feel refreshed," I say, picking up my own mug. The steam curls against my face. "I feel jet-lagged and stressed and like my pores are still sweating sunscreen."

He laughs. "That tracks."

I take a sip of coffee. "But it was beautiful. Warm. Everything smelled like flowers and salt and sunscreen. And the conference actually had good food, which shocked me."

"So worth the trip?"

I hesitate, my thumb running along the rim of my mug. "Parts of it." I'd like to stop there, pretend everything is fine, hold on to my dignity before the rest of it crashes in.

Mark gives me a knowing look but doesn't press. Instead, he says, "Speaking of trips, Sam took Nicky for his checkup yesterday."

That pulls me out of my head. "How's my favorite nephew?"

"Giant," Mark says with a proud smile. "Nine months old and already convinced he's ready to walk. He spent the entire appointment trying to climb the exam table."

I laugh, picturing Nicky's chubby hands grabbing everything in sight. "That sounds about right."

"He weighs twenty-four pounds now," he adds. "The pediatrician said he's thriving. Sam cried."

"Aww…" My heart squeezes. "I miss him. I feel like he does something new every week."

"He does." Mark rubs the back of his neck. "And Sam is starting to get nervous."

I tilt my head. "About what?"

"Going back to work," he says. "She's got three months left on maternity leave, and she's already stressing."

I frown. "About childcare?"

"Yeah." He exhales slowly. "She's called daycares, looked at home options, interviewed two people... She hates all of it. She doesn't want to leave him with anyone. But at the same time, she's going crazy without adult conversations about something other than the color of poop in the diaper."

"That's a hard one," I say, swirling the coffee in my mug. "Leaving your child with a stranger is terrifying, but I think I'd be a better mother if I worked."

"She keeps saying she'll never be able to walk out the door on her first day." He gives me a tired smile. "And honestly, I don't know how we're going to make it work if we don't find someone soon."

"Do you need help?" I ask quietly.

He shrugs. "I don't know. We just need someone good. Someone who won't freak Sam out. Someone who can handle Nicky without panicking if he shoves a Lego up his nose."

I laugh under my breath. "Sounds like a unicorn nanny."

"Exactly."

I reach across the table. "You'll find someone. Sam isn't unreasonable. She's just a mom. She'll know the right person when she sees them."

He nods, but worry still shadows his eyes. "I hope so."

I take another sip and try to give him a reassuring smile. "You will. We'll figure it out."

He nods, and for a moment, the weight on his shoulders seems to ease. Then he studies me again. "You look wiped."

"I am." I try for a joke, but my voice comes out thin. "This week has been hell."

He waits. And here we are again.

My brother has always been like this, giving me space to circle around the hard stuff. I take a big drink of coffee, because even though it's scalding, it gives me something to do with my hands.

Finally, because I see no way out of this and because deep down I want to, I tell him about the debacle with my hotel room and hooking up with Alaric, which was confusing on its own, and then running into Jeannine at the airport, the moment that sparked the worst re-entry to real life possible. "The gossip has gotten out of control." My throat tightens. "What started as a few whispers has turned into this whole story about me spending a lusty week in Hawaii with the hospital footing the bill. People actually said those words. *Lusty week*. And every time I walk out of my office, they go silent. I know they're talking about me. I can feel it."

Mark's jaw ticks. "People who have nothing going on like to pick someone to talk about. This is about them, not you."

"It doesn't feel that way." I rub my forehead. "Every step I take feels like someone is waiting for me to mess up. I let my guard down. I knew better. I never should have…" My mouth closes on the rest.

He raises his brow. "I always thought Alaric was different from the others you dated. He treated you well."

Something stabs hot under my ribs. "*He left me*. That's the part everyone forgets. He left."

Mark reaches across the table and taps the back of my hand with his fingertips. "Have you talked to him? Since you got back?"

"I was going to. He's texted." I look into the swirl of my coffee. "But now? I swear people are actually watching us. Like they're waiting to catch us together. I think they're staking out our houses."

Mark laughs, a startled burst. "Liz, it's not that bad."

I meet his eyes. "It feels exactly that bad. I'm worried I'm going to be in trouble for this. We worked at that conference. It wasn't a lust-filled week."

"Then you don't have anything to worry about, do you?" After a moment, he softens. "All right. Let's say, worst-case scenario, you can always go back to Vancouver. Or try Calgary. Or Toronto. Or if you need somewhere immediate, you can move into our spare bedroom. Sam would love it if you wanted to take some time off and watch Nicky when she went back to work. You don't even have to warn us. Just show up with a bag."

The idea of leaving Paradise squeezes something inside me, like someone pressing a fist against my sternum. "I don't want to go anywhere. But if my boss hears the wrong thing or believes this rumor, what am I supposed to do? How do I fix that?"

"You'll figure it out," he says. "You always do."

I wish I believed him.

I finish my coffee quickly because the warmth is the only thing keeping me from shaking. Then we stand, and Mark pulls me into a hug. For a second, my cheek presses against his shoulder, and I feel like I might break open if I let myself stay there too long.

We say goodbye, and I head back to work on autopilot. But I feel better after talking to Mark. This is why I moved here. I have support.

When I step into my office, I place my bag on the floor, sit down, and pull Hudson's project toward me. Numbers, charts, projections, budgets. Things that usually calm me.

I open the spreadsheet I asked Misty to send over yesterday. The columns fill the screen, rows of numbers lining up like soldiers. At first, everything looks normal.

Then my eyes catch the occupancy totals, and a jolt of confusion runs through me. These numbers show the hospital at capacity every single night. Not just full, overfull. These numbers would have people in hallways. Overflow patients. Crowding so severe we should be in incident-command mode. The press would be all over us. We should be holding emergency meetings. Staff should be complaining. There should be chaos.

But I've seen none of that.

I frown, scroll up, scroll down. The numbers stay wrong.

This cannot be real.

I lean back in my chair. My heart thuds. Something is wrong.

The file includes no notes from Misty, no warnings that the data source changed. Nothing to suggest these numbers are preliminary.

Just this file. This file that could destroy me if I sent it on.

My fingers tighten around my pencil, and it snaps in my hand.

I push back my chair and stand.

On my way out, one more detail slams into me. This isn't the first time. The slides Hudson needed from me for a leadership meeting—they were full of errors, something I brushed off as a mistake because I didn't want to believe anything worse. But now, it's happening again.

I clutch the pages and head down the stairs to Emergency, needing someone who can tell me I am imagining things, that I'm tired, that the numbers got mixed up.

As I enter, nurses call out, a stretcher rolls past, a baby cries. And standing at the center of it, typing on a computer at the nurse's station is Greyson Paradise.

He looks up when I approach.

"Hey," he says, eyebrows rising slightly. "Everything all right?"

"Not really." My voice shakes. I slide the papers toward him. "I need you to look at something."

He scans the first few lines, his brows slamming down almost instantly. "No. These aren't even close. Not even in the same ballpark."

My stomach drops.

He turns back to the monitor, fingers flying over the keys. "Let me pull the actuals." He clicks a few times, then pivots the screen toward me. "This is what we've been running."

I lean closer.

His numbers are calm. Reasonable. Normal.

Nothing like mine.

"What the hell?" I whisper.

Greyson looks at me again, eyes narrowing. "Where did you get these?"

"Misty pulled them. I don't know. I don't know anything right now." I press a hand to my forehead. "If I had handed this to Hudson, I'd be done. Completely done."

Greyson's voice softens. "Here, let's get you the right numbers."

I nod, but it feels like my head is floating somewhere above my body. "Thanks for checking."

I turn before he can say anything else because if he's kind, if he asks if I'm okay, I might crack in the middle of Emergency.

The walk back to my office feels like miles. My pulse thumps in my ears, and every step makes the knot in my stomach tighter. What am I going to do? How do I sort this out? I need someone who believes me.

By the time I get back to my desk, the numbers have blurred on the page. My hands tremble as I sit, pull out my phone, and text Trinity.

Me: Can I come over tonight?

Her response appears almost instantly.

Trinity: Of course. I'm giving you a key. Come over whenever you need to.

My throat tightens. I set my phone down and look at the clock. 3:12 p.m. I have to find something to do with myself.

Time crawls, but I update the numbers in the report and start to second guess everything Misty has ever given me. When five o'clock comes, I gather my things as fast as I can because I can't risk running into her on the way out. Not today.

I walk home, dump my bag inside, and head immediately to my car. I drop into the driver's seat and sit there, gripping the wheel so tightly my knuckles go white.

I came to Paradise for more responsibility. I hoped for better balance, a place where I could belong, where my work and my life could finally make sense together. I never expected this level of politicking. At North Vancouver, I never saw anything this brutal.

I spent a week in Hawaii, and somehow, everything went

sideways. Then, this mistake could have ended me for good.

Not just the job. The entire life I've been building here.

I drop my forehead against the steering wheel and breathe until the pressure behind my eyes eases enough for me to get it together.

I text her that I'm on the way and drive to Trinity's, my stomach in knots. She and Theo are in the lobby of her building when I arrive, her face tight with concern.

Theo runs into my arms, and we walk to the elevator. He wiggles out of my grip when the doors close, and Trinity looks at me. "What happened?"

I shake my head until the doors open into her living area.

I walk out into the living room and kick off my shoes, the familiar comfort of her space doing nothing to settle the dread clawing at my ribs. "It's Misty," I say. "She's trying to sabotage me."

Trinity's eyebrows pull together. "Liz, that's a big accusation."

"I know." My voice cracks. "But it's true. I asked her for a spreadsheet, and the numbers she sent me weren't just off. They were wrong on purpose. Greyson pulled the real stats. They're nowhere close."

She sinks onto the couch, rubbing her hands together. "I'm having a hard time believing she'd go that far."

I drop beside her. "You said yourself that she wanted my job."

"She did," Trinity admits. "She wanted it more than anyone. But she wasn't even close to being qualified. Hudson told her that, so she knows. Doing something like this… I didn't think she was that devious."

"I didn't either," I whisper. "But it's been something at every turn." I pull in a shaky breath. "Trin, you know my room situation was messed up in Hawaii, and when I asked her about not booking me a room for the conference, she got very upset and told me I'd *asked* her not to book it. Why would she say that? She was supposed to transfer Hudson's reservation to me. We never talked about the room. She just told me everything was transferred and gave me the travel file. Why would she do that?"

For the first time, Trinity's disbelief cracks. Her eyes widen with something that looks an awful lot like recognition.

"Oh my God," she whispers.

My panic rises. "There's no innocent explanation," I finish. "She wants me gone."

Trinity covers her mouth with her hand. The fight drains out of her skepticism. "Oh, Liz…"

Finally. She believes me.

"I moved here for this job. For more responsibility. To be closer to you and to Mark, and Sam and Nicky. I wanted a life here. And now, one week at a conference and this level of sabotage are the things that might ruin my career."

"We're going to get this figured out."

I stand abruptly because the room feels too small. "How does this happen? How does a work trip turn into…all of this?"

Trinity rises too and reaches for my arm. "Hey. Breathe."

"I can't." The words spill out, breathless. "I can't lose this. Not after everything I gave up to come here. Not after finally feeling like I could find a place to belong. Now, Hudson will think Alaric slept with me so he wouldn't have to do his CMEs, and Misty is feeding him lies, and the numbers are a disaster, and—"

"Liz." She squeezes my arm. "You're not alone in this."

Tears burn the back of my throat, but I swallow them down. "It feels like I am."

She pulls me into a hug before I can fall apart. "We'll figure this out. I promise."

Her words settle against me, warm and steady. But worry still swirls beneath my skin. Coming to Paradise was supposed to be the beginning. Instead, it feels like it might be the end.

Twenty-three

Liz

Dinner with Trinity and Theo makes me feel better. By the time I leave, I have a plan that tomorrow I'm going to talk to Hudson and let him know what's going on. *I can do this.*

As I walk in my front door, my phone buzzes. I need to talk to Alaric, and I'm hopeful it's him. I'm ready to do that as well.

But it's an email meeting request from Hudson.

Tomorrow morning at seven.

Friday morning, seven a.m., long before anyone is in the office.

My breath leaves my body. Hudson never schedules meetings at seven. Never.

I swallow hard as panic surges through me.

And then I text Alaric. It's way overdue.

Me: Jeannine has been spreading rumors about us, and I think Hudson is going to fire me in the morning. Also, Misty is sabotaging me.

He calls within seconds.

I answer. "Hey."

"What happened?" His voice is tense, protective. It brings emotion to my throat immediately.

I flop down on the couch and tell him everything. The gossip. The looks in the hall. The spreadsheet nightmare. Greyson's reaction. The surprise meeting tomorrow morning that feels like an execution.

He listens without interrupting, then says quietly, "Liz. I'm sorry."

"I should have told Hudson we used to date," I whisper. "I should have been honest."

"No, Liz." His voice is firm. "People don't tell their bosses every detail of their personal lives. You didn't hide anything that mattered. You did nothing wrong."

"It doesn't feel that way."

"Do you want me to talk to him?"

"No." I shake my head, even though he can't see it. "The fix has to come from me."

He exhales. "I hate that you're going through this."

My eyes sting. "I'll be okay."

He doesn't call me a liar. "I'm here if you need anything. Even if it's just to hear someone breathe."

"Thank you."

"Do you want me to come over? I can bring you your favorite dessert—McDonald's apple pie and a Diet Coke."

That makes me smile. "No thank you. But I'm really grateful you offered."

"I can just come over and hold you."

I shake my head, grinning now. "That will only complicate this."

"I'm here for you. I know our return from Hawaii hasn't

been what we'd hoped, but I want us to get back to where we were before I left Vancouver."

"I don't know right now," I tell him with a deep sigh. "I'm not sure how that's possible. But I've got to get this figured out, or I'll be the one leaving this time."

"I'm here for you," he says again, and I hear the break in his voice.

"Thank you," I whisper. "Goodnight."

I hang up before I say anything stupid.

I run a bath, hoping the lavender in my bath salts will calm me, but my mind continues to race. I sit until the water is cold and my fingers are raisins.

If I bring up Misty's behavior now, will it look like I'm making excuses? Nobody believes the girl under investigation when she suddenly starts pointing at someone else.

I drag myself out of the bath and get into bed, but sleep doesn't come. Every rumor, every look, every imagined consequence keeps replaying. I twist the blankets. Turn over. Sit up. Lie down again. Nothing helps.

When dawn comes, my heartbeat is still a jittery, uneven thud. My eyes are puffy with dark circles. Still, I move forward to face the day. I smooth my clothes, pull my hair back, and leave quietly.

The hospital is bustling when I arrive, with the graveyard and morning shifts converging. I don't look at anyone. I go straight to the elevator and take it to my floor.

Hudson's office feels too bright when I walk in.

He gestures to the chair. "Thank you for coming early."

I nod and sit, hands clasped in my lap.

"Your work has been excellent," he begins. "You've made

an impact in a very short time." His mouth tightens. "However, I have concerns regarding your ethics."

My stomach drops so fast it's like the floor disappears. An ethics violation ruins careers. Not just here. Everywhere.

"I didn't expect you to sleep with Dr. Dempsey in order to ensure he completed his CMEs," he continues.

I stare at him. "That's not what happened."

He asks about the shared room. I explain that they didn't have a reservation for me and the entire island was full.

"Misty told me you didn't need a room."

I almost choke. "I never said that."

"Liz, why did you do this?"

"I didn't ask her to cancel the room. As far as I knew, she'd transferred your reservation over to me. I would have stayed somewhere else if I could. They had a Comicon on the island, and everything was booked solid. I couldn't find any other place to stay. Dr. Dempsey offered to share his room. I didn't know what else to do."

He sighs. "I need to talk to some people. I have to protect the hospital, Liz. I need clarity before I make any decisions. For now, I'm asking you to take the week off. Paid."

I stand somehow. "I understand. Thank you."

I leave without showing my panic and walk home before driving straight to Trinity's.

It's not even eight o'clock, and Trinity's in the lobby like she's been waiting.

"Hudson's questioning my ethics," I say, voice shaking.

She pulls me inside. "No. Absolutely not."

She holds up sheets of data, flips through them, and swears. "I looked these over again. These aren't mistakes. These are meant to hurt you."

My throat aches. "What if this ends my contract? How do I explain this hole in my résumé? What if coming here was a mistake?"

She takes my hands. "You did nothing wrong. I'm going to Hudson. Today."

A tear escapes. She hugs me tight.

"You can't stop me," she says, fiercely. "This is terrible. You didn't have anywhere else to stay on Kauai. And what's worse, it's a problem someone intentionally created."

I nod. I know I can't stop her, and I don't want to. Hope flickers. Trinity's the reason I have this job. Hopefully, she can be the reason the truth comes out and I keep it.

She cups my face, searching my eyes like she's trying to read the whole story. Then she hooks her arm through mine, and she and Theo lead me to the elevator.

"You're not going through this alone," she adds.

I nod, but it still feels like I'm standing on the edge of a cliff, wind pushing at my back.

Upstairs, I sit on her couch because my legs feel shaky. She finds something for Theo to entertain himself with and sits beside me, her leg pressed against mine.

"Tell me again," she says softly. "Start from the beginning."

So I do—the numbers for the board slides being off, the hotel room debacle, the flight issue, the spreadsheet and Greyson's frown. Misty's numbers—wrong on purpose, enough to make me look incompetent or malicious.

Saying it out loud feels like peeling off skin.

Trinity's jaw tightens, eyes sparking. "That woman." She shakes the spreadsheet. "She should be ashamed."

"I don't think she is."

"She wanted the job," Trinity says. "She wanted it badly. But this? This is something else."

"I know." My voice wavers. "And now, it looks like I'm the problem."

"You're not the problem."

"I might as well be if Hudson believes her."

Trinity squeezes my hand. "It's going to be fine."

I let out a humorless laugh. "You can't promise that."

"No, but I can promise I'm going to talk to him. I know him. I work with him. He listens. And he trusts me. He just needs all the facts."

My throat tightens. "I don't want you pulled into this."

"I already am," she says softly. "You're my best friend. Anyone who picks a fight with you gets me too." She stands abruptly. "I'm going today."

"It doesn't change the fact that I slept with Alaric while I was making sure he got his CMEs." I shake my head.

"I know. But we fix what we can." She disappears down the hall, shoulders squared.

I sink deeper into the couch and rest my head against the back.

Theo wanders over, hands me his teddy bear, and climbs into my lap. His small weight cracks something in my heart.

"Can you stay here with Theo?" Trinity asks when she returns. "Or I can run him up to Paradise Hill and leave him with Vicky and Trace." She walks back out, fastening an earring, then stops. "I think he wants you to stay."

"Do you want to hang out with me today?" I ask him.

"I'll stay with Theo."

She grabs her bag and keys. "I'll text you as soon as I know anything."

"Okay."

She hugs us both. "Don't go anywhere."

"We'll be here."

When she leaves, the silence settles. I stare at the elevator long after the doors close.

The quiet descends, but instead of calming me, it makes the noise in my head louder. The fridge hums faintly, and Theo hops down. After a minute, I can hear him talking to his trains as he plays.

I go over everything again, replaying conversations, details, and the subtle looks I didn't want to notice at the time. I've spent my entire career trying to be good. Steady. To make things better. I've never been reckless or jeopardized anyone's trust.

After a little while, Theo falls asleep, and I lay him in his bed.

Time moves slowly.

I go to the kitchen and run cold water over my wrists. The shock makes me feel more energized. I drink a glass of water slowly until my shaking eases.

Sitting, pacing, breathing—nothing helps. My mind loops until it exhausts itself.

After nearly an hour, I move to the window and stare at the bridge over Black Bear Lake. Cars pass. A woman walks her dog along the waterfront. A jogger runs by.

Everything looks normal out there. Completely normal.

How can everything look normal when my entire life feels like it's hanging by a thread?

I sit again, curling into the couch cushions, letting myself feel the weight of it—the fear, the humiliation, the betrayal.

I think about the job I left behind. The risks I took. The hope I carried when I moved to Paradise.

I press my palms over my eyes and breathe.

My phone sits on the table. I pull it toward me. No messages from Trinity, Mark, Hudson, or Alaric.

I scroll through old texts with Alaric. Years ago. Hawaii. Last night. Every message holds a piece of something unfinished. Something dangerous.

How did everything get so messy so fast? How did I walk back into the fire with him? And why do I still want to reach for him now?

Twenty-four

Alaric

Dot's usually feels warm, scented with the kind of comfort you can inhale, but this morning even the smell sits wrong, too sweet and heavy. I'm here to meet my sisters for Friday morning breakfast, but I've already decided not to tell them what Evie said last week when I got home or about her ramblings when she called in the middle of the night last night. Worrying them like that has to be her job. Not mine.

I spot Sera and Josie in a booth near the back. They're not talking. They're not drinking their coffee. They're just sitting, pressed close, their bodies angled toward each other like they're bracing against wind.

Neither of them looks up until I'm almost at the table.

I slide in across from them. The vinyl groans. Josie's arms

are clamped tight across her chest, and Sera keeps turning her empty mug in small, repetitive circles. The way they look at me—sharp, worried—stirs something cold in my gut.

I try for something like lightness. "Morning."

Josie raises an eyebrow. "You look like hell."

She's not wrong. I slept maybe an hour. I couldn't settle after Evie's middle-of-the-night, frantic, splintered tone she gets when she's convinced the world is tilting against her.

The server comes over with a fresh carafe of coffee and some water for tea, and she takes our order. I go for my usual ham and cheese omelet.

When she leaves, I drop a tea bag into the hot water. But the mug just warms my hands while the rest of me stays cold.

Sera leans forward, putting her elbows on the table. Her gaze flicks toward the window as if she's checking for shadows. "We need to talk about Evie."

My spine tightens. "What happened?" I ask, though I probably already know.

Josie and Sera exchange a look, the kind siblings use when they're deciding who has to drop the bomb.

Josie exhales first, rubbing her forehead. "She called me at two this morning. Screaming."

My stomach tightens. "About what?"

"Me." She gives a humorless laugh. "She said I'm leaking internal documents to the police because she saw me carrying a clipboard." She shakes her head. "I was doing inventory, Ric. A clipboard doesn't mean espionage."

Sera rubs her temples. "Then she called me. Said someone in the family is betraying her. Then in the middle of her rant, she decided all of us are betraying her. She kept saying she could feel it 'in her bones.'"

My breath goes shallow. Evie used that same phrase with me last night. Over and over.

"Seems she locked herself in the office after I left yesterday," Sera goes on. "She changed the meeting schedule, fired the tasting room manager, and canceled the spring shipment of seedlings I've been working on for three months."

I blink, trying to make sense of the words. "She canceled it?"

"I got the notification at four this morning," Sera says.

Josie shifts forward, her shoulders curled inward. "And that's not the worst part. She told me the Paradise family bribed inspectors to shut down our expansion. She said it as if she had proof. When I asked for it, she said she didn't need any because she 'knows how they think.'"

A cold line of dread slides down my spine. This isn't stress or worry. This is full-blown paranoia.

I drag a hand down my face. "She's escalating."

"She's unraveling," Sera whispers, staring at the table.

Josie leans closer, lowering her voice. "The police were at the vineyard again yesterday, asking questions. She thinks they're stalking her."

The booth feels smaller by the second.

"If she keeps going like this, she's going to blow everything up," Josie says. "The vineyard. All of us."

Sera looks at me with tired eyes. "What do we do?"

I don't have an answer. Not one that doesn't break something else in the process. My hands tighten around the mug. "I'll talk to her."

Sera gives me a soft, almost sympathetic look. "The only person she trusts right now is Dylan."

That doesn't make any sense. I try not to react, but my jaw tightens anyway.

"She told me yesterday that you've been 'too quiet'," Josie says. "Like you're hiding something."

"Too quiet?"

She shrugs helplessly. "She's twisting everything."

The knot in my chest pulls tighter. I should have seen this coming. I should have pulled her back before she jumped so far off the rails none of us can touch her anymore.

Sera folds her hands on the table. "If she's charged with a crime, we won't be able to protect her."

The word lands like a punch. "You think they have something?" I ask.

"They keep showing up," Josie says. "And it's not to taste wine."

"Do you think she did something?"

Sera and Josie exchange another look.

"We don't want to believe she's behind this," Sera says. "Grandpa sold that parcel of land in block seventy-three to Paradise Hill decades ago. But she's been telling people possession makes it ours. And we think Zach Paradise, Dylan, and Scott may have helped her with the sabotage. The entire valley is taking sides, and she's burned so many bridges, they're lining up against us."

I lean back, stunned. "You think she manipulated them?"

"When is she not trying to manipulate us?" Sera shrugs one shoulder. "Zach just found out he's our half-brother, and she immediately started chirping her bitterness into his ear. Dylan and Scott will do anything she asks if they think she'll change her will."

My stomach sinks. "What will you do if she burns everything down?"

Josie folds her arms tighter. "Go north to Dad's. Grapes are already planted. We'll probably join him. He tells us all the time he'd love it if we came up."

"It'll kill us, though," Sera whispers. "All the work we've done for ten years. Gone."

"Literally or figuratively?" I ask.

"Dylan and Scott have talked about turning the winery into a pot farm," Sera says.

I rub a hand over my face. *Jesus.*

When I look back at them, there's fear in their eyes. Real fear, something that's rooted in a childhood built on instability and a mother who spent years trying to stay in Evie's good graces while Evie lit matches around everything.

"I'll try talking to her again," I say. "I'll go to the house. Get her to sit down. If I can just—"

"No," Sera says gently, and the softness is what kills me. "You can't fix her."

With that, the fight leaves me. She's right. I know she's right. Evie doesn't want to be fixed. She wants to be right.

Josie touches my hand. "We're not asking you to fix her. We just need you to see how bad it is."

I swallow. "It's bad."

Sera nods, resigned. "Then we deal with it together."

"Do we bring in Addie and Ginny too?" I'm not sure if that helps or hurts. Ginny is married to a Paradise, and Addie walked away from all of this. She's an artist with a sensitive soul and couldn't take the manipulation Evie dished out. So she left.

"No," Sera says. "We can bring them in later. But for now, it's just the three of us."

For a moment, none of us speaks. The morning rolls on around us—plates clinking, someone laughing, the hiss of the grill. It all feels too normal for what's happening.

The server brings our plates, but none of us touches them.

Josie pushes her oatmeal away. "I can't eat."

"Me neither," Sera murmurs, setting her fork down.

I try one bite. The omelet I love turns to paste in my mouth. I shove the plate aside.

Josie's phone buzzes. She glances down, then pales. "It's Mom. Evie's already at the vineyard. She's in a mood."

Sera grabs her bag. "I should get there before she fires someone else."

Josie stands, bracing herself on the table. "She'll fire me next."

I reach out, steadying her wrist. "She won't."

"You don't know that," she whispers.

Sera touches her arm. "Come on. The more people around her, the less damage she does."

I'm not sure that's true, but I keep it to myself.

They gather their things with shaky movements, two grown women who look, for a moment, like scared kids.

Sera pauses halfway to the door. "Are you coming?"

"In a minute. I need to think."

They nod and don't argue. That tells me everything.

When they leave, I take a breath, drop some bills on the table to cover our breakfast, and walk outside. The air is cold, and I stand on the sidewalk and inhale until my lungs ache.

Evie is unraveling.

The police are circling.

And my family is terrified.

My phone buzzes with a call from Trinity.

Dread shoots straight through me all over again. I answer before the second ring. "Trinity?"

"Alaric… I'm sorry to call so early."

Something pulls tight in my chest. "What's wrong?"

"Hudson called Liz in early this morning," she says. "It didn't go well."

My heartbeat kicks up. "What happened?"

"It was bad." Her voice breaks. "Misty's been stirring things up. The gossip is awful. Hudson put her on paid leave this week. We don't know what he's going to do. I'm going in to see him at the hospital. I need to be sure he has all the facts."

I close my eyes. She's only in this mess because of me.

"I'll fix this," I tell Trinity, already walking toward my car. "I promise."

Twenty-five

Liz

The elevator doors open and Trinity steps inside, smiling carefully. She stands in the entry for a few seconds like she's debating whether she needs another breath before speaking. Her bag slips off her shoulder as she walks into the living room, and I can see the tension pinched along her mouth.

I push myself upright on the couch. "Hey. Theo did great. He's sleeping. What happened with you?"

She sets her bag beside the armchair, smoothing the strap. "I was able to meet with Hudson."

"Okay," I say. "And?"

Trinity sits across from me. "He listened," she says. "He really listened."

My breath doesn't quite make it all the way out.

"I told him what Misty did," she continues. "Everything. The room situation, the numbers she changed, the way she handled all of it." She pauses, rubbing her thumb along the edge of her jeans. "I laid it all out."

"What did he say?" My voice catches.

"He asked why you hadn't come to him from the beginning."

My stomach drops. "I thought it was just a mistake. I didn't want to make it something it wasn't. And once I realized it kept happening, I was in this mess."

"I told him that," she says, nodding. "And I told him you weren't hiding anything. You were processing it in real time with me. I reminded him that he sent you there to make sure Alaric completed his CMEs, which he did. I told him that what adults do during their off hours is their business. I even reminded him that Greg York and Abby Newland met at a conference and now they're married, so acting like two coworkers getting together is scandalous doesn't make sense."

A flicker of hope sparks in my chest.

Trinity smiles again. "He said he'd review everything himself. Talk to people. Follow up. And he apologized if you felt unsupported."

Relief washes through me, but it's still a little shaky. "So I'm not fired?"

"I don't think so," she says. "But he needs time."

Time. I nod and try to steady my breathing. "Thank you."

"You don't have to thank me," she murmurs. "I did what was right."

I press my hand to my chest, trying to ease the ache under my ribs.

She takes my hand, squeezing gently. "You'll get through this. One way or another."

I nod and tell her I'll get out of her way, but Trinity insists that I stay. Without any other pressing options, I agree. The rest of the morning crawls, though things brighten a bit when Theo gets up and we feed him lunch. But by afternoon, the minutes fold into each other. Trinity stays close, sitting at the end of the couch with her legs pulled up, flipping through a magazine I don't think she's actually reading.

My phone buzzes, and the vibration feels electrified. I snatch for it, breath tight.

It's a group message from work about scheduling. I tuck the phone under the pillow again and press my palms over my face.

"You're spiraling," Trinity says softly.

"I know."

She nudges my leg with her foot. "Tea?"

"No. I just want this to be over."

"It will be," she says.

Maybe.

Another hour passes in slow, dragging pieces. I shift on the couch, trying to find a position that doesn't make my skin feel too tight. Eventually, when Theo naps again, my head drops onto Trinity's shoulder. She wraps her arm around me without hesitation, her fingers smoothing a line down my arm. The scent of her laundry detergent drifts up—soft, floral, familiar. It helps in a way I can't explain.

My thoughts drift back to when I first took this job, when everything felt promising and open. When Hudson trusted me. When I trusted myself. I feel the loss of that certainty like a bruise.

In the late afternoon, Trinity stands and moves into the kitchen, where cabinets open and close. Something soft lands on the counter, and she returns with a small bowl of fruit, the colors bright under the living room light.

"Eat," she says, offering it.

"I'm not hungry."

"I didn't ask."

I take the bowl and pick up a piece of melon. The taste barely registers, but Trinity waits until I swallow before she relaxes back into the cushion.

Another buzz hits my phone. This one rattles straight through my rib cage.

I reach for it with trembling fingers. A message from Hudson.

I show it to Trinity before opening it, unable to face the words alone.

She moves closer, her shoulder brushing mine. "We'll look together," she says.

My thumb swipes across the screen.

Liz,
Please meet with me Monday morning at nine. I would like to discuss next steps and clarify several matters.

The words blur, then slowly sharpen.

"Monday at nine," I say. I have the weekend to manage all these unknowns.

"That's a good sign," Trinity says. "If he were firing you, it would've happened today."

"I don't know," I murmur.

She cups my chin, tilting my face toward hers. "Hey. You still have ground to stand on. That's what this means."

A foothold. Barely. But something.

I read the message again, then again, waiting for it to shift into something more solid. It doesn't. "Should I respond?"

"Yes. Tell him thank you and that you'll be there."

My fingers move automatically and hit send.

And I do feel a little better. Now, I know when something is going to happen.

Trinity leans into me again, shoulder against mine. "Whatever happens on Monday, you don't face it alone."

Her words settle into the fragile parts of me. "Thank you."

"Always."

I go back to my fruit and then take the empty bowl to the sink, rinsing it carefully. My hands tremble as I set it on the drying rack. A tear slips off my chin before I can stop it. I swipe it away.

"I'm scared," I say softly when I return to the couch.

"I know," she says. "But you're brave."

"No, I'm not."

"You are," she insists. "You walked into Hudson's office without knowing what waited for you. You told the truth when it would've been easier to say nothing. That's brave."

"It didn't feel like it."

"Real bravery never feels like bravery in the moment."

There's a crash from Theo's playroom, and he's making all sorts of car noises.

That makes me smile, but I close my eyes. "I miss how simple everything was before Hawaii," I admit.

"I know," she says.

"And I miss knowing where I stood with people."

"That will come back. You'll find that again."

I look out at the lake, which looks like glass. "I'm not sure."

"You will," she says. "People who tell the truth always outlast the ones who lie."

I want to believe her. I want that so badly it aches.

Another buzz from my phone feels like an electric shock. My whole body jerks upright. Trinity straightens too.

Alaric: I'm thinking about you. Call me if you need anything. I mean anything.

"Is it Alaric?" Trinity asks.

"Yes."

"You can call him."

"I don't think I can right now." I don't trust myself to sound composed if I hear his voice. And once I lose that, I don't know how to get it back.

"Okay," she says. "You don't have to."

I set the phone aside and curl inward, drawing my knees close. Trinity pulls the blanket over me, smoothing it around my shoulders.

Time drifts. The late light fades to evening, softening the

edges of the room. I lose track of minutes, of breaths, of where the day ends and the evening begins. But something finally settles inside me. This hasn't destroyed me. It bruised me. Shook something loose. But I'm still here.

When Trinity walks me to the elevator after dinner, she pulls me into a slow, warm hug. "Tomorrow is a new day," she whispers. "Make sure you do something this weekend. Promise me you won't stay holed up in your house."

"I promise," I say, holding onto her for a beat longer.

On my drive home, my thoughts still circle, but more slowly now, anchored by the thin thread of hope Trinity left in my hands.

I'm not done. I'm not defeated.

Monday at nine, I'll walk back into Hudson's office.

And I believe I might make it through.

Twenty-six

Alaric

My last Monday appointment wraps up a few minutes early, but I barely register the win. I shake the patient's hand, give the usual reassurance, and the second the door closes behind them, I'm already typing my notes at a pace that would probably concern any of my colleagues. I pretend I'm being efficient, but I know exactly what I'm doing.

Liz spent the weekend at her brother's, and we talked last night as she drove home. This morning she met with Hudson, but I haven't heard from her and don't know what he said. I've been anxious all day, though she's agreed to come over tonight.

In the meantime, I'm still replaying the phone call I had with Hudson on Friday about sharing a room with Liz. I told him I was sure Misty had canceled her room reservation on purpose.

He wasn't happy to hear it, but he needed to.

Just thinking about Liz sends a pulse through my chest. Hope. Nerves. Something that feels too close to longing. I try not to look like a man rushing through his day so he can get home and not screw anything up, but yeah… That's exactly what I'm doing.

I finish charting, log off, grab my coat, and head for the parking lot. I want to be home before she arrives, with dinner ordered and the place looking halfway decent. Everything needs to feel easy for her.

The drive is a blur, full of red lights and too-loud thoughts.

She said yes and agreed to come over without any hesitation. That has to be a good sign. I tighten my hands around the wheel when the memory of Hawaii slips in, soft and warm. The weight of her beside me at night. The way her breathing leveled mine. I didn't realize how much I'd missed that until I had it again.

God, I want her to stay tonight. Even if it's just sleep. Especially if it's just sleep.

But beneath that hope sits a quiet knot of anxiety. I need to hear what conditions Hudson put on her after everything with Misty. She sounded steady when she texted earlier, but Liz never shows cracks unless she chooses to.

I pull into my driveway and hurry inside. The house looks lived in, which is a polite way of saying I should've picked everything up two days ago. The suitcase with my CME materials is still unopened in the hall, so I tuck it into my home office. I toss blankets over the couch, fold the throw in a way that could generously be called "attempted tidy," load a few dishes into the dishwasher, and gather the stack of journal articles teetering on my armchair.

I order dinner from the Thai place I like while wiping down the counter. We had a favorite place in Vancouver, and this is even better. It's something comforting, and I can't mess it up. As the order confirms, I finally stop moving.

The house is too quiet.

I glance at the window, expecting headlights already. I'm terrified they'll show up before I'm ready, and I worry they won't show up at all.

I run a hand through my hair and tell myself to breathe, to be normal, to stop acting like a teenager waiting for his crush. She's coming. She said she's coming.

I flip the switch to the gas fireplace, straighten one last pillow, and force myself to sit down.

All that's left now is waiting.

I've only been sitting for a minute when headlights sweep across the curtains, a bright arc gliding over the living room wall. My breath catches. *It's her.*

I stand too quickly, cross the room in a few steps, and pull open the front door before she can knock.

Liz stands on the top step in a dark pantsuit that fits her so well I lose my words for a second. Her hair is smooth and glossy, her face pink with cold. She looks calm and composed and utterly beautiful.

"Hi," she says.

Something in me loosens. "Hi."

She smiles and steps inside, bringing the faint scent of jasmine with her.

"You look beautiful," I say before I can overthink it.

Her eyes sparkle. "Thank you. Today was…actually a good day."

I take her coat and hang it over the back of a chair. She glances around the living room, taking in the straightened cushions and wiped counters, and the corner of her mouth lifts like she can see every frantic step I took to make the place presentable.

I shrug, trying not to seem too pleased with myself. "Dinner's on the way."

"Good," she says. "I'm starving."

The lightness in her voice warms my chest. She didn't just come over. She wants to be here.

She sets her purse down and leans against the kitchen

island, her expression shifting with a slower breath. I can already tell she's replaying something.

"So," I say, settling beside her. "It was a good day?"

She lets out a breath. "When I got in this morning, Hudson was waiting, and he wasn't alone."

My stomach tightens. "HR?"

She nods. "A woman named Mara Kelly. Polite. Serious. They wanted to go over everything that's been happening with Misty."

I stay quiet and let her talk.

"I walked them through the whole thing," she says. "I had taken notes, which helped. I told them about the wild numbers she gave me. The inflated figures she sent me for Hudson's presentation. The hotel room mess. All of it."

I shake my head. That really was a campaign of terror.

"They asked why I didn't tell Hudson earlier," she continues. "And I told them the truth. I thought they were careless mistakes, oversights. People make mistakes. I didn't want to humiliate Misty or ruin our working relationship. I'm the new hire. Calling someone out who'd been there longer felt…risky. Like I'd come in guns blazing to embarrass her instead of being a team player."

She pauses, her throat working like she's swallowing something sharp. "I thought being quiet would keep things smooth," she continues after a moment. "That if I double-checked her work and fixed the numbers, everything would level out and we'd move forward. But when she lied about me telling her I didn't need a hotel room, I realized none of this was careless. None of it."

A low burn of anger stirs in me. "I'm sorry."

She shakes her head. "There's nothing for you to be sorry about. But they're still investigating. And they'll probably come to you."

I rub my jaw. "I already spoke with Hudson."

Her eyebrows shoot up. "You did?"

"Yeah. Friday afternoon."

She steps closer without seeming to mean to. "What did you say?"

"The truth," I tell her. "That when we arrived, you expected a room. That you tried to get another, but you couldn't. I told them there was no way I'd let you stay with a stranger. And that the gossip going around is complete garbage."

She exhales something that's almost a laugh, her shoulders lowering. "You said all that?"

"I did. And I reminded them that I paid for my own room and didn't charge the hospital a cent. My professional allowance just covered the conference. And I told them I have every single handout and workbook from every session I attended if they want to verify anything."

Her mouth curves. "You didn't."

"Oh, I absolutely did. I had to buy a suitcase just to get it all home."

She laughs, and it slides straight into the part of me that's been stressed about this. "You went to bat for me," she whispers.

"Of course, I did."

She smiles warmly, maybe even blushes a bit, but dinner arrives, breaking the moment.

I answer the door and grab the bags, and she helps unpack everything. We sit side by side at the island, plates angled toward each other.

"Thai basil chicken and pad thai," she gushes. "My favorite comfort food."

We eat in comfortable near-silence for a while until she sets her fork down and wipes her mouth.

"How's your family?" she asks. "What's going on with them?"

I push a piece of chicken around my plate. "I'm worried about my sisters."

She tilts her head. "What's going on?"

"They've put years into the vineyard. Sacrifice. Sweat. Everything." My jaw tightens. "And my grandmother is coming undone. She's more and more irrational, and she might give the vineyard to our cousins."

Liz's mouth falls open. "Why?"

"Because she thrives on chaos. She's a narcissist who finds it fun when she pits everyone against each other. That's who she's always been."

Liz frowns. "But the vineyard is your family's legacy."

"Well, I'm sure my cousins haven't told her their plan for when they're in charge."

"What is the plan?"

"Dylan and Scott want to bulldoze everything and put in a pot farm."

Liz lets out a shocked laugh. "You're kidding."

"I wish. They're already running the numbers."

She shakes her head. "And Evie doesn't know?"

"I don't think so. But maybe telling her will make her rethink changing her will. Or maybe it's too late." I stare down at my plate. "I'm starting to realize I hate her. I know *hate* is a strong word. But all her games and the ways she's always testing us? She's the reason I became a therapist. I needed to find out why I was so screwed up."

"You're not screwed up." Her voice is soft but firm. She waits a beat, then adds, "I overheard people talking in the cafeteria today. About the Dempsey and Paradise feud."

I blow out a slow breath. "Outside of the government and the hospital, our families are the largest private employers in the valley. Everybody feels it."

"Wow," she whispers. "That's a lot."

"It is," I say. "And I hate that my sisters are caught in the middle."

She brushes her fingers across my forearm. "I'm sorry," she says.

I nod, swallowing the pressure building in my throat.

We finish eating and move around each other easily as we clear the dishes. When the counters are clean and the house feels calm, I nod toward the living room.

"Come on," I say. "I have dessert."

She raises an eyebrow. "You made dessert?"

"I'm not that reckless." I laugh, walking to the kitchen as Liz moves to the couch.

I grab the paper bag from the counter and set it on the coffee table.

Her eyes narrow. "What is that?"

"Only the greatest dessert known to man."

She opens the flap and freezes. "You didn't."

"Oh, I did."

She lifts out the McDonald's apple pie like it's made of gold. Then she laughs, bright and warm. "You're the only person on earth who knows this is my favorite."

"I'm not most people."

She unwraps it and takes a big bite, eyes closing like it's bliss. "You win," she says.

"I like winning."

I pull out the one for myself—after confirming she's not going to need to eat them both—and we enjoy them together, crumbs falling onto napkins, the fire crackling. When we're done, I toss the wrappers and move back to the couch.

She shifts closer to me, not accidentally this time. I lift my arm slowly, giving her space to choose. She nestles into me like it's the most natural thing in the world, her head finding my shoulder, her hand curling gently at the hem of my shirt.

"Is this okay?" I ask.

"Yeah," she whispers. "It's good."

Good doesn't cover it. The fire hums softly, bathing the room in warmth. Her breathing evens out against my chest, steady and soft. My entire body settles in a way it hasn't since Hawaii.

Her hand slides across my stomach, fingers curling lightly in the fabric of my shirt. "You should do this more," she murmurs.

"Do what?"

"Relax," she says. "Let someone take care of you sometimes."

I give a quiet laugh. "You're not taking care of me."

She lifts her head just enough to meet my eyes. "Aren't I?"

The question lands right where all my defenses used to live, and a light shines in the dark corners. Maybe she is.

She settles back down, fitting her body to mine again. The fire glows. And everything inside me moves into place, like a truth I've been avoiding for years.

If she stays the night, I know I'll sleep. If she doesn't, I still get this.

I close my eyes and let myself hope she stays.

Twenty-seven

Liz

Alaric and I have spent the last three nights together, and we seem to be finding a groove. Fantastic sex every night. Coffee for me and tea for him every morning. Brushing our teeth side by side. His voice drifting from room to room like it belongs in the air around me. It feels so much like the version of us that existed before he left me to move here that, sometimes, I have to remind myself to breathe.

And maybe that's why the empty chair beside mine in the leadership meeting this afternoon hits so hard. He doesn't miss staff meetings without reason. My mind goes where it shouldn't, and I hope his sisters are fine. Has Evie gone off the rails again?

He knew this meeting mattered. He knew CME compliance was on the agenda. Still, his seat stays empty as people shuffle papers and settle in. I keep glancing at the door with this stupid little flicker of hope, and every time it's not him, my heart sinks a little.

The CEO moves through operational updates. I nod, but nothing registers. All I can see is the empty chair. Everything seemed fine when we left this morning, so it feels careless that Alaric isn't here now. Thoughtless. Like I'm the only one holding the weight of consequences while he assumes everything will work itself out.

And the worst part is the tiny, humiliating sting of regret. I let myself believe we were finding our way back, that we understood each other. But honestly, what has changed since he left four years ago? He's still living in fear of his family. I let things get too easy, too familiar. I should've protected myself better. Been smarter.

When the CEO shifts to CME hours and looks my way for my report, I sit straighter. "All providers have met their CME requirements," I tell the room. "The last of the verifications came in this morning."

It should be simple.

But Will Morris, head of radiology, decides it won't be.

"Given that you're sleeping with Dr. Dempsey," he says, voice dripping with smugness, "I'm not sure your confirmation is objective."

Heat burns up my neck. For a split second, I imagine Alaric sitting beside me. A steadying presence. A quiet hand under the table. A simple, grounding look that tells me I'm not alone. Would Morris even have said that if Alaric were here?

The ache that floods through me is worse than the humiliation.

No one speaks. No one defends me. Hudson doesn't even look me in the eye.

I wish desperately that Trinity was here, but I refuse to fold. "The conference verified all attendance and learning hours. He brought back every course material required. All documentation has been reviewed."

"Has anyone else verified that he did the work?" Will presses, eyes gleaming.

"That's the standard process."

"And he's not here today," Will adds, feigning concern. "Suspicious timing."

The jab lands right in my chest.

The CEO clears his throat. "Let's have Hudson perform an internal review as well."

Will smiles like he just won something. "Ethics matter."

I keep my expression neutral, but humiliation crawls across my skin like fire ants. People file out, pretending not to have witnessed a spectacle, and I'm left standing alone with my bag, trying to hold myself together.

Back in my office, I sit at my desk, staring at my computer screen without seeing a damn thing. It's late enough in the day that I could probably get away with leaving, but right now I'm shaking with a mix of anger and shame.

My phone buzzes.

Alaric: Mikey's after work? A drink?

Doesn't seem like there's been a family emergency, so what is his reason for missing the staff meeting? And he wants a drink? He has no idea what kind of mess I just dragged myself through.

Me: Fine. I could certainly use one. I'm leaving now. See you there.

Mikey's is loud and crowded, which doesn't help my mood. I spot Alaric at a high-top near the window, looking relaxed, drink in hand. His eyes light up when he sees me, which only fans my flames.

He stands, smiling. "Hey. You okay? You look like you had a rough day."

I pull out my chair and sit. "Where were you at two o'clock?"

He blinks. "In my office. Catching up on charts."

"Should you have been somewhere else?"

He pauses, thinking. "The leadership meeting?"

He says this as if it's trivia, like it slipped his mind. My face likely reflects my opinion of that.

"I was behind," he adds quickly. "I figured they wouldn't need me. CME verification goes straight to the province. I brought home everything they could want."

"Well, because you weren't there, Will Morris tore into you and dragged me down too."

His expression shifts. "He said something?"

"He questioned my ethics," I say, heat rising in my face. "My ability to do my job. He brought us up in the middle of the meeting like a weapon."

Alaric's jaw tightens. "I didn't think—"

"No. You didn't." My voice rises before I can stop it.

A couple at the next table look over.

"You assume everything will sort itself out," I say, trying to stay steady. "You believe everyone will be reasonable. And when they're not, I'm the one left standing in front of the firing squad."

His shoulders tense. "Liz, that's not fair—"

"Isn't it?"

He opens his mouth, closes it again, frustration flashing across his face. "I didn't skip the meeting because I don't care. I skipped it because I'm behind, and I thought it wasn't urgent."

"Everything feels urgent when it's exploding in my face," I snap.

More people turn toward us. I feel the attention prickling along my skin.

Alaric leans forward, voice low. "I don't know what you want me to say. I can't be perfect. I'm trying."

"I don't need perfect," I tell him. "I needed you to show up. That's it. Show up for the job. For yourself. For me."

He recoils a little.

There's a long, brittle pause, then he says, "You think I don't try? You think I don't care about how I'm seen here? About how you're seen? I'm drowning, Liz. I came back to hundreds of charts, a backlog of patients, three consults that should've been handled while I was away—"

"Don't put this on your workload," I cut in. "I'm drowning too. But I didn't skip the one thing I was responsible for today."

His jaw clenches. A muscle jumps near his temple. "So that's what this is," he says. "You think I'm unreliable."

I swallow, throat tight. "Today? Yes. I do. And not for the first time," I can't help adding.

Alaric's face shutters, but not in anger—in hurt. "I can't believe you'd say that."

"Well, I can't believe you didn't show up," I fire back. "Not after everything we've been rebuilding. Not after this week. Not after—" I stop myself, the words too close to the bone. "Being involved with you looks like an ethics issue."

He looks away first, breath unsteady. "I didn't know you still saw me that way," he says. "Like someone who walks out."

My breath stutters. But I'm too raw to take it back.

He stands abruptly, the stool scraping the floor. "I don't know how to fix something I didn't even know was breaking." He grabs his coat and walks out of Mikey's without looking back.

I sit stunned, my pulse pounding in my ears as I try to process what just happened.

People stare. Then they look away, pretending they weren't listening.

My hands tremble as I gather my things.

When I get outside, his car is gone. I didn't expect him to walk away so easily, but tonight, the outside pressures have finally broken us open. And the pieces didn't fall anywhere close together.

Twenty-eight

Alaric

The next morning, my head is still full of Liz, even though I promised myself I would lock it away before my first appointment. I'm usually good at compartmentalizing, but right now, every thought feels sharp. Every breath catches on the memory of walking out.

Alicia, my patient, sits across from me with her hands clasped in her lap, her shoulders rounded like she's trying to make herself smaller. "It's just so quiet now," she says. "The girls were always here. The noise. The mess. There was life in the house. And now, it's just me and James, and he doesn't need me the way they did."

I nod and stay with her, even as my thoughts keep drifting toward my phone in the other room and Liz's silence. "It makes sense," I tell her gently. "Everything changed at once. It's normal to feel unsteady."

She exhales. "I don't know who I am without being their mom."

A familiar vibration rumbles through the wall behind me. I left my office door cracked just enough that I can hear it. My phone on the desk in the next room buzzes again. And again. The steady thump against the wood tells me it's not one message. It's a stream. Family. Only they text like that. The insistent sound punches at the same raw place Liz scraped open.

I force my attention back to my office. "You've spent twenty years caring for other people," I remind her. "It's natural to lose track of what you need. What if this is a chance to rediscover things you set aside?"

She blinks at me, eyes going glassy. "I wouldn't even know where to start."

"That's okay," I assure her. "You don't have to know today. Try asking yourself a different question. Not what you should be doing, but what you want. What interests you? What makes you curious or excited? Even small things count."

Another buzz shakes the silence. It's insistent enough that even Alicia glances toward the door.

"Sorry," I say, offering an apologetic smile. "It's been one of those mornings." I keep my expression easy and neutral, even though my stomach keeps dropping.

Alicia draws a steadier breath. "I used to paint," she says. "Before the girls were born. I wasn't very good, but I loved it."

I smile. "That sounds like a start."

She smiles too, and the panic she walked in with loosens its hold. Something like possibility takes its place.

By the time we wrap up, she's sitting taller and her breathing is calmer. These are the moments that usually settle me, remind me that my work matters.

Today, it barely reaches me. My own anxiety remains lodged behind every breath.

When she leaves, I close the door behind her and force myself to take a deep breath before I walk into the adjoining office and pick up my phone.

In my family group chat, there are twelve missed messages and six missed calls. I look at the last one.

Sera: Her press conference is on the CTV website.

A headline preview sits in one of the texts like a fist to the gut.

Evelyn Dempsey Subpoenaed

My thumb barely brushes the screen before the group chat opens in a burst of frantic messages.

Sera: Holy hell, turn on CTV right now.

Josie: Is she serious? Is this real?

Addie: I'm shaking.

Ginny: This is going to make Sunday night dinner interesting. Shit. It almost makes me want to be there. But not enough to actually go.

My stomach tightens as I tap the link.

The video opens on a press conference outside City Hall. A podium with Black Bear Vineyard's crest bolted to the front. And then Evelyn Dempsey steps into frame.

Her hair is perfect, her expression carved from stone. She looks like she's at a coronation instead of responding to a subpoena. The crowd behind her shifts, but she stands completely still. I know that posture. It's the one she uses when she's about to lie.

"Good afternoon," she says, voice like a blade. "I want to address the baseless accusations circulating today."

I sink into my chair with my pulse thudding in my throat.

"I have been informed that Nicole McQuarrie," she continues, stepping closer to the microphone, "a known Paradise cousin and a Crown prosecutor, has orchestrated a smear campaign against me and my family."

My jaw tightens.

Sera: She is naming her on camera.

Evelyn leans into the podium like she's daring someone to challenge her. "There is absolutely no merit to the allegations brought against me. None. This is yet another attempt by the Paradise family to weaponize the government to undermine our business and reputation," she says.

I rub a hand across my forehead. "Oh God," I breathe.

"They poisoned our water supply," she says with cold certainty. "They killed our prize-winning grapes. And now, they're trying to hide behind this subpoena, hoping to paint us as criminals instead of victims."

My breath stops. For a few seconds, I can't move. My clinical brain notes the detached delivery, the lack of micro expressions, the textbook narcissistic reframing. She believes her story the moment she says it.

Yes, the water contamination happened, and it destroyed a block of vines. But she leaves out the part where the Paradise family came forward immediately. They told her themselves. They compensated her fully. They believed someone was trying to start a war between us, and they were ready to make sure it didn't happen.

But now, she's lighting the match herself.

"Jesus, Evie," I whisper.

She keeps talking and spinning the story into a polished attack, calling Nicole a political opportunist and painting herself as a woman under siege. It's high-level con that bulldozes truth into the ground and plants flags on the wreckage.

When the video ends, my phone lights up again.

Sera: Evie just called. This isn't a request but a demand from her, not me. Be at dinner tonight. Mandatory. Her words.

Josie: Except Ginny.

Addie: I'm not going. She's already disinherited me multiple times. Ginny, if you want to meet, let me know.

Ginny: It's a gift that I married a Paradise. Addie, come over here for dinner, and we can gossip and be rowdy while they're all being verbally pummeled.

Josie: Can I come? I don't think she'll miss me.

Sera: Oh yes, she will. Alaric, I know she wants you there, but you don't have to come. However, Josie and I could really use your support tonight.

My thumb hovers over the keyboard. My mind races. The woman I saw on screen wasn't just deflecting. She was rewriting history with a steady hand and believing it.

Alaric: I'll be there after my last patient and rounds.

Sera sends a string of kiss emojis.

I lock my phone and sit for a moment. The echo of Evelyn's voice still hangs in the air. I've always known she was capable of distorting and pushing and intimidating. But this is something else. Something dangerous. I don't know that she can come back from this.

I turn my phone face down on the desk, like that alone can shut out everything Evelyn just unleashed. It doesn't. The room still feels too tight. I take a long breath, the way I teach patients to do when their anxiety spikes. It barely makes a difference.

Liz flashes through my mind again. Her face when I walked out. Her cutting words. The universe feels tilted.

I still have two appointments before rounds. I still have people who need me to be the version of myself who isn't gutted by Liz and horrified by my grandmother going nuclear on live TV. I straighten my shoulders and go to the door just as my next patient arrives.

It's a teenager, quiet and withdrawn, with eyes that dart everywhere. He's struggling with panic attacks at school, and today, he's barely holding it together. I coax him into breathing with me and help him unravel the thought spiral he's trapped in. For a few minutes, I manage to push Evelyn aside. This kid needs calm. So I build calm with slow questions and quiet space and the reassurance that he's not broken or alone or failing.

But when he leaves, the calm goes with him.

My next appointment is a couple dealing with grief after losing a parent. They sit close together with their hands knotted tight. They speak about guilt and fear and the ache that won't let go. Normally, this work grounds me, bringing me back to something human and true. Today, I just feel numb, like I'm saying the words but not actually making a connection.

By the time we finish the session, the sky outside my office window has softened into late afternoon. I check the time, grab my white coat, and head to the hospital for rounds. There, the halls are loud with shift change and the beeping rhythm of monitors and nurses trading updates. At least, things make sense. People get hurt. They heal. They fight to survive instead of turning on each other.

Even here, my mind keeps sliding back to that podium and the cold gleam in Evelyn's eyes, the glint I recognize from every textbook case study on authoritarian leadership.

I move through each room and check vitals and reassure families and speak with nurses. I do my job. I do it well. But there's a tension I can't shake.

When rounds end, the sky has turned violet. The air smells like pine and smoke from a fireplace. A normal evening. A quiet one.

But I know mine won't be.

I pull out my keys and look back at the hospital lights. Dinner with Evie. Mandatory. She's already drawn her battle lines. And I'm walking into the middle of it.

A few minutes later, I pull into the driveway at Black Bear Vineyard, and the whole property glows in harsh artificial light. Floodlights blaze along the main house brighter than I've ever seen them, like Evie is warding off an attack she thinks is coming. Or welcoming one.

I kill the engine and sit for a second with my palms pressed to the steering wheel. The place looks more like a fortified compound than my grandmother's home. Cars line the circular drive. Expensive ones. Unfamiliar ones. The kind lawyers drive when they get paid too much to tell someone powerful what they want to hear.

I step out into the cool night air with my breath puffing white. The gravel crunches under my shoes as I walk up the front steps. Even before I open the door, I hear voices. Low. Urgent. The clipped rhythm of people trying to keep up with a hurricane.

I push the door open.

Evelyn is in the sitting room, pacing like a general. Three lawyers sit scattered around her with laptops open and stacks of documents spread everywhere.

Evie's voice slices through the air. "They think they are coming for me. They think they are coming for this family." She gestures sharply, rings flashing under the chandelier. "They do not know who they are dealing with."

All the cousins are here too. Dylan and his brothers, Logan and Matthew. Their sister Kaitlyn. My cousin Scott Porter and his brothers, Mike, Eric, and Joey. They stand silent and stiff against the walls like soldiers waiting for orders. I can see the hunger in Dylan's eyes. The calculation in Logan's. The dull anticipation in the others'. They would raze the vines tomorrow if she handed them the keys.

Evie turns at the sound of my footsteps. "Good. You are finally here." She gestures with a flick of her wrist. "We are moving to the dining room. Now."

I glance toward the lawyers, and one gives me a look that's somewhere between *run* and *save us*.

Evelyn snaps her fingers. "Come on. There's work to do."

"Work?" I echo under my breath.

As if she's not standing in the middle of a legal disaster she created. She's dragging our entire family into her mess, as if it's reasonable. To her, it seems this is business as usual.

I follow her down the hall. The house smells like meatloaf, mashed potatoes, and fresh bread. Normally, the place feels lived in. Tonight, it seems like a stage set, a battleground polished until you can't see the cracks beneath.

I catch sight of the dining table as we approach. Plates set. Wine poured. Two chairs at the far end conspicuously absent—Addie's and Ginny's. A double punishment disguised as tradition despite not being invited.

Evie stops at the head of the table and grips the back of her seat like it's a throne. She meets my eyes. "Sit down," she says. "We are about to begin."

The moment I sit, the room shifts. The doors close behind me with a soft click. My sisters are lined up along the side of the table, trying and failing to look relaxed. Sera twists her napkin. Josie sits stiffly, with white knuckles around her glass. She keeps looking at the empty spots like she wants Ginny and Addie to walk in anyway.

Across the room, the cousins stand in a tense line—Dylan with his chin high, Logan with his arms crossed, Matthew with his jaw clenched. Kaitlyn watches all of us with sharp eyes, and Scott is probably already imagining the vines bulldozed and replaced with marijuana. His brothers just look ready to nod at anything Evie demands.

She waits until we're quiet. She lifts her glass, though not for a toast. More like someone holding evidence.

"This family is under attack," she says. "The Paradise family has been trying to destroy us for generations, and now, they are using the Crown to do it."

Josie swallows. Sera doesn't seem to breathe.

I brace myself for what's coming.

Evie turns to Dylan first. "You. I need you front and center. You're my voice. My attack dog. You will counter every accusation publicly. No hesitation. No weakness. Not one inch given."

Dylan nods, and power flickers behind his eyes. He's twenty-six, and I have no doubt Evie told him the vineyard could be his if he performs well enough. His brothers Logan and Matthew lean in, listening like this is their moment.

She pivots to Josie. "You'll handle the political outreach. We're major donors. Call in favors. Remind every person in office who they owe. Use that smile of yours. That is why God gave it to you."

Josie manages a quick grin, but it lacks warmth. She looks like she's holding a live wire. She glances at me for half a second, fear in her eyes.

Then her gaze lands on me. Her face hardens. "You stay quiet."

My jaw tightens, but I hold my position. I can feel my sisters and cousins staring at me and waiting.

"You're not speaking publicly," Evelyn continues. "You'll operate behind the scenes. Apply pressure where it matters. Whisper in the right ears. Use that brain of yours. Psychology. Influence. Whatever it is you do."

I lift a brow. "You mean my doctorate in psychology?"

Her eyes narrow. "Don't get cute."

I sit back and let silence fill the space between us. She hates when I don't react. I let it stretch.

Evie slaps her palm against the table. The wine glasses jump. "This is a fight to the death," she says. "And if any of you think you can sit this out, think again."

Sera flinches. Josie's jaw trembles before she locks it down.

The cousins puff their chests out with barely disguised eagerness.

Evie lifts her chin. "Anyone not in lockstep with me, anyone who embarrasses this family, will be cut out of my will. Permanently." She lets the word hang. "No money. No land. No protection. And I will come after you legally if I must."

There's a beat of stunned silence.

I look around the table.

My sisters look terrified. Small. Cornered. And I know the cousins are watching them like vultures, waiting for their share.

Evie keeps talking, delivering orders like a dictator cementing her rule, but I barely hear the rest. I'm watching my sisters and the way they fold under her voice as she plays them like pieces on a board. I see the cousins stiffen with anticipation. I see the lawyers shrinking into shadows.

I can see exactly who my grandmother is and what she's capable of.

And even though every instinct tells me to stay out of this and walk away and return to the quiet in my practice and the separate life I so desperately want, I also know I can't leave my sisters alone with her.

I breathe in slowly. If Evie wants a war, she'll get one. But I won't be fighting for her.

I'll be fighting for them.

Twenty-nine

Liz

Monday mornings in early March always feel colder than they should. The wind freezes my fingers as I walk the five blocks from my rental to the hospital, sidewalks still wet from last night's rain and the bare branches overhead rattling in the breeze.

It's just after eight, the sun still low behind the ridge on the far side of Black Bear Lake, and Paradise is waking up slowly around me—cars idling at the lights, a delivery truck backing into the loading bay of the café I pass every day. The smell of roasted beans drifts into the street, warm and sweet, a sharp contrast to the chilly air cutting through my coat.

I push my hands deeper into my pockets and breathe through the unease curling in my stomach. There's another leadership meeting ahead, another round of pretending my personal life isn't unraveling.

My phone buzzes in my pocket. Trinity.

I swipe to answer. "Tell me you're calling with something normal." My words fog in the morning air.

She lets out a laugh that's a little strained. "Not even close. I just survived a grocery-store interrogation."

I wince. "Evelyn's subpoena?"

"Oh yes. Apparently, Trace is 'destroying an innocent woman.'" Trinity makes her voice high and dramatic. "And then the cashier refused to check me out. Said she didn't want to be part of whatever the Paradises are plotting."

I stop at the crosswalk, dumbfounded. "That's unhinged."

"Welcome to Paradise," she mutters. "Everyone's choosing sides."

"Because Evelyn Dempsey says so," I ask, incredulous. "I'm so sorry. You don't deserve to deal with that."

"No one in our family is asking people to pick sides," she says. "Not Vicky or Trace. Not even Tarryn, and she's got every reason to be furious because it affects the vineyard. But that hasn't stopped the gossip."

The light turns green, and the walk signal flashes. I start walking again, the hospital coming into view. "People love a spectacle. And Evelyn always makes sure she's center stage."

There's a beat of silence. Then Trinity asks, "Have you talked to Alaric since the press conference?"

My stomach tightens. "No."

"Is he slammed with this drama?"

"I don't know," I admit. "He walked out on me at Mikey's last week."

The line goes silent for a second. "Liz. Oh my God. I'm so sorry. Why didn't you tell me?"

"I don't know. I was upset with him, and I lost it. And then he walked out. I'm fine," I lie. "At least I know what caused him to leave this time."

"Still. Why didn't you tell me immediately?"

"It just happened the other day," I say, stepping around a

patch of ice. "And I don't really know how I feel. I mean, I have closure this time, which helps. But we usually get along so well. It's strange to go from that to nothing."

Trinity's voice softens. "I hate that for you. I wish I could hug you right now."

"I know. Thanks." I exhale, the hospital doors ahead of me. "I'm almost at my office. I should go."

"Call me later?"

"Of course."

I hang up and slip the phone into my pocket.

Upstairs, I push open the office door. She's unavoidable, so I decide to be professional. "Morning, Misty."

She doesn't look up from her monitor. Not even a nod. Just a stiff turn of her shoulder, like my voice is something she can dodge. She was out all last week on unpaid leave—a result of HR's findings about her conduct, I would guess; Hudson told me it had been handled—and I can't say I missed her.

I glance toward Hudson's office. The door is open, but the lights are off. It's empty. Of course, he's not there. The man shows up at the crack of dawn every day, and I'm sure he's getting ready for this morning's leadership meeting.

I continue on to my own office instead. My bag lands on the chair with a soft thud. I boot up my computer, shuffle through the pages I printed yesterday, and force myself into work mode. This leadership meeting means I need to be sharp, composed.

I run through my morning routine. Emails. Calendar. Meeting notes. A quick skim of the latest ED numbers. By the time I'm ready, my coffee is only half gone and completely cold. I toss it in the sink, grab my notebook, and straighten my blouse before heading out a few minutes before nine.

The boardroom is only a short walk down the hall, but every step is a reminder that I'm going to sit at that table and pretend I don't care whether Alaric is present.

I take a steadying breath and reach for the door.

The boardroom is already half full when I walk in. Papers shuffling, low conversations, the usual pre-meeting noise. I keep my eyes forward as I take my seat, but I can't stop myself from glancing around as the room fills. No Alaric. One empty chair.

I tell myself it's a good thing. It should make things easier, sparing me the awkwardness and the risk of my emotions slipping through in front of everyone. But my disappointment ratchets up anyway. I grip my pen until my fingers ache. I'm supposed to be moving on, and yet one empty chair derails me before the meeting even starts.

Hudson walks in a minute later, followed by the CEO, and conversation dies down. I sit straighter, tuck a loose strand of hair behind my ear and try to look like someone whose heart is not currently a slow-motion train wreck.

The meeting starts. Agenda items. Procedural updates. Financial reports. People talk around me, monotone and slow, and I nod along while drifting back to the conference in Hawaii.

Sun on my skin. Alaric's hand at my back. Our mornings spent in sessions and the afternoons exploring. Laughing over nothing. The two of us without the noise of the hospital or the never-ending gravitational pull of his family.

It felt easy. In hindsight, I can see it was dangerous. Deceptive.

Someone coughs at the far end of the table, and I blink back into the room just as the conversation shifts. My attention focuses when I hear his name.

"Dr. Dempsey's CME credits," Dr. Morris says. "We still haven't addressed the delay."

I sit up a little straighter. The mention feels like a warning.

Hudson steps in immediately. "The provincial regulation board has accepted his CME submission."

A low ripple moves through the room. Dr. Morris doesn't even try to hide his annoyance. "He should still be sanctioned for the lateness. And for not being here today."

My pen taps once against my notebook. Hard. The sound jolts me into speaking before I overthink it. "We only have three people covering psychiatry and psychology," I say. "Mental health is at the forefront right now. Emergency is seeing almost twenty mental-health-related patients a day."

Dr. Morris snorts. "And what would he do with my schedule?"

I turn toward him. "As a radiologist, you interpret images and provide diagnostic reports. Occasionally, you perform image-guided procedures. Your work is crucial, but it's not the same. His team can spend hours with patients in crisis in the emergency room. The comparison doesn't hold."

As the words leave my mouth, something twists in my chest. I hate that instinct made me protect him. I hate that it still feels natural.

Dr. Morris's mouth snaps shut.

The CEO nods. "If the provincial board accepted his CMEs, then so do we. The matter is closed."

A beat of silence follows. But the room feels different now. Not peaceful. Just resigned. People go back to their papers, clicking pens, flipping pages like we didn't just spend ten minutes dissecting the absence of the man I'm trying not to think about.

I stare at the agenda in front of me, but the words blur. My pulse is still elevated, a dull thrum at the base of my throat. I shouldn't have said anything. Or maybe I should have. I can't tell which truth makes me feel worse.

I can feel Dr. Morris glaring holes into the side of my head, but I keep my eyes on my notes, pretending I'm too busy to notice. The conversation moves on to staffing shortages, budget forecasts, and the usual bureaucratic noise.

I should be listening. I should be taking better notes. But all I can think about is the empty chair and the way my chest tightened when they said his name. Hawaii floods in like a tide I can't hold back. The way he looked at me when he thought I wasn't paying attention. The little bubble of peace we created, far away from everything that always ruins us.

The contrast feels brutal now.

A question comes my way—something about discharge delays—and I answer on autopilot. I hear the words come out of my mouth and watch people nod, but I'm detached from all of it, like I've slipped out of my body.

It's not until Hudson starts talking again that my attention anchors itself. He's explaining staffing allocations for the next quarter, and I force myself to breathe slowly and focus.

By the time the CEO calls for the next item, I'm exhausted, emotionally wrung out from pretending I'm not caught between missing Alaric and being furious that I still care.

"Next," the CEO says, shuffling papers, "we'll review the updated emergency metrics."

The meeting drones on, but I feel a tightening of my resolve. I can't keep doing this. I can't keep drifting between past and present, waiting for something that's clearly already ended. Again.

The meeting finally adjourns. Chairs scrape back. People gather their things. I stay seated one heartbeat longer than everyone else, and when I stand, my legs feel steadier than when I walked in. Not fixed. Not healed. Just...clearer. And seeing the path ahead has to be the first step in getting somewhere new.

Thirty

Alaric

I close my laptop after finishing my first morning session and sit for a breath, letting the quiet settle. The teenager I saw today, who has been angry, exhausted, and brittle in the way kids get when life forces them to grow up too fast, finally cracked her shell. She talked about missing Vancouver, about feeling like Paradise had stolen the life she knew. Her voice shook even while she tried to sound annoyed. It was the closest we've gotten to honesty.

It should feel like a win.

My phone buzzes once. Then again. The screen lights up like a fuse burning toward something inevitable.

Sera: Can you come? Now.
Sera: Evie called Dylan and Scott here.
Sera: They're yelling at us.

Josie: She's in one of her moods.

Sera: Please answer.

A knot forms in my gut.

I call to my administrator from the doorway. "I need to leave. Family emergency."

She gives me a look that says she's seen this movie too many times. "Most of Paradise already knows the Dempseys are in another storm cloud. Go."

I manage a smile, grab my coat off the hook, and walk into the hall. The leadership meeting has already started, and I should be heading toward it. Instead, I type a brief email to the CEO and CMO—clean, organized, detached from the truth.

Me: Family situation has come up. I'll miss the meeting but will follow up on all action items.

Send.

Outside, I take a steadying breath, unlock my car, and start the engine. The tension sits high across my shoulders, refusing to budge.

As I merge onto the bridge, the lake stretches out on both sides, wide and silver. On good days, that view gives me space to imagine. Today, it just reinforces what I already know. This isn't one of Evie's quick tempers. This is the anger that reshapes things.

I pass Paradise Hill—vines dormant, rows perfect, the land steady in its identity. It knows who runs it. It knows its rhythm.

Black Bear hasn't had rhythm in years. Not since my grandfather died and Evie began playing power games that burned every bridge they'd ever built. Her children scattered. The cousins turned into opportunists. And my sisters are left trying to salvage scraps of something that used to be beautiful.

The closer I get to her property, the clearer the pattern becomes, the one I've tried to ignore.

Her midnight call about tank numbers. Her accusations about "missing inventory." Her abrupt shift from praising Sera and Josie to questioning every choice they make. Her renewed contact with Dylan and Scott.

She's piecing together a story that benefits one person. Herself.

The long gravel driveway confirms it before I even park. Every cousin she could weaponize has parked in formation across the front of her house. Dylan's truck. Scott's SUV. Kaitlyn's Tesla angled like she fled a crime scene. Matthew's Jeep with the crooked bumper. Joey's sedan with the cracked headlight.

A lineup she curated.

I kill the engine, step onto the lawn, and hear shouting before I reach the door.

Inside, the scene is a staged disaster. Sera stands rigid in the sitting room, fury and hurt warring on her face. Dylan looms over her, yelling like he has a right. Scott adds barbed commentary whenever he sees an opening.

And Evie sits on the couch—poised, smoothed, almost serene.

Enjoying the show.

"Stop," I say from the doorway.

No one stops.

"Enough," I bellow.

That lands. The room snaps to silence. Evie's eyes narrow, annoyance flashing across her face.

I motion to Sera. "Kitchen."

Relief floods her features as she slips past Dylan.

"Josie too."

She steps out from the hallway, jaw tight, and follows her sister without hesitation.

I face the cousins. "Dining room. All of you."

They glance at Evie. She gives a single approving nod.

Even with her blessing, they hate being dismissed. Dylan's jaw grinds. Scott's chin lifts like he might challenge me. But whatever they see in my face pushes them through the doorway.

When the door clicks shut behind them, the room settles into a colder kind of quiet. Evie doesn't stand. She crosses one leg over the other, perfectly composed, as if waiting for me to apologize for the interruption.

"What exactly are you trying to accomplish?" I ask.

Her expression softens into something deceptively warm. "I simply asked questions," she says.

"Questions designed to ignite a fight," I point out. "And you picked the most combustible people you could find to ask them."

"Sera and Josie are not ready," she replies with certainty, as if saying it makes it fact.

"They've done everything you asked. Every certification. Every audit. Every outdated tradition you insisted on keeping. And now, you undermine them in front of the people who most want to see them fail. Why?"

Her mouth tightens. "Don't speak to me like I'm some kind of villain."

I take a step closer. "You were watching them tear each other apart. You didn't stop it. You didn't redirect. You didn't calm the room. You sat there and enjoyed it. What would you call that?"

Annoyance flares in her eyes.

"Did you know Dylan wants to scrap all the vines and plant marijuana?" I continue. "You know about Scott's debts. You know Kaitlyn has zero interest in the vineyard and every interest in easy money. These aren't protectors. They're opportunists. And you invited them here."

"They wouldn't actually—"

"They would," I say quietly. "And they will. The moment you're not here to stop them. And one day, you won't be."

Her posture stiffens.

"You built something beautiful," I add. "But you're

turning it into a battlefield because losing control scares you more than losing the vineyard."

For a split second, I see it. *Fear*. Not for the vineyard. For the power slipping through her fingers. Then the mask returns.

I'm finished. "I'm not staying for whatever this next round is." I turn.

Behind me, she calls my name, but I don't respond. That tone has dictated enough of my life.

In the dining room, the cousins hover with restless energy, waiting for direction like attack dogs denied a target.

"We're done," I say. "All of you need to leave."

Scott bristles. "Evie said—"

"Evie staged a spectacle," I cut in. "You performed. It's over."

Dylan steps forward, shoulders squared. "We have a right to know what's going on at the vineyard."

"You have a right to stay in your lane," I reply. "And interrogating the only people doing the work isn't it."

He opens his mouth again, then closes it. I sweep a look across each of them.

"Go home. Don't come back unless Sera or Josie asks you to."

Kaitlyn arches an eyebrow as she passes me. "She's going to lose it when she realizes you shut down the show."

"She'll adjust," I say.

Kaitlyn snorts—half amusement, half warning—and disappears out the front door.

I allow myself one breath before heading to the kitchen.

Sera sits at the table, gripping her mug tightly. Josie is at the sink, arms rigid, shoulders high, staring into the drain.

They both look up when I enter.

"You okay?" I ask.

Sera exhales shakily. "Now, I am."

Josie pushes off the counter, crossing her arms. "She called them here. She wound them up. And she sat there like it was a spectator sport."

"It had nothing to do with your work," I say.

"Then what did we do wrong?" Sera asks.

"Nothing," I reply. "This is about her losing control, not you losing capability."

Josie's jaw flexes. She grips the back of a chair, her knuckles white. "She's going to do it again."

"Probably," I admit. "But next time, walk away before she gets traction. Don't give her an audience. She hates silence. Use that."

Sera huffs a tired laugh. "Hard to walk away when she summons a mob."

"She won't get that chance again," I say. "I made it impossible."

They share a look…exhausted but steadier.

"I need to get back to the hospital," I tell them. "You two good here?"

Josie lifts her chin. "We are."

Sera gives a small, weary smile. "Thanks for coming."

"Always," I say, squeezing her shoulder on my way out.

Outside, the gravel sparkles in the sun, the cousins' taillights fading around the bend. Evie's house looms behind me, a perfect shell for all the chaos it contains.

I rest a hand on the roof of my car, letting the cool metal bleed some heat from my skin. Today drew a line I'm finally willing to acknowledge. This family will always test the limits. But I don't have to let those limits replace mine.

I slide into the driver's seat, text my administrator that I'm on the way back, and pull onto the road. The house disappears between the trees, shrinking with every turn.

I don't look back.

I have work waiting that doesn't demand I bleed for it—and that solves real problems, not manufactured ones.

Thirty-one

Liz

I stop at the bagel place on my way in, telling myself it's just a nice Friday gesture and not an attempt to make the week feel less tense. The paper bag is warm against my palm in the elevator, smelling like toasted everything seasoning and cinnamon sugar, and for a second, it lifts my mood.

When I push through the office door, I set the bagels on the counter and Misty doesn't even look up from her screen. Which is fine by me. A moment later, Hudson steps out of his office, shrugging into his suit jacket. He spots the bag and lets out a relieved groan. "Oh, bless you. Real breakfast." He plucks a sesame seed bagel. "This beats the protein bar I inhaled on my way out the door."

"Glad to help," I say.

I pick up my bag and start toward my office, hoping to settle in before the day gets chaotic, but Hudson's voice follows me.

"Liz? Grab your laptop and come into my office for a minute."

I pause, fingers tightening around the strap. "Sure," I say, even though the request tightens between my shoulder blades. *Now what?*

I dump my coat, switch my sneakers for heels, collect my laptop, and head toward Hudson's office.

He greets me as I enter and directs me to the small round table in the corner. Somehow, that feels more formal than sitting across from his desk. I set my laptop down and try to act like this is a normal occurrence. Just a check-in. Hopefully, it is.

"How are things going with Misty?" he asks as soon as I'm settled.

I clear my throat, keeping my voice even. "I suppose they're fine."

He gives me a look—just the smallest brow lift—but it hits its mark. "Are you still having problems with her? We can discuss this with HR."

I'm not interested in throwing her under the bus. She's done a pretty good job getting there on her own. But she's still around, so I guess that means it wasn't a fireable offense. She and I don't talk, and I don't trust her. But I've already told Hudson that, so I'm not sure what he wants from me. "We're trying to find our way."

"Are you using her?"

I shake my head. "Not really. I'm not used to having administrative support." The admission feels clumsy coming out. "In my last job, I did everything myself. It's a habit."

"She's your admin too," he says firmly. "She's here to support you as much as she supports me. And if you can't trust her, the three of us and HR should talk about it."

That is the last thing I want to do. So I nod, even though the thought of leaning on Misty makes my throat tight. "I'll try to delegate," I tell him. "I know I need to do better with that."

Hudson studies me for a moment, and I fold my hands in my lap so I don't fidget. I want to be someone who trusts my team members, someone who doesn't feel like every number might be wrong unless I triple-check it myself. I guess this is him telling me I have to try.

"Good," he says eventually. "Let's make sure you're set up to succeed."

I nod again.

He reaches for a pair of binders and slides them across the table. The top one is thick enough that the clasp barely closes.

"These are projects I haven't been able to get to," he explains.

I straighten the first binder and flip it open. "Drug trials?"

"I tried to manage this, but I fell behind. We need to get caught up with the numbers, picking up where we left off last year so we can get paid." He leans back, rubbing his jaw. "They bring in good revenue, but they're admin heavy—coordination, timelines, regulatory oversight. We won't see any money if we can't get them done."

There's a spreadsheet clipped to the inside cover. My brain recoils on instinct. I keep my face neutral. "I can take it on," I say, though it comes out closer to *this is fine, I guess.*

His gaze shifts to the second binder. "This one's more in your wheelhouse."

I lift it, and my heart leaps when I see the header. *Strategic Planning – Staffing Review.*

"You hit a nerve on Monday," he says. "Behavioral Health is understaffed. We all know it. But no one's taken the time to quantify just how much. HR needs a partner who can dig in without getting political about it."

Political. The word sticks like a burr. Every department is struggling to hire. It's not a matter of people dragging their feet on opening requisitions. It's a shortage of workers. A real one. But I love detangling problems like this. The messier, the better.

"That partner would be you," he adds.

And just like that, I'm awake in a way I haven't been in weeks. "This is important," I say, flipping through pages. "This could change service delivery. Access. Budgeting. Everything."

"Exactly."

I close the binder, energized. My whole body feels like it's leaning forward.

Hudson smiles. "Knew you'd like that one."

I push my chair back. "I'll get started." I close my laptop and stand, but his voice stops me cold.

"Liz," he says quietly. "One more thing."

I look back, and the shift in his expression drains the warmth out of me.

"Your relationship with Dr. Dempsey."

My pulse jumps. "What about it?"

"You have a history," he says. Not a question.

I exhale slowly. "We do. We knew each other in North Vancouver. We dated for a while."

Hudson nods like he expected that. "And now?"

"We're not dating," I tell him. The full truth has more layers than I want to unpack with my boss on a Friday morning.

His shoulders loosen. His relief is subtle but not subtle enough that I miss it. It stings.

Before I can decide what that means, he says, "The Paradise–Dempsey dynamic is a big deal here in the valley."

I nod. "I think I've gotten a taste of it."

"Your best friend is a Paradise," he says. "Dr. Dempsey is a Dempsey. Two very different worlds. Very old conflicts." He lets out a breath. "And with Evelyn Dempsey under investigation by the Crown prosecutor, it's going to get uglier."

My brain stumbles. "What does that have to do with me?"

"Everything." His voice lowers. "Your position is funded by the Paradise Family Foundation. Several people in leadership who backed your hire are also funded by that foundation."

Something cold slides down my spine. "I didn't know that."

"That's why I'm telling you," he says. "When this rivalry

blows—and it's a runaway train right now—there'll be fallout. I don't want you caught in it. Keep your head down. Focus on your work. Don't get tangled in anything that makes people question where you stand."

His words land in a way he probably doesn't realize. Anger ignites inside me. People have decided things for me before. People have taken my choices away. I'm not letting that happen again.

Hudson is still looking at me, and it takes a moment before the pieces click together. I'm expected to be in the Paradise camp. Because of Trinity. Because of the foundation. Because of optics.

And Alaric? He's on the wrong side.

I knew the tension existed. I didn't understand how far it reached until now.

I manage a slow nod. "Okay. I understand."

But the truth is I don't. Not fully. Not comfortably.

Hudson gives a final, quiet "Good," and I pick up the binders with hands that feel too warm and too light at the same time.

I leave his office feeling like the floor has shifted under me, like I need a minute to steady myself, but the building won't give it.

I go back to my office, close the door halfway, and set both binders on my desk. The strategic planning one practically vibrates with possibility. I pull up the hospital intranet, diving right into department charts. Fifteen department heads. Dozens of units. Staffing levels that make absolutely no sense. The kind of puzzle that makes my brain itch in the best way.

The drug trials binder sits to the side of my desk like a sad, heavy math assignment I pretend not to see.

But my mind keeps drifting—back to Hudson's warning, back to the funding I didn't know about, back to the fact that someone is keeping track of who I spend time with and that it matters.

My job is paid for by Trinity's family. People expect that to mean something.

A slow, hot frustration climbs into my chest. I hate the politics and the sides and the idea that the valley has already decided where I belong when I'm still trying to figure that out myself.

When the workweek finally ends, I pack up and walk home. My body feels worn from thinking too hard about things that don't have easy answers. Inside, I drop my bag on the floor, stand in the quiet for three seconds, then grab my keys. I can't sit still. If I stay here, I'm going to drown in my own thoughts.

I get in my car and just drive. The valley stretches out around me in the darkness. The roads wind along the lake and through the tall pines, and I let the motion settle me a little, enough to breathe.

I don't even realize where I'm headed until I pull up in front of Trinity's building. My jaw tightens. Of course I ended up here. She's the person I always reach for when things feel too heavy.

I call her, and she picks up on the second ring.

"I'm out front," I tell her.

"We're at the new house," she says. "Come over. I'll give you a tour."

I drive ten minutes along the shoreline. When I get close, the construction site is lit by floodlights and looks like a giant skeleton of concrete and framing. The house is going to be enormous. I climb out of my car, and Theo barrels toward me with a yellow bulldozer in his hand.

"Liz!" he yells as he throws his arms around me.

The hug warms something that's been cold all day. Trinity joins us with her hands in her pockets and a tired smile.

"If someone had told me how obsessed little boys are with

trucks and bulldozers, I would've found a construction site ages ago," she says. "He'll watch them for hours."

I laugh, and we take a slow walk around the construction. Trinity points out future rooms and where the windows will overlook the valley. It's going to be beautiful.

"You up for a drink at Paradise Grill?" she asks.

"Sure."

We get into her SUV and drive up to the vineyard restaurant. Theo runs off to the main house to see his grandparents, and Trinity and I grab a corner booth in the bar. We order Italian sodas, and once the server walks away, Trinity fixes me with a look.

"All right. What happened? Why did you show up at my house?"

I tell her everything. The meeting with Hudson. The questions about Alaric. The foundation funding. The warning about family politics. When I ask if she pulled strings to get me hired, her face goes slack.

"No," she says firmly. "I had no idea the foundation paid for your job. It's run by one of Greyson's cousins. They fund all sorts of things across the valley, and none of it has anything to do with me. I recommended you because you're perfect for the work."

I believe her, but that doesn't erase the weight of Hudson's warning. I tell her he made it sound like I'm in the Paradise camp by default.

She rolls her eyes and grabs my hand. "You don't belong to anyone," she says. "And Hudson shouldn't have dragged you into something that isn't yours."

Her words ease some of the pressure inside me. I nod gratefully, though my reality remains what it is.

She changes the subject and asks about the projects I was given today. I tell her every detail about the strategic planning review and how excited I am. She beams. The drug trials get a less-enthusiastic reaction, which I completely agree with, but she still insists I'll do great.

Then Trinity takes a slow sip of her soda. "So," she says. "Have you talked to him?"

Him is Alaric, and I look down at the condensation on my glass. "I haven't," I admit.

Her brows lift.

"With everything going on with Evelyn…" I trail off. "He has a lot on his plate."

Trinity watches me for a moment longer than is comfortable. I brace for a follow-up. A suggestion. A warning.

But she just reaches across the table and taps my knuckles. "Okay."

She lets the silence sit between us, and it feels like support instead of pressure.

I smile gratefully, and eventually, she squeezes my hand. "If you want to reach out to Alaric, you should. Don't let Hudson decide that for you. I'll check with Greyson and his cousin and make sure your job isn't at risk because of who you talk to or date."

Emotion rises in my throat before I can stop it. It's ridiculous, but that is a concern. "Thank you."

We finish our drinks and talk about the house and Theo and random things that make the world feel a little easier. When it's time to go, she hugs me tight, and I promise to see her again soon.

On the drive home, my mind feels more settled. I walk inside, change into soft clothes, heat up a frozen lasagna that doesn't taste anything like lasagna, and finally wash my face and slide into bed.

I'm better than I was earlier, but the unease remains at the edge of my thoughts—the idea that other people are watching my connections, that they think my involvement with Alaric is something to worry about, that they want me to pick a side in something that has nothing to do with me.

I lie in the dark, letting the quiet fill the room. I'm not letting anyone else choose my loyalties for me. But this whole situation is already more complicated than I ever wanted it to be.

Thirty-two

Alaric

Once again, my phone won't stop vibrating. It skitters across the corner of my desk, as if it's trying to escape, and every time the screen lights up, my thoughts scatter. It's late on a Friday night, and I'm still here because I'm supposed to be finishing patient notes, but I've just read the same sentence four times without absorbing a word.

Another alert. Then another. I finally give in and turn the phone over.

It's a news clip. Evelyn again. She's standing at a microphone outside the tasting room, wrapped in her heavy wool coat, looking small and delicate in a way that's absolutely intentional. *Crown Corporation Investigates Evelyn Dempsey as Paradise Clan Circles*

Of course, she's framing it that way.

Another notification drops, a community post exploding

with comments. Then my phone buzzes again.

Sera: Can you talk to Evie? Please. She's making it worse.

Josie: Can you get her to stop? Dylan's losing it, and the town is turning on us.

I set the phone down and lean back, staring at the ceiling, trying to breathe. I'm trained for chaos. I'm good at talking people down. I know how to keep things calm.

But my own family imploding like this is different.

The screen lights up again, and I make the mistake of watching the full clip. Evelyn grips the podium like she's bracing against the wind, her voice thin and trembly as she says, "I'm just one old woman trying to protect what my family built."

The crowd cheers. Signs wave. People I've known my whole life stand there like she's leading a crusade. She knows how to work a crowd. She's been doing it for years. Small. Frail. Brilliant at getting people to act in her defense.

I shut the clip off before the reporters can spin it any further. But then my phone actually rings. Barry Portman, our family attorney.

I hit speaker. "Tell me you're calling with something normal."

"I wish," he says. "It's bad."

"How bad?"

"Bad enough that I stepped out of my daughter's engagement dinner." Paper shuffles on his end. "I'm hearing the Crown believes Dylan's acting as a foot soldier for your grandmother. People are talking about it tonight."

My eyes widen. I mean, seems correct, but not the message Evelyn wants out there. "Foot soldier? Seriously?"

"Yep. And it gets worse. Someone overheard Scott at Iron Horse bragging about 'taking the Paradise family down a peg.' Half the bar heard."

"Great," I mutter. "Just what we need."

Barry lowers his voice. "This is exactly what Max and Trace Paradise want. Chaos. And Evelyn's feeding right into it."

I clear my throat. "I'll call you back."

"Alaric—"

"I need a minute."

He doesn't push. He just sighs, tired and resigned, and hangs up.

Another vibration hits my phone before I can lower my hand. A new text. Another comment thread. Someone has tagged me. Pressure builds behind my eyes, making my head throb.

The notifications keep coming, and stupidly, I click one.

Someone has shared a photo of Sera from a school fundraiser. She looks sweet, harmless, just standing there holding brownies. The caption underneath makes my stomach roil.

Funny how she's pretending to be innocent when her family's sabotaging the town.

I scroll, and it gets worse. Comments tearing into her, dragging Josie into it, accusing them of playing dumb, of protecting the guilty, of whatever else the town wants to believe.

Then there's a picture of Josie unloading barrels behind the winery. Someone captioned it, *Hard to trust the wine when the winemaker condones sabotage.*

I shut the screen off so fast my thumb stings. I try calling both of them—Sera, then Josie. They don't pick up. Their phones probably look exactly like mine, buzzing nonstop with accusations.

I sit on the couch and lean forward, elbows on my knees, trying to get air into my lungs. Everything's spinning. Evelyn's theatrics. Dylan's recklessness. Scott's stupidity. The town choosing sides.

I'm so goddamn tired of all these problems my grandmother has manufactured—or at least magnified. And the only voice I want to hear, the only one that could quiet all of this for even a second, is Liz's.

I look over at my computer screen. The unfinished patient notes blink on the monitor like they're impatient with me. I ignore them and turn back to my phone instead. One more alert rolls across the top. I swipe it away and tap Liz's name.

She answers on the second ring. "Alaric? Are you okay?"

I can tell she was sleeping, but her voice is warm and gentle, and suddenly, I don't know how to keep my answer light. It almost makes everything worse.

"No," I tell her. "I'm not okay."

"What happened?"

How to explain? "Evie's been giving speeches all over town. Dylan's name is everywhere. Scott's bragging. And people are going after Sera and Josie like they're personally responsible for every problem in the valley."

Liz listens without interrupting. I'm close to unraveling, and if I do it now, she'll hear all of it, get a front-row seat to the part of me that's scared and exhausted and failing at holding my family together.

"It's a mess," I finally conclude. "I'm trying to keep up, but I can't."

"What do you need?" she asks.

The question hits like a blow.

What I need is comfort. Someone to tell me I'm not failing. Someone to sit in the quiet with me. I need her. But the thought of letting her know all that makes something inside me panic.

So I don't have an answer. The silence stretches until the frustration in my chest turns sharp. "I shouldn't have called," I say.

"Alaric—"

"I mean it. I can't handle one more thing. I shouldn't drag you into this." My voice breaks, tight and strained. "Reigniting our relationship was a mistake."

The second the words leave my mouth, regret chases after them. I can feel the hurt silence on her end like it's pressing against my skin. *What the hell is wrong with me?*

Before she can say anything, before I hear the

disappointment in her voice, I end the call.

The silence afterward is brutal.

I set the phone beside me. That was the last thing I should've done. But I'm already drowning, and I can't reach for her without pulling her under with me.

The phone buzzes again, but I don't check it. Whether it's Barry or Sera or Liz, I don't have anything left. I stand, pace halfway across the room, then return to sink back down again.

I feel like a shell of myself. My family has become more than I can manage, and now I've screwed things up—at least three separate times—with the one person who hasn't asked me to be anything more than human.

I get up again and walk to the window, resting my forehead against the cool glass. "This is all going to get worse before it gets better," I mumble.

With that, I shut the lights off, grab my coat, and pocket my phone. Evie needs to understand that all she's doing is making it worse. Everything's slipping out of my hands, and I have no idea how to stop the rest from falling apart.

My phone rings at 2:31 a.m.

The glow from the screen throws a pale rectangle of light across the ceiling.

I blink, disoriented, until the screen lights up again. My eyes sting with tiredness, and the cold creeps under the blanket as I turn toward the nightstand.

Of course, it's Evie.

We talked earlier at her house, but she remained convinced she was in the right. I begged her to listen to what the community is saying, but it didn't work. And now this. She only calls like this when she's spiraling. Or furious. Or both. My heartbeat kicks up as I swipe to answer. "Evie?"

She doesn't bother with hello. "You've seen it, haven't you?"

There's a tremor in her voice that lifts the hair on the back of my neck.

I sit up. "Seen what?"

"Oh, don't play dumb," she snaps. "The coverage. The glowing praise. The human-interest fluff about Tarryn Paradise saving the valley's precious vines. They found a powdery mildew on some vines they purchased, and they handled it so perfectly, so publicly, so transparently." She spits the words like they're poison. Her breath hitches.

I close my eyes. "Evie, it's two thirty in the morning—"

"And I suppose that's a reason not to care?" she cuts in. "Every news station is talking about them. Every reporter is calling them responsible leaders. Meanwhile, only one reporter bothered to come to my press conference yesterday."

Her voice breaks. Not with sadness, but with rage contained too long.

I don't tell her it's because nothing she says is new. Or that everyone can see she's just shitting all over the Paradise family. I tried that earlier. She waved it all off.

"They don't care about the truth," she says. "They don't care that I'm being framed. They only care about the shiny story in front of them." The words tumble out faster, like she's struggling to keep up with her own thoughts.

"Evie—"

"And you," she snaps. "You're doing nothing. Nothing. You're sitting there while the Paradise family paints themselves as heroes and lets this valley believe I'm the villain."

I press my palm to my forehead. "I can't go out and give statements. You know that. I'd lose my license." My fingers dig into my hair.

She scoffs. "Rules. Ethics. You hide behind those like a child behind a curtain." She pauses, then adds, "Your girlfriend doesn't seem to care much about ethics."

Heat flashes through me, and then disappears, leaving a cold hollow behind. "What are you talking about?"

"Oh, please." She inhales, long and shaky. "Don't insult me. Someone leaked that the Paradise family compensated us for the damaged block. No one in this family would betray me like that. So who does that leave?" Her voice climbs just a little too high on the last word.

The word *girlfriend* clangs around in my head. Wrong and out of date. I sit straighter. "Evie, Liz didn't leak anything. She doesn't even know—"

"She doesn't know?" Evie cuts in, incredulous. "She absolutely knows. The compensation, the poisoned well, the water testing. Someone told her. And I know it wasn't anyone at the vineyard. They know better."

"Evie—" My throat feels dry.

Breathe in. Count to four. Breathe out. Count to four.

"So that leaves you." Her voice turns cold. "Did you tell her? Did you open your mouth about Zach's sabotage?"

"I didn't," I say. "I didn't tell her anything." My hand tightens around the phone. It's the truth.

The Paradise family caught their cousin sabotaging the well that sits between our properties. They came clean and have been compensating us for what happened. Evie's just been leaving that part out.

"Then how did the reporter know that 'According to a source close to the families, the Paradise well was deliberately sabotaged by Zach Paradise, a Dempsey cousin'?" Evie demands, apparently reading from a recent article.

"Liz didn't leak anything," I repeat. "And the Paradise family has every incentive to get that out there themselves. It makes them look generous. Cooperative. Clean." The last word tastes bitter.

I get silence in return. Not agreement. Offended silence. It stretches long enough that I can hear my pulse thudding in my ears.

"I won't have anyone undermine me," she says. "I won't

have you rewriting my reality to defend some girl you've known five minutes."

Liz isn't some girl, and it's been a lot longer than five minutes, but I don't correct her. It would pour gasoline on open flame. And it doesn't matter at this point anyway.

My grandmother drops her voice into that low, dangerous tone she uses when she wants to hurt someone into obedience. "You do remember," she says, "that I can disinherit you. And your sisters. All of you. With a signature. A moment."

My jaw tightens. "Evie…"

"No," she says. "Don't test me. I can cut you out of this family as easily as I cut vines in the spring. Don't think I won't."

What does she think she has that I want? "Evie, look," I say carefully. "I'm on your side. I want the truth to come out. I want this to be over. I'll help however I can, within reason. Just slow down. Breathe. Please." The psychologist in me wants to guide her back from the edge, but the grandson already knows she'll refuse to be led.

A long pause. I hear her breathing, uneven and ragged.

"You should have defended me," she says. "You should have been out front."

"I'm sorry," I tell her. The words sit heavy in my mouth, heavier in my chest.

She exhales. "Good. Then maybe there's hope for you yet."

An abrupt click snaps in my ear, and the line goes dead. I sit in the dark, staring at nothing. Her voice was off tonight. More frantic. More paranoid. The investigation is eating at her mind, chewing through her composure. And the valley's sudden love for the Paradise family only stokes her fear.

Evie said Liz knew about the Paradises' compensation. About the well. And I'm pretty sure, yeah, we talked about the Zach situation in Hawaii. It was one of those nights where everything spilled out too easily. I can still see us on that balcony, the ocean dark and loud. My guard lower than it should've been.

Would Liz tell someone?

Would she say something without realizing what it

implied?

I don't know.

But it shouldn't matter. There are a million ways that information could have gotten out there. My grandmother can't control everyone, and she shouldn't expect me to fall in line.

As she unravels, though, she seems to believe just the opposite.

Thirty-three

Liz

On Saturday morning, I arrive to find Trinity already in a booth by the front window of Dot's Diner, hands cupped around a mug, staring outside like she's waiting for something she isn't sure will come. She looks tired.

I slide into the seat across from her. "Hey."

She startles. "Hey. Sorry. My brain's a little…loud today."

"Totally get it." I shrug out of my coat and drape it beside me.

Tom Callahan, the diner's owner, swings by the table. "Katie will be your server," he tells us. "She'll be right with you." He holds up the coffee pot. "Coffee?" He fills both our mugs as we nod, and then Katie arrives.

"Do you know what you want?" she asks.

We put in our usual orders, and when she leaves, Trinity

stirs her coffee, watching the spoon move in slow circles. "How are you?" she asks, glancing up.

"Still feeling overwhelmed by work, but better—on that front at least." I take a sip from my mug.

"Have you heard from Alaric?"

My stomach tightens. "Yeah. Last night."

"And?"

"I don't know." I push out a breath. "He called, and I could tell something was wrong, so I asked him what he needed. I could hear how exhausted he was. He unloaded a bunch of stuff about his grandmother, and then after a minute, he said he shouldn't have called."

She gives me a look. "Then why did he?"

"I think… I think he was confirming we had broken up." The words squeeze my heart. "Because right after that, he said '*reigniting our relationship was a mistake*.' And then he hung up."

Her eyebrows shoot up. "He hung up on you?"

"Yep."

"Did he call back?"

"No." I swallow. "I waited. I kept checking my phone. I thought maybe he'd realize how it sounded or that he didn't mean it. But there was nothing."

Trinity's expression sharpens. "What did that feel like? In the moment?"

I shake my head. "It felt like the room shrank. I just sat there. I couldn't even think straight. I kept rereading our old texts like I was trying to remind myself that he cared once. And every time I thought about calling him back, it was like my throat closed. I don't want to chase someone who doesn't want to talk to me anymore, but I also can't accept that he meant it. I barely slept. I kept waking up and checking my phone like an absolute idiot."

Trinity sighs. "That's not him being thoughtless. That's him overwhelmed."

"I don't want to be one more thing he has to carry."

"You're not," she says softly.

Before I can respond, Katie drops off our plates, making a joke about feeding "both of you" as she taps the table near Trinity. Trinity manages a faint smile before Katie moves on.

"I think it has to be his family. Grey says he's never seen the valley like this," Trinity murmurs, slicing into her pancakes. "Not even when they were kids."

"It's that bad?"

"It's worse." She shakes her head. "Back then, it was simple. Paradise kids on one side of the cafeteria, Dempsey kids on the other. No crossing the line. Now, it's like every person in Black Bear is choosing a side and sharpening their pitchforks."

My chest tightens. "Because of the sabotage?"

"Because of everything." She counts on her fingers. "Spoilage of an entire chardonnay vat—someone introduced contaminants into the tank. Equipment failures. Water issues—blocked irrigation lines, well levels dropping. Break-ins. Theft. The dying vines. Half the town is panicking, and the other half thinks it's all planned." She pauses, rubbing her forehead. "Tarryn told me yesterday that two of her vineyard workers got into a screaming match in the parking lot over which family is '*ruining the valley*'. People are choosing sides in the grocery store. Someone made a comment to Elise at the hardware store about how the '*Paradises think they're untouchable*.' It's like everyone has lost their damn minds."

"And you think someone's orchestrating it?"

"We think Grey's Uncle Max is stirring things up." Her voice dips. "He was arrested, and he's claimed he was working with Evelyn."

That doesn't sound right. "They hate each other."

She shrugs. "They don't need to like each other. They just need to want the same people weakened. The enemy of my enemy is my friend."

A cold ripple passes through me. "So they're aligned?"

"She denies it, but they could be working together in their own way."

"And the police?" I ask, glancing around.

"They interviewed my in-laws. And then Tarryn. And Elise. But they aren't treating any of them as a suspect. They're trying to build a timeline. They've asked about every complaint, every issue. It doesn't seem like just one person behind it."

"So…coordinated?"

"Maybe. Or someone creating enough chaos that it feels like multiple sources."

I swallow. "How much can they prove?"

"I don't know." She rubs her temples. "This feud started with a land fight eight generations ago. Even naming the town Paradise was petty."

I stare at her. "Why hold on to something that only hurts everyone?"

"Because letting go feels like losing."

I lean back, the weight of it all settling—Max, Evie, police interviews, the town fracturing, Alaric's voice breaking over the phone. Maybe that does offer some insight into his behavior. But I still have no idea what to do.

I shift gears. "How are you?" I ask Trinity. "Not the feud. You."

She blinks. "Me?"

"Yes."

Her mouth softens. "My morning sickness is easing." Her hand goes to her belly. "And…I think the baby's a girl."

Warmth spreads through me. "Really?"

"The doctor slipped and said she. I haven't told anyone."

"That's huge."

She looks down, her cheeks warming. "I like keeping it to myself for now."

"Your secret stays with me."

She exhales. "Greyson's trying to be subtle, but he's already making name lists."

"That's adorable."

"It really is." She smiles. "I'm so glad to feel human again. I haven't woken up nauseous in three days. I can drink coffee without gagging. And—" She sighs. "I didn't realize how tense

I'd been until the nausea finally started to fade. My whole body feels different. Softer. Less clenched."

"That's amazing."

"It is." Her eyes brighten. "Theo practiced holding a doll the other night. And he told me he's ready to be a big brother."

The laugh that escapes me feels lighter than anything in days.

With that, Trinity picks up her fork and turns more intentionally to her food.

When we finish breakfast, we hug in the parking lot.

"Let me know if you hear from Alaric again," she says.

"I will."

"And you're not alone."

I nod and head off. After a quick grocery stop, I go home. I've put off work for long enough.

The house is quiet as I kick off my boots, hang my coat, and set the drug trials file and my laptop on the kitchen table.

The binders seem to stare at me.

"Okay," I mutter. "Round two."

I open the binder and start wading through trial protocols, budgets, reporting schedules, and spreadsheets. I start a new document—Drug Trials: Liz's Brain—and begin mapping what I understand.

Hours bleed together. My coffee goes cold. My neck aches. The numbers don't match anything in our systems, and I don't even see half the doctors listed in our employee directory.

This really sucks.

I reread one section of the reporting requirements five times and still can't tell if it's referencing a federal policy or an internal guideline someone invented. I scroll back to the spreadsheet and try to match the funds tracked to the corresponding protocols. They don't match. They don't even come close.

And then—buried in a secondary tab—there's a tiny, half-hidden note Hudson left himself, a reference to where he pulls the raw data from before formatting it.

"Oh," I breathe. "There you are."

A small win, but still a win. Enough to remind me I'm not completely lost. And I'd like to keep pushing until I've fixed everything alone, pretending that I get it. But I promised Hudson I'd start delegating, and I'm not ignoring red flags any longer. I need to bring in Misty. Perhaps she'll actually be helpful...

I open a new email.

Hi Misty,
I've been reviewing the drug trials binder Hudson passed along. Could we schedule some time early this week to walk through it together? Even thirty minutes would help.
Thanks,
Liz

I hit send, and a second later, my inbox pings.

But the message is not from Misty. It's from Alaric.

My heart thuds so hard it sends a pulse through my hands. I grip the edge of the table. I'm not sure if I want to open it or shut the laptop and throw it across the room.

"Okay," I whisper. "One thing at a time."

And then I click.

Thirty-four

Alaric

I should be in a session with my regular Tuesday-morning patients, but instead, I'm walking into a police interview. Maybe that's just as well, as Liz hasn't been far from my mind since last night. I handled our call badly, and ending it the way I did was worse. I sent a short email apology—no explanations, no defenses—because she didn't deserve to be cut off like that. But I don't know if she'll respond. I don't particularly expect her to, yet even as I try to focus on my grandmother and what's in front of me, Liz stays present in my mind, a quiet reminder of something I left unfinished.

I step into the conference room at the police station, where the detectives have reluctantly agreed to let me sit in. I'm not sure if that's a good thing or not, but my grandmother is eighty-three years old, and this way I'll have a firsthand account of what's happening, not just her spin later.

The detectives haven't even settled in their seats before Evelyn takes control. She walks straight to the head of the table and sits down like she called the meeting. Her coat stays on. So does her scarf. She has no intention of getting comfortable.

David Graham, her lawyer, drops into the chair beside her and stacks his files in a neat row. He thinks the calm, organized routine hides the tension in his jaw. It doesn't. I see every twitch.

I take the seat to Evie's left, close enough to track every shift in her breathing. In the hallway, she told me to stay quiet. "*Let me handle this,*" she said.

The older detective begins trying to run through his script.

Evelyn interrupts with a flick of her hand. "I know how interrogations work. Skip to the part where you accuse me of something."

He bristles. "Mrs. Dempsey, this is a formal interview—"

"Exactly why we shouldn't waste time pretending otherwise."

Graham adjusts his glasses, a polite signal for her to dial it back. She ignores him.

The older detective opens his notebook like it's a shield and tries to begin with something simple. "Let's walk through your timeline on Saturday, August twenty-fourth. Between eight and—"

Evelyn doesn't let him finish. "I was home. Working. You already have the emails I sent at 8:14, 8:27, and 8:39." She gestures toward his notes. "If your office missed them, that's your issue, not mine."

His jaw tightens. "We still need verbal confirmation."

"You have it," she says.

The younger detective tries a different angle. "What about the calls regarding the irrigation permit? Did you receive—"

"I discarded them," she replies before he finishes. She adjusts the cuffs of her coat like the question bores her. "None came from Graham or the county office, which means they didn't warrant my time. Again, something you'd know if you'd reviewed the documentation already sent."

The detective glances at Graham, probably hoping for backup, but Graham simply folds his hands and keeps his expression neutral. He knows better than to interrupt Evelyn when she's in this mood.

The older detective leans in, trying to regain footing. "Mrs. Dempsey, we need you to answer the questions directly, not talk circles around them."

"I'm answering directly," she says. "You're the ones struggling to keep up."

A flush creeps up his neck. The younger detective fidgets with his pen, taps it once against the paper, then thinks better of it.

They move on to the financials, but neither detective has fully recovered from her pace. "There were flagged transfers—"

"Routine," she interrupts, still in that smooth, unhurried tone. "Seasonal payroll adjustments, vendor invoices, supply orders tied to harvest prep. It's all in the financial package your office received almost two weeks ago."

The older detective hesitates. That pause gives her everything she wants. Her spine lengthens, her shoulders settle, and she folds her hands.

"If you plan to imply misconduct," she tells him, "at least come prepared with something substantive. You're floating in generalities, and I don't entertain fishing expeditions."

The younger detective shifts again, this time with a flicker of embarrassment. His eyes drop to his notes, but I can tell he isn't reading them. He's recalibrating, trying to decide how to redirect a conversation that slipped away from him ten minutes ago.

The quiet between them deepens until it becomes its own presence in the room. Evie doesn't rush to fill it. She lets it stand, controlled and unbroken, with the same patience she uses on boardrooms and auditors.

No one speaks.

Evelyn's gaze cuts between the detectives like someone evaluating candidates for a job they're not qualified for. She has always been measured and in control, but I can tell there's a tension beneath it today. Her breath is slightly too shallow. Her fingers are too still. Her posture is a touch tighter than usual. She looks invincible, but I know better. Her body telegraphs the strain in ways she thinks no one notices.

The detectives certainly don't. They exchange a look that carries frustration, irritation, and a hint of professional embarrassment. They expected defensiveness. They didn't expect someone who treats their interview like an inconvenience in her schedule.

Evelyn is winning the room easily. She's also pushing herself far harder than she should. Her control is flawless, but the cost of holding it is starting to show. The longer this goes, the more my worry for her increases.

She's not going to let up. She's not going to slow down. And the detectives are outmatched enough that they're only going to escalate.

The older detective clears his throat, like he's swallowing something sour. He straightens a stack of forms in front of him, buying time. "Let's move on," he says, "to communications between you and your operations team the week before the fire."

Evelyn folds her hands. "Go ahead."

He hesitates, reading whatever is on the top page with a frown. "We've reviewed a series of internal emails that raise concerns about the level of tension between you and your vineyard staff, specifically regarding the new irrigation system. There were disagreements about—"

"There are always disagreements," she says, calm and clipped. "That's what happens when you oversee people who mistake opinions for expertise."

The younger detective chokes back a snort and tries to hide it by pretending to adjust his notes. His partner shoots him a look sharp enough to cut glass.

Evelyn doesn't acknowledge either of them.

"We've also spoken with several employees who felt you were, how was it phrased?" The detective glances at his notes.

"Overly involved in the day-to-day operations."

"I own the vineyard," she replies. "Being involved is my job."

He tries again. "Some described your behavior as controlling."

"I bet they wouldn't say that about a man." She snorts. "Some people can't tell the difference between leadership and micromanagement because they've never experienced the former."

He pushes forward. "Mrs. Dempsey, we're not here to criticize your management style. We're trying to understand the circumstances leading up to the fire at the Paradise Hill cottage."

"Then ask better questions," she says.

He visibly swallows irritation. "Fine. Here's a better question." He leans forward. "Why did you override two separate staff recommendations to delay the installation of the new irrigation lines?"

Graham tenses beside her. He's preparing to intervene.

Evelyn doesn't give him the chance. "Because the recommendations were based on outdated information and fear of change," she says. "The vineyard needed the upgrade. We were already behind schedule."

"Behind schedule," the detective repeats, like he's holding the phrase up to the light. "Because of staffing shortages. Because of vendor delays. Because—"

"Yes," she says. "Those things happen. This is agriculture, not aerospace engineering."

He flips a page. "One of your staff indicated that you were *obsessed* with getting the lines installed before the end of the month."

"That staff member also once tried to prune a block of pinot as if it were merlot after a weekend bender," she says. "Do you want to continue citing him as a credible source?"

The younger detective's pen stops mid-scratch. He inhales like he's bracing for the next blow.

The older detective's patience thins. "Mrs. Dempsey—"

She raises a hand. Just two inches. Enough to stop him. "Detective, you keep circling the same point, hoping I'll eventually contradict myself. I won't. If you have actual evidence tying me to a fire, present it. Otherwise, this line of questioning is wasting everyone's time."

His face tightens. He doesn't like being called out, especially not with Graham sitting there. The younger detective's shoulders have slumped, like he's realized they walked into the wrong kind of storm.

I suspect she's not being entirely honest, but nonetheless, my grandmother is brilliant, commanding, and relentless. Everything she has always been.

She's also still pushing herself too hard. Her skin is paling under her makeup.

The older detective finally leans back, breaking eye contact. It's the closest he'll come to admitting she has outmaneuvered him. He tries a new approach. "All right, then let's talk about the fire's point of origin."

Evelyn stills. It's small, but I know her tells. Her fingers tighten around each other for a heartbeat before she smooths them flat again.

He notices the stillness too. And he pounces.

"Your staff mentioned you were especially focused on the northeast blocks the week before the fire."

That area is next to Paradise Hill and has a view of the cottage.

She keeps her voice even. "I'm focused on every block."

"But you were seen there late," he says. "Multiple times. After hours."

Her jaw flexes. Not anger. Not fear. Something controlled and private. "I was inspecting the irrigation installation," she says. "I do that often."

The younger detective sits up a little straighter, perhaps sensing opportunity. "Mrs. Dempsey, did you or did you not have any reason to be near the origin point of that fire the night it occurred?"

Graham inhales sharply, ready to object.

Evelyn gets there first. "No."

The older detective tilts his head. "You're sure?"

Her eyes narrow. "I don't use words I'm not sure of."

Silence settles across the table.

She's holding the line. But I can feel her standing on the edge of something she won't admit to.

Seems the detectives sense it too. And that makes them bold.

The older one leans in. "Mrs. Dempsey, I'm going to ask you directly. Is there anything you haven't told us, anything at all, that might explain your presence in that area before the fire started?"

Evelyn's smile is small and deliberate. "Detective, if I had been within twenty feet of that fire, you wouldn't need to ask. You'd have already found it on the Paradise Hill camera feeds."

The younger detective closes his file with a frustrated snap.

But they push harder. Ask whether she's been under pressure. Whether she's overwhelmed. Whether she's handling the business alone.

She slaps her palm against the table. "Overwhelmed? I run a vineyard. I'm not climbing Everest in heels."

"Evie—" I try, unable to help myself.

Her head turns slowly. One look shuts me up.

She stands, but it's too fast. Her hand skids along the table for balance. She tries to wave me off, but her fingers wobble, and her knees buckle a second later.

"Evie!"

I'm out of my chair, catching her before she hits the floor. Her head falls back against my arm, her breathing shallow.

"Call for an ambulance!" I bark. "Don't just stand there. Move."

The detectives freeze. Graham curses under his breath and fumbles for his phone.

A few minutes later, paramedics flood the room, and the

whole thing turns into organized chaos—oxygen mask, vitals check, questions thrown too fast for me to answer.

I crouch beside her, tapping her cheek. "Open your eyes. Come on. Open them."

She doesn't react.

They lift her onto a gurney. Leaving the two detectives behind, I follow, my heart pounding. They wheel her into the hallway, monitors beeping, paramedics shouting numbers that sound wrong.

Then something in the reflection of the wall monitor catches me.

A tiny movement.

Her eyelid flicks.

I surge forward and grab the gurney rail. "Stop."

The paramedic blinks at me. "Sir, we need to—"

"I said stop the gurney."

They hesitate. Evelyn's fingers curl, barely but deliberately, like she's checking that I'm watching.

My stomach bottoms out, and heat flashes through me. I lean down, my voice low and shaking. "If you're faking, say something. Right now."

Her lashes don't lift, but her mouth tightens just enough to confirm it.

Rage detonates. "You've got to be kidding me," I whisper. "You terrified me. You—"

Graham reaches us, breathless. "Ric, she needed an exit strategy—"

"Oh, don't defend her," I snap. "She played you. She played all of us."

Evelyn cracks one eye open, just barely. "Lower your voice."

I stare at her, furious. "That's what you have to say?"

"It worked," she murmurs, like this is a board meeting and she just out-negotiated a rival.

"You could've told me," I say. "You could've warned me. You didn't have to—"

"I improvised," she says.

"I thought you were dying."

That stops her. For a single beat, guilt flickers through her expression. It fades as quickly as it showed.

"I knew you would help," she says quietly.

"That's not an excuse."

The paramedics shift uncomfortably. One clears his throat. "We still need to run vitals. Even if this was…strategic."

Evelyn waves them forward as if they're housekeeping. "Do whatever you need to do."

I back away before I say something I can't take back. My hands shake, adrenaline still hammering through me.

Evelyn looks over as the paramedics adjust her mask. "Alaric," she says calmly, like none of this happened. "Pull yourself together. We have work to do."

"Oh, I'm together," I say, looking at the woman who faked a collapse to manipulate an interrogation and didn't think twice about what it would do to me. "And we're going to have a very different conversation when you're not on a gurney."

Her lips twitch like she finds that amusing.

Thirty-five

Liz

It takes Misty all week to make time to meet with me. But on Friday morning, she finally hovers outside my office door, clutching the drug trials binder like it offended her. Eventually, she crosses the room and settles into the chair across from me. It's the end of a long week where every attempt to meet turned into a cancellation or a sudden "*something came up*."

I figure I have nothing left to lose with her, so I'm going to be straightforward. "I know you wanted this job," I begin, keeping my voice calm. "And I know it didn't feel fair that I got it."

Her expression tightens before she reins it in. "It wasn't fair. I've been doing your job for years. I have a degree in hospital administration. And when the position came up? I wasn't considered. Not seriously." The hurt in her voice is palpable. This is something she's been carrying quietly because no one asked.

"I get why you're angry," I say. "And I agree that it wasn't handled well." I keep my hands flat on the table. "But if you still want to advance your career, I'd like to help you get there, and that only happens if we work well together."

Misty exhales, tension easing. She nods. "Okay."

We open the binder, and she shifts closer to guide me through everything—how new clinical trials come through the system, where she pulls the criteria lists, which physicians respond and which ones need persistent follow-up, how to navigate the electronic records without missing critical data. Her expertise shows in every sentence. I listen, letting her explain without interrupting.

At one point, I lean back, overwhelmed by the sheer volume of work. "This is a full-time job," I say.

"We're behind," she agrees. "Really behind. It'll take a lot to catch up."

I close the binder halfway and meet her eyes. "Can I be honest with you?"

She stiffens slightly. "Okay."

"I've caught bad numbers in everything you've given me or that I've asked you for. Every file. Every report."

Her face flushes a slow, painful red. She doesn't look away. "I know." Her voice is stripped bare. "I wasn't doing my best. I was angry with you. And at Hudson. And I let that color everything. It wasn't professional. I'm sorry."

Something inside me eases. "Thank you. How about we rebuild our working relationship? You begin where the tracking stopped on this project and clean things up. I'll handle the current month and work backward, and we'll meet in the middle. When we're done, we'll trade and check each other's work. Two sets of eyes. Clean slate."

She looks at me for a long moment, and then she nods. "That works. I like that."

I close the binder. "Great. Let's do it."

When she leaves, her steps are lighter, and the room feels different. This task—and probably a lot of others—will be much more manageable with someone reliable to share the load.

And there's no time like the present, so I open the file on my laptop and begin working through the hierarchy of hospital employees, making notes on what I'm seeing and what's missing.

Sometime later, Hudson taps lightly on my doorframe. He doesn't step inside, just leans in the way he always does, checking to see whether I'm buried in paperwork. "You're still coming tonight, right?"

I look up. "To the fundraiser? Yes. I'll be there."

He folds his arms. "Good. It's a big night. The board likes to see full participation."

"I know," I say. "I'm looking forward to it."

The lie sits oddly in my chest, too warm and too tight. I wish I could tell him the truth, that I'm doing my best to show up even though I don't feel ready.

He studies me quietly. "Are you okay?"

"Long week," I tell him. "But I'm fine. I had a great meeting with Misty earlier today."

He seems to accept that. "That's good. Don't be late. Registration opens at six."

"I won't."

He begins to leave, and then glances back. "And Liz? Good job with Misty."

The compliment surprises me. "Thank you. I think we're getting somewhere."

When he's gone, I sit back and let myself settle. The fundraiser looms, but now, I have a game plan and a path forward that I don't have to manage alone.

By five o'clock, my head is buzzing with a strange mix of fatigue and anticipation. I walk home quickly, knowing that if I slow down, I might talk myself out of going this evening. I thought I'd have Alaric at my side tonight.

When I get home, I focus on what's ahead and go straight to the closet.

The dress is a deep, almost-black blue with thin spaghetti straps and a fitted bodice that definitely requires Spanx. I pull it on and smooth the fabric over my hips. In the mirror, it looks better than I expected—simple but elegant.

I plug in my hot rollers and work through my hair before turning to my makeup. The routine steadies me, and after a few minutes, the face looking back feels composed, even if something beneath it isn't.

My phone rings just as I'm finishing my smoky eyes. *Trinity*. I pick up without greeting her. "Please tell me you're not already there," I say.

She lets out a thin laugh. "I'm sorry. I'm not feeling well enough to go. This baby is kicking my ass."

I freeze. "What?"

"I'm exhausted," she admits. "I don't want you to go alone. I know you'll know people there, but Ryker and Ginny offered to pick you up. They have a limo."

A pulse of disappointment moves through me. I'd counted on her company. But Trinity never calls for help unless she truly needs it.

"Okay, thank you. Don't worry about me," I say. "Rest. And tomorrow night, I'll watch Theo so you and Greyson can attend the dinner with his family."

"You're the best," she murmurs. "Have fun tonight. And don't let Ryker talk you into anything questionable."

"No promises."

After we hang up, I take out the rollers, letting my hair fall in soft curls, then grab my pink pashmina and wrap it around my shoulders. As I slip into my heels, the doorbell rings.

Ryker stands on my porch like he's auditioning for a whiskey ad—hands in his pockets, easy smile, hair perfectly tousled. His eyes sweep over me with warm appreciation. "Trinity didn't tell me I'd need riot gear to fend off half the hospital," he says.

I roll my eyes. "Please don't start."

"I'm complimenting," he says. "And also warning you

about Steve Julian. Keep a five-foot radius. Preferably ten. He's the hospital man-whore and will zero in on you."

I laugh, and it feels good. "He filled the job after you got married," I jab as I lock up and follow him to the SUV.

He opens the door. "He always had the job."

Ginny's waiting in the back of the limo. "You look gorgeous!" she shrieks as I enter. "Trinity's devastated that she's missing this."

I climb in as Ryker follows. "Her morning sickness has been ruthless," I say. "She needs a quiet night."

"I know," Ginny says, turning to face me. She chatters about Trinity's nesting instincts, her grandmother's drama, and a spreadsheet that refuses to behave. Her brightness fills the car, and watching her and Ryker together—the teasing, the shared rhythm—makes something twist inside me. That kind of closeness feels far away tonight.

When we pull up at the Delta Hotel, the entry glows with soft gold lights. Valets weave around guests in gowns and tailored suits. Ginny sighs happily when she spots the floral archway.

"My mother-in-law thinks this hotel is cold," she says. "But look at it. It's beautiful."

The driver stops at the front, and Ryker jumps out first to hold the door for Ginny and me with exaggerated chivalry. "Ready?"

"Not entirely."

He grins. "Perfect."

Inside, the ballroom is gorgeous, and the hotel doesn't feel cold at all—spring blooms in tall glass columns, green up-lighting, soft music. Ginny keeps hold of my arm as we head to check-in. I straighten my back, slipping into the version of myself I use at hospital events—presentable, composed, unruffled.

We're barely through the entrance when Janna Tayler from HR, the organizer of this event, spots me. She waves, clipboard in hand, headset tucked under her hair. "Liz!" She hugs me. "Thank you for coming. You look incredible."

"Thank you. This is beautiful."

She gestures to the man beside her. "My husband, John Chappell."

I smile as I recognize him. He's a neurologist at the hospital.

He offers a polite nod. We exchange pleasantries while Janna scans the room like she's waiting for a fire. It comes—figuratively—when someone waves frantically from across the room.

She sighs and touches John's arm. "Duty calls."

He nods and follows her. "Excuse us."

I wave them off and take a moment to admire the room before parting ways with Ginny and Ryker to head toward my table. The space feels alive—glamorous without being showy, elegant without being stiff. Couples move easily through the space.

My table is near the center, close enough to the stage to seem important. As I ease into my seat, the woman beside me offers a bright smile.

"You must be Liz," she says. "I'm Kathy. Roger's wife."

For a second, I blink. "It's nice to meet you," I tell her. "I forget Hudson's first name is Roger."

She laughs. "Everyone does. I almost didn't take his last name, but my maiden name was Schwarzkopf, and no one could pronounce it, let alone spell it, so Hudson won in the end."

She's warm, magnetic in a quiet way. I like her immediately.

Everyone makes it to the table, but the chair on my right stays empty. I try not to notice, but it tugs at me—what could have been, who should have been beside me. I force my attention back to Kathy as she talks about her kids and a disastrous past gala moment involving flaming meringue.

When the welcome begins, my mind drifts. I spot Janna and John near the front, leaning in as they whisper. They look easy together—comfortable, connected—a pairing that works.

It stings. Why did everything with Alaric twist itself into

complication? Why did we let something good become something impossible?

Hudson joins us, and dinner arrives—chicken, potatoes, green beans. I make myself eat a few bites. I smile when expected, nod when appropriate, and eventually try not to get lost in the swirl of couples heading toward the dance floor. But I can't help noticing the way people soften when they dance with someone they trust. After a few minutes, I reach down to find my bag under the table.

Kathy looks over. "You're not staying for dancing?"

"I should head out," I say. "Early morning tomorrow."

She gives me a knowing smile. "It was lovely to meet you."

Hudson bids me goodnight as well, and I gather my scarf and excuse myself. No one seems to notice me slipping out. Everyone's already halfway to the bar or wrapped around their partner on the dance floor.

The hallway is cooler, quieter. I pull up the rideshare app and step outside. The air is soft against my skin, carrying a hint of rain. My car arrives quickly, and I sink into the backseat, watching the hotel recede behind me. Only then do I text Ryker and Ginny to let them know I've gone.

The ride home is calm, almost meditative. When I reach my house, I thank the driver and step out, the cool air brushing my collarbone where my scarf has slipped.

Inside, the house is silent again. I stand for a moment, taking off my heels. I made it through the event. I showed up and did what I was supposed to.

But as I inhale the quiet, truth settles over me with a clarity I can't soften.

I miss Alaric. And pretending otherwise is becoming its own kind of heartbreak.

Thirty-six

Liz

I pull into my brother Mark's driveway a little after ten, sunlight bright off the windshield. It should feel like a normal Saturday, as we've done this several times since I came to town. As usual I've showed up in leggings and an old sweater, and I'll probably drink too much coffee while Nicky toddles from room to room, pushing trucks and babbling to himself. But I still feel a little off. There's a heaviness in my chest I can't shake, and I don't know what to do about it.

Nicky and Mark meet me on the sidewalk, and Nicky takes my hand to lead me in. When his excitement settles, Sam stops scurrying, and we're all seated at the kitchen table, Mark's attention returns to me. He pours me a cup of coffee and leans back, arms crossing in that familiar way that says he's done waiting for me to volunteer information.

"Did you stay long last night?" he asks.

"Long enough," I say, keeping it breezy.

Sam puts a stack of pancakes in front of me. "You left early, didn't you?"

My shrug feels stiff. "I stayed until everyone was off to dance with their partners."

Mark grunts softly. "Which means you didn't want to be there."

"It was fine," I repeat.

Nicky presses into my side, humming to himself as he drags a crayon in messy loops across a piece of paper Sam has slid in front of him. His weight is warm and unguarded, the simple trust of it amazing to me.

Mark clears his throat. "You know you don't have to pretend with us."

I keep my eyes on my coffee. "I'm not pretending."

Except I am. And they both know it.

Sam nudges my plate. "Eat a little. You'll feel better."

I take a bite to appease her, but the food sits heavy. My mind drifts back to last night.

Mark taps his fork against his plate. "So," he says, "what actually happened?"

"Nothing. Really. I just wasn't feeling it. I'm new here, and I didn't feel like explaining over and over who I was and why I left Vancouver."

Sam studies my face in that soft, steady way of hers.

"It was just one of those nights," I continue. "Crowded. Loud. Everyone seemed to know everyone." I shake my head. "It wasn't dramatic. I just felt out of place without a date, so I left."

Mark leans forward. "How come you didn't bring a date?"

"I don't really know anyone," I say. "Trinity was supposed to come, but she wasn't feeling well. I rode there with her brother-in-law and his wife, but they were seated elsewhere, and my coworkers were all there with their partners."

He doesn't respond right away.

I set my fork down. "It just...didn't feel good, being there by myself."

Mark's gaze sharpens—not judgment, just recognition. "You felt alone."

"Yeah," I say quietly. "I guess I did."

Sam reaches across the table and rests her fingers around my wrist. "You could've called."

"And had you come rescue me?" I huff. "Not a chance."

Mark wipes his hands on a towel and drapes it over the back of his chair.

"Liz," he says, "you don't have to pretend this move hasn't been harder than you expected."

I open my mouth, but he shakes his head.

"You've always been the one who steps in," he continues. "At work. With us. With Mom. You smooth things over. Hold everything together."

Sam nods. "You do so much for everyone."

"And you don't let anyone take care of you," he adds.

I look between them, eyes wide.

Sam covers my hand with hers. "You deserve the same care you give everyone else."

My throat tightens.

Sam gives my hand a gentle squeeze. Mark leans back, satisfied but not smug.

"It's not complicated," Sam says softly. "You're lonely. Not because you don't have people, but because you're not letting yourself want more."

That pulls a groan from me. "It feels like I've been on autopilot," I admit. "Work, home, repeat. Everyone else is living, and I'm just…orbiting around their lives."

"Then change the orbit," she says.

Nicky climbs into my lap without warning, warm and a little sticky, pressing his cheek against my shoulder.

"Stay," he says softly.

I laugh, the sound surprised out of me, and kiss the top of his head. "I'm not leaving yet, and I'll always be back soon, sweetheart."

Mark smiles.

"You're allowed to want a life," Sam says.

"I want something real," I agree.

"Then let yourself have it," she replies.

As breakfast winds down, I feel calmer, though I'm still not sure what I want to do. Nicky toddles off toward the living room, chanting something about trucks, leaving syrupy fingerprints on my sleeve.

I help Sam clear the plates while Mark dries his hands.

"What are you doing for the rest of the day?" she asks.

"Not much," I tell her. "I'm going to Trinity's later to watch Theo so she and Greyson can do something with his family. Until then…nothing."

"Good." She bumps my elbow. "Give yourself a quiet afternoon."

Mark walks me to the door and pauses before opening it.

"You're allowed to want things," he says softly. "In your real life."

I let out a breath. "I know."

"I'm not sure you do," he says. "But you will."

"I'm trying," I say.

"That's all I want."

Nicky barrels into me for one last hug, arms wrapping around my thighs. I hold him close.

"Bye, Izzie," he says, waving before the hug even ends.

"I'll be back soon," I promise.

By the time I pull into Trinity and Greyson's condo driveway, the afternoon has settled into that quiet, in-between light where shadows stretch long across the lawn. I'm early by almost an hour. But she told me to come anytime, and after this morning, sitting alone at home felt like slipping backward.

I ring her unit out of habit even though she always tells me not to bother. She buzzes me in and Trinity meets at the elevator with Theo balanced on one hip, his small hand fisted in her sweater.

"You're early," she says, smiling. "Good. I'm so sorry about last night."

Theo reaches out the second he sees me. I take him without thinking, settling his warm little body against mine. He smells like apple slices and whatever toddler lotion Trinity buys in bulk.

"It worked out."

Her eyes sharpen a little at that. She steps back to let me in. "Rough day?"

"I'm just figuring some things out."

She nods without demanding information. She pulls her hair into a loose ponytail as she walks toward the kitchen. "Greyson's with his family already. I'm supposed to go meet them, but then Theo refused his nap and found the markers."

I follow her, Theo bobbing gently against my shoulder. "How bad was it?"

She points to a faint green smear on her jeans. "Let's just say Crayola owes me."

Theo pats my cheek and whispers something that sounds like "truck." I nod as if I understand him because that's what he wants.

Trinity stops at the counter and looks at me again, her expression questioning. "Are you sure you're okay?" she asks.

I shift Theo's weight in my arms. "I will be."

"Do you want to talk about it?"

"Maybe later," I say. "I'm still figuring out what I'm feeling."

She accepts that. It's one of the things I love most about her. She's intuitive without being invasive.

"Well," she says, "you're here now. That's something."

"It is."

She grabs her purse and coat. "If you don't mind, I think I'll go ahead and go. Theo's already eaten. He'll want to play for a while, and then he'll crash. If he gets fussy, sit with him in the rocker."

"I've got him," I assure her.

She pauses, watching me. "You seem…softer today."

"I had breakfast with Mark and Sam."

She steps closer and squeezes my arm. "Let yourself lean a little, Liz. You don't have to do everything alone."

Her words land almost exactly where Mark's did. I'm so lucky to have these supports.

"I'm trying," I say.

"Good." She grabs her keys. "Because you deserve more than just surviving."

I look down at Theo, who is now gently tugging on my necklace like he's testing its limits.

"Yeah," I agree. "I'm starting to believe that."

And I'd like to be walking toward something instead of just standing still.

Thirty-seven

Alaric

My phone rings just as I'm settling in with my tea at my desk. Josie's calling early enough on a Saturday that I'm worried before I even answer.

"Hey," I say in greeting. "Is everything okay?"

Josie doesn't waste time. "She's still in bed this morning."

I know exactly who she means. A knot forms in my stomach. "Is she pouting?"

Josie sighs. "I don't think this is a stunt. She sounds tired, not evasive, just worn down. Of course, I didn't know she was going to pretend to pass out at the police questioning."

I pinch the bridge of my nose. I rode with Evie to the hospital yesterday in the ambulance, furious the whole time. I told her she couldn't keep pulling escape hatches every time consequences got close. She didn't fight me. Didn't argue. She just absorbed it.

And then she slipped out of the hospital as soon as the wheels on the gurney hit the ground. Graham opened the car door, she got in, and that was that. Left me standing in the ambulance bay. I haven't spoken to her since.

I sit back. "So what's happening now?"

"Well," Josie says, "she's…asking for you."

That part throws me. Evie rarely asks for anything unless it strategically benefits her. "She said that?"

"Yes. Directly." Josie hesitates. "I wouldn't call if it wasn't important."

I look over my desk—half-finished notes, unread emails, the week ahead pressing at the edges of my mind. *I'm behind. I don't have time for this*. I also know I'm going.

"Okay," I tell her. "I'll come by."

Josie exhales. "Thank you. I'll let her know."

I gather my things and swear to myself that I'll get back to my work as soon as I can. And then I go out to my SUV.

I leave the parking garage a few minutes later and travel toward the bridge. The lake is calm beneath a thin layer of haze, the surface silvered and still. I follow the curve of the shoreline and try to convince myself this is just Evie being Evie—nothing to be too worried about.

But why do I keep showing up when every interaction ends the same way? She pushes. I bend. She pulls. I follow. A rhythm I learned too young and haven't managed to unlearn. I don't know if I'm going out of concern or obligation. I just know I'm tired of pretending this doesn't get to me.

The road curves past the marina. I grip the wheel a little tighter.

Josie meets me at the front door before I can knock. She looks like she hasn't slept, arms folded tight across her ribs.

"Thanks for coming," she says.

I nod and step inside. I'm instantly back to my childhood. The Dempsey house has always been curated within an inch of its life—no fingerprints, no clutter, nothing out of place. Even now, with everything unraveling around Evie, the home still presents as immaculate.

I spent so many afternoons here before my father was pushed out. Running through the hallways. Sneaking cookies. Sitting at the edge of adult conversations I didn't understand. And then one day, it stopped. The doors that had always been open clicked shut, and no one said my father's name again unless it was to cast him as the villain.

Then the focus became her other son, my uncle Franklin—Dylan, Kaitlyn, Logan, and Matthew's father. He was the center of her attention for over a year until she disinherited him.

She then moved to her daughter, Eleanor, and that lasted only about two weeks before she was removed from the family and Evie's focus moved to me. With her blessing, I went away to UBC in Vancouver to study viticulture and oenology. But then I took an elective class in psychology my first semester and changed my major. I realized how fucked up my family was, and I knew the wine business wasn't for me. I didn't tell her for a while, and by the time I did, Sera and Josie were working for her, so she took it a little better than she would have otherwise. But she was still mad. She's been trying to get me back into the fold ever since.

I follow Josie down the hallway, footsteps soft on the runner. We pass the old portraits. Evie in her prime, sharp-eyed and regal. My father beside her in the early frames before he disappeared.

"Is she awake?" I ask.

"I think so," Josie says. "She's been quiet, but I told her you were coming."

I nod, and we continue to the door at the end of the hall, the primary suite Evie has claimed as her throne room for as long as I can remember.

Josie gives a small, apologetic sigh and pushes the door open. Then she steps aside, letting me enter alone.

The room is dim, the curtains half-closed. I pause, steadying myself. This house holds many versions of me, and none of them knows what to do with the woman waiting on the other side of this silence.

I move toward the bed.

Evie is propped against a stack of pillows, covers smoothed to her waist, eyes closed as if she's posing for a portrait of serenity. It's unsettling. She's never been serene a day in her life.

I pull up a chair and look at her. I can hear her breathing—steady, controlled, nothing like someone who can't get out of bed. She's just choosing not to. Her hair is brushed, her lipstick faint but present. Even her flannel robe is arranged as if a stylist had a hand in it. A small tremor moves through her fingers as she adjusts the blanket.

This isn't an illness. This is theater layered over time catching up with her.

"Sorry," I say. "Wasn't sure if you were awake."

"I'm in bed, not in a coma." Her eyes open. "You look disappointed."

"I'm not disappointed." I study her face. "Just trying to understand what's going on. Josie said you haven't gotten up."

She presses her lips together, annoyed. "Josie shouldn't have called you."

"She said you asked for me," I remind her.

Evie lifts one shoulder. "I said your name. That apparently counts as an invitation in this house."

I hold her gaze. "Are you actually not feeling well?"

She sniffs, offended. "I am eighty-two years old. I've earned the right to stay in bed if I choose."

Of course, she turns it into a power statement. Even under a comforter, she negotiates for the upper hand.

I lean forward, forearms on my knees. "You asked for me," I repeat. "Why?"

She studies me, probably arranging her words. Finally, she says, "Because, sometimes, it's useful to know who will show up."

There it is. Vulnerability dressed as strategy.

"Fine," I say softly. "I'm here. What do you need?"

Evie relaxes, as if my presence restores something in her. She closes her eyes, not in rest, but in triumph she thinks I can't see.

"So," she says, "tell me what my family is doing."

There's the first hook.

"Everyone's managing," I offer.

She huffs. "Non-answer."

"It's the truth."

Her eyes flick open. "My children don't know what they're doing. And the grandchildren are worse. They think there's a mystery that requires posturing." Her gaze narrows. "What are they saying?"

I hold her stare. "I feel certain you already know."

Evie smiles, though not warmly. "And at the hospital? What are you hearing about my little…incident?"

"Episode," I say. "That's what people are calling it."

She accepts the terminology with a regal nod. "And?"

"People are curious, confused, trying to figure out why you collapsed in the middle of a police interview and walked out ten minutes later."

She lifts her chin. "I needed an exit."

"I know," I say. "You told me."

Her eyes soften—not remorse, just recognition. "You were angry with me."

"I was honest with you."

Evie studies me, as if I'm a problem she's trying to solve. "You think I manipulate you."

"I know you do," I say evenly. "You manipulate everyone."

Her fingers tighten around the blanket. "Yet here you are."

"Because Josie called," I tell her. "Not because you staged another issue. And not because you whispered my name when you knew she'd overhear."

Her lips curve, tasting the truth. "You showed up. That matters more than why."

I sit back. Such a simple sentence, carrying a lifetime of

expectation—her belief that proximity equals loyalty, and loyalty equals usefulness.

"I worry about you, you know," she says after a moment. "You don't make it easy to care."

There it is, the slide from strategy into guilt.

"I'm fine," I tell her. "You don't need to worry about me."

She closes her eyes again, but the expression isn't peaceful. It's calculating. She's taking inventory. Measuring what landed.

For the first time, I'm not pulled in. I'm just watching her, seeing it from the outside. She's not the myth, not the matriarch, not the architect. She's just a woman who's spent her life bending the world and doesn't know how to stop.

Her brow tightens. "Something's different."

She's right. But I'm not ready to say what changed.

Evie settles deeper into the pillows. She's tracking me through lowered lashes, waiting for me to fall back into the rhythm, the one where she speaks and I absorb.

For most of my life, that was enough. Not today.

She lets a few seconds pass. "You're quiet," she says.

"I'm thinking."

"That's usually when you get yourself into trouble."

I almost smile. It would be easy to fall into the old dance. "I'm not in trouble," I assure her. "Not this time."

She shifts, seeming irritated by my calm. "Then say what's on your mind."

She only wants the version of my truth she can use. Still, I draw a slow breath.

"I've spent a long time letting other people decide who I need to be," I tell her. "You. Dad. Everyone after. I've spent years running from anything that looks like love because I didn't trust myself to choose it. Or keep it."

She blinks, seeming surprised I'm offering this without her coaxing.

"And?" she presses.

"And I'm done with that," I say. "I'm done repeating patterns that never belonged to me."

Evie's expression tightens—the faintest recoil. "You think I made you this way," she says.

"I think I let you shape more of me than I should have," I answer. "That's on me, not you."

Her fingers twitch. A crack in the armor. "You don't have to push me out to grow up."

"I'm not pushing you out." I hold her gaze. "I'm stepping away. That's different. I told you years ago I didn't want this."

"I never changed my will. You're still set to inherit the vineyard."

"I don't want it."

"That's why you're listed."

"It should be Sera and Josie."

Something crosses her face, her breath catching. For a heartbeat, she looks not offended but startled. Does she think my education and career are just a ruse to show my independence before I give in and take over the vineyard? She's delusional.

We sit in suspended quiet. Even the air feels paused. Then Evie looks away first. Perhaps she's recalibrating, rewriting her understanding of me.

"You've always been difficult," she mutters, but without sting. Something else flickers—maybe respect, maybe fear, maybe both.

I rise from the chair. Not dramatic. Not angry. Just choosing to stand. "I'll check on you tonight," I tell her. "Get some rest."

She doesn't argue. She just watches me.

I leave the room with a strange clarity. I'm not walking away, still carrying her as a burden. I'm simply walking away.

Thirty-eight

Liz

I stare at my phone, as if locked in some sort of battle of wills. After my lack of a date at the fundraiser last weekend, I know I should do something. I've opened and closed Unsingle, the dating app, at least six times, but I've yet to set up a profile.

It was another long day at work, though, and now, I'm home alone. Again.

Trinity's voice drifts through my mind, steady and annoyingly right. She keeps telling me to get out more, to meet people the way I used to back in Vancouver.

But I was lighter then, not stuck in place waiting for someone else to sort out their emotional mess. Still, the more I think about it, the more I know she's right.

I brushed her off, but maybe that was a mistake. I even

joked about how terrible my last dating-app experience was. I told her Paradise was too small and too interconnected and too full of people who knew each other's business before breakfast.

But here I am two days later, and now, her advice is wearing down the resistance I had left.

The sign-in page glows up at me. I take a breath and scroll through the profile photos it shows as examples. It's mostly local scenery shots and bad-lighting selfies. I hesitate. Then curiosity wins. I tap the option that lets you browse anonymously before joining.

Faces slide across the screen. People just use first names, and that makes me feel a little better. I see a nurse from the fourth floor, one of the imaging techs, a paramedic I've seen in the ED bay once or twice, and then a firefighter who was at one of the Paradise family parties. He wore a red flannel shirt and had the kind of smile that made everyone feel welcome. I remember thinking he looked like the type who would help someone change a tire in the rain. He's leaning against a work truck in his photo. His dog sits at his feet in another. His profile is simple and warm.

I let out a slow breath. This doesn't feel as awful as I expected. No one is leering. No one is trying too hard. It's just people looking for connection.

It's time to walk toward something else instead of waiting for Alaric to decide which direction he wants to look. I want a life that keeps moving.

I go back to the profile-creation page and scroll through my photos. Most are work shots or crooked selfies with Trinity where we're both laughing too hard to look decent. I stop on one where I'm in a soft sweater, hair down, standing near the water at Black Bear Lake. It's calm and natural. I look like myself, not the version who's trying to impress anyone. Just me.

I upload it and watch the bar crawl across the screen. My pulse ticks up as the profile preview appears. I add a short line about liking coffee, quiet mornings, and people who can laugh at themselves. I keep editing until it reads the way I want to feel—

steady, open, ready for something uncomplicated.

My thumb hovers over the final confirmation. I almost chicken out again.

Then I think about Alaric being lost in the drama of his family, too busy holding up Evie's world to notice mine tipping sideways. I don't think he can help it. His life is complicated. His family is loud. But I can't keep shrinking my own life, trying to fit into a gap I'm hoping he leaves open.

I tap confirm.

The screen shifts and welcomes me in.

I smile, feeling like I chose myself for the first time in a long time. It's a soft kind of brave, a quiet kind of hopeful.

A message pops up from the app. Someone liked my profile.

I laugh under my breath. Of course, that's how this works. You wait forever for one man to notice you, and the second you step forward into something else, the world gives you a tiny wink and a nudge.

I close the app and set the phone on the table. Tomorrow, I'll decide what to do next. Tonight, it's enough that I tried.

I slept well last night for the first time in a while. And this morning I don't feel a wave of regret or want to immediately delete the app before too many people notice me there. Instead, I feel strangely light. The thought of checking my phone brings a flicker of curiosity rather than dread.

When I log in, there are four notifications. I stare at the number and shake my head because that's three more than I expected after the one last night. I swipe them open while I sip my coffee. One is a wave from a guy who lives down in Black Bear. Too far.

The next like is from Brian, the firefighter I recognized last night. His profile has a simple message.

Brian: Hey. Funny enough, we've probably been at the same events around town without even knowing it. I'm a total morning person, so I'm usually up before the sun. The lake's my favorite place to unwind.

I smile at the screen. The tone is easy, like an actual human talking to me instead of some performative dating-app version of himself.

The next is Josh, a nurse from the hospital. I've seen him in the cafeteria, but we've never spoken. His message is short.

Josh: Really like that photo of you by the water. Is that Black Bear Lake?

His spelling is correct, his punctuation intentional—little signs he actually read my profile. The message feels polite. Friendly in a way I didn't expect.

The final message opens while I'm scrolling.

Dylan: Hey there. I run my own business here in town. My photo's from one of the vineyards—figured it was more fun than a selfie.

Me: Hello.

Three conversations start at once, which is overwhelming in a good way. I answer in short, honest lines, and they all respond quickly.

Brian: What do you like to do on weekends?

Josh: How long have you lived in Paradise?

Dylan: I like my morning coffee the way I like my days—strong, warm, and not trying to test me.

That makes me laugh.

None of these exchanges feel like they're trying to push for anything. I'm allowed to be curious without making promises.

I pause in the middle of typing and glance at the clock. I'm going to be late if I don't get moving, but I don't feel overly concerned. The morning doesn't feel like something I have to muscle through. It feels open. That has nothing to do with romance and everything to do with the fact that for once I'm not waiting for my life to orbit around someone else's timeline.

Brian: Would you be up for grabbing coffee?

My breath catches. I'm not sure why this part lands differently. It's simple. It's real. It's someone who is not tangled in a storm of family chaos seeing me clearly enough to ask.

Me: I'm not sure about my schedule this week, but I'm open to talking.

It's honest and safe and hopefully still forward enough to keep the door cracked.

The second I hit send, my phone lights up again. Josh sends another message. Dylan responds with a laughing line.

But it's too much to juggle while getting ready for work, so I silence notifications and place my phone on the table.

I finish my coffee with a smile that feels completely unforced. Whatever is going to happen next can wait. I'll get there when I'm ready for it.

I dress quickly and head into work. The walk is brisk, my heart is thumping, and I'm feeling good about myself. In the elevator line, I accept coffee invitations from all three men over the next several days. A tiny pulse of nerves spikes as I imagine actually sitting across from each of them, but I push past it because this is what choosing myself looks like.

When I get upstairs, Misty's already at her desk, her hair pulled into a loose knot and her glasses low on her nose.

"Morning," I say as I set my bag down.

She glances up with a small smile. "Morning. Are we still good for ten o'clock?"

"Yes." I need to put a few finishing touches on what I promised her, but that's more than enough time.

With a wave, I close myself into my office, and while my computer boots up, I text Trinity.

Me: I took your advice and joined a dating app last night. I already have three dates this week.

Trinity: That's great. Who are they and what do they do?

Me: I only have first names, and I believe it's a firefighter, a nurse, and a small-business owner. I'll keep you posted.

Trinity: 💋

I respond to a few emails and get everything updated for Misty. I hope I got this right. There's a knock on my door right at ten, and I wave her in.

"I was going to get a cup of coffee. Would you like one?" she asks.

I'm sure she sees my obvious surprise. "Um, yes. Sure. Black is great."

"I'll be right back."

She's gone just long enough for me to straighten my desk so I can focus on this meeting.

She hands me the coffee and takes a seat.

"It's so much colder here than it is in Vancouver. Thank you."

She nods. "I agree. The higher elevation means the valley

gets colder."

I set out my binder. "How did it go?"

Misty reaches into a folder and hands me a stack of printed reports. They're clipped neatly. There are no crooked pages, no half-filled cells. It takes me a second to understand what I'm looking at. "I got the data caught up," she says. "We still need to do the reporting, which takes longer, but this gets us there faster."

I blink because we only agreed to do this last week. I expected maybe two months of data populated, not a full handoff.

"This is the current month," I say, feeling like a slacker.

Misty nods. "And this is the last year. All updated."

My mouth actually falls open. *The entire previous year*? Clean. Formatted. Balanced. I flip through the pages and look at her again. "How did you get all this done?"

She shrugs. "I sat down this weekend and knocked it out. I just needed some uninterrupted time, and I fell into a rhythm."

I turn the pages again because I need to verify that my eyes are not lying. The formulas are corrected. The entries are cleaned. The rolling totals flow the way they're supposed to. I press my thumb against the corner of the stack and shake my head.

"It took me all weekend to get the current month updated," I tell her.

Misty smiles at that. Not smug. Not defensive. Just pleased that she delivered what I asked. "I like this kind of work," she says. "Once the framework is in place, the rest is straightforward."

As I sit with the stack in my hands, I let a single thought rise to the surface. The information wasn't correct before. What I didn't know was whether that was due to carelessness or something else. But this version of Misty is capable and trying, and I can see that now.

We go over what we've put together, and the meeting winds down with nothing more than a few notes about what she wants to handle next. I tell her I'll go through everything today and confirm the data, but the truth is already settling in. This is good. Better than good. This is the first time since I arrived that I have a partner who can help me be better at my job. Things may finally turn a corner.

Once she's gone, I open the spreadsheet on my laptop and begin verifying entries. Each line that checks out widens my smile.

By the time lunch rolls around, my eyes are a little blurry. I shut my laptop and stretch before heading to the cafeteria. The smell of soup and grilled bread drifts into the hallway as I step inside. I pick up a salad and a tea, already planning to eat quietly in a corner while I sort through messages that have nothing to do with work.

A nurse with dark hair pulled into a sleek ponytail waves me down near the dessert case. She walks over with a warm smile.

"You're Liz, right?" she asks. "I'm Maggie Chu. I work on fourth."

I return her smile. "Nice to meet you."

She leans in a little. "I saw you on Unsingle last night. I hope that's not weird. This town is small. When someone new pops up, they stand out."

I feel my face warm, but Maggie laughs softly and shakes her head.

"Don't be embarrassed. It's actually great. There are so few women on there. Men outnumber us by a mile in this valley."

She gestures toward an empty table by the window. "Come have lunch with me. I can give you the rundown if you want it."

I follow because her tone is light and inviting, and I could use a little company today. We sit across from each other, and Maggie opens her yogurt while giving me a curious look.

"So, how is it going so far? Any luck?"

I laugh. "More than I thought. I actually have three coffee dates lined up."

Her eyebrows lift. "That sounds about right. Men on this

app are eager. And bored. And convinced that their next great love is hiding within a ten-mile radius."

Her teasing makes me laugh again.

"The nice thing is you get to be selective," she says. "Do not say yes to anyone unless the vibe feels easy. And always meet them in a public place. Everyone knows everyone. It keeps things comfortable."

"That makes sense," I say. "I figured coffee was a safe start."

"It's the best start," she says with a nod. "No pressure. No long meals. No expectations. If you like them, you can stay longer. If you don't, you have an easy exit."

I take a bite of my salad and relax into the conversation. Maggie talks about her own experiences with Unsingle. Some dates were sweet. Some were bland. One ended abruptly when the man realized she often worked the night shift and assumed that meant she wouldn't be spontaneous. She laughs at that, and I laugh with her.

"It can be fun if you go in with an open mind," Maggie says. "Just treat it like meeting people. Nothing more. If something comes of it, that's great. If not, you still had a coffee and got out of the house."

I nod. That's all I want from this, a way to step forward instead of waiting for someone else's storm to clear.

We finish lunch and gather our trays, and Maggie gives my arm a quick squeeze.

"If you ever need a wingwoman or someone to debrief with, I'm around," she says. "And if any of these guys get weird, come find me. I have a sixth sense for trouble."

"Thank you," I say. "Really."

"Of course." She smiles and waves as we go our separate ways. "Welcome to the club."

Thirty-nine

Alaric

My grandmother called this morning and asked me to join her for dinner this evening. After our difficult encounter earlier this week, I expected silence. Instead, she's kept talking to me. That alone feels like a win. Maybe tonight I can convince her to take my name out of the will and put Sera and Josie where they belong. All I know is it can't be my cousins who inherit the vineyard—and it shouldn't be me.

I pull into her driveway, expecting a quiet Friday night, maybe a chance to make some real progress. But once I stop the car, I just stare. Every light in the house is on. There are too many cars packed into the driveway—all of my cousins are here. She didn't tell me anyone else was coming.

A quiet dinner was never the plan.

I grip the steering wheel. It feels stupid to hesitate, but

something in my body recognizes the setup before my brain admits it. There's a familiar tightening under my ribs, the same place that always braces before one of her storms. I should turn around now and walk away. I can't keep doing this with her. But practically speaking, my absence only gives Dylan and Scott an advantage. I can't let Sera and Josie down. So I get out of my car, trying to ignore the fact that once again, this is what I always do.

I walk up the steps, my neck tight. I push open the door, and Evie is already at the head of the table, several of my cousins seated around her. She has her wool suit coat on and a scarf wrapped around her neck. She doesn't stand or greet me. She just watches me walk in.

"Did you get lost?" she asks, her voice smooth, the practiced version she uses when she wants the insult to sound playful.

"I'm on time," I tell her.

"Then you're late," she mutters, perfectly pitched so it carries across the room.

I step closer and take in the scope of things. Sera's place. Josie's. Dylan's. Matthew's. Mine. All set and waiting. At least I wasn't last.

She didn't mention any of this when she called earlier to remind me about the evening.

She tracks my gaze and offers a small, tight smile that isn't warm in any way. It feels like a warning. "Sit," she says. "We're just waiting on your sisters and the rest of your cousins."

I move to the chair she always keeps open for me at her left, close enough for her to tug me in when she needs me. But not close enough to make it look like I have any actual power at this table. I lower myself into the seat and feel the familiar pinch in my throat. Sitting here feels like I'm making a choice I swore I wouldn't keep making. But I can't abandon my sisters.

I try to relax my shoulders, but the effort falls short. I rest my hands on the table and try to pretend I don't feel the shift in the air. Something is coming. I can sense it.

And Evie looks ready.

The front door opens again, and Sera steps inside. She moves, as if she's late even though she isn't. "Hi," she says, a little breathless.

"You're finally here," Evie notes, and Sera's posture shrinks by an inch.

Sera's cheeks go pink before she even takes off her coat. She's hoping tonight will go better than the last few weeks have.

It won't.

Sera slips into the chair beside Evie, the one closest to her right hand. Her shoulders lift and settle, and she smooths her napkin with nervous fingers. She keeps touching the edge of her phone and then pulling her hand back like she's scolding herself for needing the comfort.

Another minute passes before the door opens again and Josie appears. Her smile is warmer, softer, almost hopeful. It fades the moment Evie's eyes land on her.

"You look tired," Evie says.

Josie shrugs. "Long day."

"Then try doing it better," Evie says lightly.

Breathe in. Count to four. Breathe out. Count to four.

Josie crosses the room and sits next to me. She folds her napkin once and sets her hands in her lap.

She glances at me, worry or warning in her eyes. But I can't do anything with it. Not now. Not with Evie coiled the way she is.

Dylan finally strolls in. He has a loose, easy swagger that makes him seem amused by everything. "Evening," he says with a grin.

"You're late," Evie snaps.

He drops his phone onto the table and flicks it into a spin. Evie watches it whirl. Her jaw tightens. Dylan sees it but pretends he doesn't. He thrives on the reaction.

"Traffic," he lies.

"There's no traffic in Paradise," Josie says under her breath.

"That's what made it so surprising," Dylan shoots back.

Scott follows with quiet steps, the exact opposite of his cousin. He keeps his head down and takes the seat next to Josie.

"Hi, Ric," he murmurs.

"Hey," I say. "Rough day?"

He gives a small shrug. "Just the usual."

Scott folds his arms, scanning the table with a half-smile that dares someone to challenge him. He hasn't said a word yet, but he's already set the hostile-takeover tone. With the room now full around us, the tension thickens. Evie has shaped this entire evening into some kind of test.

The servers move into the room with the first course, setting plates in front of each of us. But no one reaches for their fork. No one speaks.

Not until she gives the signal.

Evie lifts her chin and surveys the table. She looks satisfied in a way that makes my skin feel too tight. This is exactly what she wanted, the entire room watching, waiting, trying to anticipate her next move.

I let my gaze drift over the table. The pressure builds, like the air before a thunderclap. Evie sits straighter, fingers tapping on the stem of her wine glass. No words. Just a small click of her nails against the crystal.

She has our attention. And every part of me wants to be anywhere else. Most of us are just poking at the food, but Dylan and Matthew dive right in to clean their plates.

After a few minutes, Evie lifts her glass and holds it there like she's calling a meeting to order.

"Updates," she says.

Sera jumps first. She always does. Her voice wavers as she explains something about the community board and the letters they've started sending. She tries to talk strategy and upcoming deadlines.

"I thought maybe if we scheduled—" Sera says.

Evie cuts her off.

"You're letting them set the pace. You sound unsure."

Sera blinks. "I'm not unsure. I just—"

"You're apologizing," Evie says. "You don't even hear yourself anymore."

Breathe in. Count to four. Breathe out. Count to four.

Sera swallows and tries again. She barely gets three words out before Evie slices her open a second time.

"That's enough. If you can't speak with conviction, then don't speak at all."

Sera's shoulders cave in. She nods. It's habit at this point, not agreement.

Josie steps up next. Her voice is steadier. She talks about the community backlash and the conversations happening online after Evie's recent questioning by the police. She's trying to sound informed and calm.

"I've been tracking the messaging," Josie says. "There's a pattern forming, and we might need to—"

"You're spinning too many possibilities," Evie interrupts. "Stop trying to predict every angle and act."

Josie stiffens, lifts her chin, but swallows whatever she wanted to say.

Dylan watches them, his face a mask. He taps his fork against his plate, a sharp metallic sound.

"Well, at least you're thinking," he mutters toward Josie. "More than I can say for Sera."

Sera flinches. "Can you not tonight?" she whispers.

"Why?" Dylan whispers back. "We're all here for the roast."

"Enough," Josie warns.

Dylan smirks.

Evie sets her fork down.

"Dylan," she says. "Tell me why I should keep you involved at all."

His grin fades. "What?"

"You heard me."

He tries to brush it off. "Because I'm delightful?"

Evie doesn't move. She watches like she's waiting for him to understand something about himself he never will.

He straightens. "I've got meetings lined up tomorrow. I'll bring you something concrete."

Evie doesn't blink. "You'd better."

Silence settles over the table. No one moves more than necessary. Even breathing feels risky. The servers sense it too, gliding along the walls without a clink or scrape.

The next round of plates appears. When a salad is set in front of Sera, and only Sera, something in me ignites. Evie only does this when she's decided Sera needs "managing." It's the same move she used when Sera was a teenager, already cracking under her expectations. A flash of Sera crying in my passenger seat jolts through me. She gives me a tiny shake of her head—*don't.*

But I can't just sit here. "How are the vines looking, Sera?" I ask.

"They're starting to push," she murmurs. "But it's early. One frost and we'll be chasing damage for months." Her fork trembles. She pretends it doesn't. I play along.

No one is really eating. Forks lift only to move the food around, plates staying fuller than they should. Sera pushes a cherry tomato to the side. Josie saws bread. Dylan pauses mid-bite, as if he's waiting for a blast.

Evie alone eats with appetite, her gaze drifting from face to face, using silence the way some people use knives. A conversation tries to start, then dies.

Twice someone lifts a fork, and Evie asks a question sharp enough to stop them mid-motion—first Sera, then Josie. Each lowers their hand, flustered, and Evie watches the misstep like it's a confirmation.

Eventually, the servers return to clear plates, though most of the food remains untouched. Dylan shifts closer. He waits until Evie looks away before leaning in my direction.

"I've got a coffee date tomorrow," he murmurs.

I keep my eyes on the tablecloth. "Why are you telling me this?"

"With your friend Liz."

My breath stutters. The word lands like a punch in the direct and humiliating way only family can manage. Dylan sees it. He was waiting for it. His smile bends, slow and satisfied, right at the edge of my vision where I can't ignore it.

"She's out on the Unsingle," he adds. "Thought you'd want to know."

I don't look at him. I don't give him a single inch. But I'm sure my reaction is obvious because it feels like someone hooked a finger into something tender inside me and twisted.

Dylan leans back with a lazy ease that makes my teeth grind. He stretches his arm along the back of his chair like he's settling into a private victory. Whatever happens with Evie, he got exactly what he came for.

Evie's gaze snaps to me. She likely senses the tension. "Alaric," she says. "You're quiet."

It's not concern. It's suspicion.

"I'm listening," I say.

"That's a first," she scoffs.

A spike of heat hits the back of my neck, but I force my expression still. She studies me for a moment, then turns her attention back to her wine.

I'm angry with myself for falling for it. I came here expecting dinner with my grandmother, believing we could have a real discussion, not another performance. I know how she operates, yet some part of me thought this time would be different, that maybe she realized something earlier this week. But once again, I'm disappointed—with her and with myself for expecting more.

But that's not what's sitting heaviest with me now.

Liz is dating. She's moving on with a life that doesn't include me, and I've missed my chance to be part of it. That's the thing I don't know how to absorb.

The evening ends the way it always does, once Evie gets her grandchildren to fall in line behind her, she flicks her hand in a dismissive wave, and that's the signal. Chairs scrape back. Napkins fall. No one lingers.

Sera gathers her things with shaky hands and slips out fast, like staying another second might invite round two.

Josie moves more slowly. She looks at Evie, then me, then the table—her face blank in that protective way she uses when she's hurt and doesn't want it showing. Matthew waits until she steps aside, then bolts the moment there's a clear path.

"Goodnight," he murmurs as he passes.

"'Night, Matt."

Dylan leaves last, tossing me a look that's somewhere between smug and curious. "You okay there, Ric?" he whispers.

I look right past him, and eventually, he wanders out, hands in his pockets, humming like the whole evening has been entertainment.

I stay seated after the room empties. It's quiet now but not peaceful. The tension clings to the walls. I try a slow breath. It doesn't help.

Liz is out there living again—dating, moving forward, stepping into something new. I should be happy for her. I want to be. Instead, I'm sitting in a house where I'm treated like a piece on Evie's game board.

I push back from the table and stand. The staff move in to clear what's left, and I make a point to thank them. It's the only polite thing happening in this house tonight.

As I move toward the hall, Evie watches me from her chair. "You seem off," she says.

"I'm fine," I answer.

"You're lying."

I don't respond. I don't give her anything to pry open.

"Goodnight," I tell her as I go.

The air outside is a shock to the lungs after the heaviness inside. I breathe it in until my shoulders drop.

I can't keep repeating the same patterns and expect the ache in my chest to resolve on its own. Evie will always be Evie. That will never change. I know this, so if someone is going to be different, it has to be me.

And on that note, my brain shifts gears. Liz is moving on.

If I don't meet that challenge head-on, I will lose her for good.

As they always have, both of these problems have the same solution—start making the choices that are right for me and going after the life I want.

Forty

Alaric

I check the mirrors out of habit as I speed away from Evie's house, but I don't remember pulling out of the driveway. I could almost laugh at myself, though, because for once, it has nothing to do with Evie.

Dylan's words are what keeps replaying in my head, sharper every time.

Liz is on Unsingle. She matched with Dylan. They have a date.

I grip the wheel, jaw clenched, struggling to pull in a full breath. I have really messed this up.

I imagine her profile photo, imagine her smiling at someone who isn't me. The pressure in my chest spikes. I should have told her what I wanted. I should have stopped pretending distance would protect her. I pushed her away until she finally believed me.

A memory flashes—her sitting on the edge of my desk,

laughing as her hair slipped over her shoulder. The faint scent of vanilla on my shirt after she brushed past me. Her voice, her hand on my arm, the way she watched me when she thought I wasn't looking.

I'm not okay with this. I'm not okay with her moving on. I'm not okay with someone else getting the version of her I threw away.

Jealousy simmers in my stomach. I hate how it feels—petty, ugly—but the thought of Dylan sitting across from her makes me physically ill. The rush of shame soon follows. I've lost any right to feel this way. I walked away, leaving a mess in my wake.

I loosen my grip on the wheel, coaxing blood back into my fingers, then tighten it again. I want her. I never stopped wanting her.

The road straightens, and clarity descends. I'm done pretending this is fine, that it's for the best. I'm done living with less than what I truly want.

I want Liz, and I'm going to fight for her.

I turn onto my street, and the houses look the same, but somehow, everything is different. I told myself Liz would be better off without the mess I carry, that she deserved someone steady. I convinced myself that letting her go was the right thing. It was a lie.

The car glides past my driveway before I register it. I screech to a stop, pull over, and rest my forehead against the wheel. My hands shake, not with anger but fear.

What if I've already lost her?

I lift my head. Again, I imagine Liz sitting across from someone else, laughing with someone else, giving someone else what she was trying to give me. If she goes on that date, it will be because I stayed silent.

So I can't do that.

I straighten in my seat and breathe until I feel steadier. She deserves steadiness. Honesty. A man who doesn't disappear when things get hard.

I reach for my phone. *We need to talk* forms in my mind,

but it looks weak—another half-step. I set the phone face down on the seat.

I know what I need to do. I'm going to see her, be honest with her, and finally quit hiding. I grip the wheel and pull away from the curb again, making a U-turn.

I ease into my driveway and stop with the engine running. The house feels far away, as if walking inside would undo the clarity I reached on the drive. I grab my phone and scroll to Trinity because she's the only one who will tell me the truth without twisting it.

When she answers, her voice is warm but alert. "Alaric? What happened? Is everything okay?"

I take a breath. "Did Liz say anything to you about dating again?"

A pause settles over the line. My stomach knots.

"Why are you asking me that?"

"Because Dylan said something tonight, and I need to know if it's true." My voice roughens. "Is she seeing someone?"

Another pause. "She told me she was trying Unsingle," Trinity says after a moment. "She said she needed to stop waiting for things to change."

I have to nod. That's exactly right. "Did she tell you who she matched with?"

"She said she had plans to meet three guys for coffee. She didn't tell me names."

I shut my eyes and press my forehead against the steering wheel.

"If this is upsetting you," Trinity says, "you might want to ask yourself why."

"I know," I tell her. "I should have told her everything a long time ago."

"Then tell her now," Trinity suggests immediately. "Before she talks herself into something else."

I thank her, we end the call, and the car falls silent. I shift into reverse, back out of the driveway, and go to get this done.

Paradise is quiet as I drive. Porch lights glow in soft circles.

Here and there, windows shine with hints of people finishing their days. None of it reaches me. The only thing I can think of is Liz, my heartbeat urging me forward.

I stop at the four-way intersection downtown, which sits empty. I picture Liz opening her door. The surprise, the guarded look, the way she squares her shoulders when she's preparing for disappointment. Often because of me.

I turn onto her street and slow as I approach her house, then I see movement near the walkway.

A guy—I think the one I saw her with at Dot's not long after she moved here—stands beside her on the porch steps. Liz has her hands tucked into her coat pockets, and her shoulders seem relaxed. He says something that makes her smile.

I come to a stop across the street, and she doesn't seem to notice me. She's focused on him.

He touches her elbow lightly as he says goodnight. It's respectful. Familiar. Comfortable. The kind of gesture that tells me they've spent more than a few minutes together.

She watches him get into his truck. He gives a small wave when he's settled, and she returns it before turning toward her door.

I stay in the shadow of a maple tree until her porch light clicks off and the house returns to its usual stillness.

There's no anger in me. Just emptiness. There's no space left for pretending. While I hesitated, someone else stepped in. Now, I don't know what fighting for her looks like or if I need to accept that it's too late. I only know that the way I've been living isn't working, and I remind myself yet again that the only thing I can change is me.

Forty-one

Liz

Hudson's office is warm when I step inside, and two coffees wait on the small round table, a quiet gesture he uses to soften these weekly meetings.

"Morning," he says.

"Morning." I sit across from him at the table, my notebook ready, my stomach a little shaky with nerves. We've been over most of this information, and I spent half of yesterday tightening these slides, but presenting them always makes the stakes feel higher.

He shuts his laptop and gives me his full attention. "Ready when you are."

I open my binder. "First full draft of the HR and succession findings."

"Show me."

I slide the chart over. "Staffing looks different from what most people assume."

His eyes catch on the red blocks. "That much?"

"Most of it is nursing," I say. "Several units are close to unsafe ratios. We knew it anecdotally, but the data spells it out."

He nods as he absorbs that, then gestures for the next page.

"Physicians are short in a few areas too," I say. "Not as severe, but enough to create pressure."

He nods until he flips again. "Overstaffed?"

"Just in small pockets," I clarify. "It's nothing anyone's doing wrong. The workload just doesn't match the way they're structured anymore."

Hudson leans back, processing. "I didn't realize certain departments ran that light."

"Most people don't," I say. "When one team's drowning, everyone assumes it's universal."

He flips through the packet again. "This is solid work, Liz."

Relief loosens my shoulders. "Thank you."

He taps the binder. "All right. Solutions."

I turn to the blue tab. "HR's recommending targeted recruiting and stronger retention efforts. We have candidates in the pipeline, but not enough to stabilize the gaps long term."

He scans the notes. "Pipeline expansion makes sense, but the budget has to match."

"We can't move forward without leadership sign-off," I agree. "And hiring before burnout is always cheaper than hiring after someone has burned out. We're starting to see the early signs. The sick calls were up last month. Charting lagged behind shifts by hours. Nothing catastrophic, just enough friction to show how thin everyone is stretched."

He listens without flinching. It's one of the things I respect about him.

"What else?" he asks.

"Better onboarding," I say. "Mentorship. Structured

support. It keeps new hires from getting swallowed up on day one."

"That tracks," he says. "You've built a strong case, but can we fund it?"

"We can't do this piecemeal."

"You're right."

There's something warm in his tone, but I keep my expression neutral.

He's quiet for a moment, and then closes the binder. "I have a couple of ideas for how to frame this, but it needs a wider audience."

I nod, expecting him to ask for a briefing or a summary.

He doesn't break eye contact. "The leadership team first," he says. "And then the board. I'd like you to present it."

My breath catches. "To the board?"

Hudson nods. "You're the one who built this. You understand it better than anyone else. They need to hear it from you."

I sit back, trying to absorb this. I've sat in on board meetings before, tucked in at the far end of the room, taking notes or updating a project tracker. But presenting? Speaking directly to them? That's something else entirely. "I don't usually… That's not typically my role," I say, not protesting, just trying to catch up to the size of what he's asking.

"You're ready," he says. No pep talk. No grand speech. Just quiet certainty.

There's something grounding in that. Under my nerves, a ribbon of pride starts to unfurl. "Okay," I say after a moment. "If that's what you need, I'll do it."

His mouth curves. "Good. The leadership team will meet later this week, and then you can start preparing the version you'll present to the board. I'll review it with you before we schedule anything."

I nod, still feeling a bit shocked. *Presenting to the board. Me.*

Hudson reaches for his mug, but his eyes stay on mine. "You're doing excellent work, Liz. It's time people beyond this office see it."

Heat moves through me. I close the binder and try my best not to look like I'm floating. "Thank you," I tell him. "Let's make it happen."

Hudson nods and shifts in his chair, flipping to the other binder. "All right," he says. "Let's talk about the drug trial project. Where are we on that?"

I straighten. "Actually…we're in a good place."

His brow lifts, and he seems skeptical. *Fair enough.* The project was a disaster the first time we opened the files—years of inconsistent documentation, half-finished summaries, and approvals buried in the wrong folders.

"Misty caught everything up," I explain. "She organized the backlog, updated all the required documentation, and flagged a few discrepancies. It's fully current now."

Hudson's expression shifts. "Misty did that?"

"Yes. She's proved very helpful."

"That's good to know, though I'm not sure I want to reward her yet," he mutters.

"I get it," I say. "But we've had some good conversations, and the work is being done well consistently. This isn't a one-off burst of effort. She's been on top of it every day."

He taps the binder, frowning slightly.

"As you know, this is a heavily administrative project," I explain. "It needs someone who can devote the time to it, especially if we're hoping to attract more drug trials. Those bring in real money. Money we can put toward staffing and recruitment."

He looks up. He's listening now, really listening.

"Misty has a degree in hospital administration," I continue. "She wants this, and she has an aptitude for it. If we're smart, we'll train her. She's an employee worth developing."

He seems thoughtful. "Do you really think she can handle more responsibility?"

"I do. I think she already is," I say. "I'll keep an eye on her work, and if I see anything change, I'll address it quickly."

Hudson studies the binder and flips through some of the pages. Then he nods. "Let's talk to her." He stands and crosses to the door, peeking out into the reception area. I can hear the clicking of her keyboard before he even says her name.

"Misty? Can you join us for a minute?"

There's a beat of silence, then the soft scrape of her chair. She steps into the doorway with her shoulders pulled tight, hands clasped in front of her. Given our start, I understand her hesitation.

Hudson gestures toward the empty chair across from him. "Come sit."

Her eyes flick briefly to me, searching for a clue, and I smile, trying to be encouraging. I don't want her to think this is a trap.

Hudson taps the drug trial binder on the table. "Liz tells me you've been handling this project."

Misty's lips part, as if she's waiting for the rest of the sentence, waiting for the criticism she's sure will follow.

"She says you jumped in and really helped," he adds.

Misty's face softens. She exhales and sits a little straighter. "It was a great project to work on," she says. "I liked getting everything organized. It helped that Liz had already started the structure for it."

The comment warms something in me. It's the first time she's acknowledged my effort without reservation.

Hudson nods. "Good. Because I'd like you to take it over for a while."

Her eyes widen. "Full time?"

"Not exclusively," he clarifies. "But I want to see how you manage this along with your other duties. If future trials come in, we'll need someone who can keep the process tight."

Misty's hesitation melts into excitement so quickly it feels like watching the sun break through clouds. "I'd love to. Actually, I've already seen two upcoming trials in the pipeline—one for neurology and another for GLP-1s. I bookmarked them in case they're relevant, and it's something we're interested in."

Hudson's gaze moves to me, seeming impressed despite himself. "That's good initiative," he tells her. "Plan on joining our weekly project meetings. We'll go through everything together."

"Of course," she says. "Thank you. Really."

Misty rises, and Hudson lets me know we've finished as well. He opens his laptop and dismisses us with a nod. Misty clutches the binder to her chest, as if it's proof she didn't imagine all of this.

I'm halfway to my chair when I hear her soft footsteps behind me. Misty pauses in the doorway, then takes a breath and steps in.

"Liz?" she says.

I swivel to face her. "Yeah?"

"I just… I wanted to say thank you. For everything in there. For saying good things about me. And for giving me a chance after I didn't give you one."

"You're welcome," I tell her. "You've more than shown what you can do. I'm glad you took on the project. It matters."

She shifts the binder into one hand so she can tuck a strand of hair behind her ear. "I didn't expect Hudson to ask me to come to the weekly meetings or to trust me with this much."

"You earned that." I shrug. "You did the work. I'm just the one who noticed."

Her breath catches on a tiny laugh, relieved. "Still. Thank you."

I nod toward the binder. "You're going to do great. At my last job, managing these trials was a full-time role. The fact that you've picked it up this quickly says a lot."

Her face brightens. "Really?"

"Really."

"Okay. I'll…get to it then."

She steps out of my office and crosses back to her desk.

I watch her for a moment. This has been a good morning. Hudson is trusting me with the leadership and board presentations, and Misty has a new project she can be proud of. The office feels balanced in a way it hasn't since I arrived.

Next up is reviewing my notes for this week's presentation to the leadership team and figuring out what, if anything, needs to be tweaked for the board. The morning has left me optimistic, and the work feels manageable instead of overwhelming.

My phone buzzes against the desk. It's a missed call notification, and when I check the log, I see Alaric's name. He tried reaching me twice last night. No voicemail. No text. Just two calls I didn't hear.

I study the screen, unsure why the sight of his name slows me down. Nothing about those calls changes the work in front of me or the path I've chosen for myself, but they linger in my awareness anyway.

I put the phone face down. I need to finish preparing, and there's still a full day of other work ahead of me. Whatever he wants can wait until I have the space to think about it. If it was urgent or work-related, he'd leave a message, right?

I take a slow breath and return to my notes, focusing myself on the part of my life that finally feels like it's moving forward.

Forty-two

Liz

The glow of the Friday afternoon sun warms the side of my face as I skim through the last set of notes from this morning's leadership presentation, refining them to send to Hudson for the board. And I'm still reveling in the win—one of those rare days where the work feels like it's all falling into place.

A knock sounds at my office door, and I look up, expecting Hudson or maybe one of the unit coordinators with a question. Instead, Alaric fills the doorway, one hand braced lightly against the frame, the other holding a familiar paper cup.

He steps in and hands me a London Fog—a creamy tea latte made with Earl Grey, steamed milk, and vanilla—something I splurge on occasionally when the day has gone long.

For a second, I forget how to move. He's never just appeared in my office like this, and certainly not with something that says he remembered a detail I barely mentioned out loud. I haven't seen or heard from him in weeks. *What is this about?*

"Hi," I manage.

"I thought you could use that," he says.

I take a sip, and the steam curls up, comforting and familiar. I feel warm all over. "Thank you. I'm surprised to see you, but this is exactly what I needed."

He nods, pulls out the chair opposite mine, and sits. No hesitation. No hovering in the doorway the way he usually does when he's keeping his distance. He settles in, knees angled toward me, posture relaxed.

I try to gather my thoughts, but he's watching me with a quiet focus I'm not used to. It's disarming—and warming me in a way I didn't expect.

"I didn't mean to interrupt," he says.

"You're not." I clear my throat. "I was just wrapping up."

He nods but doesn't move to leave. And I realize I don't want him to.

Alaric rests his forearms on the chair arms, attention still fixed on me. There's no rush in the way he looks at me and none of the usual guarded distance he keeps with anyone who isn't a patient or one of his sisters. This difference feels deliberate.

"Sorry I missed this morning's leadership meeting," he says. "I heard great things about your presentation."

"Oh?" I try to keep my tone level and resist making a joke about how he hasn't been so great about attending the leadership meetings for a while now.

"More than great, actually," he continues. "Your staffing plan is sharp. Practical. And it's going to make a real difference for mental health, especially if we move toward a new clinic with more practitioners."

"That means a lot," I say quietly. "Thank you."

He nods. "Hudson mentioned that you've created a structure that actually supports people instead of just checking boxes. My team's going to benefit from it."

His directness sends a ripple through me. He's always

been respectful, cooperative when it matters, but this feels different, like he sees not just the project, but the strategy and the weight I've been carrying, the work I love to do.

"I didn't realize you'd been talking to Hudson about the plan," I say.

"He brought it up," Alaric answers. "And I make sure to listen when something concerns my department."

I nod. "Well…I'm glad it seems useful. The board needs to buy in as well, and Hudson's throwing me into the fire to present to them."

Alaric lets out a quiet laugh. "He knows you can handle it."

The sun shifts across my desk, a bright slash of light catching my screen and my face. I blink against the glare, trying not to squint, but Alaric notices.

His eyes move toward the window. Then he rises. "Hang on," he murmurs.

He adjusts the blinds until I'm shielded from the light. It's a small gesture, but I appreciate it. He saw that I was straining and fixed it.

"Better?" he asks.

"Much," I say.

He returns to the chair, scooting a little closer than before. It makes me wonder what, exactly, he came here for. After a moment, the silence feels strangely intimate. I'm aware of him. He's clearly aware of me. And the balance between us has shifted, as if he's not holding himself quite as tightly.

Alaric glances at my hands wrapped around the tea, and then looks back up. His gaze doesn't skim over me the way it usually does. He lingers, thoughtful. There's a pause that feels like he's choosing his words.

"I didn't say it earlier," he finally says. "But congratulations."

A flutter moves under my ribs. He isn't someone who throws around praise. "Thank you. It felt good today. Better than I expected."

"I'm sorry I missed it, though I know you were steady, clear, and you got them to listen."

I shift in my chair, trying to ground myself in metrics and timelines, but this kind of attention makes it hard to slide back into that safe, practical space.

"You should give yourself full credit for that," he adds.

"I'm working on it," I say.

Alaric nods, and I can feel him weighing something. His fingers flex on the arm of the chair, a small tell.

For a moment, it seems like he's about to say something that could tip the whole conversation into new territory. But whatever it is, he isn't ready to put it out there.

I let out a slow breath.

When he finally stands, I feel the moment release. I look up at him, doing my best to seem composed. Professional. Normal.

He takes a step toward the door and turns back to me, expression open. "I stopped by your place last night. But I wasn't sure if you were home."

I nod, my mind racing to decipher what that might mean. "Depends on what time it was. My brother took me out to dinner."

He studies me for a moment. "Ahh, okay. It's great that he's there for you."

He's smiling big now. *Why is he so happy about that?*

I stand to walk him to the door, and he thanks me for my time, which is a little odd, since he doesn't seem to have been here on official business.

"Tomorrow, my family has an event at the vineyard to celebrate the start of the season. We do it every year. Would you like to join me?"

I'm supposed to have two coffee dates in the morning tomorrow. I feel a little sweaty just thinking about it. "What time is it?"

"I can pick you up at two," he offers.

I feel as though I should see where this is taking us. Or I

want to, anyway. "Sure."

"Great, I'll see you then."

I step back into my office, feeling a little bewildered. I'm not sure what he's up to, but I'm going to go with the flow. Back at my desk, I try to find the thread of what I was working on before he walked in. It takes longer than it should, and finally I find my phone and pull up the dating app. Suddenly, I need to postpone those coffee dates in the morning.

Forty-three

Alaric

The courtyard tent glows with warm light in a slight rain as the celebration of the start of the growing season settles into its annual rhythm. People from the community, our employees, and even staff from other wineries drift from table to table with glasses of our new releases, and the murmur of conversation rises under the canvas roof. I stand beside Liz near the back where we can see the lectern clearly. Evie has insisted on addressing everyone here, something she hasn't done in years. That puts a knot in my stomach.

Also swirling in my stomach is the fact that yesterday started with a plan to have a real conversation with Liz and ended with me extending an invitation that interrupted more than it clarified, leaving everything unfinished. She's here with me now, but I'm still not sure what that means.

I push the thought aside. This isn't the moment for it. Whatever is happening with Evie this afternoon will probably need my full attention.

Evie steps up to the microphone with the confidence she wears like a birthright. Her suit is immaculate, and the crowd quiets without being asked. Whatever else she is, Evie knows how to command a room.

"Thank you for being here," she begins. "We're entering what should be a remarkable season. Our vineyards are strong. Our team is stronger. And the valley, as ever, remains resilient."

A few approving nods ripple through the crowd. She feeds on that and leans toward the microphone. "We've faced challenges. Some were expected. Some were not. And through all of it, we kept our standards high. Some families can't say the same."

My jaw tightens. She doesn't have to name the Paradises. The crowd feels the implication. A few people trade glances, as if checking whether they really heard her go there this early in the speech.

She keeps talking about growth and stability, but her voice takes on a sharper edge, as if she's testing the blade she's been dying to use. "For too long, we've allowed certain influences to disrupt the balance in this valley," she says. "People who believe their history gives them license to interfere with work they don't understand."

Liz shifts beside me. Something is off. This is aggressive, even for Evie. Her shoulders have pulled higher, as if she's bracing for a hit that hasn't landed yet.

Taking a breath, Evie straightens the stack of note cards she hasn't actually looked at once. "Others might claim innocence, but I know better. I've always known better. This valley survives because of decisive action, not handwringing."

Confused glances pass through the crowd. Someone near

the front whispers behind their hand. Evie seems to notice and pushes ahead.

"Nothing we've done has ever been reckless. Everything has been deliberate. Necessary. When other vineyards have tried to undermine us, we've acted to protect what generations have built."

The murmurs start then. And it seems that's not the response she expects. For a second, her smile falters, but she props it back up and forges on.

"People pretend damage happens by accident," she says, a slight tremor in her voice. "That diseased vines appear from nowhere. That irrigation systems collapse without cause. I've never believed in coincidence. I believe in strategy."

Liz's hand brushes mine, and she looks up at me, eyebrows raised. She's never witnessed this firsthand before. Evie is slipping, and the crowd feels it. Even the servers have gone still, as if any sound might shatter what little control she has left.

Movement at the edge of the tent draws my eye. Two detectives step inside. Their timing is unmistakable. A couple of people near the entrance turn toward them with wide eyes.

When Evie sees them, she freezes mid-sentence. Something tightens in her face. She tries to force a smile, as if they're here to honor her, but it doesn't land. She clears her throat. "I can't say I'm surprised to see law enforcement here this afternoon. Someone finally decided to address the mess created by others."

A man two rows ahead murmurs, "What mess?" His wife shushes him, but she's leaning forward too, trying to catch every word.

The detectives don't speak. They just watch Evie patiently.

She grips the lectern, her expression steady. "If I authorized certain measures, it was after every alternative had been raised and dismissed. Warnings were issued. Concerns were documented. They weren't acted on by the consortium, by the community, or by the Paradise family."

A ripple of tension moves through the crowd. Someone whispers, "Approved what?"

People are connecting the dots.

She presses on, voice shaking now. "I didn't have the luxury of waiting for disaster. I intervened. I corrected what needed correcting."

Several people gasp. By now, they seem to understand exactly what she's saying. A woman near the front turns to the person beside her, eyes wide. Another covers her mouth with her hand.

Evie seems oblivious to the way her words are landing, though I can't imagine how she thought this was going to go well.

"I protected this valley," she says, almost pleading now. "Every decision I made was for all of you. While others coasted on old reputations, I did the hard work none of you wanted to touch."

The detectives step a little closer. The crowd shifts back. Even from where I stand, I can feel the temperature in the tent drop.

Evie's breathing turns uneven as her composure frays. She keeps looking from the detectives to the audience, searching for the admiration she's always been able to summon. But the faces staring back don't match the story she's telling herself. Her gaze jumps to her grandchildren, who are mostly lined up off to one side, as if she's expecting one of them to nod, stand, step forward. None of them moves.

Her voice rises. "Don't stand there acting shocked. You know what this valley asked of me. You know how much I've carried. You've watched the Paradise family sabotage us for decades and expected me to sit quietly while everything our family built falls apart."

People whisper, unsettled. One man shakes his head and mutters, "This isn't true."

The woman next to him says, "I don't think she understands what she's admitting."

Evie leans forward as if she can drag the room back under

her control through force of will. "I did what I had to do. If a few vines were damaged or a well ran dry or a shipment went missing, it's because I refused to let them destroy us. I won't apologize for that."

The detectives move to the front row, and the crowd parts without hesitation. The realization lands fully now. This isn't rumor. She is confessing, piece by piece, to the sabotage the valley has been whispering about for years.

Evie seems to realize it then—the shift in the room, the quiet withdrawal. No one speaks in her defense. Her gaze moves to her grandchildren again, accusation sharpening her expression, as though their silence has joined the charge against her.

Then real panic registers on her face. "You benefited from what I did," she says, her voice fracturing. "You praised the numbers, the harvest, the quality. You took the reward and left me to carry the consequences."

Her hand slips from the lectern, and she steadies herself, eyes wide. "I saved you. All of you."

No one responds. The room offers nothing she can hold on to.

The lead detective steps forward. "Mrs. Dempsey, we need you to come with us while we continue our investigation into the vineyard tampering."

Evie blinks, as if she misheard. "You're here for me?"

The detective doesn't have to answer. The silence does that for him. Even the people closest to her don't move or protest, and for once, I'm able to keep myself on the sidelines. It's where I've said I want to be, and the only way to be there is not to get involved. Still, it's painful. This is the smallest I've ever seen her.

Her expression falters. "You think I'm the problem? After everything those people did? After what Max started? You think any of this happened without reason?"

Her voice breaks on the last word. It feels like something is finally giving way.

The detective repeats the request, calm and even, and Evie

looks around one last time, searching for loyalty that isn't there. The betrayal on her face is unmistakable, though she's the one who brought this all on herself.

She draws a shaky breath. "You have no idea what this valley would look like without me."

As the detectives guide her away from the lectern, the tent stays largely silent, emptied of the power she used to hold in every room.

Liz slips her hand into mine, but I don't look away from Evie as she walks past. For years, this feud infused itself through every corner of the valley, around every memory we grew up with. Tonight, the story has finally revealed itself in public, the truth laid out where everyone can see it.

I always thought Evelyn Dempsey would go out fighting. I just didn't expect the fight to be with ghosts only she could see.

When the police and my grandmother disappear from view, the tent finally exhales, and conversations start again in low tones. Something old ends in that moment, something loud and long-standing. The valley feels like it's turning toward something new, something we might be able to build without Evelyn Dempsey's shadow on every decision.

As the crowd begins to scatter, Liz moves closer, steadying herself beside me. I don't reach for her, but I feel the anchor of her presence all the same.

Maybe I can build that way too.

Forty-Four

Liz

Once Evie has been escorted out, the crowd in the tent loosens. Chairs scrape. People shift, craning toward the opening as rain drums harder against the canvas overhead.

Someone mutters that she's finally gone too far. Someone else insists she didn't mean half of it, that she's under pressure. The voices overlap and tangle.

When people start leaving the cover of the tent, they do it in clusters, hesitating at the edge before stepping into the rain. Umbrellas snap open. Jackets are pulled tighter.

When it's my turn, rain slicks the pavement, reflecting the harsh white of the temporary lights. I catch fragments of conversation as I move through the scattering crowd.

"She snapped."

"She's not dangerous. She's dramatic."

"If Black Bear goes under, we're finished."

This wasn't just a publicity disaster. It's one that could ripple through every system in town. If Evie loses her grip on the valley, the fallout lands on businesses, and on paychecks. Whatever else she is, she's also a lot of people's employer.

I turn to Alaric and pull him around the corner, away from prying eyes.

"I'm really sorry," I say. "Is there anything I can do? Or maybe help with?"

He lifts his eyes to mine, and something in his expression eases. I can see how much he's been carrying alone.

"I don't want to put pressure on you," he says. "I'm just glad you're here with me. Thank you."

I nod. In the middle of everything breaking apart today, and despite the uncertainty of my footing with Alaric, I feel remarkably steady. Whatever conversation he wanted to have the other night when he came by can wait until he's standing on more solid ground.

Someone taps Alaric's shoulder, and I step back, giving them privacy to talk.

People drift toward their cars, shaking their heads as rain darkens the gravel beneath their feet. A few glance back toward the tent like they're waiting for someone to step out and say it was all just a show, an elaborate hoax. No one does.

Officers speak quietly near the entrance of the tent, rain beading on their jackets. The flashing blue lights on their cars wash the parking lot in cold color, breaking and reforming against the wet pavement.

I stand at the edge of the crowd, breathing slowly, watching the valley absorb the blow. Paradise doesn't feel quiet anymore.

I spot Sera and Josie near the side of one of the buildings, just beyond the reach of the tent lights. They've taken shelter close to a line of trees, half hidden from the crowd. Sera's shoulders shake in small, tight movements, and Josie keeps one hand over her face, like she's holding herself together by sheer will.

My feet move before I think through anything. The instinct is simple. Human. They didn't deserve any of what happened in there. As I approach them, I slow. I don't want to startle them or make this feel like another invasion. When I get close enough, Sera lifts her head. Her eyes are glassy. She looks exhausted.

"Hey," I say softly. "I'm so sorry you had to go through that in front of everyone."

Josie wipes her face with the back of her sleeve. She nods, but her voice doesn't come. Sera swallows hard and looks toward the parking lot, trying to pretend she isn't shaking.

I pull a small pack of tissues from my coat pocket and offer it without a word. Sera takes one with a tiny, strained nod. Josie takes the pack. For a moment, we stand in a quiet bubble, cut off from the noise. People walk past, glancing over with pity or curiosity, but none of that touches us here.

Sera drags in a rough breath. "She wasn't supposed to do that," she whispers.

I don't say anything. I know better than to offer quick answers or excuses. Sometimes the kindest thing you can do is let someone fall apart without rushing them back to their feet.

Josie leans into her sister. "It's never been this public," she says. Her voice cracks. "Not like that."

I nod. "I know."

We stand together for another moment, just three women trying to steady ourselves under the cold sky. And I find I don't feel like an outsider watching a disaster. I feel like someone who belongs here because I care enough to stand with the people caught in the crossfire. Even if everything about today is messy, this part feels right.

I'm still with Sera and Josie when I hear footsteps behind me. I turn, and Alaric is there. He looks like he walked through fire and hasn't checked for burns yet. His eyes are raw, but there's no anger in them. No walls. Just a man holding himself together for the people he loves.

And I am not his focus. He checks Sera from head to toe with a look only an older brother could manage. She gives him a broken nod. Josie steps to his side, and he wraps an arm around her.

"I'm here," he murmurs into her hair. "You're okay."

There's something almost reverent in the way he stands with them, despite the wreckage of the meeting still clinging to him. He looks tired in every line of his face but not defeated. He's carrying more than he ever planned to and still choosing to shield the people around him. I stay quiet. This isn't my moment.

Josie pulls back a little, wiping her eyes. "We should go home," she says.

Sera nods but doesn't move. She looks at me instead, her gratitude soft and unguarded. It makes my throat tight.

Alaric follows her gaze and finally turns to me. Something moves across his face. Surprise. Relief. A question he isn't ready to ask. He doesn't step toward me, and I don't move either, but the thread between us pulls tight.

Then Sera and Josie are pulled aside by one of their employees, something about coordinating with the police before they leave the event. When they step away, the space between Alaric and me opens like a clearing, not empty, but charged.

The cold air lifts a strand of hair across my cheek. "You didn't stop her," I say. "That couldn't have been easy."

He exhales and shakes his head. "It was overdue."

"Overdue doesn't mean painless," I tell him. "I saw what it cost you."

He looks down. "It felt like tearing out a piece of myself. And also like the only way to protect them." He looks in the direction his sisters have gone. "They're the ones continually in the line of fire."

I step a little closer. Not touching him or inviting more. But letting him know I understand what he has been wrestling with in a way I couldn't before.

"You did the right thing," I say.

He gives a rough almost-laugh. "I'm not totally sure how

to tell anymore."

"Maybe. But it's still true."

His gaze holds mine. There's a question there, maybe a hope he doesn't trust enough to voice. But something about the way he looks at me makes the cold around us feel less sharp. My heart kicks hard, not from old wounds, but from the way the understanding between us is shifting. Carefully. Slowly.

He exhales. "I think I could see what needed to happen because I'm not in the middle of it. Everyone else is too close."

I nod, and we stand there in the glow of the police lights, two people who have hurt each other and still can't look away.

In his face, I see the man I fell for, but also the man who couldn't show up when it mattered. And then the man who today did something he'd never dared to before. All these truths exist at once, shaping the way my heart reacts now.

"I used to think you walked away from me because you didn't care enough," I say. "Today made it clear your choice wasn't that simple."

His eyes fill with relief and shame. "I wanted to tell you everything back then. I wanted to be honest. But wanting and doing aren't the same. I didn't know how, and I was so afraid. Now, you know what Evelyn can be like, what dealing with her requires. You saw it today."

"I did."

He rubs the back of his neck. "I was drowning in all of it. Her expectations. The pressure. Keeping Sera and Josie safe. I didn't know how to hold on to you without breaking everything else, and I didn't want her to break you in the process."

I don't know what to say to that. As much as I understand, it wasn't his decision to make alone.

He closes his eyes a moment. "I'm not saying it was right," he adds, as if sensing my thoughts. "It wasn't. It was cowardly, and I underestimated you."

That should make me angry. It should scratch at the part of me that remembers being in Vancouver alone, looking for a future that never happened. Instead, all I feel is a soft ache. Not forgiveness, but empathy, enough to change the shape of the hurt without erasing it.

"You were conditioned to pick her," I tell him. "Even when it hurt you."

He lifts his gaze. "It hurt to let you go—every time."

That softens my heart further. "I'm not saying everything makes sense now," I whisper. "But tonight showed me something. All this time, you weren't choosing her over me. You didn't know another way."

His shoulders ease slightly. "I'm trying," he says. "To be different. To be better—whether you're in my life or not."

I nod. He isn't just a man who abandoned me. He's a man who never learned how to stand up for himself until now. He deserves one more chance, a chance to create a version of the story that could finally let both of us move forward, whether that ends in a future together or a goodbye that makes sense.

I take a slow breath. "I'm listening, Ric. I'm not promising anything. But I'm listening now."

He nods. "Thanks. I won't waste the opportunity."

The afternoon has thinned into something colder and deeper. The parking lot has emptied until the noise is just scattered murmurs near the police cars. I stand with Ric in the quiet space between our lives. The wind shifts, and I pull my coat closer, not just from the cold, but because everything inside me feels newly uncovered.

"I don't know where this leaves us," I say quietly.

"I don't either," he admits. "But you're here. And I'm here. That's a start."

A car door slams in the distance. He glances toward the sound, then back at me. The look on his face makes my breath catch. I hold his gaze and let myself believe that seeing this through is the right choice.

Sera calls his name from across the lot, and the moment breaks. He looks toward her, then back at me. There's hesitation in his eyes, and I give him a small nod. He needs to go to them.

"If you ever want to talk about her," I say, "or any of this,

I'm not on anyone's side but the truth."

"Thank you," he says.

I nod. "I'll catch a ride home. Go be with your sisters."

"Thank you," he says again, looking at them across the parking lot. "I'll be in touch."

"Goodnight, Ric."

I turn toward the gift shop building and call a rideshare. The cold settles around me as I wait, but my mind feels clear. Heavy from the day, yes, but not whirling. And as Trinity and Ginny wave me over, I smile. This place isn't quiet, simple, or easy. But that doesn't mean it isn't worth it.

Forty-five

Alaric

Sera and Josie wait near the edge of the parking lot, shoulders pressed close, both of them pale under the streetlamp as I approach. They look like they're holding themselves together with threads that keep slipping through their fingers. Seeing them so shaken squeezes something in my chest.

"Let's go," I say quietly. "We're done here."

Josie steps into me first. She doesn't cry out loud. She never has. But she tucks her forehead against my shoulder, the way she used to when we were kids, and Evie aimed her expectations like a weapon. I wrap an arm around her and pull her in. She clings for a moment, then takes a breath, trying to steady herself.

Sera doesn't move at all. She stands a few feet away, staring at nothing, hands in fists at her sides. When she finally looks over at me, her eyes are wide and glassy. "I can't believe she said all that," she whispers. "I was prepared for her to one day disown me, as she's done to so many others. I wasn't prepared for her to admit to the fire and all the sabotage of the vines."

I nod. I want to tell her it's over. I want to promise that everything is going to calm down now. But I can't. I don't know what's going to happen. "Come on," I say instead. "You don't have to think about any of that right now."

I guide them to the car. Josie slides into the backseat without letting go of my sleeve until the last second. Sera lowers herself into the passenger seat, as if her bones hurt. She keeps both hands flat on her thighs and stares out the window.

When I pull out of the lot, I check the rearview mirror and see Liz standing next to Trinity Paradise. Her hair blows across her cheek in the wind, and she tucks it behind her ear. She is forever part of this day, and I think that's a good thing. I can't shield anyone from any of this, so it's good that she knows. We can only get through it together.

I drive across the vineyard to the family houses on the south side. In the backseat, Josie sniffles once and then goes still again.

Halfway home, Sera finally speaks.

"You didn't stop her," she says. "Not like you usually do."

It isn't a question. It's a realization.

"No," I answer. "I didn't."

Sera nods and presses her forehead against the window. She doesn't say another word for the rest of the drive.

When we reach the house, Josie moves first. She climbs out of the car and drags in a long breath, trying to hide how much her hands shake. Sera lingers by the passenger door, as if she isn't sure what to do next.

I unlock the front door and get them inside. The house smells like old coffee and the citrus candle Josie burns in the kitchen. Sera sinks onto the couch and folds her knees to her chest. Josie drops into the armchair and tucks her legs under her.

In the dim light they look younger, as if years have stripped off them in one brutal day.

"Do you need anything?" I ask.

They both shake their heads.

I sit between them on the edge of the coffee table. "You did nothing wrong," I tell them. "None of this is on you. Nothing she admitted is on you."

Josie's eyes well up again. Sera exhales in a broken rush.

"I know it doesn't feel like it now, but you're going to be okay."

Sera's voice comes out thin. "Are you?"

I nod. "Absolutely. I will be."

Josie wipes her face with her sleeve. "You should go," she whispers. "You look like you need air."

I smile. She isn't pushing me away. She's giving me permission.

Sera lifts her gaze to mine. "We'll be all right. Tomorrow is another day, and we'll keep going and doing our jobs and everything else we can to keep this business afloat."

I study them. Their exhaustion is real, but so is their resolve. They're not collapsing. They're regrouping. And they're telling me, in their own way, that I don't need to hover until dawn.

"Call me if anything changes," I say.

They nod together.

I grab my jacket from the hook by the door. As I pull it on, I catch a final glimpse of them settling side by side on the couch, blanket pulled over their legs, heads tipping toward each other.

My mind is impossible to focus on the drive home, and the house is quiet when I arrive. I keep thinking about the moment I turned onto Liz's street last week and saw her with what I thought was a date at her door. I know now it was her brother, but it still stays with me, a reminder of how long I've waited to say what I need to say. And how easily someone else could step into the space I've left open.

Today wasn't the time to talk, but I know now that I don't

want any more distance between us, particularly not the kind I create because I'm afraid of bringing her fully into my life.

I sit for a moment in the stillness of my living room, hands clasped loosely, breath steadying, and the decision comes without effort.

I need to see her.

Not tomorrow. Now.

I lock the door behind me and step outside.

The drive isn't far, and for once the traffic is on my side. On the way, I try to sort out what I want to say.

A hit of caffeine is in order, so I drive through Steaming Mugs, and soon, a green tea latte and a London Fog sit in the cup holder beside me. I can smell the bergamot and vanilla even before I pick it up. I bought it without thinking, but the moment I held it in my hand, the intention was clear. It isn't a grand gesture. It's a simple one. And that seems the best place to start.

When I step out of the car, my nerves spike. This is it. She might open the door, listen to everything I say, and still decide she doesn't want me in her life. That thought sits heavy in my gut as I walk up her steps, regret and hope tangled together. But at least I'll know. This seems to be a day forged in fire, so I might as well get it all out there at once.

Still, as I reach the bottom step, I think about turning around. I could tell myself this isn't the right time or that she doesn't need more weight tonight. But those excuses don't hold. She showed nothing but strength today, nothing but a willingness to be present for me.

So I knock.

I'm braced for her not to answer, but then the light inside shifts and the deadbolt clicks. The door opens, and there she is. Hair pulled back, a soft sweater hanging off her shoulder. Her eyes widen enough to tell me she didn't expect me.

"Ric."

I lift the cup. "I brought you something."

She looks at it, then at me, and I can feel the question in her silence. It isn't professional courtesy or politeness.

"Can I come in?" I ask.

She hesitates a second, perhaps checking in with herself first. *Good*. She should.

"Yeah," she says. "Come in."

I step in, and warmth closes around me. She moves back, giving me space to take off my coat. The room smells like her. Clean and soft. Something calming I've been craving.

I hand her the tea. "I wasn't sure what else to bring."

Her fingers brush mine as she takes the cup. The touch is small, but it sends a zing through my body.

"Thank you," she murmurs. She wraps her hands around it, breathing in the steam.

We take our seats in her living room, her on the loveseat and me on the couch.

"I should have done a lot of things differently," I say.

She lifts her eyes to mine.

"Back then. In Hawaii. And here too." My voice stays low. "I know I didn't give you what you needed. I didn't give you clarity or honesty when you deserved it. You weren't imagining the distance. I put it there."

She holds the cup tighter, but not like a shield, more like an anchor.

"I'm not here to make excuses," I continue. "You saw what Evelyn was like today. You saw what it's been like my whole life. I grew up thinking loyalty meant silence, that protecting her meant disappearing parts of myself. And she manipulated things so I would return." I shake my head. "You were the first thing I wanted that I knew I couldn't let her touch. There was no wiggle room. I didn't know how to hold on to you without tearing everything else apart."

She nods. "I just needed you to give me a chance, to let me in. We could have figured out what was right together."

"I know," I whisper. "I'm not here to rush anything. But when everything fell apart today, you were the one person who didn't add to the noise. You stayed steady when I couldn't, and that mattered."

Liz studies me for a long moment, her eyes bright. I recognize the tension in her jaw as it tightens, then eases again, her tell when she's weighing doubt against her own instincts and choosing to trust them.

"I didn't stay because of the vineyard," she says. "Or even your family. I stayed because you looked like you were carrying the weight of every person in that tent. I wasn't going to add to it. No one should have to do that alone."

"I'm trying to be different," I tell her. "Not just for my sisters and not out of guilt. But for myself. I've realized the only way to get the life I want is to take it, to make the choices I want to make. I can help my sisters, but I don't have to put their needs before my own. That's never been what they're asking for. So if you'll let me, I'd like to try to repair things for us too. But I'm not here to push you."

A small, warm exhale leaves her chest. She moves over next to me on the couch, still holding the tea.

"I'm listening, Ric," she says. "I'm not promising anything yet. But I'm listening now. I hear you, and I think I understand you in a way I didn't before."

I nod once. "That's enough," I tell her. "More than enough."

She looks down at the tea in her hand, then back at me with a faint, almost shy warmth I haven't seen from her in a long time.

"You remembered how I like it," she says.

"I remember more than that," I answer.

She smiles.

The space between us feels open. Not painful. Not uncertain. Just open, a place we might step into when we're ready.

"I didn't expect you to come tonight," she says. "I thought you'd be with your grandmother at the police station."

"I didn't expect to either," I admit. "Her lawyer is with her, and she'll call someone to pick her up when it's time. I don't think it will be me. But anyway, I couldn't stop thinking about you. And not in the way that made everything complicated before. In a way that made everything clearer."

She chews the inside of her cheek for a moment. "Today was a lot."

"It was," I agree. "She put things out there that can't be unsaid. She'll have to work with her attorney to figure it out."

Her breath leaves her chest slowly. "And you didn't stop her."

"I'm not sure I could have, but I realized it only prolongs the nightmare when I do. I should have stood up to her years ago or at least stopped trying to save her from herself."

"You weren't ready," she says. "You learned how to survive her, not how to confront her."

I scoot closer to her. Not too close, just enough to stop pretending there's nothing between us. "I can't promise this won't be messy," I tell her. "I'm still figuring out who I am, how I want to be. But if we try this again, I'll show up the way you need."

Liz studies me for a quiet moment. "I'm not asking for perfect. I don't even know what trying again would look like right now. But I want honesty. And consistency. I want to know I won't be the first thing dropped the moment Evie demands your attention. And that you won't decide for me what I can and can't handle."

"I won't."

Her breath catches, barely noticeable, but I see it. "I meant what I said," she says finally. "I'm listening. That's all I can offer tonight."

"And that's perfect," I tell her. "Thank you."

Her hand rests near her knee. I look at it for a moment, then let my fingers drift forward until they touch hers. She doesn't pull away. Instead, her fingers curl around mine, the way you reach for something you want but promised yourself you'd be careful with.

We sit together in the soft glow of her living room, hands lightly joined, the tea cooling on the table. There's no rush. No urgency. Just two people finding the space between what was broken and what might come next.

Forty-six

Liz

The Sunday morning light slips through the blinds before I'm ready for it. I roll onto my back and blink up at the ceiling, waiting for the pieces of last night to settle in the right places.

It doesn't come in a rush. It comes in layers. The meeting. Evie's voice cracking in front of the valley. Ric standing alone in the middle of chaos. The way he looked at me in the parking lot like he didn't know how to breathe. And then the knock on my door hours later, soft enough to be hesitant, steady enough to mean something.

As I walk to the kitchen, my gaze drifts to the little table near the couch. The empty paper cup sits exactly where he left it. I didn't move it last night. I didn't want to. The faint scent of bergamot still lingers when I reach for it, the steam long gone but the memory warm. Emotion moves through my chest. It feels like holding a moment I wasn't expecting to get back.

I set the cup down and draw in a slow breath, letting myself feel it. Last night didn't fix everything, but it shifted something.

I pad into the kitchen. The floor is cool under my feet as I move through my morning routine, filling the coffeepot and reaching for my favorite mug, the one with the tiny lavender sprigs painted near the rim.

The coffee maker clicks and sizzles as the coffee fills the pot. I lean against the counter and wrap my arms around myself. I'm tired but not in the drained, brittle way I've grown used to since things with Ric fell apart. This tired feels softer. Earned. Like something inside me finally stopped bracing.

The coffee finishes, and I fill my mug. The warmth rises into my face, pulling me back to the moment he stood in my doorway with the cups in his hands. He looked nervous in a way he never lets himself look. And when he spoke, the honesty in his voice was a revelation, more effective than any explanation he could have offered months ago. *"You weren't imagining the distance. I put it there."*

I close my eyes. I can finally absorb this without being pulled under. He didn't ask for forgiveness or try to soften what he'd done. He told me the truth because he understood that silence had been what caused the damage.

The coffee cools enough for me to sip it, and I take the mug to the couch and pull my knees up, the blanket draped over the back falling across my lap. I breathe into the quiet, and the truth of the matter slowly comes into focus. I wanted him to come, even if I hadn't been ready to admit it. And he did. Not out of obligation, or pressure, or habit, but because he chose to.

I lean back against the cushions and let out a breath. I feel like I'm waking up a version of myself I haven't been in a long time, someone who isn't bracing for disappointment, someone who can sit in a quiet morning and let herself want something again.

I'm not ready to run toward him. But I'm ready not to run

away.

I'm halfway through my second cup of coffee when I hear footsteps on the porch followed by a quick knock. Not polite. Not tentative. It says the person on the other side has already let themselves in emotionally, even if the door's still closed.

I open it, and Trinity stands holding a paper bag that smells like fresh pastries. Her hair is in a messy bun, and she's wearing sunglasses, even though it's barely nine in the morning.

She lifts the bag, as if it explains everything. "This seemed like a morning for carbs."

I step aside, and she breezes past me the way she always does, immediately comfortable in my house. She sets the bag on the counter and pulls out two cinnamon twists, pushing one toward me.

She studies my face over a bite of pastry. "So. Want to tell me why I woke up at seven feeling like the valley had shifted on its axis?"

I give her a look. "You're not psychic."

"No. But I have very good emotional Wi-Fi where you're concerned." She squints at me. "You seem calmer than you should after last night. That's either a miracle or a man."

I take a slow breath. "Ric came over."

Her eyebrows lift. "Ric? We're back to calling him Ric?"

"It wasn't what you're thinking."

"I'm not thinking anything," she says, even though she absolutely is. "I'm just listening with my entire face."

I lean against the counter. "He showed up with a London Fog and apologized. And he didn't try to rush or smooth things over. He just talked—honestly."

Trinity's chewing slows. "And how did that feel?"

"Unexpected." I pause. "Good and scary. Better than I was prepared for."

She nods, as if she's fitting this new information into a map of me she's been updating for years. "Did he take responsibility? Real responsibility? Or the pretty version men use when they think partial accountability counts as emotional growth."

"He took responsibility," I say. "Fully."

She lets out a quiet whistle. "About time."

I don't disagree.

I walk over to the couch, and she follows with her pastry. She sits sideways, one knee tucked up. "Liz," she says gently. "You've been stuck since Hawaii. Scared to want or ask for anything. And honestly, I get it. You were left in the dark for way too long."

I nod. "Last night didn't fix everything, but it changed something. That and witnessing firsthand what happened at Black Bear yesterday. I don't know what trying again looks like yet, but I'm not shutting the door."

Trinity smiles, soft and proud. "Good. You don't have to leap. You just have to be honest with yourself."

A small silence settles between us as we sip our coffee and eat pastries.

Then she nudges my foot with hers. "You deserve someone who shows up without you having to send a smoke signal. If he keeps doing that, maybe there's something real left to build on."

"I'm not making any promises," I say.

"I'm not asking you to." Her smile widens. "But I like that you're open to seeing where it goes. That's new."

I let out a breath. "I won't bend my life around someone again."

"Good," she says. "Hold that. Make him meet you where you are."

I nod because I know she's right. I also know this version of me wouldn't settle for anything less.

Trinity retrieves the bag and extracts another pastry. "Also, if he hurts you again, I'm egging Evie's house. I'm just putting that on the table."

Despite everything, a laugh escapes me. "Please don't."

"Oh, I won't." She grins. "Not unless necessary."

But by the time I walk to the hospital lot for work, Monday morning has picked up speed, and my stomach feels a little fluttery as I approach the building. A cluster of staff stands near the side entrance, talking in low voices. I catch pieces of their conversation as I walk by. Nothing loud. Nothing pointed. Just a community trying to make sense of the weekend's explosion.

Inside, the energy shifts again. It's busy, but with an edge. People glance up from clipboards and computer screens, eyes lingering half a second too long. Not at me specifically, but at anyone who walks by, as if everyone is trying to read everyone else's reaction.

I head for my office, hugging my planner to my chest. Misty appears at the doorway before I even reach my desk. Her hair is frizzed on one side like she got ready in the dark.

"Oh good," she says. "I was about to text you. It's already been a morning."

"That's what I figured."

She closes the door behind us. "You saw the news?"

"Which part?"

"All of it. Evelyn Dempsey went off the rails this weekend."

I let out a soft breath and nod. "I was there."

Misty's expression softens. "Are you okay?"

"I'm fine." I'm grateful that feels close to the truth.

She leaves me with a small nod, and I sit at my desk. The chaos outside doesn't feel personal, and that's new. I'm not bracing for blame. I'm not holding my breath.

A few minutes later, I go to Hudson's office for our Monday meeting. When I arrive, he's standing by the window, reading something on his tablet. He looks up as I walk in.

"There she is," he says. "I hoped you weren't hiding under

your desk."

"I thought about it."

He huffs out a laugh. "I saw you in some of the photos and the news on Saturday. You handled yourself well. That level of public meltdown would rattle most people."

"Yes, I was invited to the party, but the outcome was definitely unexpected."

"It was." He sets the tablet down. "Still, I'm glad you were there. For Alaric's sake." He lets that hang between us for a moment. "The board isn't going to involve the hospital in vineyard politics," he continues. "But it's a small town, and gossip runs faster than the speed of sound. I appreciated how calm Alaric stayed. That matters."

I nod my thanks, wondering what exactly Hudson thinks he has pieced together, and we settle down to business. Mostly, Hudson relays the board's feedback on the staffing plan. They're pleased with the direction we're taking, but every conversation lands in the same place. There simply aren't enough people. The medical shortage is real, and it impacts everything.

We break down numbers in a few areas and brainstorm a bit about ways we can be creative, but ultimately, it's just a long slog ahead. We vow to keep at it, and when we've wrapped up, he gives me a reassuring smile before dismissing me with a wave.

Back in the hallway, I feel a little steadier. People pass by with charts and coffee cups, calling out updates and delegating tasks. There's work to be done. I need to focus. I walk through it, my pace even, my heart quiet.

When I reach my office again, my phone buzzes. I set my planner down and pick it up, expecting a message from Misty or a calendar alert.

It's a text.

Alaric: How are you today?

My breath catches, something warm rising from my chest to my throat. I read the message twice. It's simple. No pressure.

No assumptions. Just him checking in. I sit down slowly. Despite everything else he has going on, he's stayed present.

My fingers hover for a moment before I type.

Me: I'm okay. I hope you are too.

I set the phone face down on my desk and breathe. I can feel the difference between emotional noise and emotional clarity. And clarity feels good. It feels earned. It lets me hear my own thoughts again.

Something is shifting. Not fast. Not sweeping. Just small and true.

I'm deep in searching for ways to be more efficient with the staffing plan when I look up and find the sky sliding toward dusk. It's time to walk home. The day felt long, but not in the draining way I expected when I first woke up. There was a lot to get done, but I managed. I feel on top of things, rather than pulled in by the chaos of the weekend.

The house looks the same as it always does when I get back. But I feel different tonight. Lighter. I walk up the path and pause on the porch. The wood creaks under my weight, and a cold breeze brushes across my cheek. I unlock the door and step into the soft quiet of the entryway. I hang up my coat and move into the living room. The blanket is still draped over the couch the way I left it this morning.

I lower myself onto the cushions, which give the way they always do, soft but supportive. I tuck my legs under me and pull the blanket across my lap.

I set my phone on the coffee table and stare at it for a moment, not because I'm waiting for a message but because I'm thinking about the one I sent earlier. I expected to feel anxious after hitting send. I expected the familiar tightening in my chest, the uncertainty that always used to follow anything involving Alaric.

None of that showed up.

I pick up the phone and reopen our conversation. His message still sits at the top.

Alaric: I'm good. My calendar is packed today, but you're never far from my thoughts.

With my reply right below it.

Me: Same with me.

Simple. Honest. Without the guardedness I've carried for months. I want to keep moving forward. So I respond again.

Me: I just got home if you want to talk, or we can talk tomorrow.

I hit send and set the phone back on the table, flipping on the TV.

I'm watching *Crave* and considering my dinner options when the knock comes. It's soft enough that I almost miss it, just a muted tap against the door.

I pull the blanket aside and stand. I walk over and rest my hand on the knob for a brief moment, letting my breath steady. Then I open the door.

Ric stands on the porch, shoulders hunched against the cold. His hands stay tucked in his pockets, and the porch light casts a faint glow across his face. His eyes lift to mine. "Hi," he says.

"Hi," I answer.

He lets out a slow breath and stays where he is. "I wasn't sure if I should come. I didn't want to push. I just didn't want the night to end without seeing you."

I ease the door open wider. "You're not pushing."

His expression shifts with relief, and he nods once. "I won't stay," he adds. "I only wanted you to know I'm here. And I meant everything I said on Saturday night."

The cold air curls around us, mixing with the warmth of the house behind me. "I'm glad you came," I tell him.

He gives me a small smile. "I'll see you tomorrow."

"Wait," I say.

I don't explain or justify, I just step closer to him. My hand curls into the front of his coat, sliding beneath the fabric until I feel the solid heat of his chest. His breath catches as I pull him down and kiss him—sure, deliberate.

For a heartbeat, he doesn't move. Surprise stills him, his body locked between instinct and restraint. Then his hands come up, one settling at my waist, the other sliding to the back of my neck, as if he's afraid I might disappear if he doesn't hold me there.

The kiss deepens, slow and consuming. Not rushed, not clumsy, stealing breath and thought alike. His mouth is warm, sure, answering me with everything he didn't say this weekend. I feel it in the way he leans in, in the quiet sound he makes against my lips like he's been holding himself together for too long.

The cold air fades. The world narrows.

I press closer, my body fitting against his in a way that feels familiar and new all at once. His grip tightens. When he pulls back to breathe, he rests his forehead against mine.

"Liz," he murmurs.

I don't give him space to retreat. I kiss along his jaw, feel the way his breath stutters, the way his control frays at the edges. His hands slide under my sweater, warm against my back, pulling me flush against him like he's done pretending this isn't exactly where he wants to be.

"I wasn't going to stay," he says quietly.

"I know," I say, my mouth brushing his. "That's why I stopped you."

I pull him into the house, and he kisses me again, deeper this time, unguarded. His back hits the wall, my hands in his hair, his mouth on mine like he's finally letting himself feel everything at once. There's urgency now. Heat. When he lifts me, my legs wrap around his waist, and we move deeper into the house, as if him staying was never a question at all.

He carries me down the hall without breaking the kiss and nudges the bedroom door open with his shoulder, the room dim except for the spill of light from the hall behind us. He sets me down gently at the edge of the bed.

His gaze drags over low, steady again but thinner now, stretched tight with need. "Is this okay?" he asks.

I nod, fingers already working at the buttons of his coat. "It's more than okay."

That's all the permission he needs.

He eases my sweater over my head, slowly enough that the brush of fabric against my skin feels deliberate. His hands feather over my skin, and he pops the clasp on my bra. Once it's gone, thumbs trace my nipples as they harden to his touch. When his mouth follows, pressing warm kisses along my collarbone, I tilt my head back. The sound he makes is quiet, almost reverent.

He straightens just long enough to shed his jacket and shirt, like he doesn't want distance any longer than necessary. When he comes back to me, his hands are warm, sure, slipping to my hips, guiding me back until my legs hit the mattress.

I sit, then recline as he follows, bracing himself over me. His mouth trails a slow path downward, each kiss unhurried, intentional.

When he slides my jeans free, his knuckles skim my skin, sending a shiver through me. His eyes flick up to mine, dark and intent, a question and a promise all at once.

"You still good?" he murmurs.

"Please," I beg, pulling him back to me.

He smiles against my mouth, and any lingering hesitation disappears with the weight of him, the heat, the way his hands trace over me, as if they've been waiting for this moment.

"What do you want?"

"Only you." Gasping for breath, my eyes roll back as he places his mouth directly over my nipple. He gently clamps his teeth around the sensitive flesh until my body hardens beneath his touch.

"Oh, fuck," I groan. A strong pulse beats between my legs, and a white spark of light flashes behind my eyes. I feel ridiculously turned on, with liquid pooling in my swollen pussy.

"Mmmm," he murmurs.

A thrill passes through my body as his tongue darts over my skin. After ensuring the other nipple isn't left out, he migrates farther down my body.

"I need you inside me. Please," I beg.

"So demanding," he says, looking up at me, his tongue lazily circling my bellybutton. Hooking his thumbs inside my silk panties, he pulls them down my legs, eventually casting them aside.

"You're incredibly sexy, Ms. Ward." His lips drop to my bare pussy, and he inhales deeply.

"I need you," I reply, pulling him up until we're face to face.

I bite him softly on the shoulder and push him back into the duvet. I caress my way down his body, over his taut stomach and down the line of downy hair that eventually disappears into bare smoothness under his boxer shorts. Pulling his last remaining garment down and away from his body, I'm thrilled to uncover his erection. Using the tips of my fingers, I take my time stroking up his thighs and over his balls, reveling in his sharp intake of breath as my hand moves up his thick, solid shaft. I close my eyes and moan softly at the feel of Ric's incredible cock, which I stroke softly with the palm of my hand.

When he places his hand on the inside of my knee, I jump. But this quickly turns to anticipation as he encourages my legs farther apart.

"I've dreamed of you splayed out like this in bed, and it didn't do you any justice." He groans as I circle my wet thumb over the engorged head of his cock.

With the lightest of touches, he runs his fingers along my inner thigh, the look on his face telling me he's fully aware of the desperate tension he's causing in my body. When he reaches my swollen lips, he brushes across them before caressing the opposite thigh. I'm panting noisily now, and my grip around him tightens.

Ric trails his fingers toward the pool of liquid between my legs. As he pushes one finger inside, I cry out. He slides his finger forward until he reaches the base of my clit. He holds his finger in place, applying exquisite pressure and allowing the tension to build.

"Fuck me." I exhale through gritted teeth.

"Expletive or request?" he asks.

"Either…both—" I moan as Ric adds his thumb to the mix, positioning it at the top of my clit and making a small circular motion.

"What about a condom?" he asks.

I prop myself up on my elbows. "I'm on birth control, and I haven't been with anyone except you since long before I moved to town. I'm clean."

His expression softens, and he presses a quick kiss to my forehead. "You're the only one I've been with in over a year. Are you okay going without one?"

"Yes." The word is barely out before I'm pulling him to me.

His hand fists in my hair, tipping my head back as his mouth crashes into mine. The kiss is hot and messy, tongues sliding, teeth scraping, all urgency and need. I moan into his mouth, my hips lifting on instinct, and he groans like he's been waiting to hear that sound.

He begins to ramp up the pressure, and I can feel the early signs of an orgasm building inside my body.

"I need to feel you," I demand.

Suddenly, his hand clamps around my wrist, preventing me from stroking him any further. He maneuvers me on the bed, leaning over me. As he drops his mouth to mine, I wind my legs around his waist, pulling him closer. Moving his hand between our bodies, he positions himself and pushes just slightly inside me.

Breaking our kiss, he gazes into my eyes. Without a word, he begins to slide farther into my tight, desperate, quivering body.

"Oh…my…God," I groan as he buries himself, every wonderful ridge and curve of him feeling gloriously magnified. I close my eyes and take in the sensation.

"Look at me," Ric orders. "I want you to keep watching." He smiles as he continues to sink into my tight, twitching body until he's buried to the hilt. I take a sharp breath, aware that I'm currently being stretched wide and loving every second of it. Rocking his hips, Ric pulls partway out before pushing himself forward once again.

I groan as my internal muscles clench around his solid mass. Once again, Ric retreats, pausing for a short time before thrusting again. I cry out, a ferociously strong orgasm building with every stroke.

"I want to see you lose control," he breathes, partly pulling out once more, forcing me to wait for the overwhelming sensation I know is coming when he plows himself back into my body. "You," he says, slamming himself into me and pulling back. "Are…so…fuck…ing…sex…y." He thrusts his hips with each syllable muttered.

"Oh, God! Please don't stop!' I beg as I begin to scale the heights of my orgasm. "Please. Please."

"You want it hard?" Ric grunts.

With a pleading groan, I nod, unable to find the words to respond.

"Hold tight, then."

With a hand out to brace himself, he hooks one of my legs over his shoulder, opening my body wide to him. He thrusts long and hard with a rhythm that pushes me toward the dizzy heights of my all-consuming orgasm. Just before my release, when my body is tense and set to explode, Ric sucks his thumb into his mouth and then rolls it gently around my clit. At the same time, he speeds up his thrusting hips until I'm launched into a noisy, violent orgasm.

As pleasure crashes through my body, Ric stays still, allowing my internal muscles to contract in waves around his rock-hard cock. Then just as I'm starting to recover, he resumes circling his thumb and rocking his hips.

"Oh, no! No!" I moan as Ric pushes my body immediately back towards a second orgasm.

Showing no mercy, he pushes me beyond the boundaries of any pleasure I've previously experienced. When I begin to tire, he drops his mouth to my nipples and clamps down. I roar in response, the sensation a jumpstart to my fatiguing body. A short while later, his thrusts become much less controlled.

"I'm sorry… I'm going to come…"

He groans, and I can feel a change in his thick cock within me. My body clenches even more tightly around him in response.

"Oh, God!" I shriek as he slams himself harder and harder into me and my muscles spasm into yet another orgasm. With a final thrust, Ric roars as he pumps his cum deep inside my body. We collapse onto the bed, and he drops his lips to mine and kisses me tenderly, on and on.

We're both beyond spent and breathing raggedly. Ric pulls a blanket over us, and I spoon against his body.

"Always and forever," I hear him mumble as I drift off to sleep.

Forty-seven

Alaric

Three months later

Last night, Liz and I had a nice dinner out, and I'm more and more convinced that we've settled into a good place. She's moved out of the cottage she was renting and into my house like this is where we were always meant to be. I don't ever want to spend another night without her.

Evie, on the other hand, has spent the last three months going back and forth with the police. Somehow, she's not in jail, but that's only because she's Evelyn Dempsey. And even so, our world has been shaken up. My sisters and cousins have all been questioned. We're waiting for the shoe to drop when the Crown finally gets all their evidence in line.

I should be getting ready for work, but I'm sitting at the

kitchen table with a mug of green tea that's gone cold. Outside, the sky hasn't decided whether it wants to turn gray or stay blue. My phone vibrates across the wood, and I recognize the number before I even pick it up.

I already know what they're going to say.

The officer's voice is calm and measured. There's no urgency now, only procedure. He informs me that my grandmother was taken into custody without resistance. She was processed. She'll be transferred to the regional facility this afternoon. The district attorney will make a statement later.

I thank him, set the phone down, and breathe through a heaviness that doesn't belong in my chest, yet has lived there most of my life.

For a moment, I stay seated, trying to feel the ground under my feet. The tea tastes bitter when I swallow, but it anchors me enough to stand and reach for my jacket. I need to get to Sera and Josie. The vineyard is going to be chaos with the press. I'm halfway down the hall when I hear a soft noise behind me.

Liz steps into the kitchen, ready for another day at the hospital. The morning light touches her hair, and the look on her face tells me she already knows what's happened.

"Was it the police?" she asks.

I nod.

Her hand slides over mine. The warmth of her touch pulls something tight inside me.

"You should go to them," she says. "I'll join you if you'd like."

I want to tell her she doesn't have to. I want to tell her she's already done more for me than anyone. I don't say any of that. I just nod again and let her fingertips brush against my palm before we gather our things and step outside.

"I'd like to make a stop on the way," she says as we get in the car.

She directs me to her favorite bakery, and she's in and out in a minute. Now, the car is full of the scent of cinnamon and warm bread.

We drive on to Sera and Josie's house, and I park on the gravel driveway and sit for a second, staring at the front window. The curtains are open. It's a small thing, but I know what it means. They aren't hiding today.

Inside, Josie's sitting at the kitchen table with a mug she hasn't touched. Her eyes are red but dry. She looks up the moment she hears me, and something in her breaks. Not loudly. Not dramatically. Just a soft collapse of breath as I pull her into my arms.

Sera stands by the counter, arms folded tight across her chest. She meets my gaze, and for a heartbeat, her expression softens. Her anger has built a shell around her for months, but today, it looks cracked at the edges. "We knew it was coming," she says.

I nod. I did too, but knowing hasn't made it easier.

I stand with them, one hand on Josie's shoulder, the other reaching for Sera's. I tell them they're not alone. I tell them I'm here. They listen, but more importantly, they lean in.

Liz sets the bakery bag on the table and rests a gentle hand on Josie's back. Josie's breath hitches once, then steadies. Liz looks at me, her eyes calm, clear, and quietly protective. She's here the way she's been here for weeks for all of us, steady and sure, a presence that makes the room feel less brittle.

"Thank you for coming," Sera says to Liz.

"Of course," Liz answers.

After a few minutes, Addie and Ginny arrive. And we hold on to each other all over again. There's no talking or forced comfort. Just the six of us in the quiet kitchen while the morning proceeds around us. It feels like the beginning of something, like a life where we're not holding our breath all the time.

I look at my sisters. Then at Liz. I feel something like peace take shape inside my chest. We don't know what Evie's arrest means. She told all of us she was ready for whatever fake news was going to do. But this morning we don't talk about it. We sit together and eat our cinnamon rolls, drinking coffee and tea.

The vineyard is awake and busy by the time we leave my

sisters. The fruit is set and the canopies are growing, so there's much to be done. The July air outside is warm, and it feels clean. Liz slips her hand into mine as we walk to the car.

I drive us to the hospital with the windows cracked. The road unwinds in front of us, and neither of us speaks. There's no need to fill the silence.

We each go our own way when we get to work, but Liz leans over and kisses me before she starts down the hall. "Let me know if you hear anything else."

I squeeze her hand. "Promise. And I can make something for dinner tonight."

She smiles. "I'll order takeout."

Back at home at the end of the day, we move to the living room where she curls against one end of the couch, knees tucked. I sit beside her, close enough to feel the heat coming off her. The fading light washes across her face, soft and warm, catching on the tiny lines of worry.

I trace the back of my fingers along her arm. "Are you okay?"

She looks at me, her expression open in a way I'm still getting used to. "I'm all right. I'm more worried about your sisters."

"They'll be all right," I say. "It'll take time. But they're stronger than they think."

"And you," she says quietly.

I lean back. "I'll get there too. Today was…a lot. But it needed to happen. And now, it's done. No more anticipating."

She nods, as if she understands every piece of what I'm not saying. She's been doing that more lately. Seeing me without trying to fix anything, meeting me where I am instead of where I should be. It's a kind of care I didn't know I needed until I had it.

"You were good with them this morning," she says. "They needed you."

I nod. "I spent a long time stepping around the worst parts of this family. Today felt like facing it head on."

"You did," she answers. "And you didn't fall apart."

I reach for her hand, threading my fingers through hers. She shifts closer, head resting against my shoulder. Her hair brushes my jaw, and the scent of her shampoo settles the rest of the tension under my ribs.

We sit like that for a long time.

After a while, she lifts her head to look at me. "You didn't have to do this alone."

"I know," I say. "I just didn't know how to let anyone in without losing myself." I breathe out, slow and steady. "It's different now."

"It is," she says. "For both of us."

The last of the daylight fades, leaving the room washed in gray-blue.

I press a small kiss to her hair. "I'm glad you're here."

"I'm not going anywhere."

She leans into me with an ease we both once thought we'd lost, and knowing she's found it again with me brings gratitude I feel to my core.

Today was heavy. Tomorrow might be too. But this is growing into something that won't break under pressure. And I want whatever comes next.

Liz spoke with Hudson yesterday after we got to the hospital and told him I was going to need some time away from the press—and she was going to join me. Miraculously, he agreed to give us Friday off. He's gradually stopped being so defensive about our relationship. Once he realized that apart from Evie, the current generation of Dempseys and Paradises are doing a much better job of sharing space with one another, he let go of the idea that being involved with me somehow means Liz is putting the funding for her position in danger. So, instead of working today, we're out in the fresh air. We're not going far, just out to Big White, but it's enough distance to breathe without feeling the weight of the last few months.

I drive us along the lake as the sun climbs higher, the water catching the light in long streaks that look almost metallic. Liz watches the shoreline through the window, her fingers resting loosely against mine on the console.

My dad's cabin sits at the edge of a narrow inlet, tucked between tall pines that sway just enough to break the stillness. It isn't fancy—two rooms, a small deck, a view that stretches across the water like a slow exhale. When I see it again, a hush settles inside me. There's something about this place that feels like hitting a reset button.

I unlock the door, and Liz steps inside. The smile that moves across her lips makes the entire drive worth it.

We spend the afternoon doing nothing that would count as productive. We walk the path behind the cabin. We sit on the deck with mugs of tea. We let the lake do most of the talking. Every once in a while, she reaches for my hand, and each time, something in my chest loosens a little more.

As the sun starts to drop, I build a small fire in the stone pit outside. The air cools fast in the valley once the light fades. Liz wraps herself in a blanket and sits close, her shoulder brushing mine. The fire pops and crackles, throwing a warm glow across her face. She tucks her hair behind her ear, and I watch the way the light catches the gold in her eyes.

"You look like you're thinking," she says.

"I am."

"About Evie?"

"Yes, and the mess she created."

She shifts so she can see me better. "Tell me."

I look at the fire for a moment before meeting her gaze. "I keep thinking about how long it took me to get here. Not to the cabin, but to this place with you, where I'm not hiding from myself or pretending I'm fine while I push you away."

Her expression softens. "You don't have to pretend with me."

"I know," I say. "That's what's different."

She reaches for my hand under the blanket.

"I spent most of my life reacting," I explain. "To my family. To expectations. To fear. I didn't know how to choose for myself or how to hold onto something good without assuming I'd break it."

"You didn't ruin anything," she says.

"I came close."

She shakes her head. "You learned."

I breathe in the scent of the fire, the sharp cold rolling off the water. The world feels small and steady. "I love this with you," I tell her. "The way we fit when we're not running from anything. The way we talk. The way we don't talk. The way I feel when I wake up with you next to me." I pause. "I love who I am when I'm with you."

Her eyes pull me closer without either of us moving.

"I want a life where I get to come home to you," I say quietly. "I want that every day."

She inhales slowly, the blanket shifting with her breath. "Ric…"

I'm not on one knee. There's no ring in my pocket. There's no plan. It doesn't feel like a performance. It feels like the truth.

"I want to marry you," I tell her. "Not because it fixes anything or erases the past. But because you're the person I want beside me while I build whatever comes next."

The fire pops softly. The lake carries the sound away. Liz looks at me for a long, still moment. Her eyes shine, but she's not crying.

She touches my cheek, her palm warm against my skin.

"Yes," she whispers. "I want that life too."

I exhale.

She rests her forehead against mine. The moment isn't dramatic, and it doesn't need to be. It's quiet and honest and completely ours. It feels exactly right.

Epilogue

Liz

Two months later

It's a Friday night in September when Trinity and Greyson pull up outside our house. I notice right away that something feels off, even before I'm fully in the car. Trinity doesn't turn around to smile at me the way she usually does, and Greyson barely glances away from the steering wheel. They're quiet in that careful, controlled way that usually means they've been circling the same argument for a while.

We pull away from the curb, and the silence stretches.

I sit back and watch the neighborhood slide past my window. Porch lights flick on one by one as dusk settles in. A couple walks their dog across the street. Somewhere nearby, a garage door rattles open. Everything feels normal, which only makes the tension inside the car more pronounced.

Trinity stares out her window as if she's counting streetlights. Greyson keeps both hands on the wheel, posture stiff, eyes fixed on the road ahead.

I register all of it, then leave them be, instead letting my attention drift to the thing that's been needling me since this afternoon. I really don't want to cook tonight.

I tried calling Ric before they arrived. Straight to voicemail. I tried again once we were halfway down the block, telling myself the first one didn't count. Same result. I picture him in his office, shoulders hunched as he works through charts, completely unaware that I'm irritated over something as small and domestic as dinner.

I know it's not fair. I know he's busy. It still gets under my skin, a low-grade irritation I can't quite shake.

"So," I say eventually, because I can't sit in silence anymore. "What exactly are we doing at the courthouse?"

Trinity's shoulders lift slightly before she answers. "Just something quick for Tarryn and Trace."

Greyson's sister and father. They run Paradise Hill Vineyard.

Greyson nods like that explains everything.

It doesn't help my mood.

We're supposed to be grabbing drinks tonight. Ric couldn't come, which already had me on edge. My mind drifts, unhelpfully, toward Evie and the chaos she's left behind. Even when she's not actively causing trouble, she lingers like a shadow that never fully lifts.

The courthouse comes into view as we turn the corner, its stone façade lit from below, solid and imposing against the darkening sky. This isn't a place you swing by casually. It's where things get decided. Where words turn permanent.

Greyson pulls up along the curb and parks. The engine cuts off, and he gets out immediately. Trinity turns toward me, one hand already reaching for the door handle.

"You guys go ahead," I say. "I'll wait here."

She freezes, like I've disrupted something carefully

planned. "No," she says quickly. "You should come in. We don't know how long it'll take."

I glance around at the nearly empty parking lot. There's no movement, no activity, nothing to suggest this will take more than a few minutes.

"I'm fine," I tell her. "I'll just sit for a minute."

I reach for my phone again, thumb hovering as I try Ric once more. Straight to voicemail. My jaw tightens. He knows I hate this feeling, the sense of details just out of reach.

Trinity shifts closer, lowering her voice. "I'm nervous."

That makes me look more closely at her.

Her hands are clasped together, fingers twisting slowly, like she's working through something she hasn't said yet. It's subtle, but it's not like her.

"Nervous about what?" I ask. "Has someone been arrested?"

She swallows. "I just need my best friend. Can you come hold my hand?"

Something in me softens. Trinity doesn't get nervous like this. She's the steady one, the person who walks into chaos and figures out how to manage it. If she needs me, I'm not staying in the car.

I let out a breath and open the door. "Fine. But if this ends with jury duty, I'm blaming you."

She smiles faintly and laces her fingers through mine the moment my feet hit the pavement, as if she's afraid I'll change my mind.

Halfway across the plaza, Trinity stops.

"Maybe you should touch up your lipstick."

I turn to her slowly. "Why would I need lipstick?"

She gives me a smile that doesn't quite land. "It's looking a bit faded."

She must be more nervous than she's letting on if she's worried about what I look like.

Inside, the courthouse is quiet in that after-hours way that makes every sound feel amplified. Our footsteps echo as we move down the hallway.

"Are you sure they're even open?" I ask Greyson.

"Yeah," he says easily. "We just need to grab something from the judge."

That explanation doesn't help, but before I can press, Greyson stops in front of a judge's chambers and knocks once before opening the door.

I follow them inside and stop.

For a moment, my brain refuses to cooperate. It takes in shapes and color before meaning. People standing too close together. There's a low murmur of breath and shifting weight.

Then the room comes into focus.

Ginny stands near the window, arms crossed loosely, a smile pulling at her mouth. Ryker leans against the wall beside her, posture casual but eyes sharp, watching me more than the room. Addie stands closer to the center, hands clasped in front of her. Josie's eyes are glossy, and Sera looks like she's vibrating with contained energy, rocking slightly on her heels.

Against one wall, Mark and Sam stand shoulder to shoulder. Why on Earth would they be here? Sam gives me a small nod, like she's silently telling me I'm not in trouble, that this isn't bad news.

But this is too many people for a courthouse office. Too much intention packed into a space that's supposed to be neutral.

My pulse picks up.

Then Nicky spots me. "Aunt Izzie!"

He launches himself across the room, a burst of movement that breaks the tension instantly. He skids to a stop in front of me, arms flung wide, face lit up like this is the best surprise he's had all week.

"Did you see?" he asks breathlessly. "I'm dressed up. Uncle Ric said I had to be very good today, and I am being very good."

Laughter ripples through the room. Nicky spins once, then twice, bowing so deeply he almost tips over before dropping into a dramatic crouch, clearly waiting for applause.

I laugh despite myself. "You look very handsome."

He beams, then darts back to Mark and Sam, whispering loudly that he nailed it before flashing me a thumbs-up.

When I finally look up again, my gaze finds Alaric.

He's standing a few feet away, hands at his sides, watching me carefully, like he's giving me time to take all of this in.

He looks different. Not dressed up exactly, but nicer than what he wears to work. Intentional. His expression is open, steady, and entirely focused on me.

My mind scrambles for an explanation. This isn't a hearing. No one looks tense or defensive—no anger, no bracing for fallout. "Is everything okay?" I ask because it feels like the only safe question. "Is someone sick?"

Ric shakes his head. "Everyone's fine."

I glance back at the others, trying to read their faces. Ginny's smile softens. Josie wipes her eyes as if she's already lost a quiet battle with emotion. Sera bites her lip, clearly fighting the urge to say something.

I become suddenly aware of myself again—of my dress, perfectly acceptable for work but not exactly…this. Of my flats. I smooth my hands over my skirt, then stop when I realize I'm doing it.

"What's going on?" I ask quietly.

Ric steps closer, but he doesn't touch me yet. "I don't want you to feel rushed," he says. "I want you to have a minute."

My throat tightens. The room feels very still now, like everyone else has faded into the background. I can hear my heartbeat. The quiet rustle of clothing as someone shifts.

Whatever this is, it's about me.

"This probably feels like a lot," Ric says quietly.

I let out a shaky breath. "That's one way to put it."

A few people smile behind him, but no one interrupts.

"I know you didn't wake up this morning thinking you'd be standing in a courthouse after hours with your entire life staring back at you."

That earns a small, helpless laugh from me. "I didn't even change my shoes."

His mouth curves, but his eyes stay serious. "I noticed. You still look beautiful."

The words land gently, not like flattery but like fact. I glance down at my dress again, aware of how ordinary it is. How unceremonious. How me. A part of me wonders if I should feel embarrassed. Another part realizes I don't want to change anything.

Ric steps closer and takes my hands. "I didn't want this to feel hurried," he says. "But I also didn't want to wait for some future version of our lives where everything is magically quieter and easier."

My chest tightens.

"We keep saying we'll slow down someday," he goes on. "After the next deadline. After the next crisis. After the next thing settles. But life doesn't work that way, and I don't want to look back and realize we kept choosing later when what we meant was afraid."

I swallow hard.

"I know this is fast," he says. "And it's okay if you need a second to catch up to it."

I nod. My mind races ahead, tripping over practical thoughts I didn't invite. Tomorrow. Work. My calendar. His schedule. The fact that I didn't call my mother. The absurdity of being here in flats, hair pulled back, no warning, no buildup.

And underneath all of it is another truth. I'm scared, not because this feels wrong, but because it feels like something I could lose.

Then I look at him.

The man who knows how I take my coffee. Who leaves the light on for me when I work late. Who doesn't flinch when things get complicated. Who shows up, even when it's inconvenient.

Fear loosens its grip.

Ric exhales and lowers himself to one knee.

The room quiets, not in shock, but in recognition.

"I didn't choose tonight because it was easy," he says. "I chose it because it's real. Because it looks like us. Busy. Slightly imperfect. Surrounded by the most important people in our lives."

He reaches into his pocket. The ring rests in his palm, an antique emerald-cut diamond, deep and clear, set in a band that looks like it's already lived a life.

"This was Evie's," he says quietly. "My grandfather gave it to her."

My chest tightens, but he doesn't let the moment tip too far.

"I'm sorry she's not here," he adds. No explanations. No justifications. He lets the truth stand.

Then he looks back up at me, eyes steady. "I promise to choose you every day. On the loud days and the quiet ones. When work gets heavy. When life doesn't slow down the way we wish it would."

My eyes burn.

"So I'm asking you," he continues, "not because it's convenient. Not because everyone's here. But because I don't want another ordinary day to pass without you knowing exactly where you stand with me." He pauses. "Will you marry me?"

My mind flips through everything that should make this harder than it feels. The speed of it. The practicality of it. The part of me that likes a plan and a little warning before life changes shape.

But I already live with him. I already choose him in the small, ordinary ways. We've already agreed to this. It just wasn't official. This isn't a leap. It's a step forward.

"Yes," I say finally. "I want to marry you."

The words don't echo. They don't explode. They land softly between us, exactly where they belong.

Relief crosses his face first. Not triumph. Not excitement. Relief, like he's been holding his breath. "Okay," he says quietly, as if he's acknowledging something sacred. "Okay."

He doesn't stand right away. He doesn't look around the

room. He keeps his focus on me and reaches for my hand, which is trembling just slightly now that the decision has been spoken aloud. "May I?" he asks.

I nod.

He slides the ring onto my finger, and the stone catches the light as it settles into place, cool against my skin before warming almost immediately.

It fits. Not just physically. Emotionally. Like it's been waiting for me, not the other way around.

For a few seconds, it feels like we're alone.

Then the room exhales.

Cheers rise around us, warm and full, not startling but celebratory. Someone claps. Someone laughs. Someone wipes at their eyes. Nicky's voice cuts through it all, loud and delighted.

"She said yes! She said yes!"

That's when Ric stands.

He pulls me into his arms, holding me close enough that my forehead presses into his shoulder, grounding me as the world rushes back in. I feel his breath against my hair. His hand firm at my back.

"Are you okay?" he murmurs.

I laugh, overwhelmed in the best way. "I think so."

"You don't have to do anything else tonight," he says. "Just stay right here with me."

That's when I let it in, the quiet joy and certainty that come with knowing the choice is already made.

When I pull back, the faces around us come into focus again.

Ginny is grinning openly now. Ryker claps like he's at a game he's deeply invested in. Josie dabs at her eyes, and Sera still looks like she might vibrate out of her skin.

Trinity steps forward and wraps her arms around me, squeezing tight. "You're marrying him," she says, like she needs to hear it twice.

"I am," I reply, and the words still feel new and wonderful.

Ric slips his hand back into mine, his thumb brushing over the ring. When the noise softens and the room settles again, he turns slightly, still keeping me close. "There's someone I want you to meet."

I follow his gaze to the man standing quietly near the desk, waiting patiently.

"This is my cousin, Gordon West," Ric says. "He's a judge."

I blink. Once. Then again. "A judge," I repeat, mostly to myself.

Gordon offers a small smile. "Nice to finally meet you."

Something in my stomach flips. Not panic, exactly, but awareness, a door I thought was closed has suddenly opened all the way.

Ric squeezes my hand. "He can marry us right now. If you want."

If I want.

I glance down at my hand, at the ring catching the courthouse light. I think about my dress. About the fact that I didn't even think to wear earrings. About how nothing about tonight looks the way I might have imagined this moment if I'd been planning it.

And then I realize something else.

If I had planned it, I would've been stressed. I would've overthought every detail. I would've worried about timing and expectations and whether everything looked right.

This doesn't feel like that.

This feels like standing still in the middle of a life that's already moving.

"I didn't expect this," I admit quietly.

"I know," Ric says. "That's why I wanted you to choose it, not get swept into it."

I look up at him and see the patience in his face, the care he's taking not to assume anything beyond the question itself. My chest loosens.

"I'm wearing my work dress," I say, almost laughing.

"And flats."

"I love that," he replies without hesitation. "You look like you."

I glance around the room. At the people who already know us, who have seen us tired and distracted and trying to juggle too much. At Trinity, watching me closely, ready to step in if I wobble. At Nicky, perched on the edge of a chair, eyes wide, fully invested in whatever happens next.

The idea of waiting suddenly feels stranger than the idea of doing this now.

"Okay," I say, surprising myself. "Let's do it."

The shift in the room is immediate, as if everyone understands this moment deserves quiet.

Gordon gestures toward the center of the room. "Whenever you're ready."

Ric turns to face me, both of my hands in his now. For a moment, we just stand there, breathing each other in.

"This doesn't have to be long," Gordon says. "But it should be intentional."

I nod. That feels exactly right.

He begins slowly, his voice steady and warm. "Love doesn't announce itself in grand gestures. It shows up in ordinary days, in shared responsibility, in the decision to keep choosing one another."

I listen, but I'm also aware of Ric's thumbs tracing small circles against my hands, grounding me as my emotions threaten to spill over.

When Gordon asks Ric to speak, he takes a breath first.

"I promise to keep choosing you," Ric says, eyes locked on mine. "Not just when it's easy or exciting, but when we're tired and distracted and stretched thin. I promise to show up, even when life gets loud. Especially then."

My throat tightens.

When it's my turn, I don't reach for something eloquent. I reach for something true. "I promise to stand with you," I say. "To build a life that makes room for both of us. To keep coming back to what matters, even when we get pulled in a dozen directions."

Gordon nods, satisfied. When he pronounces us married, the words don't feel ceremonial so much as inevitable.

Ric leans in and kisses me slowly, like there's nowhere else we need to be.

For a moment, everything else falls away. Then the room comes back—laughter, applause, Nicky clapping too hard and grinning like he's just witnessed magic.

Ric rests his forehead against mine. "You okay?"

I smile, surprised by how steady I feel. "I'm really okay."

Then Nicky breaks the spell. "Is it over yet?" he asks loudly, eyes wide.

Ric smiles over at him. "Yes."

Nicky's face lights up like this is the best possible answer. "Cake?" he asks, nodding seriously, then immediately starts clapping, as if he's decided that's the correct response.

That seems to give everyone permission.

The room fills with sound, applause and laughter rising together. Trinity is the first to step forward, wrapping her arms around me. "You're married," she says.

I laugh, breathless and a little stunned. "Apparently."

Ginny hugs me next, quick and fierce. Josie presses her hand to her mouth, eyes shining, then pulls me in carefully. Sera bounces in place before deciding on a hug that's all energy and excitement.

Through it all, Ric stays close. One hand at my back. One hand finding mine again whenever the space opens up. It's quiet reassurance, like he knows exactly how unsteady joy can feel when it arrives in a rush.

When the noise finally softens, we drift back into a loose circle. Someone pulls out a phone. There's talk of photos. Of dinner. Of how fast the word is going to spread once people realize what happened here tonight.

I glance down at my hand again, at the ring catching the light. This time it doesn't feel surreal. It feels settled, like it's where it's meant to be.

Ric notices and smiles. "Are you good?"

I nod. "I keep thinking I should feel overwhelmed."

"And?"

"I don't," I admit. "I feel calm. Happy."

We're standing close again when he leans in, his voice low enough that only I can hear it. "I have one more surprise."

I lift an eyebrow. "I feel like we've met our quota for the evening."

He smiles. "This one's for later."

I wait.

"We leave in the morning," he says. "Early."

I blink. "We what?"

"Havana," he says gently, like he doesn't want to startle me. "A week. Hudson and Misty helped plan it."

I stare at him, then laugh, the sound breaking free before I can stop it. "You stopped answering your phone."

"I had to," he says. "You would've figured it out."

"Of course, I would have."

He presses his forehead to mine. "I didn't want to wait another day," he says quietly. "For any of it."

"I didn't either," I realize. "I just didn't know it yet."

Later, when we finally step outside into the cool night air, the courthouse behind us and our families lingering nearby, I let myself lean into him fully. His arm wraps around my shoulders, like it's always done that.

"I've never been happier," I tell him.

He smiles into my hair. "Good. Because this is just the beginning."

Thank you for reading *Dr. Dempsey*. I'm so glad you spent time in Black Bear Valley with Ric and Liz. If you'd like to see the original breakup scene between them—the one that happened long before this story began—you can find it here https://dl.bookfunnel.com/lebzfvbmmq. Or, if you're ready to stay in the valley a little longer, keep reading for a preview of *Dr. Anderson*, where Addie and Luc's story begins.

Dr. Anderson

Addie

The sand is still warm as I move toward the fire, toes digging in for balance. Driftwood burns in a crooked ring at the annual bonfire, and Black Bear Lake spreads out behind it, dark and glass-smooth, the moon floating on the surface, bright and steady. The air smells like smoke and sunscreen and wine that came straight out of a bottle without touching a glass. I breathe it in, the night settling around me. This is my favorite part of summer, the one that still belongs to us. Before it gets packaged and sold.

The start of summer in Black Bear Valley isn't just a party. It's a marker.

Next week, the tourists will start showing up in earnest

around town in Paradise. The early ones are already here, but soon things will tip from quiet to crowded. Traffic slows. Tasting rooms fill. Questions get repetitive. At the same time, the vineyards hit the stretch where everything matters. Growth turns serious. Long days stack up.

But tonight is the breath before all of that, before everything turns watched and weighted again—including me.

Most of the town has turned out for the occasion. You can tell by how conversations overlap without effort, how nobody bothers with introductions. Music drifts from a speaker that's seen better days, and laughter carries down the beach. Someone closer to the water is already dancing, shoes abandoned in a heap, body loose like tomorrow can wait.

"Look at that man," Emma orders, shoving my shoulder as I come to stand next to her. "The one over there at the edge of the fire. Holy guacamole, he's sex on a stick and hot, hot, hot."

I shove back against my best friend, Emma Patel, and follow her line of sight. The man she's looking at is indeed something to behold. He has dark, messy hair that contrasts with his pale skin, brooding blue eyes, and his body… I fan myself. His T-shirt is stretched over his arms and chest, and his shorts highlight his massive package.

I push a stray curl behind my ear. My hair's slipping loose from the braid I put in this afternoon, and my favorite bohemian skirt dusts the sand every time I move. My smile is wide and unguarded. This is me when I'm not trying to manage anything. Barefoot. A little chaotic. Fully present.

I lean over. "How much you want to bet he stuffed a sock in his shorts?"

She looks him up and down with a nod. "No way is he that big."

Just then he turns our way and smiles. When he makes eye contact with me, I smile back.

It seems to encourage him. He makes his way closer. "Hello, ladies."

"Hi," Emma offers.

"What brings you here?" he asks.

"We're celebrating the start of summer," she says.

"I like that. May I celebrate with you?"

"If you can keep up." Emma grabs my hand and tugs me closer to the fire, toward the noise and all the people who know my name. I go willingly, laughing as I stumble, shoulders loose, chest light.

I may have been born a Dempsey, a name that comes with a lot of baggage in this town, but I walked away from the family business and drama—or I've tried to, at least. I hear whispers of my grandmother's name as I cross the sand because she's suddenly back in the news. Evie doesn't do anything quietly, and her long-running rivalry with the Paradise family has always been volatile. It's history, land, legacy, and a grudge that never cooled. News articles like to dress it up as "competing visions" or "old vineyard disputes," but that's polite fiction. This is about two families who've been circling each other for generations, each convinced the valley would be better if the other would just back off. Evie never does. Neither do the Paradises. And I want nothing to do with any of it.

"Looks like you found something interesting," I say, nodding toward the guy's glass of wine. "Are you just pretending you're not here to join the party?"

One corner of his mouth lifts. "Someone has to make sure the fire behaves."

"Bold assumption that it needs to be you," I say. "We're very responsible."

His eyes move over my body. "I can tell."

I shift closer to the fire. "You don't seem like you're from around here."

"And you are?"

"Painfully," I confirm. "Which means I know this party is the calm before everything goes crazy."

"Tourists," he says, without missing a beat.

"And vines," I add.

That does it. His attention sharpens, focused in a way that

feels intentional rather than reactive. "Do you work for one of the vineyards?"

"No. But I've lived here my whole life. I know how this town works."

"How lucky for me."

I laugh. And he lets the sound carry instead of rushing to fill it, like he's in no hurry to move past the moment.

"Are you always this serious at parties?" I ask.

"Only when I'm paying attention."

I tilt my head. "And right now?"

His smile comes easier this time. "I definitely am."

Something tightens between us, not a spark so much as a steady pull. I register it, name it, and decide it doesn't get to affect anything unless I let it.

The fire pops behind us. Music swells, then fades. He just holds my gaze.

How can I refuse that kind of interest?

Emma picks up her almost-empty glass of wine and takes a big swig. "My name is Simran, and this is Maryanne."

I chuckle that she's using our fake bar names. She's out to tease this poor guy. I almost feel sorry for him. Maybe.

"Nice to meet you both. My name's Anderson." He leans toward my ear and whispers, "It's not a sock. Care to feel for yourself?"

I'm shocked that he heard us across the fire, but I manage to keep myself upright. "Thanks," I tell him. "But I typically keep my hands to myself until I've had at least a few drinks."

"Let's get you both some new drinks," he suggests.

I roll my eyes. "Laying it on a little thick, aren't you?"

"Trust me, nothing is little, and you did say that's what you need to verify that I don't stuff my shorts with socks."

I shake my head and smile. He puts his arm around me, and his hand rests against my back. I feel the electric charge shoot right to my core. While his forwardness should have me throwing what's left of my drink in his face, instead I'm quite turned on.

"So, what do you both do for work?" he asks.

This is where Emma shines. Watching her spin a web of deceit is quite something. "I teach fourth grade at Our Lady of the Vines Catholic School," she says. "And Maryanne is a nurse."

He grins. "So it's either hot for teacher or naughty nurse?"

Damn, he's good. That's our joke. I might actually like this guy.

Emma swears that men don't like smart women, so in situations like this, we downplay our brains. In fact, Emma has her PhD in aeronautical engineering and recently received several million dollars in funding so she and her team can build rockets. I also have a degree in engineering, but these days I'm a watercolorist and artist.

Anderson leads the way, and we wander over to the makeshift bar that Mikey's has set up for the bonfire. Terry Lawrence, the regular bartender at Mikey's who has just transported himself to the sand for the evening, shakes his head when he sees me. He always calls Emma Trouble One and me Trouble Two. Anderson orders a red wine for himself, Emma indicates that she'll have the same, and I step up to the bar and order a Sex on the Beach.

Terry pours two glasses of Black Bear—my family's vineyard—and then makes me my drink. As he hands it to me, he mouths, "*Be careful.*"

"Thanks for the drink." I wink and smile at him.

"Do you know him?" Anderson asks as we walk back toward the fire.

"It's a small town. We know almost everyone here," Emma replies.

I raise my glass to him. "To an evening of fun."

His eyes lock with mine. "I'll drink to that."

Emma clears her throat. "Well, I heard someone mention s'mores. I'm off to find out if I can snag one or three of them."

Emma doesn't eat many sweets, so I know what she's doing. She gives me a look that's equal parts permission and promise of interrogation later, and then drifts toward the far side of the bonfire, already halfway back into the crowd.

Just like that, it's only us.

I take a deep pull of my Sex on the Beach. I need to cool off.

"Tell me more about you." Anderson's voice in my ear makes my nipples pebble.

Damn. I shrug. "There's not much to tell. I work at the hospital as a surgical nurse. What about you? What brings you to Paradise?"

"I suppose…" He doesn't look at me. "I'd never been, and I wanted to check it out."

New faces don't slip past the locals unnoticed, not when you've grown up here, not when your life intersects with the same people over and over again in different places. Anderson doesn't connect to anything familiar. No shared history. No stories trailing him. Which means he's temporary.

An early tourist, he's here to enjoy the lake while it's still quiet and the wine before the tasting rooms fill up. Paddleboard in the mornings. Drink well in the afternoons. Then leave before the crowd turns relentless. That narrative settles easily. Safe. Contained. A beginning with a built-in end.

He doesn't step closer right away. He lets the heat from the fire do the work as we sip our drinks. He lets the space between us tighten until I'm the one who shifts.

When he does move, it's unhurried. His hand settles at my waist, firm enough to anchor me, warm through the thin fabric of my skirt. His mouth finds mine without warning and without hesitation, open and intent, tongue sliding in like he already knows I won't stop him.

I don't.

The kiss is deep and unapologetic, not rushed but hungry, his tongue stroking slowly and thoroughly, like he's setting the tone instead of asking permission. My hands fist in his shirt, pulling him closer, my body lighting up in a way that's immediate and unmistakable.

When he finally pulls back, it's only far enough to breathe, his forehead resting against mine, his mouth still brushing mine like he's not done.

There's no smile. No joke.

Just heat, fully awake, and the clear understanding that something has shifted.

I don't want to spend the night with him. I just want the heat.

"There's a hotel just across the street," he murmurs.

"I was thinking down the beach," I reply. "Toward the marina."

He smiles. "I like the way you think."

I do too.

People tend to drift the other way, toward the bridge, toward the noise. The marina stays quieter, the trees thick enough to swallow sound. I lace my fingers through his and lead him off the sand, into the shadow of the pines. I barely have time to turn before his mouth is on mine again, deliberate and hungry.

His kiss isn't wild. It's controlled, tongue sliding in with intent instead of urgency. Heat pools low and heavy, my pulse kicking up like it's been waiting for permission.

I break the kiss. "I want to see you."

A slow smile curves his mouth. "You will."

He turns me toward the tree, pressing me forward, his hands settling at my hips like he's mapping me. The bark is rough under my palms as he pushes my skirt up, exposing skin inch by inch, taking his time like he knows exactly what it does to me. His mouth traces the inside of my thigh, unhurried, reverent, and I groan before I can stop myself. He pulls my panties aside, and his tongue dances across my clit as I hold my breath.

"You're already wet," he murmurs, not sounding surprised.

I am. Fully. Openly. There's no pretending otherwise.

He slides my panties down and spreads my legs, his fingers easing inside me. I drop my head back, breath breaking as he sets a rhythm that isn't rushed or sloppy. It's purposeful. Like he's learning me.

"You like being touched like this," he says, more observation than question.

"Yes," I say, because there's no point in lying now.

His thumb circles my clit, steady and precise, the pressure building until my legs start to shake. He grips my ass, smacking one cheek hard enough to sting, and the sharp contrast snaps something open inside me. My response is instinctive. I press back into his hand, wanting more, asking without words.

"That's it," he murmurs. "Stay right there."

He keeps his mouth where it is, his tongue slow and deliberate, circling and retreating just enough that my hips start to chase him without permission. Each time I get close, he eases back, changes the pressure, drags it out until my thighs are shaking and my breath is coming in uneven pulls. My hands brace against the bark, fingers digging in as the tension coils tighter and tighter, until I can't hold myself still anymore. When he finally gives me exactly what I need, it breaks through me all at once—sharp, overwhelming, stealing the air from my lungs as my body opens completely around the sensation.

And he doesn't stop.

He stays close, grounding me as the aftershocks roll through, his mouth following the slick trail between my thighs like he intends to remember the taste. When he lifts his head, his eyes are dark and intent.

"You're beautiful like this," he says.

That's when I drop to my knees.

I undo his shorts slowly, deliberately, watching his reaction instead of pretending I'm overwhelmed by it. There is no sock. No illusion. He's just big, hard and flushed, the weight of him solid in my hand.

"So," he says, voice low, "now what are you going to do with me?"

I answer by licking the tip, enjoying the way his breath catches as I take him deeper, inch by inch, letting my mouth learn the weight and shape of him without hurry. My tongue slides along the underside, lingering where he's most sensitive, and the low sound he makes tells me I've found exactly what I was looking for. I hollow my cheeks slightly, letting the pressure build, easing back just enough to make him tense before taking him in again.

His hand comes to my hair, not pushing, just there, warm and steady as he steps closer, crowding my space until my shoulders brush the bark behind me. My hands brace at his thighs, my mouth working him with slow intention, letting the pace stay mine. The sounds of the beach are swallowed by the trees as he groans my fake name under his breath and I feel the control in him start to slip.

He pulls me up before it tips too far, hands firm as he turns me, guiding me forward until my palms find the tree again. He pushes my skirt out of the way. I hear him behind me, the quiet shift of movement, and when I glance back he's tearing the condom open. He rolls it on, his grip tight, controlled, like he's making a point of not rushing what comes next. By the time he steps back in close, my anticipation is sharp and coiled, my body already bracing for the moment he finally presses into me.

When he pushes inside, it stretches me in a way that makes my vision blur. I moan, bracing myself as he fills me completely, the sensation overwhelming and perfect all at once.

"That's it," he murmurs, hands firm at my hips. "I've got you."

He begins slowly, allowing me to adjust to his size. Once he's fully seated, he sets a pace that's relentless but controlled, each thrust hitting exactly where I need it. Pleasure builds again, faster this time, hotter, until my body betrays me completely. I come hard, shaking, the sensation rolling through me in waves I can't stop.

He follows, breath rough, body tight against mine, holding me steady as his release crests and breaks.

Later, when my legs finally remember how to work, I make my way back to the beach alone, skin humming, body loose and satisfied in a way I haven't felt in a long time.

No numbers exchanged. No names repeated. Just heat,

clean and contained.

I text Emma.

Me: No sock.

Emma: Did you get his number?

Me: Nope. He's temporary.

And that's exactly enough.

Preorder **Dr. Anderson** now at **https://geni.us/dranderson** and be first to read Luc and Addie's story when it releases in April 2026. If the book is already out when you see this, the same link will take you straight to the page where you can borrow it in Kindle Unlimited or purchase your copy. Happy reading!

Thank you

Canada is my home by choice. My family moved here for work, but we stayed because we fell in love—with the people, the landscape, and the healthcare system that quietly shapes so many lives every day. It's one of the reasons writing about doctors felt like such a natural place for my stories to live.

Both the *Brothers Paradise* and *Dempsey Follies* series take place in the fictional Black Bear Valley. But if you ever find yourself wandering through British Columbia's wine country, especially the Okanagan Valley, you may notice some familiar echoes in the vineyards, lakes, and small towns that inspired these pages.

Thank you for reading, and I hope you enjoyed the ride.

Every book begins with readers who are willing to open the first page of something new. Thank you for giving this story—and this new series—a place on your shelf and in your time. When you read, recommend a book, or share it with someone else, you help these characters travel farther than I ever could on my own.

My husband deserves more credit than he'll ever ask for. Writing a novel has a way of taking over the rhythm of a house, and you've always understood that. You give me the space to disappear into a story and the steady ground to return to when the work is done.

To my boys—thank you for believing in what I do, even if these aren't the books you'd choose to read yourselves. Your confidence, quiet as it is, means more to me than you probably know.

A special thank you to Jessica Royer Oken. Your editorial eye challenges the story in all the right ways while protecting its heart. You have a rare ability to strengthen the work without losing the voice behind it.

And thank you to Courtnay, Linda, Iris, Nancy, and Diana for the careful final pass every book needs. Your attention and respect for the reader's experience help ensure the story arrives the way it should.

Books may be written in quiet rooms, but they reach the world because of the people who stand behind them. I'm grateful to everyone who helped bring this one to life.

Thank you for being here at the start of the Dempsey Follies.
XO XO
Gracie

Books by Grace Maxwell

Men of Mercy

Doctor of the Heart (Paisley & Davis)
Doctor of Women (Nadine & Michael)
Doctor of Sports (Eliza & Steve)
Doctor of Beauty(Laine & Jack)
Men of Mercy Box Set

Mercy Medical Emergency

Doctor Delight (Tori & Griffin)
Doctor Bossy (Amelia & Kent)
Doctor Rebel (Lucy & Chance)
Doctor Enemy (Ava & Roman)
Previously released as *A Doctor for Valentines* in "Love is in the Air, Vol 3"
Doctor Tyrant (Hailey & Christian)
Mercy Medical Emergency Box Set

Brothers Paradise

Dr. Greyson (Trinity & Greyson)
Dr. Beckett (Sadie & Beckett)
Dr. Ryker (Ginny & Ryker)
EMT Declan (Tarryn & Declan)
Dr. Kingston (Elise & Kingston)

Dempsey Follies

Dr Dempsey (Liz & Ric)
Dr. Anderson (Addie & Luc)

www.ingramcontent.com/pod-product-compliance
Lightning Source LLC
LaVergne TN
LVHW010632110826
845149LV00014B/2830